# Night of the Crescent Moon

by

M. Flagg

*The Champion Chronicles,*
*Book Four*

The Wild Rose Press, Inc.
PO Box 708
Adams Basin, NY 14410-0708
Visit us at www.thewildrosepress.com

Publishing History
First Edition, 2024
Trade Paperback ISBN 978-1-5092-5688-4
Digital ISBN 978-1-5092-5689-1

*The Champion Chronicles, Book Four*
Published in the United States of America

## Dedication

For my sister Linda. For my children RM and Kara.
For those who carry loss in their hearts forever.

Just like that, she knew. Something or someone had used dark magic. But why? And above all, how? Because unwritten laws were very clear in every dimension. And with portals closed to the human world, whatever managed to lock down a human's mind didn't do so randomly. It had been a specific assault, which meant it had a plan. She literally reeled, hitting the side of the door to support her body. She took a deep breath and then another. How long had it been since her senses had gone this crazy? Not. Ever. She was positive.

Chapter 1

Dark Spell

"Antsy... Restless... Feels like you're doing jumping jacks in your skin, my brother?" Christopher Forbes stared at the sleeping monitor in front of him and not at his best friend who asked the question. *Yeah. Trev nailed it.* "Yo... I'm talking to you, Chris," Trev nudged. "You got all kinds of good shit going for you. Plus, you're a real head-turner walking down the street."

He ignored that last comment. "But that's how I feel." *And lately? All the time.* "Now I've got work to do."

"Yeah, yeah, like finishing one routine report is gonna make a difference. Hey bro, we've already secured our niche on the corporate ladder, even though we kings of the late shift don't dress the part and answer to no one, my man. Our plan's tight, okay?"

Neither of them did suits and ties. That's why this shift remained their domain. Jeans and soft shirts their preferred version of corporate wear. "Yeah. I get it. I've got to start this report."

Trev chuckled. "You can do it with your eyes closed, my man. What you really need is some quality chill time," Trev said with a little more gravity in his voice. "Like we always say, having the company's best interest in mind means never updating the old resume.

Damn. We are the best and brightest. HR dudes think we do no wrong. So take some chill time."

"Sure. Right after I finish the report," he answered, hoping to end the conversation. If he had special powers, he'd will this crazy tension out of his shoulders. It had been there all week, and every time he tried to concentrate his mind wandered. This had never happened before. And he didn't need an amateur therapy session with his best friend.

"Look. It's the beginning of the month, and there aren't any issues tonight," Trev said with a stretch, leaning far back in his lumbar support chair personally picked for long hours of screen work. "I'm only saying—"

"Yeah. I know what you're saying," Chris replied, feeling more and more like a mad dog at the end of a chain.

"I can handle it, my brother, if you need some chill time."

He shook his head. "No. I'm good."

"You are not good. Listen to me. Go. I've got the report."

"What if—"

"What if what? Some overseas clients can't call up payroll docs from the cloud? I've got this. And since you don't want to discuss restless and antsy, just get up and go."

Friends since high school and now partners for years, their work ethic and thoroughness with clients had secured them a huge corner office overlooking a handpicked row of reps, whose names they knew and had personally hired. They were both by the book and reliable. Company men through and through. But even squinting, he couldn't focus on the columns that swam across the screen. "Okay. You win. I'll do a half-personal and come back for end-of-shift closeout."

"I can handle that, too."

"I know you can."

"So why am I still seeing you?"

He eyed his partner across the office at the other desk before he blew out a breath. Made quick work of clicking the entry for personal time in the portal. Maybe Trev was right. A couple extra hours to clear his head and be right back here Sunday evening. Seemed like a plan. As if reading his mind, Trev said, "I'll do weekend night email coverage, too."

"No need to. I'll log in."

"Nope, no, and nada. Deal with whatever shit's throwing you off your game. So, we good?" his friend added with an easy smile.

He nodded with a grin as he stood. *Without a doubt, I'm done for the night,* he thought pulling off the headset to fully disconnect from all real-time drama in the client world.

"See you Monday evening but call if anything comes up."

"Keisha's taking the baby to her mom's for the weekend, so all I've got on the schedule is leaf blowing and watching football. Listen. You be good, my brother. Take care of you. And don't catch that crazy-ass flu shit flying around out there," Trev added with a finger wag. "People are dropping like dead flies."

He thought about news reports all over social media. But antsy and restless weren't flu symptoms. He had no fever. No stomach pains. What ailed him had to be in his head. *Maybe get out of the city and spend the weekend doing yard work at the house in Jersey? Maybe put up a profile on some dating app and get a personal life?* He couldn't even make up his mind about what to do. Sure. His social life suffered because of night shift hours. But he had weekends free and it never got in the way before. *Restless. Antsy.* No other words described what rumbled through his soul like rolling thunder.

He took the elevator to freedom, leaving behind all the unmanageable catastrophes his team often wrestled with. He thought about small businesses trying to come back from stock market fluctuations or the crazier shit like this year's rampant flu epidemic racing across the country like a wildfire out of control. Everyone felt edgy.

*Yeah, a vacation somewhere at some remote Scottish hotel in the Highlands.* For years he used vacation time to spend with his elderly parents. They'd been well into their forties when they adopted him. Had given him a great life. But they'd both been gone two years already. He shifted his weight as a chill ran through him. No. He had grieved, dealt with the loss, and had moved on full of loving memories.

*Antsy. Restless. How has whatever this is gotten so bad so quickly?* So much so that Trev had seen it in him. *It's only natural,* he told himself, *because we go way back.* But those two words—exactly what he had been thinking—came out of Trev as if he had read his mind. *Shit.* Still lost in thought, he stepped out of the elevator and into the lobby.

"Done for the night, Mr. Forbes?"

He almost jumped out of his skin and then stared at the guard at the front desk. "Yeah," he answered, pulling out of a foggy haze, something he never experienced, either.

"You feeling all right? There's a nasty bug going around."

"Yeah. I'm okay," he answered. The security guard unlocked the glass door at the side of the revolving behemoth. "Thanks," he said with a half-smile before standing on the empty sidewalk to take in a deep breath.

The October air smelled fresh and clean, something unusual for midtown Manhattan. High above the towering buildings one could actually see stars in the sky tonight, sense the stillness halfway between midnight and dawn. He crossed the street and headed up the next block. Thrusting his hands in the pockets of his jeans, he let out a sigh. *Just. Plain. Restless.*

Maybe he *did* need to find someone special because twenty-five and single was one thing. But thirty-five and single sometimes felt like a life-sentence. The dating pool had thinned for him. And more often than not, he could almost sense the woman not right for him. That didn't stop him from trying, though. He just hadn't found the right one yet. As he walked, he wondered if his future was like these dark Broadway theaters… where the plays had already closed. *I really need a drink tonight. Let the brain shut down for a few.* He'd never been a barfly; didn't do the club scene. Definitely not in the pre-dawn hours.

Yet he strode down the empty street as if someone kept pulling his arm. Turning down a side street off Broadway, his eye caught a glittery sign halfway down the block. Stopping beneath it, Chris looked up. *Destiny* it read in neon letters. *Yeah, so what is mine?* Intrigued by the thought, he shrugged and approached the door.

The bouncer looked like he belonged with the WWF. The huge cover-charge shocked him. "I just want one drink," he argued, aware of the odd, grinding music coming from somewhere within.

"It's mandatory," the bouncer barked.

*Kiss my ass,* he thought pulling out a credit card from his wallet. And after a quick swipe, the big-foot monster moved aside. As he tucked his wallet into the back pocket of his jeans, he studied the glittery papered walls. Bejeweled crescent moons and five-pointed stars reflected from high-hat lights strategically placed like a path before he took the stairs down.

The club had a wide-open underground space with four square columns. It had a curved bar with a continual barrage of customers being served simultaneously by very attractive bartenders, more than half of them women with tight, low-cut shirts that looked like a second skin. Black leather couches lined the walls, all of them occupied. He'd never seen so many haute couture dresses and suits in one place before. And yeah, obviously he looked *really* underdressed for this place. People stood in groups drinking and talking while the dance floor appeared full as well. A new song started, the music unique, almost erotic, performed on low strings. The melody swirled around as if to engulf the crowd, hypnotizing, lilting… Probably on purpose.

He scanned the groin-grinding dancers. Laser-like flashes bouncing off expensive watches, dripping diamond necklaces, and every other type of priceless gem. These were the rich and beautiful— and he didn't fit in. But he made his way to the bar, ordered scotch on the rocks and downed it. Then he found the perfect dark column to lean against. As the song ended, the sound of a woman laughing caught his eye. He scanned the dance floor before quickly doubling back to a feminine laugh.

She was a stunning, gorgeous woman, blonde and petite, with eyes that sparkled. As if the world stopped spinning and time stood still, Chris couldn't look away when she glanced at him.

Three men surrounded her, so he shifted to the right. And when one of the men moved aside, his back stiffened. Just his luck. Executives from his company. The way they leaned into her bothered him, as if they owned her or perhaps, she owned them. She sure looked gorgeous enough. She moved closer to where he stood. Of course, the three men followed. He turned aside because this would be a no-guilt eavesdrop. Every employee knew that the company upheld a high moral code.

"I don't care what your qualifications are, babe, you're hired. I'll make you my personal assistant," one man said holding out a card with two fingers. "Name your salary and I'll double it just to look at you every day." The two other buffoons, one the head of HR, laughed as they raised their drinks.

"What the hell," Chris muttered.

"What if I want to run my own department," he heard her ask.

"Not a problem. Like I said, name your salary," the head of HR replied.

*What a friggin' lie, not to mention false hiring practice.* The man did a half-turn as if to look around, maybe to see if anyone heard him, and Chris pushed back into the shadows. Shit, if they saw him then this excursion to *Destiny* could turn into a dangerous one. And hearing this type of not-so-normal offer? *Who the hell gets to name their price or double their salary. It's a highly respected company totally on the up and up.*

One that believed in signed moral clauses. Is this *really* how they do business?

Although he'd only had one drink, he felt lightheaded. He could choke on the amount of weird in this club. When a new song pounded a heady rhythm that thrummed in his chest, working his way through the dazzling dancing crowd, Chris headed up the stairs to the exit.

This information could come back to bite him. If they recognized him. If they *seriously* recruited this way... *If only God knows what else.* These execs, jacked up on booze and a very *iffy* what-else, could escort him out the door with his work-life in a cardboard box on Monday. He took the stairs mulling over these questions and more. But... that beautiful, drop-dead gorgeous woman, the way her wide eyes met his stayed in mind.

The closer he got to the doorway, the faster his thoughts split in two. Found it hard to concentrate on the more important issue. He had worked hard for this position. So had Trev. Would they fire him, too? Suddenly feeling more woozy, he made it out to the street and leaned against an old-fashioned lamppost outside *Destiny's* door. How long would it take before one of them came out to confront him? And that woman... what if she tried to get away from them and had no one to help? He closed his eyes thinking, *go back inside for her or get the fuck out of here.* But he couldn't move.

"Are you okay?"

Chris glanced over and down to his left. He couldn't respond, too enamored by such astounding beauty, her alabaster skin made more desirable by the soft glow of the lamplight. Long blonde hair seemed to shimmer against her perfect shoulders. Her full breasts heaved with every breath and looking up at him, the blue of her eyes resembled a summer sky. She asked again, and this time he replied, "Yeah. Yes. I'm fine. Thanks for asking."

"Thank me for asking," she said with a charming laugh. "You almost scared me, it took you so long to speak." He straightened up as her gaze slid back to *Destiny's* door with a jerk of her chin. "Maybe we should get away from here. Walk with me." The brush of her hand on his forearm sent a shiver up his spine. Yet always a gentleman, he offered his arm, and she took it. Together they headed to Broadway in silence.

"I'm five-foot four in bare feet."

Chris narrowed his eyes and glanced at her. "I was just thinking that."

"You didn't want those executives from your company to know you were in there."

Curious as to why she said that, he answered, "No. Not at all."

"They made you uncomfortable, so you left."

He nodded once. "Anything else you want to tell me before I say it?"

"Think a question."

*Not on your life.*

They stopped before crossing the street even though there was no traffic at this hour. Her smile enchanted him. "Are you always this concerned about morals and getting a friend fired that you go weak-kneed? Were you really worried about me?"

"This is a very weird first conversation," he replied, not knowing what else to say. Because it was.

"Then let's begin again," she said with a laugh that

almost tinkled. They walked farther down Broadway, turned onto an empty block with theaters. "My name is Aurora."

He smiled, captured by her lovely eyes. "Hello, Aurora."

"Hello, Chris. So very pleased to make your acquaintance."

Had he told her his name? He couldn't remember. Her hand suddenly covered his, and he couldn't recall his last thought as he drowned in her beauty, such a vision of loveliness. A split second later, they were sitting on a bench in a park he'd never noticed before. Right here in the theater district. *Freakin' odd,* he thought. The lightening sky appeared held at bay as the crescent moon brightened. A soft caressing breeze added to the lethargy of the moment. Yet here he sat on a park bench, next to the most enchanting woman he'd ever laid eyes on, and he felt strange. Blinking a few times didn't clear his mind. Her perfume, a blend of spices and flowers, enticed like an aphrodisiac. Sexy. Erotic.

"Does the scent of me turn you on?" she asked, as if they were in a tunnel with her sensual voice softly echoing off metal walls.

"Why?" he asked, like an idiot. The disorientation made him dizzy, yet Aurora smiled in a carefree manner. "Where are we? I don't recognize—"

"We are safe from all the troubles in your world."

"My... my world?"

One shoulder lifted and a grin began. "I find you worthy of me," she purred.

"Worthy... of you?" *What is she saying?*

"Don't try to understand. Just feel." Her hand slid between his knees and crept upward. Her lips met his with an urgency that could only lead to more pleasure. He found himself selfishly kissing her back, hungry for more of her. His tongue sought hers like a lightning bolt seeks water. Her hand slid higher and when she cupped against him, nature took over. Lost in a sinful fantasy, his kiss deepened.

"Touch me," she whispered as if in a dream. "This is what I want." His hand slid under her red dress. Aurora sighed a soft "yes, it's what we both want." More than seductive, she straddled his lap. "Explore. Wander. It will relieve the restlessness within."

"Restless," he whispered, her command his to follow.

"So very restless and you don't know why," she replied as if reading more than one emotion he felt rumbling beneath his skin. She nibbled his lower lip, ran her fingers through his hair. Placing her hands on his shoulders with a slow rock and a slower moan, her nails tickled his skin. And he craved more.

In the blink of an eye, she was naked. Lifting off his lap, she took his hand, and led him deep into the thicket of trees. There wasn't a single rational thought left in him. The fact that he didn't do this sort of thing. The fact that he didn't even know her. The fact that he felt compelled to follow as if in a dream state, a strange fantasy. None of it seemed real.

"Only you and I matter on this night of the crescent moon because I have chosen you." In the blink of an eye she stood at the base of a magnificent tree, it's canopy of autumn leaves rustling in a gentle breeze. Her arms stretched wide, the sway of her hips intoxicating.

He approached with no will of his own. Her wrist flicked and his clothes disappeared. Her hands ran down his body, working him in a greedy way. Hot and heavy, his body responded. Heat shimmered off her skin with a scent so erotic that he drew in deep breaths, each one more stimulating than the one before. Her leg bent around him, and she let out a purr. He was hard and ready, willing, and fully able. Thrust into overdrive, his heartrate soared. With her pinned between him and the majestic tree, he plunged into her racing toward a frenzied rhythm.

*By all the immortal sorcerers of the Second Realm, have I not picked utter perfection*, Aurora thought as he pumped and thrust. *Tall and muscular like a warlock in his prime. Chiseled features and bright-blue eyes as if he were of my realm. The length of him hard and thick to fill my fertile womb.* His head bent forward, and she breathed in the scent of his blond hair, the colored strands catching beams of moonlight.

"With power within me, dark arts delight, I fill with his seed this crescent moon night," she whispered to the archer's bow of an orb in the sky, the consent of the universe her wish and greed her sole purpose.

The passion he filled her with was a perk, never expecting *this* amount of pleasure rolling through her body. How to make it last came to mind, and with a quick incantation time itself slowed. She positively quivered with new sensations. Pure ecstasy. Once again her gaze rose to the sky. "With power within me, dark arts delight, I fill with his seed this crescent moon night."

As her captive's heartbeat raced again, she almost couldn't wait for his climax. One hand gripped her bottom. The other up against the tree. He moaned and threw back his head, pure bliss carved in his handsome features as hot seed shot out.

But she wasn't done with him yet. She watched their bodies unlock, planting a new thought in his head. "You still crave me," she whispered as he staggered back. To drown in delicious kisses. To be mounted again. She'd take it all, feeling like a goddess of the night, an erotic fantasy his human mind would never recall.

*Why not,* she thought. *A fine specimen such as he could be made to climax again.* Yes. She had chosen well. Once more and then he would rest for a lifetime. He'd be the puppet and she'd pull the strings, forever under her spell and a pawn in her destiny.

"Come," she ordered, easing her hand down his chest. He moaned with his lids low and his jaw slack. Greedy for more, she stood on her tiptoes, fisted his hair to capture his mouth. Their tongues meshed together as she slid her hand low to grip him. Erect again, she'd put it to good use. *Now for a little variety...* Turning around, her back fit perfectly to his chest. His hand reached around to cup her left breast and she sighed, rubbing her bottom to tease his erection. It felt erotic and naughty. But she could get naughtier still. They sank to their knees together, fully in sync.

Her hands hit the carpet of leaves in front of the conjured tree. Her hips jerked and bucked another invitation. When he grabbed her hips anticipation soared. This penetration felt jolting and rough. She liked it. Very much. His thrusts hard enough to make her cry out in pleasant pain. Letting her elbows give way, the erotic sense of acting submissive had her panting. When she had enough, well, not really—she intoned, "With power within me, dark arts delight, I fill with his seed this crescent moon night," for the final time as his sperm filled her.

It seemed almost a shame to steal her captive's future. But sacrifice is often necessary for greatness. She envisioned the joining of sperm and egg. She envisioned her belly growing. She envisioned herself the Mother-Queen of the Second Realm.

He gasped before collapsing on top of her. Grunting and strangely enjoying the weight of him, she took a moment before squirming out to freedom. The sex had been better than expected. No warlock had ever come like that. They never made her orgasm like she had tonight, either. *Maybe take a human servant as a lover on the side. It's doable. An easy spell.*

But… she had more to do before leaving him in this deserted alley. She stood and that slinky red dress clung to her body. She waved a hand and a vial appeared in her palm. She pulled out the stopper and went to work. A few strands of hair. A swab of saliva. She rolled him over and ran the vial over the tip of his flaccid cock before recapping it. With a second incantation another appeared, which she uncapped. She reached under her dress and filled it with his seed, then resealed that one as well. Just in case, she'd freeze this one.

*What a handsome specimen he is.* She studied his face, his toned muscles. *I have chosen well, indeed.* Her left palm waved over her victim, head to toe, in a deliberate fashion. Unless she freed his mind, this would be how he remained. For a brief second, she thought of the unwritten laws. What she had done tonight went against all of them. *To interfere with humans in their world? To cross dimensions without proper permission through a secret portal? Unthinkable and also untraceable.* She shrugged a shoulder. *Well, so what?* A sly smile began thinking about the Gatekeeper with contempt. The vampire would never know. And besides, *never* would she kowtow to silly rules or filthy vampires.

She allowed one last look at her victim. "Farewell, Christopher, thank *me* for all you've done."

Stepping away from his naked body, her hands shot wide. "I summon you open," she intoned. The air swirled and a ripple began. The small rip grew large enough to slip through. The lush, autumnal setting slowly revealed its true form. An empty space between two theaters, just blocks away from a nightclub called *Destiny*.

Chapter 2

Dark Witch

Aurora stepped into the Second Realm making sure she'd not be seen or sensed. It was her time to shine by defying the unwritten laws. With a secret incantation she sealed the portal as much as she could, until nothing more than a small rip. No one ever came so deep into the forest at the edge of the realm. No one knew of the secret portal's existence. And it would stay that way. For now. Someday far in the future, news of it would make her rich beyond belief. Selling its location to the highest bidder an exciting possibility.

With the portal so far from her cottage, she'd have to keep the dark spell going and soundlessly hike the narrow path through the forest. Cloaked in incantations to further protect from detection, she forged ahead with her red stilettos in hand becoming one with the earth, one with the thick richness of evergreen firs surrounding her. *No nosey filthy guard will find my path. No sorcerer will be the wiser. No witch will detect what might be seen as devious.* Her plan had been flawless, executed with class and perfection. Plus, she'd just proven how that slimy vampire of a Gatekeeper could be duped. A wicked grin appeared. How easy it all had been!

Was it chance or fate that they had crossed paths in the last hours before his world's sunrise? Was it chance or fate that this god of a man had found her in the club called *Destiny*? Christopher Forbes. She'd been drawn to him as if nothing else mattered. Shaking off the memory, she redoubled her efforts to focus on self-protection and entered the clearing. The clover felt soft under her feet, and with a prance she approached the three steps that led up to the porch of a quaint-looking cottage.

Before entering, she turned her face up to study the first moments of the crescent moon in the Second Realm. She scanned its narrow strip of light leading to the cottage door. A twist of her wrist slipped the lock and she entered before securing the door with a thought. Lights flickered awake without a touch. The fire in the central hearth flamed high and hot. Warm colors on the walls, thick curtains over the windows made the space her cocoon. Spells cast with intent kept her secrets within this bubble.

Legend had it that the cottage had been abandoned over thirty years ago by Gwendolyn on the night she disappeared. The warlock's body had been found inside, stabbed like fresh meat and dead for days. Realm dwellers thought the cottage cursed because of what had happened here. And crafty Gwendolyn had cloaked her actions in such a way that even the strongest magic could not penetrate her secrets. Oh, how Aurora had craved stories about the chosen witch and her boy-child when she was young. Thinking about it made her smile, imagining the drama, the sadness, the gaps between what really happened and what folklore had embellished.

With utmost care, she slithered out of the red dress and then burned it in the blazing fire along with the sexy red stilettos. She hated to part with those shoes. Naked and free, she walked through her home to the bedroom.

She held out her palm. The vial opened to let the blend of seed, hair, and saliva intertwine before it floated through the air to settle into a conjured locket. Once filled with three elements of life, it's five sides sealed. Another incantation would keep the dark spell strong and resistant to all other magic. A wave of her hand had the amulet secure around her neck.

The all-important vial of semen appeared in her palm. Strutting into the kitchen, she went to the freezer and placed it deep within. Dancing around full of pride, her eyes swept across the modern layout she had conjured. Most Second Realm homes were modest and simple. Not hers. It satisfied her to defy 'the norm,' reaching into upper-class minds for ideas and fashionable furnishings. Whether half-breed or pure-bred, many Second Realm dwellers recalled living in the human world. Those minds were the easiest to pluck a picture from.

She prepared for bed with care. Clean face covered with expensive elixirs. Hands, arms, and legs oiled with a fragrant herbal reduction she created herself. The canopy bed stood high and firm in the center of the room, and she carefully slid under the covers. Three soft pillows raised her legs, but the one under her head felt firm, comfortable. For the next forty-eight hours she'd be in a trance-like state. To ensure conception. To ensure her future.

How many witches' journals had she read? Hundreds? Thousands? Housed in the Hall of Memories near the palace, she had groveled and obeyed and submitted to the elder witches to secure the position of a Memory Keeper. It had taken years to gain their trust. But she accomplished the task. Pouring over Second

Realm records from decades of childbirth documents, she had studied each one for specific information. Important hints on how to ensure conception, how to hold a child in the womb; how to do this or that, blah-blah-blah. She even combed through forbidden tomes kept separate, as if their segregation wouldn't tarnish *The Pure-Breed Roll of Births*.

She squirmed in the bed, more comfortable now. But of course, comfort didn't matter as much as purpose. A true purpose, which was contrived, but a true one, nevertheless. And of course, she'd cheat a bit, for personal reasons like relieving herself and sips of water for sustenance. No. She wouldn't eat. And as the crescent moon grew, semen and egg would conjoin.

She visualized tonight's most impressive outcome. Sensual. Supple. Mesmerizing... The thoughts placed in everyone encountered tonight. None in the club had escaped her charm, and it had been so very easy to bend a human mind. One night of erotic sex to fill her with living seed. One night to be remembered only by her.

She had studied and planned. Planned and studied. Not for decades had Second Realm dwellers felt any sort of excitement. Her plan would bring it back. A snap of her fingers produced her private journal. Once more she read the excerpt from the *Book of Calipha*...

*Here in the Second Realm, the Night of the Crescent Moon shall be a time most holy. Between the hours of dusk and dawn, the chosen ones will merge and become one, bearing fruit to further the race of wizard and witch alike.*

*Here in the Second Realm, the warlock and witch shall surrender the boy-child to the rulers of the realm. He shall be the holy one, the future of our race, the purest of the pure.*

*Here in the Second Realm, when the new warrior reaches Enlightenment, he will sacrifice himself to ensure the rulers of the realm's immortality.*

*Thus, it is written. Thus, mote it be.*

Closing her journal, a hand waved to conceal it. Hundreds of crescent moons had come and gone without the prophesied child. Yes. Change was necessary. The sorcerers had begun to show their demise in odd ways. Weather not as controlled as before. Birth population of purebred witch and warlock had declined dramatically since humans were brought to the realm as servants sixteen years ago when thousands of portals sealed shut. Seven portals were left. One on each continent. And each had a Gatekeeper. The price of portal travel was strictly limited to very few. One could say her finding a hidden portal had been more than serendipity, as if fate smiled upon only her, as if meant to be.

Other shifts had occurred. Constant gossip about spells and conjures going awry, the results often hideously pathetic. Many realm dwellers were too skittish to use dark magic, the practice considered much too greedy and subversive. Well. Not her. Then cane whispers of how the sorcerers were no longer as powerful as they used to be three decades ago. Celebrations no longer as spectacular; not well attended.

*She* was a pure-breed, born and raised in the Second Realm. When the vast migration of witch and warlock from the human world occurred, she, like many other pure-breeds, believed the realm began to deteriorate. Human servants brought with them their own miseries. They were not to be trusted. And as for the vampires in the Third Realm? Now they were truly a nasty, conniving lot… all of them.

As Aurora the Mother-Queen, she'd lobby for war with the Third Realm. The blood drinkers secretly yearned to rule all three realms. *What filth beneath my feet!* The memory of Bonfire and captured vampires blazing like torches before they burst into dust and bits of bone excited her. As a child, she loved to watch Bonfire. Pure-breeds would make the pilgrimage to the far away palace of the sorcerers. Bonfire would be reinstated for anyone who threatened the Second Realm. Vampire, human or half-breed would burn—once she ascended to Mother-Queen.

*The time has arrived.* Full of confidence, Aurora let out an exhausted sigh. It had been a productive excursion into the human world. Planning, preparation, timing. All had been perfect. She fingered the locket at her breast dreaming of what was to come.

Chapter 3

Good Witch

Martine Kendrick had exceptional nursing skills. She was also the youngest member of the Kendrick witches, women with a powerful sixth sense, users of good magic. Super smart, feisty, and one hell of an ER nurse, Martine loved the energy on the shift from dusk to dawn. St. Francis Hospital implemented the specialized in-between shift for two additional nurses a month ago because of this wicked, early flu season. Not having to think twice, she volunteered for an immediate schedule change. She craved being busy at work. And with everything in her personal life keeping her stuck in the in-between, it suited her mental and emotional state like something custom-made for comfort.

Dottie, her favorite co-worker for the past four years, came to the nurses' station looking dead on her feet. Short, round and usually full of energy, the look on her face read frazzled. "Did you hear the EMS's call, M?"

She gave a grin and two thumbs up. "Sure did. Cubicle Q is prepped."

"It's another reroute, so call it quaint or quirky—" then they said together, "we nurses of the in-between are ready to roll." Dottie nodded with a snort as Martine raced down the left corridor to meet the ambulance diverted from St. Claire's with another John Doe.

Lately, there had been a bumper crop of patients just before daybreak. Waiting inside the ER doors, Martine closed her eyes and focused her mind. With the ambulance still minutes away, she honed in on the new JD with little effort because there was a huge difference between a knife wound or some poor homeless guy with a taste for mixing drugs and alcohol. Her sixth sense told her the male in transit hadn't been in a traffic accident. In fact, the unusual way she clutched her stethoscope said there might be something different about this one. Funny. She could usually link her mind to victims in transport, but this one gave off nothing at all.

Probing deeper, she stifled a quick gasp. Pain slammed into her forehead and at the base of her neck in a weird way. This didn't feel right. It felt other-worldly—out-of-the-ordinary. Definitely not her normal reaction sensed with some random act of violence.

Just like that, she knew. Something or someone had used dark magic. But why? And above all, how? Because unwritten laws were very clear in every dimension. And with portals closed to the human world, whatever managed to lock down a human's mind didn't do so randomly. It had been a specific assault, which meant it had a plan. She literally reeled, hitting the side of the door to support her body. She took a deep breath and then another. How long had it been since her senses had gone this crazy? Not. Ever. She was positive.

Certain facts became crystal clear. For the human mind to be so locked in pain, the perpetrator had to be powerful. Plus, to leave the victim in such a void proved malicious intent beyond a doubt. Vampires couldn't do something like this, although she'd be sure to scan the man's body for bite marks. Also, this type of mind violation spoke to the perpetrator's intelligence and ability level. Again, not a vampiric signature. *No. Couldn't be a vampire.* She didn't sense this even remotely possible, which meant one thing. *Outlawed dark magic practiced in the Second Realm. A dark witch or warlock, neither welcome in the innocent human world. But how did one get through the portal?* Maybe she was wrong.

But that last thought sent a shiver down her spine burning at the small of her back. Portal travel wreaks havoc on a human body. *Is that why I can't sense anything in this man's mind? Had he escaped from the Second Realm? But how?* She knew of only one person who had experienced portal travel and survived. He had only been about thirteen at the time. Closing her eyes she whispered, "Lukas," and immediately regretted saying his name out loud. They had stopped talking five years ago, and no, she wouldn't pick up a phone to ask Lu about it. Besides, he probably wouldn't even speak to her after the way she had purposely pushed him out of her life. *Let it go, M, opening that can of worms is not an option.*

No. *Maybe I'm totally off base.* How could a witch scramble a man's brain like that? *And it isn't even a full moon, which juices a witch's power like a half dozen shots of Italian espresso.* Obviously, the cure wouldn't be found within modern human medicine. She shook her head. Why make an innocent suffer? His thoughts could have just been wiped clean. He might have a headache for a while, but he'd resume normal life within weeks. Dark magic packed a powerful kick. That user would undeniably suffer. *We live by a code of honor: Do no living creature harm.*

She locked the mental rambling down as the ambulance backed up to the ER doors and whispered, "By all that is good, help me figure this out." The doors of the ambulance opened. Two of the best EMS workers she knew brought the stretcher to the ground. Hitting the ER door release she watched them slide wide. "And a very good morning to you, M," Tim said, one of the crew who had the best smile in the city. She liked him. He had a good soul.

"Hey good lookin'," she replied with a slight smirk, "Whacha' got cookin' for us?"

"This is a weird one for sure. Where to?"

With a tilt of her head to the left, she replied, "Cubicle Quirky is prepped. Lead the way and I'm right behind." Looking down, already sick to her stomach, she focused on the victim. Her pulse raced and sweat dotted her brow... not her usual reaction. *Which means I have to save him.* Like a silent vow to the universe itself, commitment shot through her heart. Her sixth sense quivered with anticipation like a warning or a plea when she looked at him again. At least serendipity landed this one on her shift. Between magic and her medical skills, he had a fighting chance. And she would do her best.

"M? Are you with us," she heard Tim say.

"Right here," she replied as they settled the JD into Cubicle Q's bed.

Tim shook his head. "Damn. And it's not even a full moon."

"I know," she replied, studying her new patient. Off the cuff and for no reason at all she added, "It's a crescent moon?"

"Yeah. It is."

25

Again, her sixth sense hummed. Old witches' tales raced through her brain like flipped pages in a children's book. Rhymes, prophecies about birth and death during the crescent moon. Old, wise witches had some really freaky stories. Taking his blood pressure, she asked, "What do you have so far?"

"Vitals are strong. No marks or bruises. BP was good in the field. I'm guessing somewhere in his mid-thirties, but we found no ID on him. Guess his wallet was stolen along with his clothes. He was unconscious when we got there."

"Who called it in?"

"Some neighborhood watch people saw him lying in an alley around dawn and called it in."

"Where did you find him?"

"In a space between two theaters off of Broadway. Naked as the day he was born."

"No clothes or anything around?"

"Nope."

"And no signs of a fight?"

"None."

An eyebrow rose. "So just a good-looking man naked and unconscious in an alley with no identification whatsoever."

He gave a shrug. "Maybe a hook-up gone wrong?"

"Not my department. Did the sarge in charge take photos and prints?"

Ready to leave, Tim answered, "Yep. Want me to keep you posted?"

"No. I'm sure they'll assign a detective." She checked the IV-drip of fluids as tonight's ER doctor entered the cubicle. Short, stubby, and oh-so-sweet, Forster was one of the best.

"His vitals are good," Martine offered before he asked the question. "CT Scan of his head?"

"Rush it," Doc Forster added with a nod. "Any trauma to his body?"

"Nothing we can see."

"All right, then." He scratched his head, "Let's get the scan and see what's going on inside. Full blood panel, too." He swiped his finger across the all-important electronic tablet poking boxes before scribbling an unreadable signature.

"I'd like to stay with this one," Martine stated.

"Sure," he replied as he left.

*So what's your story, JD, and why did you end up here tonight?* She always gave a full one-hundred percent, just like her co-workers. But this case felt like something more than a mystery... the kind that makes your head hurt and your stomach sour. Whatever happened to John Doe had to be based in the supernatural. Something sinister and selfish, which went against good magic everywhere.

Martine stared at her co-worker on the in-between shift, and within seconds, Dottie glanced her way. "I'm staying with the Cubicle Quirky case until he gets a CT scan."

"No worries," Dottie fired back. The mid-forties mother of two let out a sigh. "Do you want help taking him?"

"Nope. I can handle it."

Dottie eyed him, head to toe. "Oh boy, not hard to look at. Who is he?"

"Damned if anyone knows." Watching Dottie leave, her new patient's handsome features, his fit and trim build weren't lost on her, either. She didn't get print model or construction worker; sensed his good looks genetic. *Maybe a lawyer or accountant.* Once the police did their job, she'd find out. One thing was certain, though. If dark magic had been used on him there would be damage the eye could not see. Although his features stayed relaxed as if in a deep, sound sleep, in reality, his brain held chaos with explosions of pain scrambling every nerve.

"Psychic investigation, here I come," she whispered. Could she reverse the spell? Messing with someone else's magic often had ugly consequences. "Too risky," she mumbled. Unlocking the bed's wheels she studied John Doe again. He looked perfectly healthy. But looks were often deceptive. First and foremost, an innocent had been violated. *Sad, really… just how fragile the human mind actually is.* "But I've got you now," she whispered, pulling the bed out of the cubicle. If fate brought him to her, then she was on board.

Steering the bed down the corridor she went through another set of doors, made a right then a quick left to the scan pavilion. "Is this our JD?" the technician asked.

"Yep. I'll stay during the scan."

"No problem," the tech answered. He prepped John Doe with care as Martine watched from the booth. And when the technician joined her, they observed the scan process together.

The realization got her back up, made bitterness stir within as if it could swell up high and gush. Already knowing the answer, she asked anyway, "See anything unusual?"

"No. Everything looks good," was the dreaded answer as the process came to conclusion. Obviously, he had done enough of these. If something looked wonky, the tech would see it as well. "Okay. You can take him."

Martine cleared her throat. "Thanks. Have a good rest of shift." He helped her get JD settled on the rolling bed and fixed the cotton blanket around him. The deception of peaceful sleep cut like a knife as she pushed her patient out of the scan pavilion and back to Cubicle Quirky.

****

Dottie gripped the foot of the bed locking it in place. "So... surprise, surprise. No room at the inn this morning, handsome," she whispered as if he were awake and alert.

"No bed?" Martine asked.

"Not a one. Johnny is staying right here for a while."

"Oh," she replied with a bit of relief. "I told Doc Forster I wanted to stay on this one. Can you handle the others?"

"What others?" Dottie chuckled. "It's almost peaceful now. I've got a broken arm waiting for release papers in Cubicle Sweet and a dementia case going on about crescent rolls or something like that in Cubicle Treat. No worries. Stay with your man."

*Crescent rolls or crescent moon?* "Wait. Can you stay with him a minute? I really have to pee."

"Sure. Take your time. No one's going anywhere in a hurry."

Once outside the curtain, she raced down the thirty feet to Cubicle T. An old woman lay shivering, blanketed to her chin. The unfocussed stare intrigued Martine, and she approached without a sound. But then her sixth sense did that tingle thing again. Without a doubt, this was no ordinary dementia case. They shared magic-knowledge. She felt certain. *Tell me of the crescent moon*, she whispered to the woman's mind.

The old one whimpered. Stray whisps of gray hair appeared full of static as she shook her head. Her eyes stayed wide, glazed over as a solitary tear edged its way down the side of her wrinkled face. *A dark witch came through a secret space between two giants. She wooed the man as only a dark witch can. To steal his future. To steal his seed on the night of the crescent moon.* "Fornication," she moaned low and harsh. "Human seed is taken for a purpose. I know. This is truth."

Holding her brittle hands, Martine leaned closer. "Rest, my sister."

"You must save him."

"I will. With all the good magic I know. This I vow. Now rest."

A slight nod happened before the old one closed her eyes murmuring, "Look to the legend."

Were there other old ones as powerful as her grandmother? She'd have to ask her mother. Straightening her back, slipping out of the cubicle without a sound, Martine shook her head wondering how she could make such a promise. Perhaps the old one *had* been strong in her day. Perhaps her mind lapsed in and out of reality after years of protecting humans from the dark magic practitioners who often preyed upon the weak. And yet, JD didn't appear weak-minded in the least. She took a cleansing breath and exhaled before opening the curtain to Cubicle Q.

"Thanks, Dottie. All better."

Her co-worker gave an understanding grin. "I'll leave you two alone." She patted Martine's arm. "He really is a handsome one, M. You think the coma is permanent?"

"I don't know, Dottie. Just want to make him comfortable, you know?"

"Sure, honey. Maybe use some of that sixth sense of yours, right? I'm two cubicles away if you need another break."

"Thanks, but I'm good."

"You think you'll stay after your shift?"

"I'm not sure yet."

"Well, let me know."

"Sure thing," she replied.

Once alone, Martine checked his vitals and notated his chart on the patient tablet. She brought her mouth close to his ear. "My name is Martine Kendrick. I know something unnatural happened to you. I'll try to ease your pain. If you understand, think yes and give me a sign." Her heart absolutely sank when no response came. If the spell was weak, he would have been able to think the word. With renewed focus she placed a hand over his forehead and willed him strength. An ever so slight twitch of his eyes happened. "Good job. Let my voice guide you to a place of rest. Ease away from the pain," she whispered three times. But the dark spell cloaked his psyche. At times, she'd pull back, yet the twists and turns remained a chaotic maze holding his brain captive. The old one's words came to mind… *Seed. Fornication. Look to the legends…* Easing away from the patient, she sank into the chair at his side. Legends. Legends and folklore about the Second Realm. She shook her head and whispered, "No. It can't be. It shouldn't be." Her stomach rolled and her heart raced.

What if his mind never could be freed? She thought about scores of humans in facilities, all over the world, whose minds had once been altered by dark magic, many of them diagnosed mentally ill or locked away in prisons. Had John Doe been a good man? She didn't sense even an ounce of evil within him.

Legends and folklore. How foolish of any witch to interrupt a human life for the greedy purpose of fulfilling a stupid legend. Yes, there is always some grains of truth in a legend. *But which is which?* She closed her eyes and whispered, "Please do not let this be true."

\*\*\*\*

Dottie poked her head in with a cheerful, "Shift's over, M." Coming all the way into Cubicle Q, added, "M? Are you okay?"

She managed a weary smile and a slow nod. "Yep. Just tired."

"You look drained."

"That too," she added with a small laugh.

"Jose's right down the hall at the nurses' station. I have the car today. It's grocery time. I can give you a lift home." Martine looked at John Doe and then back at Dottie. "He'll be fine," her co-worker whispered in a concerned tone. "He isn't going anywhere for now and he looks, well, sort of peaceful."

*But he isn't*, Martine thought and then suddenly yawned.

"Ya see? Now that's a sign as your mother would say. Let me get you safe and sound back to Kendrick House. Catch some Zzzzs. Have a nice hot shower and a hot meal before you're right back here for another in-between shift. What do you say?"

It did sound heavenly. "You sold me. Take me with you."

"And don't worry, I already told the day supervisor about our dear John here. She'll keep an eye on him. So will Jose. I even asked him to text you if there's a change."

"Jeez, Dottie," she replied with a chuckle, "motherly super skills just radiate all over the place. But seriously, thanks for doing that."

"You're very welcome. Say good-bye and let's hit the morning traffic."

Martine touched the side of John Doe's face. *Rest. Let peace enter your mind.* Dottie was right. He was very handsome.

Chapter 4

Mother and Daughter

Kendrick House looked like every other brownstone on the city block. A well-kept home with many brick steps leading up to a glossy dark-wood door. A classy autumn wreath of dried flowers and herbs graced the etched glass window on the upper half of it. The knob was an old-fashion one of polished brass, but the keyhole gave away the fact that all had been updated and now very secure.

Flowerpots lined the steps, filled with seasonal mums of various colors. In the summer, the pots held miniature roses, again, of various colors. In the winter, small evergreens lined the steps up to the door. In the spring, hearty Hosta were interspersed with snapdragons, only the bright purple ones.

The ordinary often hides the extraordinary. Inside, a small foyer led to a set of polished stairs straight ahead. Floors of hardwood gave off a sheen of sheer beauty. A mix of classic and functional modern could be seen in every room. Fine Persian carpets woven with colorful patterns set off the living room and dining area. The kitchen, blending old world charm with up-to-date appliances, was at the back of the brownstone. It overlooked a twenty-by-twenty-foot garden. Upstairs had three bedrooms and a large bathroom. Martine's room faced the street. Her mother's bedroom was at the back of the house.

The bedroom between mother and daughter had been her grandmother's, Martha Kendrick, the matriarch of their family. Her renowned skills as a young witch dated back to Granny Martha's childhood. In Martha's memory, that bedroom had been turned into a study. Martine called it her personal link to the greatness of her grandmother's extensive skills. Mary, her mother, rarely came into the room, so Martine appropriated the space as hers alone, like a sanctuary where she felt connected to other powerful female ancestors who had lived here long before she'd been born.

Dottie pulled into an empty spot right in front of the brownstone, even though parking spaces were as rare as finding a flea on a shaggy dog. Almost at the point of total exhaustion from the past fourteen hours and still thinking about her patient, Martine rolled her tense shoulders. "Thanks for the ride, Dottie."

"What are friends for, right? Listen, make sure you eat and then get some quality rest."

Grateful for the genuine concern and that her co-worker hadn't added the usual 'and you're too thin,' she nodded once. "Sure. Will do."

"You think maybe taking tonight off is a possibility?"

"Don't worry. I'll be clear-headed after some sleep. See you after sunset."

"Do you want me to swing by and pick you up?"

"Nah. I like to Uber in." The real reason? So she could be alone with her thoughts— because figuring out how to help her new patient wasn't going to be easy-peasy.

"Okay, but if you change your mind, just shoot me a text."

"Will do," she replied, getting out of the car. Waiting while Dottie pulled away, she gave a small smile and a quick wave. Her co-worker was a gentle soul, a truly good person who had enough on her plate as a single parent.

Turning, she let out a sigh and walked up the stone steps lined with colorful mums. For years, autumn had been her favorite season, watching leaves change the air smelling crisp as humid summer days fade away. Not to mention Halloween and Samhain. Dances and festivals to celebrate the end of harvest and the beginning of the dark months. But four years ago, all of that changed. Autumn meant time to grieve her personal loss. In private. All alone.

Tired as hell and reaching into her bag for the house key, she stood with one foot on the first brick step and took a moment. The breeze tickled against her cheeks as if to awaken the devastating memory. It had been a morning just like this when she lost her daughter. She blew out a sharp breath as if to push away the memory that tore open her heart. *Just put one foot in front of the other*, she thought as she walked up the steps.

She unlocked the etched door. Walking inside, she reset the alarm system. Of course, her keys went right back into her handbag, which she placed on a small table in the foyer. Shrugging out of the dark purple hooded cardigan, one of her all-time favorites, she hung it on a coat hook.

Did she feel hungry? Never much these days. Especially in October. When John Doe arrived, she completely forgot about the plastic container in her locker behind the nurses' station. Couldn't even recall where she had placed her last cup of coffee. Her patient's critical state unnerved her again. Pulling out her cell phone, she thought to text Jose, a great nurse and a real team player to boot. Instead, her finger landed on the call icon. It didn't matter. She'd leave a voice mail, but then Jose answered with a hearty, "*Hola Emita*, what can I do you for?"

Her mouth slid into a smirk. "I didn't expect you to answer."

"Eh, we're slow right now. *Digame*, who is our sleeping beauty?"

"How do you know that's why I called?"

"Ooh, he's some good looker. You think he's my type?"

She chuckled. "I don't know."

"Sure you do, *Emita mia*, you got wicked skills, girl. What are they telling you?"

*Very intuitive,* she thought, answering. "I'm too tired," with a little laugh. "Any change in his condition?"

"*Nada.* BP steady, no erratic heartbeat, and still comatose. I just catheterized him. Urine is clear."

"That's good news. Keep an eye on him for me, will you?"

"Why? You fallin' for our patient or something?"

"You wish, right?"

"Hey, my *abuelita* says alone over thirty is an old maid, you know?"

"Stop trying to give me a happily-ever-after. I'm just concerned. No ID yet?"

"No. I think the local police precinct is pretty overwhelmed with all the *stupido* cuts. Plus, this crazy flu is hitting cops hard. Want me to text if we get a name?"

"Sure. And if there's any change in his condition. I appreciate it."

"No problem. Eat. Make sure you eat, and then get some sleep."

The concern was genuine, and she answered with a soft, "I promise. See you tonight." They'd do an overlap because face-to-face discussion turned out to be far superior to reading updates on a tablet. And Jose never left before updating the relief.

Slipping her phone into her scrub's pocket, she sensed it an unexpected blessing to have all these wonderful professionals on her team. They'd become an extended family she had grown to cherish. Maybe she owed her sanity to them as well. *Today, JD is in good hands.*

Walking through the living room and dining area, she entered the kitchen and gripped the granite counter. Would exhaustion win out over hunger? "Not today," she muttered, pushing herself to head for the fridge. She took out yesterday's pasta with broccoli, the container of grated parmesan and a tub of whipped butter. Just enough energy to fix the plate meant using the microwave instead of heating it on the stove. The next rumble of her stomach confirmed she made the right decision. Fiddling with the ingredients, she placed the dish in the microwave and hit two minutes. Her mind was fried. Her senses dull. She reached for a glass from the kitchen cabinet and filled it with filtered water from the fridge.

Usually, she'd brew a cup of coffee. Not today. She drank deeply, only coming up for air when the steady beep of the microwave sounded. Generous amounts of cheese and butter went on the pasta and broccoli, but it didn't make her mouth water. Before moving from the counter, she whispered while opening the breadbox, "Italian bread, please let there be Italian bread," and to her delight, a fresh loaf stood ready and waiting. Breaking off the heel, she picked up her plate and sat at the kitchen table.

A full minute passed before she stopped playing with her food. She had lost a lot of weight, which, considering her once-curvy figure, didn't look healthy. Spearing a piece of broccoli and one piece of macaroni, she got it to her mouth. The blend of textures made her eyes roll. Heavenly. Heavenly food prepared to perfection. Her brain needed a rest from the puzzling predicament of her patient. *So steering clear of anything other than chewing and swallowing is progress.*

But what exactly happened to John Doe? What misguided witch managed to slip into the human world looking for sex in all the wrong places? Had she been here before? Had she, maybe, known him already? If so, was he complicit? *Maybe I'm getting this all wrong, because maybe he wanted to impregnate her on the night of a crescent moon?* Yet, she didn't sense it true, and she always relied on what she sensed.

*He could actually pass for a warlock.* Her own father had been a warlock. Blond and tall just like JD. She put down the fork and pulled her raven-black hair out of the bushy bun, letting it splay across her shoulders. Then swiveled her neck from side to side. If some witch entered this dimension, well, that spelled trouble with a capital T—with dark and deadly written all over it. *The legend of conceiving and delivering during crescent moons. It had meaning.* Digging her fork into a piece of pasta, she stared at it.

"Don't play with your food. Put a forkful in your mouth and chew."

Yanked out of her reverie, Martine almost slid off the kitchen chair and stared up at her mother. "Okay, Mare," she replied using her favorite term of endearment before spearing a piece of broccoli as well.

"Good. You're going to do that over and over again until the plate's clean. Then we have to talk." Tall and statuesque, her mother came off formidable and bossy. The tone of voice? All chest and not a hint of the maternal. All business, which meant whether or not she wanted to fall into bed and hug a pillow, well, it wouldn't happen.

Mary Kendrick easily read her daughter. "It sure as hell isn't happening," she replied full of concern, which didn't show in her voice or on her face. Sitting across from her stubborn daughter, Mary leaned forward with her folded arms secure on the table. It didn't matter what time she got to the gallery. She'd watch every forkful of food go in until that plate was clean. Respectful of Martine's privacy, Mary usually stayed out of her mind. Not this morning. As the silence continued, *"mommy dearest through and through"* came across loud and clear. Probably, on purpose. "Don't think of me like that. I never said you couldn't use wire hangers, although you should use wood. Clothes hang better. When I was young, my mother said I resembled a young Jane Russell. Never, *never* Joan Crawford—ugh!"

Her daughter swallowed, sipped some water, and took another bite. *She's too thin. Everyone sees it.* Sorrow and loss can do unspeakable damage. *After four tedious years, it's always more than visible in early*

*October.*

The fork clanged on the table. "I need a break. Let the food hit my stomach, Mare. I swear I'll eat more. Cross my heart."

"Yeah, so uncross your feet." She shook her head. "Jesus Christ. Of all the hospitals in New York City, they have to bring him to yours? On your shift? Right near the end of it, so you had ample time to get involved. To try and walk his mind."

Her daughter pushed the plate to the center of the table, perfectly placed between them. "As it is, so shall it be," she stated without emotion.

Mary shook her head slowly. "No. No way. This is trouble, Martine. You never should have walked his mind. You can't get yourself involved with whatever a dark witch has in store for him."

"I had to, especially after I talked to the old one."

"What old one?"

"She was in one of the ER cubicles. She has dementia, but, boy, her mind is a hundred-percent when she's lucid."

"Did you recognize her?"

"No, but she's one of us. Fighting for all that is good, yadayadyada…."

"And she told you about—"

"I saw it in her mind. We had the unspoken kind of conversation. You know. Like the ones you and I have. I heard her loud and clear."

Curious about what her daughter knew and proud of her powerful talents, Mary asked, "So what did she say?"

"Something about a dark witch slipping into our world, and you know she wasn't the friendly Tabitha type. She mentioned the crescent moon. And she used the word fornication. Piecing it all together, between the legend and what was in her mind, I get dark witch on a fertility mission. Having sex with a human for the specific purpose of getting pregnant. Jeez. I hope the old one makes it because she looked pretty weak."

"And the old one just happened to be at the ER, at the same time as your John Doe. At the very hospital you work in."

"One and the same."

"Martine. I urge you to listen to me. You shouldn't get involved."

"Too late. I see need. I help."

"I don't care."

"But I do," she replied, more intense than usual. "Mare, he's an innocent. Used in a terrible way."

"You don't know that, and you aren't going to stick around him to find out." She didn't care if she looked like a cat ready to pounce on an unsuspecting mouse in the house. "The violation of Unwritten Law is never acceptable. The bitch purposely jumped dimensions, knew what she wanted and went for it. We all sensed something, it was the only topic of discussion in our healing circle last night." She had to convince her, saying with a sigh, "Martine. You're jumping into something you can't fix. Again."

"You're crossing a line, Mare."

"No I'm not. I know what you carry in your heart, in your soul. I know the sadness, the devastation."

"It's not what you think."

"Honey, it's exactly what I know to be true. You can't interfere because he's marked by her. She can find him and use him again if she wants to… if what they did last night doesn't result in conception."

The shake of her daughter's head was predictable, also unwise. "It's a ridiculous piece of folklore. The night of the crescent moon crap. How does it go again? I remember you and Granny Martha saying it on All Hallows Eve, like a fairytale turned nightmare or something."

Mary recalled the stories as well, whispering the rhyme. "On the night of the crescent moon, a male child strong will be conceived. And after all his time within, 'twill be on the night of a crescent moon received." She rubbed her forehead and let out a sigh. "It's been said Second Realm witches and warlocks believe this child will be raised like a prince and then sacrificed for the sake of the immortal sorcerers."

Her daughter's hand flew up in the air. "It's bullshit fantasy and folklore. Special births and sacrifice. Pfft!"

With a tilt of her head, Mary studied her daughter. *Too thin and too stubborn.* "Whatever you may or may not believe, if there are issues in the Second Realm, let's say a move against the Third Realm vampires? The next ones they're coming after are those of us who chose to stay in the human world."

Fire lit her daughter's wide, dark eyes, which appeared larger with her cheeks so hollow and pale. "Stop, Mare. Just stop."

"You're very powerful in your command of magic. Also, very smart in the way you think and the way you feel out a situation. You know our ways and our rules forbid us to interfere. We use what we've been given for the good of humankind. We cloak our involvement for a purpose. We don't interfere. We stand down." There. It was said and on the table like the plate between them.

"Good witch ways and all that is right. Yeah. I get

it. But, stand down? No. I won't stand down. You can stand down. The damn healing circles can stand down. But not me. He is an innocent."

Sensing the fury in her daughter, she answered, "You still blame them, don't you?"

"Of course, I blame them," Martine shouted, shooting up and out of the kitchen chair. "Because of some stupid old witch's tale—"

"Martine—"

"I didn't plan it! It wasn't on purpose that I got pregnant during a crescent moon. And when I went into premature labor on the night of a crescent moon, *your* healing circle did nothing to stop it!" Her daughter's body shook. Full of grief. For the past four years, Mary relived the tragedy, too, but kept it to herself. Yet loss is loss. It changes you forever.

"Take a breath, honey, take a sip of water. Please sit back down. My love for you filters through time and space. What happened... that it happened during the crescent moon was just coincidence."

"I'll never forgive them," her daughter hissed.

"Martine," she said like a gentle command, and her daughter eased back into the kitchen chair with her arms crossed tight. Was it because of the physical exhaustion of an intense ER shift or being pushed to the precipice of being broken? She'd say what had to be said. "I swear by all that is true, she came too early to be saved. You're a nurse. You know it in your head as well as your heart. What happened had nothing to do with the moon or an old witch's tale. And we did use our healing powers. To save *you* when you hemorrhaged." Memories of that morning. Her daughter alone in a taxi. Test after test. Rushing to the hospital. Hours in labor. A tiny baby girl's birth that should have been a most joyous occasion turned into a horrible nightmare.

"She'd be four years old this month," her daughter whispered, the expression on her face like an empty canvas. Grief buried deep, but always right there in her eyes. And her daughter could cut you off and shut you down like an expert.

They sat in silence for a full minute before Martine unlocked her arms and laid her hands on the table. Mary covered them with her own. "Mom, I sense something in this man. Lying there so still. So captured in a dark magic spell. I knew as soon as I touched him. Something sinister and supernatural has occurred." She paused. "I live by the law to heal as a nurse. I live by the law to heal as a good witch. The craft doesn't define me like it does you. My path is different. I know it as sure as I'm sitting across from you." Pulling away, her daughter rubbed her eyes and then her hands ran down her face as she blew out a slow breath.

Ready to listen with an open mind, she said, "What is it you sense?"

"He's different. Don't ask me how I know. I just do. Because of the way I reached into his mind for just a split second."

"But you weren't able to communicate with him."

"No. I don't think he knows how we do it. Maybe that's why I tried to lock to his mind. It didn't happen the way it does when we read people. It felt intense and it didn't leave his brain like jelly."

"What did you sense?" she asked again, seeing a spark of fire in her daughter that hadn't been there in years. Helping others often lifts your own burden. Would this type of connection do it?

"Something's different about him. I know I'm right."

Mary eased back in the chair. Rarely did they see situations differently, yet the concern in her healing circle stayed in mind. If her daughter was right, then protecting him had to be the way to go. "I'll trust your judgement on this one. The call is yours. Let me know if you need any help. You know I'm always here for you." With a half-smile, she added, "You look tired."

"I need sleep."

She stood, taking Martine's plate to the sink. "I'll clean up. Do you want me to make a container for you to take tonight when you go back on shift?" Her tone softened to a warm soothe. Looking at the uneaten food, she truly hoped the answer would be yes. "I'll put some extra in, just in case you want to share with Dottie."

"No. I'll be fine."

"Sleep well."

Sensing her daughter climb the stairs slow and steady, she let out a sigh. The plate was still full. The uneaten food went straight in the trash. Placing the dish in the dishwasher, she forced herself to breathe in and out with control. By no stretch of the imagination did she feel calm. Not one bit. If Martine was right in what she sensed. If, in fact, a dark magic spell had been cast for the purpose of greed and self-aggrandizement? There would be some furious trouble brewing. Not only for the man and the dark witch. It would impact the human world. Plus, some witch or warlock crossing dimensions without permission always ended badly. Very badly.

Chapter 5

Draven

Draven, often called the Gatekeeper, stood on the barren plains in the Third Realm. Red mist swirled through the tepid air, remnants of the portal he used to travel between dimensions. After the unexpected cataclysm sixteen years ago, seven known sires and hundreds of their minion vampires took refuge here. Personally, he had never cared to sire after his own turning in 1847. He preferred human minions. Yet his origin was impeccable. Cyril, his sire, had been a powerful vampire who met an untimely end as the victim of an unprecedented event, which involved the mystically enhanced vampire—his renowned and often despised brother in blood.

Surviving the purge that had occurred in the human world, Draven had greedily taken up this coveted position of Gatekeeper. Too knowledgeable to be disenfranchised, he became the one vampire powerful enough to control the only known portal in North America. He alone knew who or what slipped in *and* out of the human world.

Tonight, his anger rose beyond fury, informed about an impossible breach less than twenty-four hours ago. He had not brought the perpetrator through. In fact, he had no idea how he or she got into the human world! The vault in his office, which contained access to the portal had remained locked. Only he could open it. This transgression belonged to someone in the Second Realm. An act of treason against unwritten laws of that realm would be dealt with. After this meeting with the seven sires who called themselves the War Council in the Third Realm, he would be tasked with hunting the fool down, finding some unknown portal, and then disposing of the body.

Moving with confidence through the barren land, purpose steadied him. Squelching this rumor, proving this type of impossibility would place him higher above all the other gatekeepers. Due to his business acumen, the sires as well as the sorcerers had acquired great wealth, more than enough to sustain both realms. And sires were far superior to those three sorcerers, so caught up in worn-out traditions and conveniently set in their ancient ways. A thin smile spread across his lips. *Ancient ways are soon to be ancient history.* The War Council had worked wonders with the Third Realm. Those vampires didn't acquiesce to spells and potions. They were physically strong, learning to sustain their strength by feeding off each other and a good supply of human blood slaves. Of course, these captured humans, all evil by nature and housed like cattle, existed mainly for the seven sires' consumption only.

Picking up his pace, he passed growing fields tilled by captives. Thousands had been thrown through the portals before they closed. Many hundred still survived. Nearing the road to the council building, his back stayed straight, his purpose renewed. The physical appearance of their realm had been a 'gift' from the three immortal sorcerers. It offered protection, a conjured design with detail that reminded him of nineteenth-century Europe. The atmosphere, purposely created, could sustain human life. The difference? Only enough sunlight to grow food for the captives, the air a constant autumnal temperature—Draven's favorite season.

The entrance to the Council building had been tooled magnificently in black marble. He adjusted his tie and buttoned his expensive suit jacket, striding past vampire guards. They knew his worth. They knew that even to dare question his purpose would result in starvation, the sires' favorite torture.

The wide doors yawned open, and he strode across the black marble room, took his seat at the other end of the wooden table. Never one to bow, he inclined his head enough to mimic respect. Herodotus, one of the oldest surviving sires met his gaze. "There has been a breach." His voice, as always, came across raspy and harsh.

"So I've been informed, Sire."

"Give us information."

"There is little at this time, however, if true, the offender came from the Second Realm. The breach was sensed by dark seers hours before human dawn. Yet the vault remained sealed."

"You will follow through."

"Yes, Sire." And he wouldn't let this rest until he had facts and answers.

"Very well. You will stay the day and catch us up on other business."

He gave a slight nod. "Although I graciously thank you for the invitation, my presence would be better served in the human world where I might gather information about the breach to present to you." The pause dragged on, and Draven grew concerned. He truly did not like staying too long in the Third Realm. Slave blood reminded him of soured wine.

"I will agree to your request upon one condition. You will return before the next phase of the moon with the location of this breach."

"Yes, Sire. As you wish, Sire."

"You continue to manipulate the markets?"

"Of course, Sire."

"And have you found a place for us in your world where we might reside?"

He looked around the table before answering with a careful, "No, Sire."

Herodotus's eyes turned to bits of coal. "And why not? We miss the hunt of humans. Need I say more?"

"No, Sire," he answered quickly to stroke the bastard's ego. "The right property has not presented itself. I wish to only present what I know will please you."

"You are the hunter, Draven. Your continent is enormous. We could easily be happy in the wilds of Canada if no state has what we require." The pause grew irritating. "Perhaps you are too wrapped up in your club business."

"No, Sire. Your needs are paramount. I will redouble my efforts, Sire."

Leaning back, Herodotus continued to study him. "Mark my words, Draven. It has been over fifteen years since I walked the night in the human world. This will not be a multi-decade self-imposed separation." His powerful fist hit the table. "I walked the human world for a thousand years without incident. To sire. To feed freely and at will. This is *more* than a desire."

"Yes, Sire," Draven replied and then bowed his head

with his hand over his unbeating heart. He wondered how many others at the council table felt the same. Probably all. These were not vacant vampires turned and let loose on humans for gaming pleasure. The sires in the room were the *crème de la crème*. The upper echelon of the demon world. They could play with the human mind and wipe memories like a warlock. Perhaps in human life they already had those gifts. Being turned simply enhanced them. Some sires only turned those who had specific traits like intense masculinity or a bendable sensuality. Rarely were women turned. And at that thought, Draven sensed the deeper reason for wanting back in the human world. Sex. Power. A new legion of vampires… Plain and simple.

He cleared his throat. "Sire, I pledge my loyalty and make the promise to see to your orders immediately upon my return." Dare he say what came to mind? *Of course. An easy remedy, although rather a small offering.* He only looked at Herodotus. "Might I suggest a walk. Just you and I?"

No bristle. None at all. Instead, an expression of curiosity crossed the notorious sire's bearded face. Herodotus rose. A wave of his hand dismissed other council members, and then with a turn, said, "Walk with me to my quarters."

He bowed deeply this time and followed. The building may look average on the outside. Inside looked like a palace as they crossed over into a private area. Tempered glass windows feet away from the outer ones. Marble hallways lined with classical art and sculpture. Thick carpeting with threads of gold woven through the patterns. Everything screamed luxury.

"What is it you wish to speak to me privately about?

State it."

"Might I offer you a night at *Destiny*?"

The sire stopped and eyeballed him. "Is this a riddle?"

"No, Sire. It is the club I own in Manhattan. You will remain undetected by Guardians of Souls within its walls. A night of pleasure can be discretely arranged." Gauging the seconds of silence and realizing he still had his head on his shoulders, he continued. "The club offers an atmosphere that may brighten your mood."

"And when could this be arranged?"

"Tomorrow at the human world's twilight. I shall meet you where the red mist begins at the end of the realm." Had Draven been human, he'd be sweating as if locked in a sauna. Placing his existence in the old sire's hands never felt a comfortable spot.

Finally, Herodotus stopped in front of a richly carved set of doors fit for a king. "Then human twilight it is."

Without wasting a beat, Draven bowed low and deep with his hand over his unbeating heart. Rarely had he jumped dimensions with a guest. But the portal was his alone to command. "Sire," he said still bowed low, "Until tomorrow's twilight."

Herodotus touched the doors, which opened onto a massive room, its masculine décor spectacular. He waited for them to close and then turned to retrace his steps. Once he passed the council chambers, he strode out the building and past the vampire guards. The trek back couldn't happen fast enough, and upon reaching the growing fields, he broke into a run. Entering the barren plains, red mist engulfed him like a heavy blanket on an autumn night.

Arriving at the portal, he whispered the incantation only known to him. The portal swirled open and he traveled through space and time, stepping into a sealed room at the end of his office. Locking the vault door behind him, he walked to his desk.

Preparations would have to be made. He'd wait until the last rays of daylight claimed the city streets. Pulling out his cell phone, he looked over the list of his minions until he found the right one. "Have a car waiting at 5:56 this evening. I wish to run some errands tonight."

\*\*\*\*

The alarm on Martine's phone buzzed an intentional, irritating set of beeps. A flick of the wrist silenced it as she sat up and scrubbed her face. Sweet, refreshing sleep had not happened, no matter how deeply her mother had entered her mind to place the suggestion. It had been a river of dreams. One of them the same nightmare. Never would she forget that fateful day. The sight of her dying daughter in her arms. It was always the first thing on her mind when she woke; the last on her mind when she fell asleep. Never would this unending grief subside in her soul. But that nightmare was hers to own and protect. The river of dreams also contained a rerun of John Doe, sensing it predestined that he had been redirected to St. Francis during her shift. Did she believe in fate? In Karma? *That's a total yes, yep, and youbetcha all rolled into one.*

Sweeping her hair out of her eyes, she pulled the coated elastic band off her wrist and turned her thick loose hair into a bushy bun. From the edge of the bed, her gaze swept the bedroom, a safe haven. Never again would she live anywhere but the home of her happy childhood. Never again would she let any man close

53

enough to tempt her, either.

She didn't crave independence anymore. Had pushed away all personal friends knowing they had nothing in common now. She refused to participate in any coven's healing circle. In her mind, they remained responsible for her baby's death, no matter what her mother said. No. Everything she needed was right here. Peace. Quiet. Together yet separate. Besides, her bond with her mother far exceeded the norm, and she knew it.

They were both powerful women. Both powerful witches. Each sought their own version of privacy, but they also had their commonalities: good magic and good sense. Yet she no longer shared her gift with others who, just like them, used magic judiciously with great care.

After a refreshing shower, Martine dressed in purple scrubs for her shift. The rich color had always been her favorite. Plus, it identified her and Dottie as the in-between shift in the ER. Going downstairs, she pulled out her phone. The app confirmed her ride mere minutes away. She left the brownstone, took a deep breath of fresh October air, and let out a sigh.

No texts meant no change in her patient. Putting her phone in the pocket of her purple cardigan, she realized it meant no new info and no answers as well. She thought about what her mother had said this morning. Why *did* she want to get herself involved? Because her patient needed her. Why spend the energy on a John Doe? Because her patient needed her. Only until he regained consciousness, though. Then he'd certainly be pushed out of her life in a quick minute. *As it is, so shall it be,* she thought as she got in the back seat of the small sedan.

That last thought had been more a realization than prediction. Her connections, those damn things like emotional attachments, meant opening her soul; redirecting energy she so desperately needed to survive. Nothing held with her. Nothing tempted or excited her. She'd let no one open the door to her heart, to her very soul. She went through the motions of living without anything grounding her. True, she had her professional life on track. But all the rest? Just motions. Empty motions. The word 'guarded' came to mind. 'Emotional exhaustion' followed at a close second.

As the car took the city streets with ease, she wished her own path could be as clear as the car's. Autopilot worked well. Up to this point. The image of the man in the hospital bed captured her attention once again. Why? What pulled her in? Was it the not knowing where you were or how you got there that resonated with her? Or the desire to right the wrongs of the universe and get him back to his destiny that poked holes through her tough outer shell? How about a moral challenge? Pick up the wounded bird and heal it before the ever-present hawk senses its next victim. *Who is that saint of lost causes?* "Saint Jude," she whispered, answering her own *Jeopardy* question. And as if that revelation spurred the proverbial horse to a dangerous rear-up, the sharp jolt slammed her body and mind back to the here and now.

The driver put the car in park. She stared out the windshield from the back seat, totally stunned. "Are you all right? Are you hurt, miss," the driver asked as he hit the key pad on the dashboard, entering 9-1-1 to report the accident. He gave the location, agreed to not leave the scene. *Waiting for the police could take an hour*, she thought as she rolled her shoulders. "Yes, I have a passenger," he answered into his phone. "It's a blue sedan. Oh. The license plate number? Of the other car?

It's a limo. Oh. Yeah. Uh, D-E-S-T-I-N-Y. It's a New York plate."

The shiver that ran up Martine's spine settled in her brain as the harsh shrieks of a police car whooped three times in rapid succession. *Wow. In record time.* Maybe she wouldn't be late for her shift after all. The driver turned to her. "Are you hurt, miss? Please answer me."

"I'm fine," she replied, a bit irritated. "Do what you have to do."

The officer spoke to the driver before leaning in the window to address her. "I'm going to ask you to step out of the car if you can, Ma'am."

"Sure," she said with a nod. Another officer stood at the back door reaching in for her arm as she got out. Then she had to smile. "So this is what you look like outside, Jerry."

"Hey, Martine. You okay? No bumps or bruises?"

"Perfectly one-hundred percent. How late for my shift will I be?"

"Not that late, give or take a half hour to get statements and process this. I'll get you there in fifteen if I use the siren." The little laugh came easy thinking Jerry a gem of a guy. One of New York's finest. Honest, patient with a strong set of morals.

"I'll take the fifteen. St. Francis gets pretty short-handed after sunset."

"Don't I know it. Just stay here while we get the info going."

Pulling the purple sweater's hood up over her head, she took in a deep breath of fresh air. The wind kicked up as if it decided, spur of the moment-like, to scream "Yo! It's autumn!" The quick gust caused a bunch of crisp multi-colored leaves, recently added to the seasonal menu, to fly around her proving just how fickle Mother Nature could be sometimes. She ran and settled with a quick lean in the closest building's doorway, hoping to shield from the next unpredictable gust.

The limo with the *Destiny* plate didn't look at all damaged, but the sedan's bumper had seriously lip-locked beneath the higher one. Both drivers were talking to the police officers. She had to wonder what kind of show-off needed this type of expensive carriage to tool around narrow city side streets. When the back door of the big, black chariot opened, what stepped out piqued her interest.

He looked tall, over six feet. Dressed with expensive taste and groomed like a model. His jet-black hair pulled back neatly and tied at the nape of his neck lent a severity to his angular features. The vivid widow's peak perfectly aligned with his straight nose and thin lips gave the impression of a powerful man. Both his carriage and stature said he enjoyed an edge of danger. The expression on his face was a do-not-disturb sign for the faint of heart, which had her sixth sense tinkling like a dinner bell. An aura of darkness shimmered off the wide shoulders of a long black overcoat. His eyes locked to hers in a compelling way, but she had no desire to read him. *Orbs of darkness, simultaneously languid and mesmerizing, like he's pondering a jump into an abyss.* She couldn't look away as he strode toward her in the doorway of the building. And those dark orbs turned out to be a really soft, warm brown.

"The driver will be fired. Rest assured, madame." His voice came from the depths of his chest. Rich, cultured with an accent hinting of Europe.

Not at all interested in his type, she replied, "It was

just an accident."

"Nonsense," he huffed as if insulted that she didn't agree with total retribution for a little fender-bender. "I pay him good wages to know how to drive. One does not back out of a parking space between two cars like a clueless beginner. This outrageous act may have brought harm to you. He will be fired."

She shrugged. "Wow. What a dramatic monologue because of a simple misjudgment. Get over yourself."

His eyes flared wide. His nostrils flared wider. "You do not know me, and you do not know my business practices. I demand perfection. If as simple a task as pulling out a parking spot is unattainable, then the man has sealed his own fate. Now move as you are blocking my way."

Stunned by his arrogance, she replied, "Oh, I'm sorry. Is this your building?" His response, or rather, the way he chose to reply, would either give him a second chance at civility or bring forth her natural desire to irk him more.

Those cocoa-colored eyes narrowed as if he actually decided to take a second and reassess the situation. "Perhaps I am the one who should say I am sorry. It was rude of me to go on as I did."

"That's a start."

"Please stand aside so I may enter my business."

"And the fate of your driver?"

"I have already decided his fate."

"And you won't reconsider?"

"Why should I?"

"Because I'm asking."

"And who exactly is asking this of me?"

"Martine. Martine Kendrick."

An eyebrow raised, and he nodded once with a bow of his head, so un-Manhattan-like. Martine looked away, not at all drawn to those intense windows to his soul. Her jaw tensed as her senses hummed, but she refused to read him thinking how he positively wreaked of malevolence. Without another word she stepped to the side as Jerry called to her. This man, whoever he was, made her uncomfortable. He seemed off somehow. Definitely dangerous.

"Ready to go," Jerry asked.

"Sure," she replied.

"You won't be too late."

"Oh my God, I didn't call in."

"They'll just have to understand. You sure you're okay?"

"Yeah, why?"

"Uh, you look a little, uh, maybe a bit paler than usual."

"Nope. I'm a-okay."

Jerry, ever the gentleman cop, took her arm, guided her into the back of the police car. "Your chariot awaits."

*Chariot... very much the opposite of that black overly-expensive limo whose back bumper doesn't even have a scratch on it.* She eyed the nervous driver as he got back into the car to park it, lining it up so he could carefully back into the empty parking space in front of the mysterious man's 'business.' Putting two and two together, Martine looked at the plate and then looked at the sign above the doorway she had stood in.

"Destiny," she whispered.

"What destiny," Jerry replied. "You think fate had something to do with the accident?"

"No. It's on the license plate."

"Yep, happening right in front of the club with the same name. Guess there's a connection."

*There always is*, Martine thought. What connection? She didn't know. But as sure as day follows night, it would reveal itself.

Chapter 6

Identities

Settled on the bed in the same position, Aurora remained in a trancelike state, oblivious to her servant's activities outside her bedroom. She had sent the girl away for three days to ensure her plan remain hidden. Although loyal, anyone could be made to talk when tortured.

At the requested hour, the servant girl entered her room, and Aurora winced at bright sunlight. "I command you to close the drapes, Anika. Now," she hissed low and deadly.

"I will not. My mistress, you said before I left that whatever your response, I have to open the drapes every morning. Plus, I made your breakfast." A weary groan came because it was true. Second Realm sun had been listed as crucial for conception in all those dusty diaries. Lowering the covers, she sat up slowly and leaned forward, obviously awaiting a fluff of the pillows behind her back. Anika made quick work of it. "Why are you so flushed, my mistress? Are you feeling ill? Do you have a fever? Shall I call a witchdoctor?"

The giggle that followed made her cringe. "Stop. Talking. I am not sick," she replied with a wave of her hand.

Anika returned with the breakfast tray, placed with

perfection on the bed—protein rich eggs, fruit, black tea, and toast. She waited until her tea was poured, and then placed a forkful of eggs on the edge of a piece of toast. Chewing slowly, she swallowed and sampled the fresh berries on her plate. "We start a new regimen today."

"A regimen?" Anika asked. "What type of regimen, my mistress?"

"We will walk two miles at an easy pace. Then I will listen to soothing music while you weed the herb garden before noon. You will prepare a healthy lunch. My preference today is a garden salad."

"Yes, my mistress."

The sweetness of the berries tasted divine, and she finished them in silence fully aware of Anika standing at attention next to the bed. "I will see no visitors."

"Yes, my mistress."

"Now leave me while I finish breakfast. I will call to you without words. Open your mind and come when you hear me. No words. Remember that. Don't have me scream your name." Anika curtsied and began to back out of the room. "Very nice. You are learning, my young friend." she offered, the crumb of a compliment sufficient. Once alone, she nibbled the toast, delighting in the task she'd surely accomplish. Sipping the last of the tea, she placed the cup on its saucer and opened her mind to her servant. Just shy of a minute, Anika entered her bedroom and curtsied saying a soft, but proud, "Yes, my mistress."

"We need to shave off many seconds when I call to you in my mind. Now prepare my bath. A warm bath. Not hot, with lavender and rose petals."

"Yes, my mistress," Anika replied taking away the tray.

Leaning back against the pillows, she thought about her plan. The girl would need to be more than ready to accompany her to the palace once her pregnancy showed. The sorcerers would demand Aurora be right under their noses. *She* could then demand anything, especially keeping those rabid guards leashed, and they would have to comply.

Noting the precise passage of minutes, she sensed her bath ready and waiting. She stood and stretched before wrapping herself in a soft silk dressing gown of pale pink before leaving the bedroom. Entering the bathroom, she fingered the locket and allowed a small smile. "I sense the temperature perfect and the scent refreshing. By the time we move to the palace, you will have everything in hand to impress the sorcerers."

"Thanks, Aurora."

In a split-second, her smile faded. "It is always *my mistress!* Am I clear?"

The girl positively shook. "Yes, but I—"

She moved in like a predator. "The sorcerers will sense deception. And they will pounce!" She dropped the dressing gown and slipped into the tub. "So much to learn. So little time."

"But you're not even with child yet."

Her eyes narrowed. "And how would you know that?"

Anika sucked in a sharp breath. "My mistress, I just… I just meant—"

"Enough," she yelled on the edge of irritation. With a flick of the wrist, the bathroom door slammed shut, locking them in the humid space. "You will *never* be so forward with me again! Because you will be tortured, judged *treasonous and hung!*" She let her last words sink in, watched tears gather in Anika's eyes before they dripped down her pale cheeks. With a flick of her wrist the door sprung open. "Go. Heat my towels."

Anika curtsied deep before leaving her alone. Another flick of her finger closed the door and she let out a slow, even breath. Planting the seed of punishment worked better than a spell.

As her body relaxed, so did her mind.

****

Already late for her shift, Martine stuffed her backpack under the patient bed in Cubicle Q. It was far more convenient than shoving it into her locker. "What'd I miss?"

"Nothing at all, but I think it's odd," Dottie whispered.

"What's odd?" she replied, already knowing where the conversation was heading.

"That they haven't moved JD to a room yet."

"I know, right?"

Dottie shook her head. "I mean, it's just weird."

"Nope, not weird because this is Cubicle Q, so it's just quirky."

"True enough. How long did it take our last Cubicle Q patient to get a bed?"

"She didn't. She was shipped off to a rehab facility two days in."

They both stared at her patient. "Well, it's this strange early flu season, and there's all these nasty viruses going around and around, especially with the weird weather patterns. Ugh," Dottie's hands flew into the air. "I swear. Snow, hail, heatwave, and summer showers all in the past two weeks. It's like we're living in Scotland or something."

Her thoughts immediately switched to someone she truly missed. Lu had moved to the Highlands after their last disastrous conversation. She pushed him out of her mind, asking, "Why Scotland?'

"I vacationed there years ago. Beautiful country, but it would start out rain, turn to snow, then sleet, and then the sun came out. All between dawn and sunset. I never knew how to dress."

Martine shrugged and shook her head. "Even the weather reports don't get it right. It's just been crazy out there." Scrolling through the patient tablet, she added, "So no changes in John Doe's condition?"

Her co-worker looked over her shoulder. "Just the same old, same old. What do you think happened to him?"

Martine let out a short laugh. "You asked that at least ten times last night."

"Well, you *do* have a unique sixth sense. There's no denying it." Dottie paused, apparently waiting for an answer.

Scanning the quagmire of his mind again, she shook her head. As if the ingredients for a cake had just been thrown in a bowl helter-skelter and nowhere close to being beaten together best described it. "My best guess, or, um, *feeling*, is something out of the ordinary."

"Must have been," Dottie replied with a bob of her head.

"I don't want him shipped off to some below-average state facility like a holding cell until there's a match on his prints or DNA."

"Do you think he's in the system?"

"No. He doesn't come off as the criminal type. I think DNA is a better way to go. You know, Dottie, those ancestry sites are really popular. Hell, who knows?"

"Maybe someone's come forward looking for a missing person. Like a wife?"

"Maybe," she said, but didn't sense it. There had been no indication he wore a ring, no contusion that said it had been wrenched off by a thief.

"Well, whatever. It's kind of nice to stroll in here every few hours and take in all this handsomeness." She moved away from the bed, but Martine remained at John Doe's side. "Gonna spend a few minutes alone with him? The night crazies haven't started coming yet."

Martine gave a nod. "I'll check his vitals and stay awhile. Come get me when the shift cranks up?" With a little wave, Dottie left, resetting the curtain behind her.

Crazy would start soon. Martine was sure of it. For the moment, though, she opened her sixth sense to the man in the bed. What had happened was in there, only shielded by a dark spell so strong, so intense, that nothing could penetrate. The witch who created this specific spell had to be well-versed in dark magic because she sensed no door, no way into his mind. Shielding the cubicle from unwanted visitors, she settled into the chair next to the bed.

Focusing again, she tried to follow each synapse, each avenue to his memories. This spell had severed all connections to conscious or unconscious thought like they'd been put through a shredder. Anger bubbled up over what had been done... so totally unnecessary. *The human mind is a thing of beauty. Perfect in its design; something to be treasured. Dark magic is cruel. Using it on an innocent? Never necessary.*

Footsteps approached with a whispered, "What the hell..." and she snapped her fingers removing the protection spell. The curtain flung open, and she smiled.

"Hi, Jerry. Come to check up on him?"

"Yeah. You too," he replied. "Feeling okay?"

"Totally. No fender-bender residual aches or pains."

"Got some info on your John Doe. Interested?"

She gave a nod, thinking, *more than you'll ever know.* "Got a name yet?"

"Christopher John Forbes. Age thirty-five. Single. No family. Parents died a few years ago."

"Wow. How sad."

"Plus, adopted through a Catholic agency so no birth parent or any other usable info. He works for a tech firm about ten blocks from where they found him. Has one close friend there, a Mister Trev Chambers. The guy seemed pretty broken up when we interviewed him. Says Forbes had been very restless last night and left early, around four in the morning."

"What about the crime scene?"

"Nothing. Not even a stray hair or any body fluids at the scene."

"Really? How odd." Her sixth sense kept tingling.

"We haven't ruled robbery out, though. Did any of your tests show anything?"

"Nothing. I saw the labs. All scans and blood tests are clean."

"I hear there are no beds, huh?"

"Not a one," she said in a professional tone. "Will the city move him to a facility?"

"Nope. Funding ran dry. Too much going on politically right now, too. I gotta run. Take care."

She gave a smile. "You too. Be safe out there, Officer." As soon as the curtain closed, her smile faded. *Not one stray hair... what if the witch has his hair, his saliva, and his semen?* All three together could be used to cast one powerful spell.

She touched her patient's hand and leaned in close. "What happened, Christopher Forbes? Who did this to you?"

She ran her fingers lightly across his forehead in a gentle way, a caring way. Hopeful for a twitch of an eye, a twitch of a finger, any signal of any type. But nothing happened. His mind had been plundered in a most unique way. One thing gave her comfort. He'd be in her care every night. As for the day shift? With a little help, he'd need a particular type of protection around the clock. Mare would agree and get in touch with them because he was an innocent. He needed their help.

Of that, she felt certain.

Chapter 7

Revelations

More than frustrated, as if staring at a blank page, Martine grabbed her cell phone to see her mother's name on the screen. She hit the green icon, not sure of how the request would be received. "I need you, Mare."

"How long were you going to wait," her mother replied.

"When did you know I'd ask for help?"

"Let's cut the small talk, dear daughter. You sense something more tonight?"

"Yeah. This really could be a fertility spell. Dense, deep and dark. I think the witch took hair, saliva, and semen."

"Ugh," her mother said before a long sigh.

"I need your help."

"You mean the collective 'your,' am I correct?"

All right. She'd admit it. "Yes. The collective 'your.' I think the old one last night knew this is of such vast importance—"

"You mean consequence," her mother interrupted.

"Importance, consequence… whatever, Mare. Someone with our other-worldly knowledge needs to be here around the clock. Someone we can trust. Maybe reach out to—"

"Got it. I'll call Deepa."

"Maybe I missed something."

"Trust your skills, Martine. You and I both know how powerful you are."

"In this dimension, sure. If there's Second Realm involvement then it's different, Mom.

"You sound unsure of yourself."

"I am," she whispered. "So here's my second request. Can you convince your healing circle to lend some support? To keep trying to get through the spell when I'm not here?"

"Sure. But you can ask them yourself. It's time, honey."

"I'd rather the ask comes from you," she whispered closing her eyes. The healing circle didn't deserve her trust anymore. Her bastard of an ex had pulled her away from them five years ago. And then the loss of her baby shattered her very soul along with any trust she had in them. The hollowness that never left had to be pushed aside, at least for the time being. Only long enough to save an innocent man from an eternity of suffering somewhere between Heaven and Hell. But she couldn't help Christopher Forbes on her own, this spell like nothing she had ever encountered before. "Please," she added even softer.

"Of course," her mother replied.

"Thanks," she said, leaving out the endearing 'Mare' that always made her mother smile. She put the cell phone in her pocket.

*Why a fertility spell?* "Ugh. That silly legend," she muttered. Hijacking her patient's mind had been the perfect crime. Her spine stiffened with an anger so deep that her head hurt.

"How are we doing tonight?"

She jumped, staring at Dottie who was suddenly next to her. "I didn't hear you come in."

"It's these new sneakers. How's handsome here?"

"The same."

"Got any more info from Officer Jerry? I heard he came by earlier."

"John Doe is Christopher Forbes. He'll be with us for a while."

"Wow. What about family?"

"None."

"Oh, that's sad. So, no one in the world misses him?"

"Looks that way. What brings you into Cubicle Q?"

"It's a slow night, thank God. I just thought I'd come take a look. And you know, see how you're doing."

Funny how Dottie sensed her low points. Her friend's bright mood and positive outlook on life always worked wonders. It calmed her, even soothed her. "I'm okay. I'd be better if he would just wake up." Dottie gave a nod before she left.

*Just waking up isn't going to happen.* She paced the cubicle more than a few times before sitting down next to her patient. It would be a very long night.

****

It took Draven nearly twelve hours to get more information. At his desk before sunset, Draven hissed into his cell phone, "There has been a breach." The owner of *Destiny* added, "it is your mission to inform me of any irregularities. You failed to do so." He listened half-heartedly to a minion's gibberish. "No. It is most certainly your fault. This will not go unpunished. Let me be clear." With his temper about to explode, Draven dialed it down enough so he could talk. "How did the dark seer say a Second Realm witch enter this dimension?"

Leaning forward, he again paused for the pissant on the other end, not interested in her blather about some unknown portal. "Hear me clearly. You will pay for not immediately informing me. If any of this brings even the slightest suspicion upon my club, upon my status in the human world, I will have your head on a Medieval pike for all dimensions to see! Fix it!"

He threw the cell phone, landing it at the precise end of his desk full of irritation, full of frustration. He'd have to wait until sunset before venturing out to comb an entire city searching for the 'where' as well as the 'how.'

Fees were paid for using the portal. Gold and precious gems easily exchanged for cash in this world. It was his brokerage, keeping fools and starry-eyed realm travelers at bay. Granting travel to the human world happened at *his* discretion. His alone. But dark witches? They were cunning. Deceptive. "Self-absorbed bitches," he hissed, wanting to grab a minion from the nightclub and take a long, hard drink from a bloated vein.

One phrase from that call stood out. *There are no unknown portals. Period.* Unknown portals were the thing of legends and folklore. Decades ago, a similar breach had been talked about. Some drivel about the Second Realm's chosen one. *Yes. Over thirty years ago, long before a multitude of dimensional portals permanently sealed shut.* His mouth quirked, vaguely recalling the Second Realm's love of gossip. Always so gullible. So steeped in 'thee' and 'thou'… 'so be it' and 'thus shall it be'… etcetera. He had no concern for ancestral crap.

For the past sixteen years, he had realm travel in

check. Never flaunting his power, he kept a low profile, safe and away from prying human eyes. Now a breach. A Second Realm dark witch meddling with a human. If dark seers sensed it, then surely the intrusion had been felt by those who practiced good magic in the human world as well. And once her victim was located, trouble would follow.

Now he *had* to get involved. With little to no alacrity, he turned to the computer on his desk scrolling back the video feed. His expression hardened. Nights ago and well after midnight, his bouncer indicated a stunning woman had waltzed into *Destiny* but couldn't recall her paying a cover-charge. His temper subsided after noticing the woman glance toward a particular column. "What do you see," he whispered to himself. He clicked on a second camera to pull up a different angle and studied the screen once, twice, and there… the image magnified with a swipe of his finger. Was it a man or a warlock? Height and coloring gave him nothing. All Second Realm pure breeds were fair of skin although different shades of blond. Assuming him human, this could be her victim.

He pulled up Camera Three, and a thin smile began. Magnification or zoom, as it was now called, a wonderful tool. He took a screen shot of the man's face. He then took a screen shot of the lovely, but devious woman. *Is she the dark witch?* Had he been a naïve fool, he would wonder who lusted after whom.

Rather irritated, he stood to reach the cell phone and then sat back down with it close to his hand as he sent the necessary photos to it. Scrolling through his contacts, he found the minion who often boasted about his many contacts. Attaching all the faces and a close up of a business card, he entered in the text box: FIND THEM! Meanwhile, he'd start his own search.

An hour later, with the help of the Internet, he had a wealth of information. The three men surrounding her worked for the same tech company in HR. "Fools," he whispered with a sneer. What made him pull up the company chart, he'd never know, yet it was a stroke of excellent luck. The photo came up on the fourth tier of the chart. Leaning back in his chair, Draven whispered, "Christopher Forbes."

When his cell phone chimed, he opened the text message and grinned ever so slightly. He now had the who and the where, and then pressed a number into the desk phone. "I want the car waiting." This driver had always been reliable, not like yesterday's idiot who was now simply another 'gift' to the vampire realm, another captive to drink and drain.

*Ah, but the woman Martine Kendrick... such intense, intelligent eyes.* A nurse, he recalled, and rather feisty as well. Natural beauty; no makeup yet stunning, albeit very thin. Not his usual type, for certain, but the way she stood up to him felt refreshing. Her mother had been mysterious and passionate, so very many years ago. "And you, Martine, are the new generation of good witch in a much-admired line." Once again, the Internet proved to be a very helpful tool in locating which hospital she worked at. Then, he simply stared at the information on the screen. "What an odd coincidence, or is it not," he whispered. He sat up straighter. Rarely did he become unnerved, but Draven shot out of the chair to pace the office. He had walked this earth too many years to believe in coincidence. *Not even remotely possible.*

\*\*\*\*

Martine came in early to meet her daytime-counterpart, a trusted Georgian nurse named Marsha. *Thankfully, Mom came through,* she thought. Their involvement meant her mother sensed the seriousness of this dark witch's intrusion into the human world. The group was known to the Kendricks and other good witches. The Georgian network held the front-line defense in the fight against evil. Some of them were ordinary people, some mystical warriors called Guardians of Souls. Others were healers like her. Most likely, the Georgians would now fund her patient's round-the-clock care at St. Francis.

The ER remained busy tonight with an overflow of flu patients. Although Martine's priority was Christopher, she had offered to help her colleagues on the other side of the ER. "All good," she said to Dottie, whose patient now had an IV line, resting quietly.

"Thanks, M. Heading back to Cubicle Q?"

"Are you sure you don't need anything else?"

"No, but isn't that crazy how they all arrived at once? It's a good thing you came in early."

Martine gave a tight smile, calling over her shoulder, "Just come get me if you need another pair of hands, Dottie," before she headed to Cubicle Q. Approaching the closed curtain, her senses went on high alert. Pulling it back, she stared at the mysterious man in disbelief.

"Nurse Kendrick," he said in that rich deep voice, "I have come to see if you are truly all right."

She studied the tall dark stranger quickly placing him outside his club. "What are you really doing here and how did you know where to find me?" Silly questions, she realized because all it took was googling

75

her name.

He gave a thin smile which fit with his handsome, angular features. "I'm guilty of using the Internet more and more these days."

"Just as I figured." But something about him bothered her, and she couldn't quite put a finger on it. He stood at the foot of the bed as still as a statue in a long black overcoat. His hands were gloved, which seemed odd for an autumn night. The tight crease of his trousers and no doubt really expensive shoes said more about him. "As you can see, I'm just fine. Exactly as I told you the other evening. By the way, did you fire your driver?"

With a tilt of his head, his gaze slid to her patient. "I have sent him to another place for another type of personal service."

*Odd, such a strange way of speaking with just a hint of European charm, and I don't even want to guess what type of job the poor driver has now.* Recalling his anger over a simple fender-bender, one could only imagine. Her eyes shifted to Christopher and then back to him.

"Your patient... is he severely injured?"

"In a way," she replied, more amused. "So now tell me, what are you really doing here?"

"You're very astute and I suspect very few things get past you. Guilty as charged." He paused with his hand over his heart and her senses tingled. "That you could have possibly been injured by someone in my employ is truly an embarrassment. And I'm sure the accident made you late for your shift. Might I make up the inconvenience with the offer of a quiet dinner and a drink, perhaps?"

Shifting her weight, she placed one hand on her hip, and full of sarcasm, replied, "Really?" Her senses clanged like cathedral bells now, and she wasn't about to let him off her radar. "And what else do you want?"

"Madame, I would never—"

"You sure as hell wouldn't," she interrupted. "I'm going to ask once again before I call security. What are you really doing here?

He folded his arms across his chest and sighed. "Again. Guilty," he admitted in a charming way. He seemed to be good at deception. Very good. As if he were a master at it. "Your patient is one Christopher Forbes."

"Do you know him?"

"Not personally. It appears he was at my club the night this happened."

Now, more than curious she asked, "How can you be sure?"

"I have security cameras. He appeared to stare at someone."

"Who?"

"It is of no significance."

"Like hell," she quickly said. "The police have no idea what happened to him. Maybe that someone knows. Maybe she did this to him."

"I never said it was a woman, Nurse Kendrick."

"Call me Martine. And I just put two and two together. A good looking man. A night club, which you own—it has to be a woman."

His broad shoulders shrugged in a non-committal way. "Today, one can never be certain."

*Oh, I'm certain.* "Okay. Whatever. You know for sure it's him?"

"I have several video feeds and camera angles."

"And so you, what, like, scanned hours of video and just happened to zero in on my patient?"

"It is the other person in the video I am interested in finding."

*So am I.* Her sixth sense kicked into high gear. When too many coincidences happened it meant something more. There had to be a link, and Mister-tall-dark-and-mysterious knew more than he let on. *Plus, there's something about him...*

"Let me apologize for disturbing you at your place of work," he quickly said.

"No. In fact, I'll take you up on that offer if it still stands, but I don't get off until dawn."

His warm eyes widened. "Oh. Dawn. Yes, well, perhaps you will be my guest for breakfast and a fresh cup of coffee? It would have to be at my club."

"Sure. I remember where it is," she quickly replied, not wanting him to rescind the invitation.

"Wonderful. My driver will wait for you right outside the emergency room entrance."

"Oh. You don't have to do that. I can Uber."

"Nonsense," he replied in a very old-fashioned manner. "I insist, Martine. My driver will be waiting." He inclined his head before leaving the cubicle.

Running after him, she called, "Wait... I don't know your name."

He turned and stared deep into her eyes, which caused another annoying tingle down her spine. "Draven. My name is Draven," he said before turning away and strolling out of the ER.

His impeccable posture, his broad shoulders and the stride so full of confidence reminded her of... "Oh, shit," she whispered. The next thought slamming into her brain felt like a meteor hitting the earth. *Only one other person has that arrogant stride and talks the way Draven does.*

The old-fashioned mannerisms so out of step with modern culture. Not to mention the proper yet charming head-bow that screams *I've walked this earth for centuries.*

*Draven is a vampire.*

Chapter 8

Rendezvous

Draven sent the limo back to *Destiny* and decided to hunt before tonight's event. He raced through the city streets, less dense with tourists due to this unresponsive flu. Of course, it didn't really matter since even on the street everyone seemed to be practicing 'social distancing.' Plus, a vampire at full speed felt like a gusty breeze to a human. Finding a gang member beating a pit bull to death, he set the dog free and drank deeply from its 'former owner.' Satisfied with his 'good' deed, as Donovan, his trusted bouncer held the door, he strode through. "Everything is prepared in the club?"

"Yes, my lord."

"There is additional security on the street?"

"Yes, my lord."

"Once the courtesans arrive, no one else comes in and no one goes out."

"Yes, my lord."

Herodotus would not be kept waiting in the thick red mist. Sires were notorious. Their patience never tested, not even by a vampire of such necessity like him. He entered his office and locked the door. Crossing the room, he entered four numbers into the vault's high-tech keypad. The heavy door swung open, and he approached the portal, waiting until the swirling portal's color deepened to a rusty red, and then stepped through to the Third Realm.

Bending low in a respectful bow, he said, "My most sincere apology, Sire, that you were kept waiting for this humble servant." He held the position as an acknowledgement of his misstep.

"Humble," Herodotus said with a snicker, "you couldn't be humble if your undead existence depended upon it. Thus, you will provide me with three lovelies for my private pleasure this night." The pause felt endless before the command to stand came. Then, to impress, Draven bowed deep once again. He locked arms with the sire and brought Herodotus through the portal.

Arrangements had been made with a specific contact, and *Destiny was* perfectly secure for this private party. It would be an all-female staff tonight. Should any part of Herodotus's club experience be unacceptable, that staff member would be slowly drained after the sire left. And he'd have the other staff members watch the macabre act of his drink and drain—to insure a deeper sense of loyalty. Or fear.

The music pulsating through the sound system stayed at low volume, the tracks specifically chosen to heighten a sexual mood. Twelve magnificent courtesans, splendidly naked, gyrated to the slow tempo of the composition. Jewels graced their earlobes and navels, their necks exposed and inviting. Handsomely clothed in a black suit, Herodotus groaned and grunted as each courtesan curtsied low until their breasts met the dancefloor. Like a king he studied the tempting flesh on display. A glass of expensive champagne was offered, which he took with a stately incline of his head.

A new composition began, and the sire chose a

particular beauty to dance with. She offered a wrist, which he brought to his mouth as their groins grinded together. His fangs slipped in for a quick taste, and then a look of approval swept across his neatly-trimmed, bearded face. When the time was right, Draven would lead the sire to a private room in his massive lair beneath the city streets for hours of sex. With a specific blend of drugs, he hoped all the women would be alive and breathing at the end of the tryst. Being such a meticulous planner, he hadn't lost one yet.

Draven made his way to the circular bar to watch the scene unfold. The next sensual tune washed over him like an ocean wave. Each chord progression, each haunting melody coupled with his favorite tempo... an erotic luxury to fill his brain. The barmaid offered herself. His fangs punctured her right wrist as he held it to his mouth. He drank deeply but slow, taking just enough to enjoy; not enough to make her woozy. Sweet and smooth, her blood trickled through his system. Pulling his fangs out, he sealed the wound with a lick and resumed his study of the sire.

As the hours dragged on, his thoughts drifted elsewhere. What would Martine be like naked beneath him? The Kendrick witches were passionate women. He knew firsthand. Would she tease and excite before he took her? Would she willingly sink to her knees and pleasure him?

Close to fully aroused... less in control, when a favorite courtesan came over, he pulled her into a dark corner. As the rhythmic bass of the sensual selection hammered his chest, he'd allow himself a little pleasure. When a second courtesan approached, he saw no reason not to double his enjoyment. His tongue swept across his fangs in anticipation.

Sensing the hour, he'd know when to move Herodotus along. With the sire's appetite for sex sated, he'd usher him back through the portal. As for right now, he'd indulge in a sexual fantasy.

Then he'd sit at his desk because he had a breakfast to plan.

\*\*\*\*

Was it hard for Martine to get Draven off her mind? Yeah. Was it hard to stop thinking about how a vampire had been standing right here with her in the ER at St. Francis? You bet. She massaged her patient's limbs with gentleness. Took his vitals and changed the IV, notating everything on the patient tablet.

How long had Draven been with Christopher before she found him standing at the foot of the bed? Was the vampire more involved with this than he let on? Touching her patient's forehead, she sensed the chaotic scramble in his brain just as she had multiple times before and during every shift. There had been no other invasions. He remained in the same shape mentally and physically as if he had been purposely placed in suspended animation. But as her sixth sense quivered, she'd have help on the next mind-walk.

"I'm here," her mother said entering cubicle Q, "And I brought help."

Martine smiled at the two women. She liked Sharon a lot. A jovial soul with goodness radiating from every pore. "Mom clued you in?"

The snug hug felt just right when she came around the bed. "I'm ready to help in any way I can," Sharon said with a warm smile.

Then Martine glanced at her mother. "I think you

and I need to talk first."

"Oh," Sharon said, "I'll go grab us coffees."

"No," she replied, "I need fresh air. We'll go outside for a few, okay? You don't mind sitting with him?"

"Of course not. Take all the time you need."

After a quick "thanks" they walked out of the cubicle and down the corridor to the ER entrance. The night felt brisk, and Martine leaned back against the building as her mother eyed her. She blew out a quick breath. 'This keeps getting weirder. Don't know where to start."

"Let me guess. You found out something."

Her eyes went wide. "A lot. My patient was at a club called *Destiny* right before this happened to him."

"Destiny? I know that club," her mother said with her eyebrows high.

"Hang on, Mare, because this gets even weirder." She told her mother about the fender-bender, about the crazy gusts of wind and then described the club owner. She looked away adding, "I sensed something strange about Draven but couldn't put my finger on it. Then, tonight, I mean, we were slammed for about an hour. When I went back to Cubicle Q, he's right there standing at the foot of Christopher's bed."

"What! Draven came *here*," her mother said, more an exclamation than question.

"Jeez, my sixth sense kept clanging but at first, I didn't know why. Plus, I think he knows the dark witch."

"Go ahead. Say it."

"There's only one other person who exudes that type of confidence, who speaks in that old-fashioned way all the time. Not to mention the charm. Oh, great Goddess of the Earth! You know what I'm saying." She stopped talking as her mother gave the dreaded nod.

"He's a vampire, and a dangerous one."

"I got vampire, but I didn't get dangerous," she said with a shrug.

"He most certainly is." Her mother walked away with a sigh before coming back. "Of course, I know him. And before you ask, yes. He and Michael had the same sire."

"What the hell, Mare? There's a connection to Michael? Not to mention now we have the Georgian Circle *and* a vampire involved?"

"The Georgian's are a no-brainer. It's a breach, Martine. A Second Realm witch coming through an unknown, undocumented portal. Draven is the Gatekeeper. He guards the only portal still active in North America. The Georgians have known it for years."

Her eyes went wide. "You're saying they accept this vampire in our dimension?"

"Yes and no," her mother said with a shake of her head. "After what happened sixteen years ago, and we can thank Michael for that one, many vampires and dark witches scurried out of the human world like rats. Those portals only opened one way and that way was out of our world. The Guardians still find vampires in hiding, thinking they can survive far from the cities. But some smart and savvy sires got away."

"And they took over the Third Realm?"

"Yes. And they stay there because Draven is the Gatekeeper. He doesn't have a soul like Michael did, does... you know what I mean. But he has innate intelligence. No one in any dimension wants the destruction of humankind. There's a rhythm to life as is."

Her eyes narrowed. "The unwritten laws don't apply

to vampires."

"No. But Draven respects the unwritten laws. He may not believe in them as we do, but nevertheless, he'd never allow a breach."

"He wants the dark witch, doesn't he?"

"Oh he wants her all right. What she did could wreak havoc in so many ways, it'll be more than your worst nightmare."

Martine stood straight, stretching her back with her hands firmly planted on her hips. "I'm having breakfast with him."

"Over my dead body," her mother quickly replied. "I just told you he's dangerous."

"But he won't hurt me. I'll protect myself."

"Bad idea, Martine."

"He has information, which can help because if we don't find the dark witch to reverse the spell, I lose my patient, and that's not happening."

Their eyes locked. "I know I can't talk you out of it. Promise me. You'll be very careful."

"I'm a big girl, Mare. And I know my skills. Plus, his charm doesn't work on me, so unless he wants to sell me into sex slavery—"

"Don't even joke about it!"

"I'll be fine." She took a deep breath sensing overwhelming concern. "Are we ready for some mind-hunting?"

"Lead the way. And let's keep your breakfast plans to ourselves, Okay?"

"Fine with me," she replied as they headed back to Cubicle Q.

Chapter 9

Connections

Collectively, the power of the three good witches surrounding Martine's patient was impressive. Sharon had proven time and again how focused her concentration could be. Hers was the generation between mother and daughter, in her late-40s, the prime of her life. Tall with a robust figure, many considered her to be the next leader of the healing circle when her mother decided to step down. Martine had to agree that the healing circle couldn't be in better hands with Sharon.

In the hours that followed, with an anchored protection spell around the cubicle to insure no intrusions, they linked their powerful minds. Like a giant snake, capable of slithering its way through a dense and dangerous jungle, they followed synapse by synapse to heal and restore. Some of them had almost connected—after more than one try. Nearing a point of exhaustion, Martine pulled out of the conjoined focus. Not happy to have to admit it, she whispered, "I think I'm tapped out for tonight."

Sharon sank down heavily into the chair with a loud huff while she and her mother sat on each side of the bed at her patient's feet. She wore a weary smile while her mother rubbed her temples. "That dark witch used some pretty strong magic on him," Sharon stated.

"I fully agree," her mother whispered. "We can do a round of never-have-I-ever with this one. Ugh. It's given me a headache."

Martine hauled herself up and took his vitals. Truly, she felt drained, which made her rethink those breakfast plans. "Maybe you shouldn't keep them," her mother whispered as Martine notated his vitals on the patient tablet. "Any physical change?"

About to state the obvious her eyes shifted to Christopher's right hand. As if their minds were still linked, both women followed her sight-line. "Oh my God," Sharon huffed.

"Mother of all, be praised," her mother added.

His pinky twitched and then his ring-finger followed. They watched the ever-so-slight movement full of awe for a full ten seconds, when, just like before these grueling hours, his body stilled once again. Then they let out long, slow breaths together. All that hope Martine had in her heart simply wafted away like smoke from a burned-out candle.

"Hours of concentrated power for two twitches," Martine muttered.

"It's a start," the ever-optimistic Sharon offered.

Mare, however, had a look on her face. "I say ditto to my daughter's take on it." She paused before adding, "How many hours were we at it? No. You don't have to tell me because at this rate, we don't have the stamina to keep this up night after night."

Stifling a yawn, Sharon replied, "We can call in the others, Mary."

Martine shook her head. "I think it's pretty clear, isn't it? The only thing that can undo this is to break the original spell completely. We need that dark witch."

"No," her mother said, followed by Sharon's tense, "Nuh-uh."

Cranky and craving a strong shot of some really high-priced whiskey to numb her nerves, Martine put up her hands with a quick, "Okay. Stop. Draven is our way to her. I know it. I feel it deep in my bones."

"No," her mother said.

"For the well-being of an innocent, Mom. He can't fault our logic."

"Even if he finds her, he won't give her up."

Sharon hustled out of the chair, color leaving her cheeks. "How does Draven fit into this? How do you even know about him, Martine?"

She studied the powerful healer, hoping the good witch wouldn't have a blood pressure episode, but then again, what better place than an ER. "Christopher met the dark witch at his club." Her eyes narrowed, adding very calm, "Breathe, Sharon, in and out, in and out." She reached over and guided the woman back into the chair, keeping two fingers on her wrist to take her pulse.

"It's not safe. It's not. Mary, tell her!" Sharon took a few breaths modeling her own. "If I'd known he was involved, I wouldn't have… I mean—"

Her mother suddenly stood behind rubbing her shoulders as if a simple act of kindness could persuade her to relax. "I know what you mean. You don't have to explain your feelings."

More for their sake than her own, Martine said, "I'm sorry I said his name, Mare. Really, I am. But if his information gets us to her, then my patient has a chance."

Her mother met her gaze as Sharon closed her eyes and continued to take slower breaths. "And I'll talk to the Georgians. They'll agree to get more involved." Her mother patted Sharon's shoulders. "Let's get some breakfast and then I'll get you home. It's close to dawn."

Plunging her fists into the edge of the bed, the good witch used it as leverage to haul herself to her feet. When she swayed, Martine grabbed her arm. Together, they released the protection spell from the cubicle.

"Text me to let me know you're home safe," she said to her mother.

"Yeah. And make sure you keep your guard up with you-know-who. Like I said, he's a real charmer."

"I wasn't born yesterday, Mare."

"Again, I'll warn you. You don't know who you're dealing with."

After seeing them to the ER exit, Martine leaned against the glass eyeing the empty corridor to her patient. *Why do I get the feeling there's more to the story about Draven? With both of them.* Too tired to follow the mystery any further, she walked back to Cubicle Q to check the IV line and notated Christopher's vitals for the final round of her shift. Scrubbing her face, drained from the multi-hour mind-walk, she willed herself more awake.

Dottie's head poked through the curtain, which looked as if it floated with no body attached. "Want a ride home today?"

"No, thanks. I've got errands to run."

"Make sure you check out the super shiny limo with a driver outside."

Her eyes went wide, but she played innocent. "Did we take in any high-profile patients?"

"Probably. Even the rich and famous are getting this crazy flu. See you tomorrow night."

"Be careful driving home, Dot," she replied.

Minutes later, a new nurse came through the curtains. Sensing her a Georgian, she also looked familiar. Trying to place the nurse, her sweet smile came off kind, almost adorable.

"Hi Martine. Nice to see you again."

Still puzzled, she said, "I'm sorry, do I know you?"

That sweet smile sailed at her once more. "Paige. Paige Virelli? We met years ago as teenagers? Deepa assigned me to rotate with Marsha."

Her eyes went wide with a shocked, "Oh my God! I didn't know you were a nurse." *A Georgian as well.* Yet the recall hit her like a punch to the heart. "I'm so sorry. It's been a long shift."

"I still keep in touch with Lu."

And *that* hit like another punch, causing a flutter in her chest as well as a jolt to her conscience. His deep dimples appearing with the slightest quirk of his mouth. Eyes an uncommon deep-blue, always full of mischief. His easy smile forcing you to give one in return. She shut down the recall dead in its tracks and sensed each new, weird connection making things more complicated.

"Right. That summer in the UK, with Jillian," she whispered, forcing a grin. "She's okay now, right?"

Paige nodded. "Lu and his father saved her life."

Martine caught Paige's memory of both Jillian and Lu. "Wow. Yeah. We met right smack in the middle of my wild-child days. And that's why you went into nursing, too."

"Seeing something like that changes you."

*Don't I know it.* She handed off the patient tablet, fighting off more memories.

Paige took it, saying, "See you at sunset, Martine."

She grabbed her oversized handbag and purple

cardigan from under Christopher's bed. Staring at Paige, she pulled up the hood and shoved her hands into its comfy deep pockets. "Text me if there's any change?"

"Sure thing."

"Oh. Jose has my cell number."

"I already have it in my phone," Paige replied, signing in on the tablet and ready to begin her shift.

Walking through the curtain of Cubicle Q, her thoughts circled back to the unprecedented event in Siena. Lu, a scrawny fifteen-year-old, had put himself in harm's way to save Jillian. Right after it happened, she had gone with her mother and grandmother to Portofino for an important funeral, overly curious to see the change in Michael. Then she met his son and they hit it off instantly, both mischievous to a fault. What followed were years of a tight, close friendship that ended in a fireball of hurt. *Don't go down that wormhole of regret. You started it and never had the nerve to apologize.* Wrapping her arms around tighter, Martine walked the quiet corridor bothered and exhausted. Seeing the limo outside the ER, she blew out a sharp breath, too tired to do a quick spell ensuring that no one saw her getting into it.

****

When the limo pulled up to the door of *Destiny,* a thin smirk crossed Martine's face. The irony of the club's name wasn't lost on her, even though she felt mentally and physically drained. Taking the driver's hand as he assisted her out of the plush backseat, she gave a soft "thanks," and took a slow walk to the entrance. Before she grabbed the handle, a beefy man who could probably make a killing as a wrestler pulled it open and stayed outside, which was a good thing because she didn't think his shoulders would fit through the door frame. Another "thanks" left her lips.

Strolling down the hallway, she took in the dramatic flair of the décor. Lights reflected off tiny stars and bejeweled walls, giving the impression that the *Destiny* experience was unique. She descended the stairs into a massive floorspace. The beefy bouncer, because what other position could someone who looked so deadly have, indicated a door at the end of the long, wide hall to her left with his arm extended. She got a good glimpse of the unisex bathrooms—all four of them as she sauntered down the hall. She could easily imagine haute-couture clad clientele being privy to more shades of elegance as they primped in front of floor to ceiling mirrors.

Reaching the end of the dimly-lit hall, a door was ajar. The brass plate on it simple: Private: Do Not Enter—which she did anyway with a one-finger push. Draven stood next to the classiest desk she'd ever seen. Dark wood with carved legs held her attention. Neat and tidy accoutrements of a businessman on top. A very large, probably super-expensive computer perfectly centered. Her focus swept the room to the other side, taking in a plush leather couch and a set of matching armchairs. On the wall behind the couch, a flat screen TV some six-feet wide. Directly across the room a vault door ornately tooled with a digital pad next to it looked large enough for someone to walk through.

"I gather you approve of the décor," Draven said with a thin grin.

*He's a looker, all right.* "Wow. Really impressive. I'll give you that." Pulling a hand out of her sweater's pocket, she readjusted her handbag on her shoulder.

"But it is not our final destination," he said, walking to another door behind his desk. When it opened rich aromas of strong coffee and bacon came at her. Her stomach growled as he entered and she followed.

The ultra-modern dining room had a huge, classy couch at the far end, albeit without windows, of course. Soft tones came from recessed lights, the décor impeccable yet very masculine like his office. The table, set for two, held an assortment of breakfast items— enough to feed a party of six.

Dressed in a classy black suit, black shirt and tie, Draven held a chair for her to sit, which she did. "I feel very underdressed," she said with a slight smile.

"Nonsense," he replied as he sat at the head of the table and to her right side. "I wasn't sure what you prefer, so my chef prepared a variety for your palate." He reached for her cup, rimmed with gold against an off-white floral pattern, and filled it three-quarters of the way with coffee. After placing it on an equally impressive gold-rimmed saucer, he filled his own. "Please help yourself. I'm sure you must be ravenous after such a long shift."

The first mouthful of coffee revived her immediately. Choosing one strip of bacon and a lovely Eggs Benedict, she picked up her knife and fork, slicing into the creamy hollandaise sauce.

He sipped his coffee, and then said, "Surely you will eat more than that, Miss Kendrick."

She dabbed her lips with the cloth napkin on her lap and eyed him. "Please compliment your chef. This is delicious. And the coffee is very good."

"Thank you. I made it myself. An old habit. I like it strong."

"So do I," she replied. Stealing a line from someone she had known since childhood, she added, "Coffee is an eternal pleasure, isn't it?"

He gave a thin smile with a slight tilt of his head as if curious. "Yes. It is most certainly an eternal pleasure."

She finished the egg portion, leaving an uneaten muffin, and then worked through the crunchy bacon cooked to perfection. After another sip of coffee, she sat back in the chair. He continued to study her with an intense expression on his face. *And a very attractive face to boot.*

"You cannot be full," he said with a certain tone of authority. "I urge you to try and eat more. Perhaps fruit. The strawberries are ripe."

She gave a half-smile, forking a berry and an orange slice as well. "And you haven't eaten a thing. I wonder why?"

"I had my breakfast just before you arrived."

*A liquid one...* "Fresh or from the blood bank?"

"Very preceptive. Knowing what I am, does it frighten you?"

"No. I have a close family friend who once had the same... affliction."

"Ah, yes. Did you know Michael and I have the same sire?"

*Who would have guessed?* "How interesting."

"And Mary, how is she? May I offer my condolence on the passing of your grandmother, Martha. I knew her as well."

"Jeez, you vampires get around. So why am I really here?"

"We might share information regarding your patient."

After she chewed a piece of the orange slice, she shrugged a shoulder. "What can I possibly tell you that you don't know, Draven? I'm sure your servants have already gathered information from multiple sources."

"I prefer to call them minions," he said in an arrogant way with a dismissive flourish of his hand.

"Tomato-tomahto… I'll bet you have sources in police departments, hospitals, banks. I could go on, but you catch my drift."

"My dear Miss Kendrick—"

"Martine. Just Martine."

"As you wish. Has Christopher Forbes awakened, Martine?"

She rolled her eyes. "Oh, please, just cut the crap. We both know he isn't in a natural coma. A dark spell created by a dark witch who most likely jumped dimensions left him like that. Mare said you're like a gatekeeper. So, this breach is your fault because you let her through." Picking up the large strawberry, she bit off the tip. It tasted sweet and she took another bite before putting it down.

"Odd that you use the same word I do. Yes. It was a breach. But I had no knowledge of it. Neither did any others in the Second and Third Realm."

"Don't even try to say she acted on her own. There are legends about crescent moon nights."

"I am aware. And I assure you, once again, this breach and what she has done goes against their unwritten laws. She acted on her own."

"And she just happens to end up here in your club. Really, Draven? Who is she?"

"We are working on it."

"Well, work harder. Because the longer my patient

is in this state, the less likely it is for him to come out of it without serious brain trauma. He is an innocent. He should have been off limits to her. She stole his future, and for what? Some stupid legend about conceiving and delivering during the crescent moon?"

"You are well informed, Martine." He paused as if to choose his words while she fiddled with expensive gold-plated silverware aligning them as they had been before she used them. "I am incensed that a dark witch breached dimensions. It is wrong. Our three realms have lived in peace for fifteen years since your... what did you call Michael? Ah, yes, your close family friend... since he created such tremendous chaos that all other portals closed."

"But you're still here."

His facial expression changed, almost as if he were shocked. "Yes. I am, and here I will stay because it is I who ensures no thirsty sires or insane underling makes its way through to the human world. I serve the higher purpose of peace between our realms."

"Yet you walk freely among so many unsuspecting humans like some gift to your kind."

"My kind? I was once human, Martine. I have walked this earth since 1847 and I have seen much more than you ever will. I have loved and lost. Like your close family friend I have avoided the stake. Some of us, and I will admit, though, not many, retain *some* sense of moral responsiveness. Let us focus on the issue at hand. You know what I am. I know you are quite powerful on your own and I will ensure that no harm comes to you... from any of *my* kind," he added on the edge of sarcasm. "I am sure you have worked your way through his mind. What have you learned?"

She blew out a long breath and shook her head. "You obviously don't listen, do you?" His arrogance, like his awesome good looks, came at her full force. His deep voice sounded almost mesmerizing, very much like Michael's. She could hem and haw or give Draven what he wanted. "The truth is, I've tried. Others came to help me try again. After hours of our pooled power all we managed to do, well, two fingers twitched," she added in defeat.

"How many were you?"

"Three pretty powerful witches."

"Your mother and who else?"

"I prefer not to say."

He leaned forward, his eyes like pools of melted chocolate. "You will tell me."

With a frown, she replied, "It doesn't work on me, Draven."

After a grin, he narrowed those dreamy eyes. "I could make you tell me."

Her back went up, saying, "No you can't, and no you won't."

He leaned in with a sniff and a smirk. "Ah… sweet, sweet Sharon."

She shrugged thinking, *Damn, he knows her scent?*

"You chose well, or rather Mary did. Sharon must have matured into a powerful healer. I remember her fortitude very well. She was quite beautiful in her twenties."

"I really don't want to take a stroll down memory lane. Not lover's lane, either." *No wonder Sharon reacted the way she did. He's a charmer, all right.* She sighed as her shoulders relaxed. "I'm sorry. I was out of line and offensive."

"Noted, Martine." He paused a moment. "What else? There is something else."

Sure that he'd find out anyway, she said, "The same night he was brought to the ER, so was an old woman, who I believe is one of us. She used the word fornication. She said the alley between two giants, and they found him in the space between two Broadway theaters. She said a witch took his seed on the night of the crescent moon." Although it had cooled, she took another sip of coffee. Draven refilled the cup as soon as she put it down. "That's all I have to give you."

Pouring coffee into his own cup, he gave a slow nod, then took a long sip and swallowed. "This dark witch remains hidden. But I have a picture of her, which I will share with you. She must not get to him again."

"I agree. So now that you know what she looks like, go get her."

He slightly smiled. "It's not that simple. I do not fit the look of a warlock."

"No. They're all tall, blond and blue-eyed. What about a half-breed?"

"No, nor a mutant. My travels to the Second Realm are only at the request of the sorcerers. A request I fully hope I will not get anytime soon."

"So send a minion or something," she replied, wondering why he hadn't already done so.

"It would take weeks for anyone fully human to become acclimated to the thin air and climate of the Second Realm. She must be found and very soon," he replied with a swipe of his hand. "Have you shared what you mentioned before with the police?"

"Of course not."

"Tell me, are you assigned to him every night-shift?"

"It's being arranged. And we know the day-nurses as well."

"Let me guess. You have involved the Georgians. That is a good move because he must be protected. And the mystical warriors, the Guardians of Souls? Are they involved?"

"I don't know, but yes, all his nurses except for me are Georgians."

"Are the Georgians financing his care?"

"Probably. With things like dark magic spells, it's best not to involve personal insurance companies. So. What else do you know about Christopher Forbes?"

"He was adopted through a private Catholic charity. Found in a church, wrapped in a blue blanket, the birth mother never identified. His adoptive parents, now deceased, were decent people who raised him well. He still keeps up their home in New Jersey. There are no incidences with the law, not even a parking ticket. He works for a very respectable international company, and he has one very close friend."

"You're not giving me anything new here." Well, he had, in fact, but she didn't let on.

He placed his coffee cup on its saucer without a sound. "I agree with what I'm sure you already sense. He is indeed an innocent."

"So then why did he come into your club in the middle of the night? I mean, it doesn't fit with his personality. Was he trolling for sex? Does he have a hidden life?"

"My staff has studied our videos for the past six months. He's not in any of them. My belief is that this visit was a one-time fluke."

"That altered his destiny."

One long finger tapped his coffee cup. "I suppose."

"What about the dark witch? Is she a regular?"

"How very perceptive of you to ask. She isn't in any other videos, either."

Taken aback, she replied, "I didn't expect that answer."

"Yes. I know. Odd, isn't it? Both of them just happened to be in here on the same night."

"At least we know she hasn't had her eyes on him before."

"It also means whatever portal she uses opens both ways. That is worrisome."

"Do you think she told anyone else about it?"

"I highly doubt it. This is knowledge she will keep to herself."

"So, it means she came into the human world with an explicit purpose. Find a man. Have sex and get pregnant."

One eyebrow raised, which completely complimented his handsome features. "There is something you said before... the old woman said she took his seed."

She shrugged, saying, "Well, they had sex."

"But the words... took his seed." He paused. "Why would she do so? I'm sure she knows the point in her cycle when fertile."

"But pregnancy may or may not occur."

"Was she, perhaps, bringing back to her realm... a....a—?"

"A backup," Martine said as she sat forward. "Crafty bitch, isn't she? Not only does she rape him—"

"I doubt it is rape," he interrupted, "Most likely he

was a willing participant already under her spell."

"Okay. Wrong choice of words, I'll admit. What you're thinking is she took his sperm back to her realm to try to impregnate herself if this sex trip didn't work. She's a *real* crafty bitch. There has to be some way to identify her."

"That, as I said, we are working on."

"What else?"

"There are many issues," he said as he looked away.

"Draven, we've shared so much information already. Tell me, please," she said, full of interest. *Maybe 'please' strokes his ego a little?*

After a pause, he said, "I will not share information about an unidentified portal with the three sorcerers who rule the realm. Only the sire's War Council is aware of the breach. No sorcerer would sanction her romp through the human world, but they might sanction the fulfillment of the legend."

She hadn't thought of that. Sitting forward, she folded her arms on the table staring at him. "Go on."

"They have a scroll which has existed in their dimension for centuries. It is worshiped as if it were prophecy from their holy book, like the Christian bible, called *The Book of Calipha*."

"What does it say? How does it fit in to all this?"

"It gives the realm written guidelines about the boy-child conceived and born on the night of the crescent moon. He will be their chosen one. At the age of enlightenment, which is believed to be thirty years of age, he will be sacrificed to ensure the immortal sorcerers continue to thrive in their realm."

Her eyes went wide as her jaw dropped. *There's that word again.* "Did you say sacrificed?"

With a slow nod, he answered, "Yes."

"Okay. The purpose of conception and birth on the night of the crescent moon is to make a baby boy. And thirty years later he's *sacrificed*?"

"I know. Archaic, isn't it? Yet look at the Christian faith with the Son of God sacrificed at the age of thirty-three."

"But that was for the sins of all," she quickly said.

"As for the Second Realm, the Chosen One's gift of his life ensures another thirty years of rejuvenated power for the three immortal sorcerers. It ensures the safety of the realm. As you said before... tomato-tomahto."

"Unbelievable," she whispered. "To grow a life, to feel life within you and then raise a child groomed for a sacrifice? How could a mother in any dimension do something so horrible? So morally wrong?" She saw her daughter in her arms struggling to take her first breaths. Grief and loss... that unbearable sorrow, always in her heart, threatened to surface.

Draven leaned close and touched her shoulder, snapping her out of her reverie. It made her jump. "You are suddenly quite pale. Eat, Martine. You must eat something."

She swallowed the acidic taste in her mouth, not about to share what had taken her out of the moment. "No. I'm full. I'm all right. I have to go." She stood as a shiver ran through her. "Thanks for breakfast and the information."

Draven stood when she wrestled getting her handbag over her arm. He came to her side assisting in a gentlemanly way. "I can do it myself," she quipped.

"Please," he simply replied, and then he did the strangest thing. He put the top two buttons of her purple cardigan through their loops. The hood settled over her hair, like an odd act of caring. "It is windy outside. You are exhausted. I wouldn't want you to catch a chill."

"Thanks," she whispered still in the ghost of a memory.

"Hand me your phone."

"Why," she asked, reaching for it in her pocket as if on autopilot. As soon as the top became visible, he took it from her. It was already unlocked.

"I am putting my cell phone number in. I will put your number into my phone after you leave. As promised, I will send her picture. Be very careful, Martine. Make sure your patient is guarded well, just in case she decides to—"

"Right," she said, cutting him off. He took hold of her elbow, which again gave away his refined manners, a throwback to a time long gone. *It never gets old, the feeling of knowing the vampire beside you had lived for centuries.* And his grip to her elbow? Steady and gentle.

"I will walk you upstairs, and I will not tolerate any protest," he said in a non-threatening tone. She didn't fight him as energy simply drained from her. In a way, truly grateful for his assistance because her joints felt stiff. He walked her through the hall of bathrooms, through the club and up the stairs. They slowed down at the last long hallway, and Draven handed her off to the beefy bouncer. Realizing he couldn't survive the daylight she turned and met his gaze.

Before she could speak, he said, "It has been my pleasure, Martine. We will meet again. I am sure. Please take care of yourself." She nodded, watched him walk away with long, confident strides.

The beefy bouncer took her hand with a soft, "Come

on, Miss," and then he went through the doorway first. As if he knew, he kept his hand at the small of her back as they walked to the limo. The driver opened the door and she settled into the plush leather seat, her eyes heavy and scratchy. Her arms and legs felt as if they wouldn't hold her up as the limo pulled away from the club called *Destiny*.

Chapter 10

A Plan

Martine's eyes eased open pulling herself to consciousness after spending most of the day in bed. Sprawled across the mattress she turned on her back. Still in her scrubs from last night's shift, she had literally dive-bombed the firm bed this morning, so exhausted that she hadn't even gotten under the covers. It wouldn't be a far stretch to say that the way she landed was the way she woke up.

Her cell phone poked out of her pocket, partially visible in the comfy cardigan, so she pulled it out to check the time. Seven solid hours of dreamless sleep didn't normally happen. She had more than enough time to shower, dress for the shift, and eat. Yawning wide, she stretched her arms above her head.

*What a shift. What an after-shift breakfast.* "What a mess," she murmured. Looking at her phone again she saw the number three on the text message icon. Clicking on the first from her mother, it simply read: How did your breakfast date go? She frowned. *It wasn't a date. More of an information swap.*

The second message came from Draven, and it had an attached photo of the dark witch along with the message: I enjoyed our breakfast together. We must do it again, and soon. Please rest and renew. Studying the photo of a beautiful woman, the fact that looks can be very deceiving came to mind. She could see how a man could be totally attracted, especially if she had set her sights on him, which probably happened with her patient. She didn't respond to Draven's message, either.

The third message came from Paige. It read: No change, vitals strong. I'll stay an extra hour or so. Meeting friends for a late dinner so take your time.

*What a God-send.* That one she answered with a simple: OK. Thanks. See you @ 7:30. Her body ached like she had sprinted up a mountain. Her brain could use a little more down-time as well—before sharing Draven's information with her mother.

Laying down her phone, she pulled herself out of bed and made her way down the hall to the bathroom. Tempted to soak in the tub, she grudgingly chose a hot shower instead. It would wake her up; prepare her for another twelve hours at Christopher's side. It would give her time to think. Standing under hot pulsating water, so many weird connections to all the people already involved in this case intrigued her. *Funny. The last time something like this happened? Sixteen years ago.* Right here in the city when she was a wild-child just shy of seventeen.

Michael's one-man battle against evil. Lu being protected and kept hidden. Portals closing. Then Guardians hunting down vampires; leaving them dust and bone. Good witches sensing the shift as evil lessened by the boat-load. Being able to assist humans without danger from dark witches, and then, the regroup of covens and healing circles to cleanse the world of demonic protagonists who normally stayed hidden. *Humans have no idea how much they benefited from a new kind of peace with those portals closed.* Had they taken this new peace for granted? Would the actions of one selfishly stupid dark witch unravel it like a kitten playing with a ball of yarn?

"Over my dead body," she huffed, vigorously rinsing shampoo from her hair. It had been a long time since she couldn't wait for Mare to get home from the gallery—so they could talk.

****

Dressed and ready for her shift, Martine hurried down the stairs. After hanging her cardigan on the coat rack in the small foyer, she walked through the living room and dining room entering the brownstone's kitchen with a small smile on her face. "How'd you get away so early, Mare," she said as a cup of fresh coffee came into her hand.

"I felt your need."

They both sat at the kitchen table at the same time. "What about the art gallery?"

"It's in the capable hands of an employee. I'm all yours, so share."

She took a mouthful of the dark-roast blend and swallowed before leaning back in the kitchen chair. "Draven certainly is a looker. You must have some history with him." When her mother didn't answer and looked away, Martine clicked her tongue. "What is it with Kendrick witches? Humans aren't interesting enough? You have to fall for vampires?"

Her mother smirked. "I think its genetic. You know it was your great-grandmother Morgan who took Michael under her protection some forty years after he reclaimed his soul."

"But she didn't fall in love with him."

"No one really knows. But your grandmother loved him like nobody's business or so I've sensed. Martha, bless her soul, never talked about Michael, but whenever we were together like some odd-ball family, you could feel the bond between them."

"Speaking of Michael, how long have you known that he and Draven have the same sire?"

Her mother shrugged. "A long, long time. They also have many of the same traits, as is often the case with powerful sires."

*And wasn't that the truth,* Martine thought, studying her mother.

"Similar good looks and a commanding presence. Not to mention the old-world charm and charisma. Draven, however, has a cruel side. He may have a moral streak or two as well, but he doesn't own his soul the way Michael did." After a ripe pause, she added, "Enough history. Tell me about breakfast."

Which Martine did, not leaving out any details. Mare seemed to listen with keen interest, her dark-brown eyes intense, her full eyebrows tight. Her shoulders stayed forward with her arms crossed on the kitchen table. Didn't ask too many questions because as Martine spoke, her mind stayed open to read, as if Mare had been sitting right beside her during breakfast.

"Good. He knows the Georgians are involved. That should clip his wings a little. Let me see the picture." She pulled up the text and handed over her phone. Her mother studied the dark witch and handed it back. "Wow. Will you look at her? No red-blooded man would walk away from that."

"Draven is very concerned about the portal she found and used."

109

"We all should be."

She shook her head as if to shrug it off. "I don't see why."

Her mother leaned forward. Her dark eyes grew even more intense. "Think back to before Michael took a serious chunk out of the sorcerer's stronghold in the human world. So many Guardians of Souls killed—the only mystical warriors who could destroy vampires. So many demons wreaking havoc. Humans selling their souls were a dime a dozen. No one safe after dark. Anywhere in the world. Portals opening, not to suck evil out—but giving evil doers free access to our dimension. It was a frightening world to those of us who know what exists."

Again she shook her head, stubbornly replying, "This dark witch isn't going around the Second Realm broadcasting it. This is one self-absorbed bitch-witch and one hidden portal."

"No, honey. Look beyond the dark witch. Nothing happening in any realm is an isolated incident. That's where Draven serves a purpose. He's not stupid. The knowledge of a hidden portal is a powerful thing. Suppose the dark witch is found and tortured until she gives up its whereabouts? Suppose she can be bought? Dark witches love wealth as much as they do power. And then there's the fact that she actually *found* a hidden portal. How many other sinister players will go hunting for one? How many vampires want to make their way through to drink and drain here again? There are *so* many things wrong about this, I can't begin to count."

Still not convinced, she asked, "Is this the real reason the Georgians are involved? Not just because an innocent life is on the line again?"

"Positively a big fat yes, because they sense it, too. The danger is endless. Besides, they've always known Draven's role involves a bit of morality. He can control the beast-within enough to think clear and rational. Don't kid yourself, though. I'm sure he uses his charm on the sorcerers as well as the vampire council in the other realms. Personal greed alone would have him keep hidden portals closed."

"I didn't get the impression of personal greed at breakfast, Mare."

"No. But I'm sure you sensed his anger with the dark witch who used the portal. And when she's found? Draven isn't going to slap her on the wrist. He won't hand her over to the sorcerers for punishment. He won't bring her to the vampire council, either. He will be lethal. Merciless—as he should be."

Martine met her blazing eyes. "And what if she's pregnant?"

Her mother leaned back and blew out a breath, her jaw tight, her lips barely apart. "We've heard rumors about how conceiving and carrying to term in the Second Realm doesn't happen often. It's like a dying race. And we all know how when a race begins to die off, just like in a fictional space novel, they try to find another home. They'll be jumping into our world in droves. Mark my words. As long as there's breath in my body, it *will not* happen. Life as we know it wouldn't survive." Then she said, "Back to my original point. It's a one-in-a-million chance the dark witch conceived."

"I believe she took his semen with her, which means she has a backup plan."

"That's why, pregnant or not, Draven will hunt her down and kill her."

111

Martine looked away. "No vampire is stupid enough to walk around the Second Realm hunting a witch. And besides, he'd stand out like a sore thumb, not looking like a warlock. Wait," she said, as she started thinking.

"What," her mother said.

*He's mystically-human like his father. He has Guardian skills. Most of all, he could pass for a warlock with ease.*

Mare's eyes narrowed as her face jutted forward. "What are you thinking, Martine?" Then her eyes shot wide while shaking a finger. "No. Oh no. Jesus Christ! Get it out of your head! No! *Not ever!*"

Martine sat back locking her arms across her chest, totally convinced. "My patient's entire future, an *innocent* life is at stake, Mom. He's blond and blue-eyed like a warlock. He's got mystical strength. The Georgians are already involved. You know he'd find her."

"Michael would never allow it! How could you even think of using Lukas like that? In another dimension, where he had been *abused* as a kid? Alone there, without any help! How *could* you, Martine!"

Stubbornly, she argued, "There's a time issue here, and my way is the only way. You've always said that he's even more powerful than any Guardian of Souls the Georgians have ever trained. He's super smart and he'd fit right in."

"No. Don't even think it."

"Christopher Forbes is as good as dead unless we reverse the spell. Lu gets to the dark witch. He gets her to show him the portal, then he brings her through to our world. We find a way to close it for good this time. Number one: Portal gone. Number two: We get the dark witch to lift the spell on my patient. Number three: The innocent is saved. Right up the Georgian's alley for the good of all mankind."

"No," her mother said low and full of fury.

*Nope, I'm not about to stop.* "We work together with Draven and the Georgians. Michael will help because Lu's involved. Once we force the dark witch to reverse the spell, Draven can have her because she deserves what she gets for doing this to an innocent! Event closed. No never-ending nightmare of anything jumping into our world to toy with humanity. It's perfect."

Her mother shook her head. "By all that is good, Martine, come up with a different idea."

"It's not an idea. It's a solid plan. I've tried to undo this wicked spell. You and Sharon tried as well. We got nowhere. Drastic times call for drastic measures, isn't that the old saying? If what you say is true, then these are the dreaded drastic times, Mare. And before you say anything else, run it by the Georgians. *And* Michael. If they say no, then we prepare for the coming doomsday. But we won't stand a chance in hell." She stood and pulled her phone out of her pocket.

"Are you calling Lukas?"

Now *that* felt like another punch in the gut. "Hell no. I'm calling an Uber and I'm going to work."

"We aren't finished discussing this."

"There is no more discussing this! We have to act. Christopher's body is going to shut down. We'll put him on life support, which has its own dangers. Suppose there's another component to this spell. Suppose once she's pregnant, the spell is designed to kill him. What happens then? Another innocent who we could have saved is… *sacrificed!*" She shook her head. *And there's that friggin' word again.* "Call Deepa, Mare. Fill her in on what we know. Share the whole doomsday picture. Then call Michael and Lukas. Just do it."

Not waiting for a response, she left her mother sitting there with her mouth open. In the foyer, she punched her arms through the purple cardigan, slung her handbag over her shoulder.

*There. Done.* Truth is brutal. She had experience with brutal truth. It slapped you in the face, and it left a mark. No. She wouldn't call Lukas. Not after all these years. Not after the way she had shut him down, so cutting and cold. Her mother had to do the right thing soon because if she didn't, more than one innocent would stare death in the face. The world would change again, and this time, not for the better.

****

As Martine walked down the left corridor of the ER to Cubicle Q, she pulled off her purple cardigan. The discussion with her mother left her more than a little anxious. She had been rough with Mare. The plan? Okay. It was a gamble. Lu would be in the line of fire from three immortal sorcerers, dark witches, and who the hell knew what else. Cruel players existed in every race, in every religion, in every realm. Entering the cubicle, Paige stood at their patient's side taking his vitals. Folding her cardigan before placing it with her handbag under the bed, she asked, "How is he tonight?"

Without looking up from the tablet, Paige replied, "No change. The phlebotomist came in two hours ago to take another sample."

"And Doctor Forster?"

"He checked on him earlier in the day. I didn't expect you for at least another half hour. Want to get some coffee or something?"

"No, I had a cup before… Wait. What is that?" Her eyes lit on a white box on the rolling tray, which had been pushed to the side.

"Someone left it for you at the check-in desk. Dottie brought it in."

Martine walked over and studied a box, a perfect one-foot cube, and it felt warm to the touch. She untied the purple ribbon wrapped around it to lift the lid. Her eyes grew wide as the aroma of roast beef and potatoes au-gratin wafted through the cubicle. Each had been labeled. A note lay over the tin wrapping and pulling it out, her eyes met Paige's.

"I thought I smelled food. Just couldn't figure out why," Paige said with a giggle in her voice, adding, "Aren't you going to read it? Or am I being too nosey."

"Not at all," she replied, rather curious herself. The stationery was crisp, the color of an eggshell. Her name looked hand-written in a script close to calligraphy. She pulled out a folded piece of matching paper. *To further insure you remain healthy, please enjoy the meal. You must eat, Martine. Draven.* Raising an eyebrow, she folded the note, placed it back in the envelope, and then slipped it into the pocket of her purple scrubs.

"I can't tell if you're happy or shocked," Paige said.

"A little of both, but mostly the latter."

Paige came over and looked inside. 'Wow. Fancy gold fork and knife, too, definitely not the cafeteria kind. I've got some time, you know, if maybe you want to—"

"No. Not hungry. I'll save it for later." Replacing the lid, she decided to be a bit nosey herself. "When did you last hear from Lukas, if you don't mind me asking?"

"Not at all," Paige replied, but her sweet smile

faded. "Jillian and I face-timed with him a month ago. Last year, we surprised him with a visit when he finished his PhD at Oxford. But he seemed very distant."

So many questions, she couldn't prioritize them. "Oh wow. I didn't know he finished it." Years ago, he had been worried about writing his dissertation—right before that ugly, one-way shouting match. All the witty texts and what they called their secret letter writing saga, abruptly ended. So did the hilarious phone calls. Who ever said a girl and a guy couldn't be best friends? They could tell each other anything, until... *You shoved him away and let thousands of gallons of muddy, murky water flood over and destroy that bridge.* She still missed him but couldn't reach out.

*Yeah, I need to know more.* "Does he still come to the states to see the two of you?"

Paige shook her head and looked away. "Not for years, since he moved to Scotland."

"Oh. Sorry. Now I'm the one being too nosey."

"No. Not at all," Paige said with a shrug. "Maybe he's seeing someone."

*Hopefully someone who cherishes him for the treasure he is.* "Probably," she said.

"You know him, he's very private, likes to keep things to himself."

"Yeah." *No. We shared everything. But hurt doesn't happen if you stay closed off. And I've become a master at it, too.* Needing to change the subject, she added, "The Georgians have to get more involved with this case."

"You know Deepa, right? The North American Continent's Researcher for the Georgians?"

"I sure do. She's a good lady. I had my mother contact her."

"She filled me in on the broader aspects of Christopher's case. I get the feeling Deepa thinks this could become a grave paranormal event."

"I'll bet she's more than right."

Paige said, "If she is, then you should tell Lukas about it, too."

*Way too much muddy, murky water...* "I'd never go over Deepa's head."

Staring down at their patient, Paige replied, "I wouldn't stand on protocol this time. His condition is going to deteriorate. It's only a matter of days." Paige glanced up at the clock.. "Oops. We're meeting up across from the Met at this great Italian restaurant. It's a long walk."

Her sixth sense clanged like a gong. "Take a cab. It's safer. The city has been on a slippery slope since this crazy flu epidemic. There aren't enough police on the streets."

Scrolling through her phone, Paige replied, "You know, you're right about that one."

"Take a cab home as well, Paige. Don't take a chance on the train or busses, and don't use the subways. I have some extra cash on me if you need."

"Thanks, but I'm fine. Have a quiet shift. You better eat that delicious dinner before it gets cold. Marsha will relieve you at six a.m. on the dot."

"Be safe with your friends."

"Text me if there's any change?"

"Sure," she replied. Already grateful for Georgian involvement, they were about to be bombarded with more information. Mare would make the request. If Lu truly was the mystical warrior her mother often marveled over, then he would help. Because like his father, Lu had a good heart.

Chapter 11

Decisions

Rarely did Mary Kendrick feel torn between two opposing factors. Rarely did she have a problem trusting her daughter's astute sixth sense. If Martine called this right, then time was of the essence. And what she now asked for would be an unprecedented alliance between good and evil. Both sides not only working together but trusting each other.

The Georgian Circle's mystical mission to rid the world of unholy evil had been paramount for over a thousand years. Their protection of the innocent far above reproach. Draven, on the other hand, represented evil across all three dimensions. Blood lust, a most powerful craving, might be disguised, but it always lurked right below the surface of his supposed civility.

As Mary entered the elevator to the Georgian penthouse, how to approach the Researcher with all this new information had her attention. Deepa Chandra was a revered Georgian. They had worked closely fifteen years ago to unravel the repercussions after a paranormal event involving young Jillian Gerhart in Siena and remained professional friends ever since. The elevator doors slid open. Her gaze locked to Deepa's as she stepped into the foyer and then followed her into the study. Sitting in front of the researcher's desk, never one to mince words, Mary simply said, "You know about the breach."

"It's on our radar, Mary."

"Good. Then what I'm about to offer you is more information. Plus, a dangerous, but possible plan to bring this event to a positive conclusion." Both women sat back. Mary ticked off the facts one by one. Deepa took copious notes, seldom interrupting as if they shared the same brainwaves. By the end of it, the Georgian researcher's legal pad appeared covered with notes with some sentences underlined, some words circled. She sent a picture of the dark witch to Deepa's cell phone and watched her reaction.

"At least we now have a face. And what's your take on Draven?"

"That's where this gets tricky. Hold on to your hat for this next part." She proceeded to explain her daughter's meeting with the Gatekeeper.

Deepa leaned forward. "Your daughter's playing with fire, Mary."

"Oh don't I know it."

"He serves his purpose, but he can turn on a dime."

"That's exactly what I told her. Martine also insists we need Lukas Malone to really bring this thing home."

Deepa threw down the pen and gripped the edge of her desk. If there had been an hour-glass in the room she would hear each grain of sand make its way down as the seconds slipped away. Obviously, Deepa looked as worried as she was.

"I know there are limits, Deepa, and this plan of hers crosses many lines, but it could work."

"Did Martine consider the psychological effect this could have on Lukas? My God, Mary." Shaking her head, added, "Beaten and brainwashed as a boy, held captive in the Second Realm for heaven's sake."

Very aware, she whispered, "I know."

"Abuse doesn't leave you. Simply *being* there could trigger a traumatic reaction."

"I agree, but we need him. Look. Draven could switch sides in a split second. Lukas is the only person *any* of us should trust to find the dark witch and bring her back to our world."

Deepa leaned forward with her lips drawn tight. "I'm not convinced."

"It all comes down to the way he looks. Signature traits of pure-breeds in the Second Realm. Blond hair, blue eyes, pale complexion. Granted, he's just about six-foot and doesn't have the height, I mean, all warlocks are at least six-foot-three. But put him in a heeled boot and he'll pass as a realm dweller. Lukas is smart off the charts. He has Michael's mystical strength and a warrior's focus. He *will* find her, Deepa, and bring her back to lift the spell on the innocent man lying comatose in St. Francis Hospital." Although not fully comfortable selling her daughter's insane plan, she remained bound by her word.

"Suppose we do this. And then what? We sign the dark witch's death certificate by handing her over to Draven?"

"That's not our concern, Deepa."

"What if she is with child? It is an innocent life."

"Then add a provision. You have facilities. House her until she delivers. Then hand her over to Draven. The child will have a human father. The sorcerers won't want the baby because he's a half-breed. And if she delivers a girl, they'll kill her immediately."

Deepa's eyes narrowed. "What makes you so sure the child will be a half-breed?"

Stunned for a second, Mary's eyes narrowed as well. "What are you saying?"

"As soon as we knew about the breach, some of our Georgian seers sensed something unusual. So our researchers dug deeper. In the *Holy Book of the Second Realm,* every thirty years like clockwork there is a boy-child conceived and birthed on the night of the crescent moon."

"I've heard the stories. There's also something we refer to as the legend of Gwendolyn."

"Yes, but we may know something you don't. Seers in this very city sensed a breach as well as a birth. In the 1980s. Thirty-five years ago, to be exact. Modern technology allows us to extrapolate compilations of their accounts."

Mary sat back with a questionable, "Okay."

"Many report it had been a distraught Gwendolyn who breached dimensions, a pure-bred witch and direct descendant of the line of Calipha who prophesizes about the birth of her boy-child. Simply knowing your child would be raised by the sorcerers and eventually sacrificed as a man would force any mother's hand. The birth of a baby boy becomes both a blessing and a curse. Seers suggested that Gwendolyn and her newborn came into our dimension—through a hidden portal. She left him in the narthex of a chapel wrapped in a blue blanket. There are references to one simply known as Mother."

"Naturally, that person took the baby in," Mary said, getting that sixth sense tingle.

Deepa nodded. "Of course. Interestingly enough, on that very night, seers sensed another woman's immeasurable sorrow, giving birth to a stillborn baby boy."

"And there's a connection between this 'Mother' person and her."

"Precisely. Yet, she and her husband brought home a newborn. Paperwork found suggests it had been a sealed, albeit legal, adoption through a religious organization."

"And what did the seers *suggest* happened to Gwendolyn?" Mary asked as her sixth sense hummed.

"That she returned to the Second Realm never to be seen again."

Her sixth sense suddenly went wild. "And how does this relate to Martine's patient?"

"Georgian researchers found multiple triangulations to Christopher Forbes's birth, confirming the night had a crescent moon." Standing, Deepa walked to the window overlooking the city. She turned and faced Mary. "If he is, in fact, Gwendolyn's son, then he is, in fact, the realm's Chosen One."

Mary shook her head. "No. It's all but impossible. I mean, the chances of that dark witch randomly having sex with her realm's Chosen One is like finding one specific grain of sand in the Atlantic Ocean, Deepa."

"Call it fate. Call it destiny. Call it the master plan of the universe."

She sat forward. "All the more reason to save him by finding the dark witch. Isn't it written in their precious document that he'll be sacrificed, which implies a death sentence for this innocent?"

"You have a point."

"And isn't that what Georgian's do? Save the innocent? Let's put the issue of the dark witch aside for a minute. The hidden portal is a danger. Only *she* knows where it is. The longer we wait on getting Lukas in there, the more chances are that she sells the information, *or* the sorcerers torture it out of her when they get wind of this. Lukas is our best chance to find her. She'll lead him to the portal, and we'll make sure it's closed for all eternity." She took a breath and blew it out slowly. "We need Lukas, Deepa."

"First, we need him to *agree* to put himself through what may be a highly traumatic task. Michael will surely have a say in the matter."

"Lukas is his own man."

"As you know, Mary, your child is your child forever. And what about Michael?"

"If anyone can keep Draven under control, it's Michael. Who better to keep a vampire in line than a former mystically-enhanced one?"

Deepa nodded once. "I will petition the Sovereign Council for approval when I am finished reviewing all the information we've discussed."

"Good. I'll call Michael."

"You know him well, Mary." Deepa paused, studying her. "Do you also have a history with Draven, or am I out of line asking the question?"

Shrugging a shoulder, she only offered, "It was a long time ago."

"Will this new alliance make you uncomfortable? Can you distance enough to think clearly?"

"Not a problem, my friend." And she meant it. "An innocent man's future is more important than my past. It's wrong to steal someone's destiny, and that's exactly what the dark witch did." She stood and walked with Deepa through the penthouse and into the foyer. "We'll work together on this one, and maybe even save our world."

"I agree, Mary. I will make the formal request and then we can plan accordingly."

Before stepping into the elevator, two powerful women smiled at each other with resolve written on both of their faces.

****

Never one to put off what could be done right now, Mary had to, unfortunately, do just that. With it being well before dawn at the Georgian Estate in England, Michael would probably spend the first ten minutes yelling at her for waking him up, anyway. In front of Deepa's building, she glanced at the doorman, walked a few feet away and then pulled out her phone. Why not run some of this by a good friend first? Sharon's very sleepy voice made her wince as she stated, "I thought you'd still be up."

"I had a long day. So many second graders puked just before dismissal that I thought they might have food poisoning from lunch."

"Oh no. Was it?"

"No. The nurse said it's this crazy flu, so I stayed late to get everything ready for all the absences next week and left everything on my desk."

"Maybe you should take a few days off."

"Oh wait. It gets better," her friend said, now sounding more awake. "Instead of checking my emails, I made dinner and ate with the girls, did a load of laundry, you know, all that good stuff. You would think I'd get a robocall or something."

"Let me guess. No school for a while?"

"They decided to close next week because of the

crazy-ass flu, and all my lesson plans and outlines for virtual lessons are sitting on my desk."

Mary winced. "Want to meet somewhere for a cup of coffee?"

"Why don't you come here? I made cinnamon buns yesterday. How about it?"

"Sounds like a plan. See you in fifteen minutes."

"Perfect," Sharon replied. "I'll make tea. We don't need coffee at this hour."

"Great," she said. Clicking the red icon, she sensed someone approach. About to whammy whoever it was, she quickly turned and stared at the doorman.

"Pardon me, miss. It's pretty late. May I hail you a taxi?"

"Sure, thanks," she replied. Two minutes later, she was on the way to Sharon's building.

****

Sitting across from her friend of many years, they sipped blueberry tea. Mary took a bite of the cinnamon bun and rolled her eyes. After a second bite, she said, "You outdid yourself. This is delicious."

"I know, right?" An open smile came at her.

"Listen, I want to run something by you."

"Shoot."

"First, I want to know what you sensed about Martine's patient."

The smile faded. "We won't be able to help him, Mare. Even if the entire healing circle works night and day. It's a very complex dark spell, isn't it?"

"Yes."

"Do you know who the witch is?" Mary pulled up the photo on her phone and showed it to Sharon.

"Never seen *her* before."

"She's from the Second Realm." A look of shock began and she added, "There's a real serious issue here. I'm calling Michael Malone in a couple of hours."

"Why? Is it really that bad? I mean, he's still got that mystical strength going for him, but why?"

After a sip, she put her teacup down on its saucer. And braced herself. "Because we need to work with Draven." Of course, Sharon paled. "I know you're still afraid of him."

"He drank from me, Mare."

"But he didn't kill you, Sharon."

"He charmed me and drank from me! He has a mean streak. He'll turn on you."

"Not with Michael around. He'll have Draven leashed like a mad dog and under control. I just spoke with Deepa Chandra. The Georgians are getting more involved. And Martine came up with a plan."

"A plan?"

"It's pretty far out there, but it might just work." She took another sip of her tea. "The scope of this could be huge. The outcome has to go our way. But we need Draven."

Sharon huffed with a quick, low 'pfft.' "Like anyone can trust him."

"We're going to have to, because this also involves an unknown portal." It took a few seconds for her friend to piece it together. "Look. If you don't feel safe—"

"I'll put one hell of a protection spell on my apartment. I mean, if it was only me, I'd leave the city for a while. But I have the girls now, and a job I really love."

"I'll make sure you have no contact with Draven. Michael never wanted to come back to this city, either, but there's a lot riding on him agreeing to help with this."

Sharon cleared her throat. "As long as I don't have to see him, then count me in."

"Thanks. But there's something else. It's not only Michael. We need his son, too."

"Lukas?" Sharon shook her head. "Keeping that boy safe while his father did what he did with those Hell-beasts all those years ago."

"He's in his thirties now, a year younger than Martine."

"So there's a *hell* of a lot riding on this."

Mary nodded. "Which is why we also need Draven."

"Michael should kick him out of this dimension and send him to that vampire realm."

She had to grin. "I don't see it happening, Sharon. Draven serves a purpose."

"But he has a mean streak."

"He's not going to come after you. That all happened, what, like twenty years ago?"

Her friend nodded once. "I saw him with Michael and just assumed they were alike."

"I know. Hell. I did too. Put him out of mind. Please."

"Easier said than done," Sharon scoffed.

*Don't I know it,* Mary thought. *She'll cast a powerful spell of protection the minute I leave and be more than cautious from sunset until dawn. Knowing Draven, I'd do the same.*

\*\*\*\*

Mary lay restless in her bed between bouts of pacing and trying to sit calm and collected in the chair next to her dresser. Over the years, every visit, every phone call with Michael Malone had been pleasant. He had settled into a comfortable life with Alana, his wife, raising twin teenage girls at the Georgian Estate in England. Given his history, Michael couldn't be classified your typical husband or father... not your typical anything. Then again, neither could Lukas, the son of a mystically-enhanced vampire and carried almost to term by a devious dark seer. Yet his unprecedented conception and birth, a birth that none could explain, had happened. Raised safely away from Michael, the boy had been found and handed over to the sorcerers in the Second Realm. They made the child feral. It took years for Michael to rescue him.

He remained a true-to-the-bone Champion against evil since wrestling back his soul with some heavenly help in 1890. Something no other vampire has ever been known to do. Then sixteen years ago, seeking retribution for what had been done to Lukas, he rained holy terror down and destroyed this continent's triumvirate of evil. It took a gruesome nine months to fulfill the Georgian Council's Document of Atonement. Then, in another mysterious event, Michael Malone found himself graced with human life. He would grow old with Alana, his true love. He would guide his troubled son out of a terrifying past and into adulthood. Lukas had grown into a fine man, a fierce mystical warrior with solid moral principles.

Wondering how to approach this request pulled Mary out of bed only to pace again. How could she ask this of either father or son? How could she tell someone she loved like a brother that his son would need to lay his life on the line in a realm that had once terrified him? Looking at her alarm clock by the bed, sensing Michael awake, the time to call had arrived. She took a deep breath and picked up her cell phone to make the call. Then she waited.

"I wondered how long it would take you to contact me."

Although rattled, just hearing his rich baritone voice made her smile. "I didn't want to wake you."

"Good call. I need a full night's sleep these days." He paused. "Tell me what's happening in that miserable city," sounded more like an order than a request.

"My sixth sense is tingling, and Martine's sixth sense is clanging like Big Ben. I think this is going to be a tough one, Michael."

"Who are the major players?"

"Right now, we've got an innocent in a comatose state, a missing dark witch who put him in it, and we need her to release him. Otherwise, he will die."

"And?"

"There's an unknown portal."

He groaned, asking, "What's the connection?"

She took a few seconds before saying, "Look up a passage in the Second Realm's *Book of Calipha*. It's an ancient rite involving the night of the crescent moon and the birth of a boy-child."

"Let me guess. This dark witch tricked someone into impregnating her. I have some experience with that. This child would be her ticket to get in tight with the realm's sorcerers."

"You got it."

"She jumped dimensions, didn't she, using this unknown portal?"

"And there's the real danger. You know how this continent's portal travel goes through one specific vampire."

"Ah, yes. Dear old Draven. How is he these days, besides filthy rich?"

"He's just as concerned."

After a groan, a growl sounded. "You've spoken to him? Are you crazy?"

She bit her lip, but it was a *must* need-to-know now. "I didn't. Martine did."

"Mary—" he said, loud and sharp.

"I know."

"Mary—" he said, louder and sharper.

Just as loud, she bit out, "She's safe, Michael."

"The hell she is! Put her on the phone right now."

"She's still at the hospital, and don't you *dare* hang up on me and call her!"

"Call her?" he said in that tone that made your stomach flip. "It's a good thing there's an ocean between us because I'd shake some sense into her! I'll be on the next flight out."

"Good. I hoped you would say that. But there's more."

"What do you mean there's more?" His voice sank to a deep rumble in his chest. She could just imagine the look on his face, and her stomach flipped again. "I'm waiting, Mare."

"We need Lukas. Come as soon as you can." Not about to listen to his rant, she ended the call and flung the phone on her bed holding on to hope that he'd take some kind of super-sonic private jet. An innocent life hung by a thread. So did the fate of the human race if that portal wasn't found, then sealed and closed—for good.

Chapter 12

Evil and Good

The minion in Draven's office had a bloody nose and multiple contusions on his face and chest. Draven relished each thready breath of air trying to weave through the minion's lungs, and then, each rattle of an exhale. He stood back wiping blood off his hands in a civilized manner, and ran the hot, wet towel over his palm. Dropping it on his desk, human blood mix with water in a glass bowl. It turned a dark shade of pink, or as he saw it, a muted shade of red.

Another moan came from the minion, which made the vampire smirk. This was his second victim of the night. He had been less brutal on the first, going straight to the drink and drain—when the first cut on the man's lip brought the old bloodlust front and center. That one had been an appetizer. With this minion, however, he chose to play with his dinner.

"I will ask one more time," he said as he turned to face the sniveling human, "What information have you gathered on the dark witch?"

This moan came out a cry. "I swear, my lord, the time stamp on the video proves she had been in the club for hours, dancing and flirting with many of your clientele."

Leaning in, he stated, "I already know that."

"And… and she only gave her name to the men shortly before she left."

"I know that as well," he said in a low hiss.

"Yes, my lord. Aurora, she called herself Aurora."

"What I see in your eyes is that you have no more information." The minion positively shook in the chair, his heart rate dangerously high. Draven straightened and gave a bored sigh. "Very well. If it is all you have to offer, then you may leave."

A quick and shaky "Thank you, my lord," came as he helped the minion stand.

"There, there,' he said in a sympathetic way, "You have no need to thank me. You have offered all you know."

Holding the minion up with a firm arm around his waist, they walked slowly to the closed office door. When the man's hand reached for the doorknob, Draven held his palm against the wood. Then 'dinner' turned with a look of pure terror as the beast-within leered with amber eyes and long, white fangs. With uncanny speed he grabbed the minion's neck and sank them deep into his jugular, drinking less greedily than he had with the first. Not swayed by gurgled screams, he preferred to focus on the thick, rich blood filling his mouth before coursing through his system. *What an unholy pleasure, the taste and scent of warm blood.* He sucked harder, deeper until the pounding heartbeat slowed and slowed until it stopped. Ripping his fangs out of the minion's neck, his eyes morphed back to those of the handsome man. Dropping the body to the floor, he walked to his desk to hit a button on the phone.

Hearing a reverent "Yes, my lord," he simply ordered, "have the mess in my office cleaned."

Without so much as a glance at the dead bodies, he pulled on his long woolen coat and left the office closing the door behind him. A slow macabre composition scored for cello and violin in the minor key filtered through the club's audio system, modern enough to tease one's sexual desires with just a hint of romance. The musician in him inhaled the ambiance of its slow tempo. Had he been in a different mood in the hours before dawn, he might have enjoyed a sexual romp with a courtesan.

Not tonight. He left the club full of humans, walked up the stairs with his head low, trying to focus on other important issues. But then Martine Kendrick came to mind. He wondered if she were as passionate as her mother in the bedroom. Approaching street-level, so many satisfying memories of Mary pulled him back in time.

The 70s had been a good decade for women, freeing the new generation from puritanical and often prosaic sexual customs. Mary's choice had been clear, opting out of those moral confines to dive head-first into craving erotic pleasures. Those nights with her had been heady and wild. Like all good things, it had come to a rather abrupt stop—by him, *not* by his brother in blood.

The bouncer held the door as he strode through. He inhaled crisp autumn air and turned up the empty street in the city that never sleeps. The cliché didn't hold one bit of truth lately. Influenza outbreaks all but crippled most businesses. Hospitals were overrun. Less police on the street. Every public service felt its affect, mostly the morgues.

Some city blocks later, he stood in the shadows and studied wrought-iron gates across the street. Police tape crisscrossed the space between two theaters, which were, of course, dark this time of night. He made his way off the pavement to them. Reaching high, he hoisted himself up and over, bringing his toned body down without a sound.

*This is where the breach happened.* His left hand swept the air. He sensed nothing. He moved around in silence… listening, feeling, waiting to sense even the smallest vibration that would reveal the portal. Nothing. Nothing at all. How had Aurora tricked the human? No one in their right mind would walk into this alley without a sense of foreboding. Had she shifted the man's reality? Conjured something more suitable for seduction?

He left the same way he entered and strode back to the club with daybreak surely on its way. Instead of going into *Destiny*, he stood across the street to watch a steady stream of customers leave. Beautiful women dressed to entice. Handsome men undressing the women in their minds. Dozens of hook-ups and one-night stands. *Yes. The women leaving are all stunning; all gorgeous.* Mixing business with pleasure, however, was not his way. He pulled out his phone, swiped through his contacts and placed a finger on a specific one. Preferring to text, he messaged his desire, then waited for a reply. In less than a minute, he had it. Catching the bouncer's eye, he strode across the street. "Was that the last of them, Donovan?"

"Yes, my lord," the bouncer replied with his hand over his heart and a bow of his bald head.

"I am expecting company. Stay on your post and show her down when she arrives. Then stand inside and wait to lock up." He didn't expect an answer. An order is an order. The trusted minion had done this many times before, knew the protocol.

Draven picked up his pace going down the stairs and through the hall to his office suite, which was perfectly in order with no trace of what had happened a few hours earlier. The air hinted fresh lemons and a trace of vanilla. He left the door ajar as he usually did when expecting company. Sinking onto the couch, he closed his eyes. Minutes later he smelled her perfume before she walked through the door. His contact's choice was perfect. The courtesan's raven-black hair reminded him of Martine. So much so that he would keep her image in mind instead of the beauty who stood before him.

"Welcome, my dear," he said with a charming grin as he stood. He held out a hand, which she took, and led the way through the door behind his desk. Once inside his hidden home beneath the city block, he led her through to the second bedroom, not the master suite. His shoulders hit the door and he unbuttoned his suit jacket before locking his arms across his chest. The well-paid woman stood at the foot of a bed. The fantasy of her being Martine had him already hard and tight against the fabric of his expensive black trousers. Slowly she stripped off her clothes. First the blouse, then a lacey bra. Her skirt slid to the floor, and she stood in waves of dark silk. The lace panties he'd take care of later. In her high red heels, she walked over with her chin high. Her feisty expression reminded him of Martine as well. He approved.

Her arms bent at the elbow and slid behind her head of loose black hair, the way he liked it. His hand drifted from one beautiful breast to the other, around and above as well. His fingers slid lower—lower still until the warmth of her core filtered through his skin. The moan she released sounded gracious, the feel of her pleasant in his palm.

*So tall and statuesque...* For a brief second his thoughts switched from daughter to mother. But no. Martine would be his next conquest. He ran an arm around her waist, and like a graceful dancer she leaned back as he explored. Her supple body excited him. The rise and fall of her breasts a thrill. He pulled his hand away and she went down on her knees.

Without saying a word, she unzipped his trousers to free his erection. He'd have sex tonight. Rough sex. Her tongue licked and teased. Perhaps she sensed his mood, and quickly took him into her mouth. Usually he'd lock his arms again. Not tonight. It was Martine's lovely long hair he fisted as the courtesan worked the length of him.

A growl began low in his throat as he mastered his fantasy.

\*\*\*\*

Martine wrapped the silverware in the cloth napkin that had been provided with Draven's dinner. Once again, she thought, *compliments to your chef*, shoving them inside her handbag under her patient's bed. She had given Christopher a sponge bath earlier; brushed his teeth and combed his hair after shaving him. All had been done with tender care knowing that underneath the appearance of a peaceful rest, he suffered.

At his side, she leaned forward in the chair and took his hand. "I'm here for you," she whispered. "I know you're in pain and I promise, we'll find her and force her to release you. I'm begging you to hold on, Christopher. Hold on to hope like never before because by all that is good, you'll get through this. I promise."

Minutes later, Dottie popped her head in. "Are you

ready? I can give you a lift."

She smiled at her co-worker. "That would be great. My relief should be here very soon."

"Great! Come get me when she arrives. I'll wait at the check-in desk."

"Was it a crazy night?"

"Umm, yes and no. It calmed down around 4 am. How's handsome doing," she asked with a jerk of her chin.

"No change."

"Jeez, that's too bad. I put him on the prayer list at my church."

She gave a nod. "Good idea." The curtain pulled open with a whoosh and both of them looked over. "Hi Marsha."

A bright smile appeared on the middle-aged woman's face. "Hi Martine. Enjoy your day off."

She looked at Marsha and shook her head. "I don't have a day off. See you tonight."

A puzzled expression came at her. "Oh. I was told that Paige is taking your shift tonight because you'll be tied up with the meeting. Have you checked your emails lately?"

Her phone was already in hand. She read the one-word text from Draven, and pulling up the last email, she eyed it, then read the brief message. "Oh. Sure. The meeting. Where is my head lately?"

Marsha shrugged. "I find myself checking emails often, especially when there's such an, um, an important personal assignment. No need to worry. We'll take good care of him."

"Wouldn't even doubt it, Marsha," she replied. Dottie's eyes darted between them. Then Martine grabbed for her purple cardigan and handbag beneath the bed. Pulling on the comfy sweater, she said to her co-worker, "Ready?"

"As ever," Dottie replied.

They walked out together and got into Dottie's car. As her co-worker put it into reverse to back out of the parking space at the side of the ER entrance, she said, "Is something going on with your patient? I know it's a strange case, but I've never seen these nurses before."

"There's a private Catholic organization picking up the bill. I help out sometimes, and I've met some of the other nurses they employ. They're all good people. Like you, Dot."

"Who are they? Maybe I've heard of them at church or read about them in our parish bulletin."

"This particular organization tends to be pretty private." She swept Dottie's mind to veer it way *way* off its current course. Otherwise, being this tired? She just might say something she shouldn't. "If it isn't grocery shopping day, how did you manage to get the car?" *Perfect*, she said to herself, listening to her colleague go on and on about her sister coming to visit for a few weeks. They chatted back and forth until Dottie pulled up in front of the brownstone.

Martine smiled. "Will you get home in time to make breakfast?"

"It's Saturday, M," Dottie said with a laugh. "The boys get to sleep in."

"Jeez. I lost track of the days."

"It's easy in our profession."

"Tell me about it." She paused. "Thanks for the lift. Are you on for Sunday?'

"No. I come back Monday night."

"Enjoy your time with the boys and your sister this weekend," she said before getting out of Dottie's car. Giving a wave, she watched her pull away and then turned to the brownstone.

Even under bright morning sun the autumn air felt chilly. Leaves danced to the ground from a huge oak on the sidewalk as she passed the colored pots of hearty mums on the front stone steps. Martine hurried through the routine of pulling out her keys, unlocking the door and resetting the alarm before shrugging off her purple cardigan.

Still full from the delicious dinner Draven had sent, she went directly upstairs to her bedroom. No alarm on her phone would be set. She'd sleep until waking up refreshed. Her handbag went on the dresser and then she stripped off her purple scrubs, rolling them into a ball to put them in the clothes hamper in her closet. She settled the terry cloth robe over her shoulders and tied it before tip-toeing out of her room and down the hall to the bathroom.

The hot shower felt heavenly as did the after-shift wind-down in her body. It had been a tense couple of days. And the idea of tonight's meeting with Deepa and possibly other Georgians had her attention. What would Deepa say about her plan? With or without the Georgians, she'd do just about anything to save her patient. And what about Lu? Had her mother called him? She stopped washing her arm, then slowly lathered up again. It didn't matter. If he was there, she'd be distant but cordial because the event takes precedence. *It has to. An innocent life is at stake.*

Would they question her about Draven? Although a thoughtful gesture to send her such a fine dinner, how truly cooperative would the vampire be? If he knew her mother, then he had to have been in the city since the 1970s, at the very least. With the meeting set with Deepa and God-only-knew-who-else for after sunset, she'd have time to do a little digging on exactly what this vampire was about. Maybe sense her way through some witchy websites for entries.

Wrapped in the terry cloth robe, she brushed her teeth and then pulled her hair out of the bushy bun, her signature hairstyle since those wild-child teenage years. *Some things never change*, she thought with a grin, *and I still prefer soft, purple pajamas over nightgowns.* She still liked the way multiple silver hoops graced her ears, the smallest hoops at the top ending with the largest low on each ear lobe. She didn't like the feel of rings on her fingers, the only necklace worn was a polished silver cross given to her by Michael Malone.

Her eyebrows knit thinking about Lu's father. Lu would find Aurora and the hidden portal. Michael would intimidate her enough to lift the spell—one of his specialties…with human or demon. *Yeah, he'll definitely convince her to lift that dark spell, all right.*

Dressed in purple pajamas, she tip-toed back to her room, closed the door and this time, pulled down the covers and settled into bed. With the black-out drapes already closed, she snuggled on her right side and hugged a pillow under the covers. It didn't take long to fall asleep. She truly felt mentally and physically exhausted.

Chapter 13

Michael

The smell of dark-roast coffee filled Martine's senses as she turned onto her back. Immediately, she winced—because the black-out drapes were wide open? She blinked again before her eyes slid to a tall figure sitting in the chair beside her bed. His long legs were crossed at the knee; his elbows planted on the chair's arms. She managed to catch the irritation on his face while his fingers stayed steepled, slowly ticking off the seconds on his lips. His dark wavy hair still touched his collar, lit perfectly by the late afternoon sun that kept just enough of his angular features hidden in the shadows.

"Good. You're awake. On the night stand is a cup of coffee and a blueberry scone from that bakery you like." The low, dark tone coupled with the clipped British accent didn't match such pleasant words. By no stretch of the imagination.

"Michael?"

"You will sit up and eat every last crumb. You're too thin, Martine. I will address that issue in good time," he said with signature arrogance. She let out an exasperated 'humph' while adjusting the pillows against the wooden headboard and sat up. He stood at her side with the plate in one hand and her favorite purple mug in the other. Dressed in all black with his sleeves rolled up, he looked both dangerous and handsome as hell.

"Why do vampire's always want to feed me? Think I'd be tastier with more meat on my bones?" The look on his face deepened, something she remembered oh-so-well, his irritation revving up to full force.

Those dark eyes framed with thick lashes narrowed. "That is not funny."

"I think it's hilarious," she replied, taking both from him. Before his next command, which was sure to be, "I said eat," she sipped the coffee, set it down on the nightstand, and gingerly took a bite of blueberry scone. She chewed slowly, deliberately, and after swallowing, gave a sarcastic, "Are you satisfied now?"

His favorite stance appeared. Arms locked across his chest. Feet slightly apart. "Not in the least, little girl."

*Uh-oh... those last two words mean business.* So with a hint of a tease, she replied, "I just can't get used to your classy accent. I guess old, *really old* habits never die."

"It's part of the human me," he said less amused. His high cheekbones and straight nose complimented thin lips, which hadn't turned into a smile. "It's been years since I've seen you, Martine. It's been many more years since I've sat here watching you sleep off those wild-child nights." She took another bite of the scone, waiting to see where this stroll down memory lane would lead. "You've been driving your mother crazy since before you could talk."

"And you've always been a thorn in my side."

"I am not," he said as a brief look of shock crossed his drop-dead handsome face. "You were a handful. More so after your father passed. From what I hear, you've revisited some of your evil ways recently."

143

She had to chuckle. "How so?"

"I recall many dangerous stunts during the wild-child years. Purple hair. Multiple piercings, the desire to ride on motorcycles, and the dreaded tattoo stage—"

"They're all very tasteful. Wanna see?"

"No. And don't interrupt. I recall the stoned bikers and the awful musicians, if you could call what they played music, just because your curiosity piqued and you liked mischief."

"I never brought home a vampire, though. I had you." She caught the thin grin before his face took on that you-know-you're-in-trouble look. He leaned forward. She took another bite of the scone. He could be very intimidating. Sometimes.

"Draven is dangerous."

After swallowing a mouthful of coffee, she replied, "Really? He's been a perfect gentleman with me."

"I can assure you it is a façade. He is not to be trusted. And yet, you were alone with him. Mary told me about your breakfast date."

"I wouldn't call it a date exactly."

"You went to his lair and had breakfast with him. Alone."

"His lair? Is that what you called your brownstone all those years ago?"

"I lived above ground, not below the dirty city streets. And it is a lair. He kills his victims there."

She went to put the plate down. He handed it back. She took it, but her eyes narrowed, really wanting to roll them, but he'd probably go ballistic and use the dreaded "little girl" line again. She bit into the scone rather brazenly, then returned it to the plate as she chewed. After another gulp of coffee, stated, "It was an information swap. That's all. A onetime deal."

His signature strides to her dresser was a sight to behold. *God. Even the back view is a thrill in those tight jeans and fitted shirt.* He fished around in her handbag and pulled out the rolled napkin with silverware. "Wow. You still have a vampire's sense of smell, don't you? I was going to wash it all before I gave it back."

Michael threw it on the bed. Of course, it landed right next to her hand, exactly where he wanted it. "Explain. And you will not want me to ask twice."

"Draven sent over dinner… to the hospital. I've no idea how it got there. Hence the line about vampires always wanting to feed me." When he turned to the closet, her mouth flew open before yelling, "Michael," which didn't stop him. In a split-second, he had the note in hand. "Super-speed's still intact, too," she muttered as he read the note and then crushed it in a perfect little ping-pong ball—with one hand. "See? No "my dear Martine' on the page or anything else to suggest anything devious."

He came back to her side, his eyes slid to the scone, and she took another bite. "You will never again be alone with him."

"I honestly can't promise that. He has more access to information about Aurora. And I won't lose my patient because of some stupid legend."

He leaned down and held her gaze. *Full-on intimidation.* "Give it to me." She placed the rolled napkin and silverware in his outstretched hand. "The note as well." She complied. "You will never again be alone with him. Is this understood?" The sharp tone complimented the determination on his face. So she gave a slow nod.

"No, not good enough, honey." Sitting on the bed, he took her hand. That he could slide from threatening to tender had always been impressive. "I'm not kidding," he added in that calm, charming baritone. "You know I love you even though you know how to push my buttons. If anything happens to you in this event, it would kill your mother, and it would break my heart." The switch back happened as his jaw tightened. "Say it out loud and mean it."

"I will never again be alone with him. I promise," she whispered.

"Good," he said as he stood. "I will hold you to your word. Now on to this eating issue. You will finish every last bite as I stand here and watch. You will eat healthy meals and finish what you are served. Well, get on with it. Finish the scone. Then out of bed. Meet us downstairs dressed for the day."

It was useless to not comply. Funny. She felt that wild-child stir again. Michael had been a big part of her life. Seeing him made her feel safe. Draven's charm hadn't worked on her. She was positive. But if he turned out to be as dangerous as Michael said, she'd believe it. After the last bit of scone, she handed him the plate, took a last sip of coffee and handed him the mug.

He gave a gorgeous smile; a very rare sight to see. "Ah, my dearest Martine, I've missed you so."

As the bedroom door closed, she blew out a long breath and sank back into the pillows piled behind her. *Everything's going to be all right now, because he's here. It's like having a secret weapon with mystical strength to combat evil... someone commanding and fierce.*

\*\*\*\*

At the kitchen table, Mary sat across from her dearest and literally life-long friend. She had grown up under the protection of Michael Malone, the notorious mystically-enhanced vampire who reclaimed his soul. Her earliest memories included him and her mother, a young widow, in deep conversation. She'd often curl to his chest as a child listening to his voice echo against her ear—making it so easy to fall asleep. It made no difference that he didn't have a heartbeat. But now, looking at Michael sitting across the table, she watched him breathe out of necessity. No one would ever know this healthy human being had a singular history spanning centuries.

"You're staring at me again, Mare," he softly said.

She chuckled with a shrug. "Every now and then it still gets to me."

A typical thin smile appeared. "It certainly is a shocker, not to be an eternal twenty-seven anymore. I don't think too many men enjoy their forties the way I do."

"You still look the same."

"I don't feel the same. Now and then there's the occasional backache."

"Ugh! Aren't they brutal?"

"They truly are." He took a sip of coffee and studied her.

"What is it you need to say?"

"You remind me so much of your mother," came out softer still.

Her eyes instantly filled. "I miss her every day."

"I do as well. Without Martha and your grandmother Morgan I'd never have been prepared to live life again, know how to love and cherish Alana and my children the way I do. I am forever in your family's debt for allowing me the privilege of being so close to all of you, accepted throughout the decades."

"Mom always said family is everything."

"I couldn't agree with her more."

"Alana's going to miss you being with us until this event is brought to a conclusion." Love for her stood right there in his dark eyes. When it came to beautiful Alana, he truly wore his heart on his sleeve. "You don't spend too much time apart."

"Just the way I like it," he replied.

Then the lines around his eyes tightened. "I've read everything the Georgians have so far, including 'what-if' scenarios Deepa sent. The passage from their holy book is bothersome. Because if this Christopher Forbes is Gwendolyn's son, then his very existence spells danger across dimensions. That this dark witch found him could be viewed as a good omen to some in her realm. Anytime ritualist belief is involved, no matter the realm, zealots are sure to surface."

"She has to be found, Michael."

"If she came through undetected then anything could come through. The portal obviously works both ways. This event could easily put the human world back to where it was before my mayhem in Manhattan. But I'm not about to involve—"

"Which is why we need Lu," Martine said, taking a seat while pushing up the sleeves of her purple sweater. "He's the only one in this little need-to-know circle who can pass for a warlock in the Second Realm."

So involved in the conversation, Mary didn't hear her daughter come in. "Martine, dial it down," she said, reading Michael's worry.

He shook his head. "Honey, what you're asking is very dangerous. This will be a trip into his past during a most terrifying time. It's taken Lukas years to put all that rage to rest. We should explore other ways."

"There's no time for that, my patient is human."

"Are you sure about that? From what I understand, he may be the sorcerers' rightful sacrificial lamb." Anger in his voice came through loud and clear. Then he glanced at her. "Mary? Tell me Martine doesn't know."

"It hasn't been proven, and Deepa can't be sure."

"She's not sure of what?" Martine asked leaning forward.

Less than eager, she looked at her daughter. "Deepa calls it a triangulation of events. They believe Christopher Forbes is the boy-child Gwendolyn birthed on the night of the crescent moon. Gwendolyn brought him through the portal to hide him."

Michael cleared his throat. "That's the reason you will not speak to Draven again. He's been known to get information out of anyone, especially women who think they are one step ahead and immune to his charm. If your patient is Gwendolyn's son, then he is the full-blooded sacrifice that will increase the sorcerers' powers. Who is to say it won't start a war between the realms? And that cannot happen." He leaned into her daughter. "If the sorcerers haven't had a blood sacrifice in over sixty years now, their powers may begin to weaken. The two conjured dimensions will shift, perhaps revealing more hidden portals. Like the one Gwendolyn found, they will be searched for by crafty dark witches and warlocks. The human world conjoins the other realms. This is where the war between vampire and witch happens."

"All the more reason for Lu to find the dark witch,"

her daughter said.

Michael smacked his hands on the table and stood up, leaning down over Martine and locked to her eyes. "Not going to happen," he firmly stated.

Mary grabbed his arm. He rarely lost his temper, and you didn't want to be on the other end of it. "Stop. Please. Both of you." But the two of them remained eye-to-eye. Although she tugged, he didn't budge. Not even an inch, as if he were made of solid rock.

*Just this once, back down, Martine. You're tenacious. So is he. Your plan will put his son in all kinds of danger. If it were me, I'd feel the same.* Her daughter turned away. Michael walked over to the kitchen counter leaning against it with his arms tight across his chest and his ankles crossed. The stand-off continued in silence, and Mary blew out a sharp breath and shook her head. She walked over to Michael, easily read fear in his heart.

"We'll discuss this plan of yours tonight," he said controlled and calm. "Deepa will send a car. Until this event comes to a successful close, Guardians will shadow both of you and keep watch over Kendrick House." Without another word, he left.

Relieved the de-escalation worked, Mary sank back into the kitchen chair and stared at her daughter until their eyes met. "You just had to push, didn't you? What the hell is wrong with you lately?"

"There's nothing wrong with me, Mare. Lu's our only hope."

Not wanting another round of fighting, Mary took herself out of the game. Something mundane like a big load of laundry would be a welcomed diversion right now.

Chapter 14

Brothers in Blood

Draven stood in the passageway where Aurora had come into the human world. He scented every single inch again, and as he had last night, sensed nothing. He turned his face up to the sky marveling at its clearness.

It had been on an October night like this that he had met his fate. He recalled his sire, now dust and bone. Cyril had singled him out. The arrogant pianist never saw it coming, too flattered and full of himself. *Perhaps a bit naïve, never believing such creatures existed.* A vampire does not recall human life. Yet he retained an astute musical ability as if those skills were etched so deeply within his brain that nothing, not even undeath, could erase them. Sitting confidently at a piano, his fingers always flew with passion over the eighty-eight keys. Chopin ballades were his favorite. Liszt's rhapsodies a close second. He had heard these pieces performed by their composers in person. In Paris. In the 1840s.They had been his equals, his inner-circle in days long gone.

Flexing his hands at his sides, he fought the frustration building within. Perhaps another night of sexual pleasure was called for. He'd consider it.

"How odd. So lost in thought that you didn't hear me jump the fence, Draven."

He stood perfectly still as a thin smile began. "It has

been years since I've heard the richness of your voice, brother. I've been worried about your current state." After clicking his tongue, added, "Humans are so very vulnerable."

"Really? Worried about me?"

Slipping his hands into the pockets of his long wool coat, he shrugged. "I have heard you resettled in merry old England. What brings you back to the city?"

"You do."

"Me?"

"Yes. You. I believe these belong to you." The rolled napkin with silverware inside landed precisely at his feet, followed by an envelope crushed into a small ball, which bounced off his shoe.

"I was a perfect gentleman with her, Michael."

"You will not speak to Martine again."

"I wondered why she didn't answer my latest text. I sent her the name of the dark witch hours ago. Her name is Aurora by the way."

"I am aware."

"Again. I will state that I was a perfect gentleman with dear Martine."

"Am I expected to believe you?"

"You have my word," he replied with his hand over his heart.

"It doesn't beat anymore, Draven. Your word is just as useless."

"Ah. As always the barb cuts deep. I know my place in the human world. I know my value."

"And I know you still enjoy the drink and drain. Human beings go missing."

"The city has been in a fast decline lately. Murders. Car-jackings. Drugs. Crime is on the rise here, or don't you read the newspapers at your happy home in the English countryside? I suppose it was with foresight that you chose not to return. Your family might not be safe on the dangerous streets of this city. Many things can change in sixteen years."

"And many things, such as you, remain the same."

With a smirk, he stated, "Another barb. Always the arrogant bastard."

"I could say the same for you."

Becoming irritated, he ran his tongue over his fangs. "Why are you here, Michael?"

"To return what's at your feet. Don't think I don't know what you're doing. You can scent her out. Lead her to believe she has the upper hand. Play all fine and proper before you decide to pounce. The parlor tricks are getting old, Draven. Martine is off limits to you. Forever."

"Protective of the Kendrick witches, aren't you?" He shook his head. "Some things never change."

"We've already agreed upon that point. Now let's move on to the next."

"And what would that be."

"Get those romantic fantasies about Martine out of your head, and I let you continue walking the earth."

"Whatever are you talking about?" The quick chuckle came off an insult, and his fists flexed, really wanting Michael's throat in his hands.

"Now, now, calm down, Draven. We aren't going to fight tonight like two men having at it, albeit rather brutally, in a dark alley. Consider this a warning."

"How so, brother?"

"I'm not your brother, Draven. Cyril is burning in Hell. I know because my son and I sent him there."

"Ah. The mystical child. How is Lukas these days?"

"If you think I have a temper, you'll not want to meet my son when he senses even the slightest threat. You'd be dust and bone before the tips of your fangs tingle."

"So he's just like you."

"Absolutely."

"I hear such pride in your voice. I can't wait to meet him." Making a mental list of all the important players to deal with now—he'd be well-prepared. Knowing the son would be involved appeared to be like a free-gift-with-purchase.

"Which is why you will play by my rules until this event is brought to a satisfactory conclusion. You will stay clear of Martine. If there is any information to be shared it will be through me. So. Let's go down the list once again. No Kendricks. No Guardians. No Georgians whatsoever. Keep up the façade as you do so well and stay clear of anyone living and breathing. Prove it, Draven. Prove you know your place in the human world and we just might keep you in the money with your portal travelers."

"You don't trust me."

"Trust is not in your vocabulary. We have a history. I know you perhaps better than you know yourself."

"I kept my word with Mary."

"Yes, you did. But I recall a rather nasty affair with a dear friend of hers. You tasted her, Draven."

"That was well over twenty years ago."

Suddenly, Michael was in his face. Draven bared his fangs, his beast-within awakened. Then he felt the point of the stake through his heavy wool coat.

"Stop the transformation. Do it now or I will end

you. Think of your fortune. Think of your prized grand piano in your underground lair. Think of all the heady sex with courtesans. All the real life passions you get to experience. All those pleasures lost if your eyes begin to turn that awesome feral-yellow." Forcing his beast-within down deep, he heard, "Good job, Draven. You are not its master, but you have learned to control it."

"When I choose to."

"Let's keep it that way."

The point of the stake eased off and his eyes locked to Michael's. "I realize the consequence of not finding the portal the dark witch used. For the human world as well as the other realms. It must be found and sealed."

Michael took a step back. "I'm glad we agree. Legend has it—"

Tossing his head, Draven replied, "I could care less about their legends."

"The dark witch must be located in their realm and brought to this dimension. She must release the man from her spell. He is an innocent."

"Innocent. Guilty… it is of no concern to me."

"What you mean is that after she lifts the spell, the location of the portal dies with her."

His eyebrows rose. "One could say that."

"Her fate is yet to be determined. Let's work on finding her first."

"And how shall we do that? You'd stick out like a dissonant chord in a harmonic composition. So would I. Neither of us could pass as a warlock or half-breed servant."

"My part in this event is you. If finding her takes us to their realm, than be warned. Do not cross me, vampire," he added in a low, murderous tone.

155

Draven sensed it a significant threat, something he didn't take lightly. Had it been any other human who spoke to him like this, he or she would be drained and dead already. That Michael still had vampiric skills spoke volumes. They were an even match.

"I will cooperate," he offered.

After backing away, Michael grabbed the top of the high fence to hoist himself over without a sound. The only difference between them? Michael Malone had a heartbeat. He didn't.

Chapter 15

Lukas

In a sullen mood, Martine spent most of Sunday alone in her room. For as long as she could remember, Sunday dinner had been a special event at Kendrick House. It dated back almost a century, to Morgan Kendrick, her great-grandmother. No matter the importance of whatever you were doing, everything stopped at five p.m. and you made your way to the table, upholding the tradition paramount. Every component of dinner had to be top-quality, and desserts just as important. If not homemade, it came from a fine bakery.

The front door stayed unlocked, all friends welcome. Michael had a running invitation to Sunday dinner, considered family. He'd arrive after sunset. Of course, he didn't partake in the delicious meals. His only sustenance had always been the blood of animals neatly packaged by specific butchers. Martine grew up knowing this about him—it didn't bother her in the least.

Already dressed for the in-between shift, which she'd take over at 7 p.m. tonight, she turned off the computer in Granny Martha's room. Leaning back in the chair, she recalled Michael's last Sunday dinner with them in May 2005. He had come off broody and distant. They all sensed it. *Days later, he destroyed three evil things. Now... evil could be on the rise again.* That her plan for this event had been forwarded to the Georgian Council satisfied her. At the long, boring meeting with Deepa Chandra last night, she'd gotten permission to read part of their file on Draven. *And some piece of work he truly is. Michael's right. Draven is very dangerous.*

She stood, *not* looking forward to Sunday dinner. For five years, she had avoided the tradition making up one creative excuse after the other. Now with Michael here, it loomed like a ghost from the past before her. She wasn't hungry, even though incredible aromas wafted up the stairs to haunt her. Since the loss of her daughter, hearty meals weren't of any interest. The memory of those last minutes of her life, not to mention the hollow hole in her heart with every sappy commercial about baby food, baby lotion or diapers. So many reminders of emptiness in everyday life.

Knowing Michael waited downstairs brought back other feelings, too. The care-free, wild-child years and his bristle when he tried to make her see reason. *A simpler time full of possibilities,* she thought as she leaned against the banister. Not at all ready, she took a deep breath. *Turn off your sixth sense, think about nothing and just go through the motions.* But the dining room wasn't being used, and walking through it, only seeing Michael already seated at the kitchen table, his presence resonated deep within her heart.

When she entered the kitchen, she came to a full stop and her jaw dropped, simply staring at someone she hadn't expected to see. His thick blond curls, now worn long, were tied at the nape of his neck, creating a loose rippled ponytail. Then he turned, revealing a thinner face and deep-blue eyes, both calm and sure. No longer wiry, he looked as fit as an athlete. Her eyes were already wide, and they began to fill. Holding her breath, she felt rooted to the floor. Unable to speak. Unable to move.

He pushed off the kitchen chair, walked over with his arms wide and a warm smile complete with magnificent dimples. They held on to each other as if both had become lost in a mist of memories. Closing her eyes didn't erase five years apart, nor the horrible way she ended their friendship. As if sensing her apprehension, his arms tightened across her back. The steady rise and fall of his chest as her head rested against him brought a strange comfort. Yet too many emotions blurred the lines, crashed into each other. She bit her lip unable to focus. He looked happy. That's all that mattered. And when he kissed her cheek, for the first time in a long time, she felt drawn to life again.

"Christ, how I've missed you, M," he whispered in her ear.

"I can't believe you're really here, Lu," she replied still tight in his arms.

"For you, I'd have walked if necessary."

Looking aside, she frowned. "Yeah, and swim across an ocean, too."

"Like I've always said, for you, anything." He held her shoulders as she pulled back, and his deep-blue eyes filled, his expression one of concern. "You're so thin. It's like you're wasting away." She glanced down, but he drew her close again. The last time they'd seen each other, she had been healthy and happy, convincing him how her new boyfriend would be her destiny, how they'd have a baby and live happily ever after. She hadn't realized it until just now. "I'm so very sorry," he whispered as if he read her thoughts.

"Let the woman go and take your seats," Michael

said. It sounded like an order, but a gentle one. "Mary slaved all day over this. And I'm hungry."

They both smiled as they stepped back from each other. He took her hand and led her to the seat next to his. With Lu on her left and Michael to her right, she closed her eyes and whispered a soft, "blessed be." Mare kept talking about something or other. Too overwhelmed to listen, Martine's heart kept skipping beats.

Michael filled her plate. "A thick slice of roasted turkey, only dark meat. One scoop of mashed potatoes and two tablespoons of cranberry sauce because it is your favorite. Six string beans and a tablespoon of corn," he said while drizzling gravy over the meat. Then he leaned in, and she met him half-way. "You have a little of everything. You must eat it all." Their eyes met, hers instantly filled again when he kissed her cheek. "I'm here now. Everything will be fine."

She nodded once, swiped the corner of her eye. *Blessed be indeed,* she told herself, and turned to see Lu smiling—at her. "When did you get in?"

"Early this afternoon. I dropped my stuff off at Dad's brownstone. Christ. I couldn't wait to shower and change. The Highland estate isn't anywhere near an airport. It took forever to get to Edinburgh for an international flight." They studied each other as if searching for something more. His shirt matched the deep-blue of his eyes. She didn't dare try to read him, too afraid of what she might sense.

She started to ask a question, but Michael cleared his throat. "We'll have plenty of time to talk after you eat."

Her eyes went wide, and so did Lu's with a similar expression on his face. Then they both shook their heads as she said to Michael, "You were never this bossy."

"I've had years of experience with dinner conversation. And years of experience as a parent now."

"Don't I know it," Lu mumbled with a mischievous grin.

"As well you should," he replied in a fatherly fashion, which made them glance at each other again.

For the first time in a long time, she found herself hungry. Dinner continued with all the "pass me this" or "please pass me that," and she ate everything Michael had served her.

Mary stood to clear the table, but Lu jumped up saying, "No. Please sit. M and I will clean up," which they did while exchanging more stolen glances and tentative smiles. Her mother talked about the gallery. Michael chatted about Alana and the twins. With the table clear and dishes in the dishwasher, Martine made the coffee while Lu brought dessert to the table.

*Now the real conversation begins,* she thought. Lu had definitely filled out, no longer thin and wiry, but muscular in a subtle sort of way. She glanced over to see him staring at her again.

"Am I correct? The Georgians approved my daughter's plan," her mother stated.

"So now we prepare," Michael answered after swallowing a mouthful of coffee.

"What's to prepare?" My plan is simple. Lu gets the dark witch, and you convince her to lift the spell on my patient. There. Easy-peasy."

Lu had a cream puff ready to pop into his mouth, which now hung in the air. "Wait. What? I do what?"

Placing her favorite purple mug down, she glared at Michael. "Didn't you tell him?"

"It's your plan. It's your ask," he answered as he raised his coffee mug before he took a drink.

She wanted to kick him under the table! *This isn't happening. We haven't spoken in years and I have to ask him?* "Really? I have a shift to get to."

"You have at least half an hour to explain. I'd start," Michael added with a typical no-nonsense expression.

Dinner suddenly felt like lead in her stomach. She pushed her dessert plate aside and turned to Lu. Not knowing what to expect, she blurted out, "The dark witch who has my patient locked in a spell is somewhere in the Second Realm. You've been there."

His brow knit, his face more than serious. "Kept by the sorcerers and I was just a kid."

"But you know the realm."

"I also know what guards do if you get caught sneaking around."

*Oh, God!. What if he says no?* Very unsure, she asked, "Can you put what happened there behind you if it means saving an innocent's life?"

Lu sat back in his chair, lacing his arms across his chest, just like his father. "Keep going. What do you need me to do?"

"Find the dark witch who did this to him."

"But there are six villages."

"Do you remember any of them?"

"I do," Michael chimed in.

Tight and narrow, her eyes slid to him. "I told you, *you* won't blend in the way Lu can." Turning back to Lu, her expression softened. "You know that pure-breed Second Realm dwellers are all blond and blue-eyed. You fit right in to, you know, snoop around."

Michael leaned forward. "It could take weeks to find

her. No. There are too many ways he'd be exposed. It's too risky."

At first she didn't know what to say and took a moment. Straightening her back, she glared at him. "Not you, me, or Mom can just slip into their realm to poke around, Michael. I sense Lu is perfect for this. And he won't be afraid to deal with Draven." She looked back at Lu admitting, "I'd die if anything happened to you. But you're my patient's only hope."

The dreaded silent thinking began. Her mother looked full of worry, Michael looked ready to kill. Lukas sat there lost in thought. Yet she saw herself pulling the sheet over Christopher Forbes' face and then wheeling his body to the hospital's morgue. *Another innocent life lost, and for what? Some stupid legend.*

"It could work," Lu finally said.

"No," Michael stated in a firm voice.

"I don't have to stay there, Dad. I can go back and forth as need be."

"No," Michael stated even firmer.

"Why not? M's right. I fit in. I know what I'm doing, and I can handle myself in a dangerous situation. Chances are the hidden portal is on the outer edge of the realm. I can start with the outer rim closest to each village and then work my way inward if need be."

"Portal travel makes you sick. We made it through and you bloody well lost everything in your stomach, all feverish and incoherent. I know you recall the feeling. What you're thinking of doing? You'll be sick for days on end in a realm where no one can help."

Lu's deep-blue eyes shot wide. "I was thirteen then, I'm thirty-one now."

"You're still my son, damn it," Michael yelled,

leaning his elbows on the table. His hands folded across his face, as if to conceal the look of realizing a parent's worst nightmare. His chest rose and fell at a rapid rate.

Martine couldn't move, but her mother rubbed his arm and whispered his name.

"Dad," Lu said in a soft, calm voice, "I'm good with this."

"You don't know what you're getting into. Anything could happen there. Anything." His eyes, dark and dangerous, bore into his son's.

"I'll take every precaution. I'll find her and bring her out." His voice stayed soft, as he broke from his father's eyes and faced her. "I'm in. I think your plan will work. We'll talk tomorrow and set things in motion."

Her mother pushed off the table first, saying, "I'll make you a plate for later," and went to the kitchen counter. Martine stood up, pulled her phone out of the pocket of her scrubs to order an Uber. The app finally pinged indicating she had three minutes.

Michael leaned back in his chair and threw his napkin onto the table. When he stood, she felt as if her "ask" of Lu would decimate the life-long bond between them. Saying nothing, she kept her gaze down to walk around him. But his hand snagged her wrist, and she told herself to keep it together when he pulled her into a hug. A tender kiss met her forehead.

"I wish there was another way. I know you're concerned." she whispered, blinking back tears.

"When you love someone, you take the good with the bad," he whispered. "Your grandmother often said that—about me."

"I swear. We'll all send our most-powerful protection with him. Every good witch we know will create a spell so strong that no friggin' sorcerer or dark seer will know Lu's there. I swear."

"You're damn straight you will," he said as he peeled her arms off. "Or you'll have me to contend with. It won't be pretty," he added with one raised eyebrow and a very thin smirk. The car service app dinged in her pocket. Mare handed her a plastic container. She turned back to look at Lu. His head stayed down, his face showed nothing as if very far away. Martine walked into the foyer, grabbed her purple cardigan, and ran out the door.

## Chapter 16

Memories

The patient hand-off with Marsha went smooth. Her shift notes on the tablet indicated no change, which was good news. If Aurora could be quickly located and the spell lifted, there would be a good chance he'd come out of this okay. Christopher's healthy life-style choices served him well, even in this unnatural state. Martine stood at the open curtain, giving her a view of the ER corridor. The hospital remained full because of this crazy flu and the ER buzzed with activity. Part of her felt guilty just having one patient. Part of her didn't. Looking over the nurses and ancillary staff, she wondered who were Georgians or Guardians sent to protect her patient. Georgians could be any profession, but Guardians were young, mystical warriors... demon hunters.

She walked back to her patient and then heard, "Christ, I totally hate hospitals."

Even though she recognized the voice, she jumped and turned with a smile. "What brings you here, Lu?"

"I want to meet Christopher Forbes." He had changed into a black shirt to match his jeans. His pale complexion and deep-blue eyes were even more pronounced in this monotone look. Now at her side, she eyed the oddly-cuffed boots that came midcalf. His focus switched from Christopher to her with a tilt of his head.

"It's been too long, M. I've really missed you, and you need to know I've never stopped caring about you."

She looked away. Just the sound of his voice touched something inside. "I've missed you too."

"I'm sorry I didn't reach out again," he whispered, the slight Scottish lilt blended with British inflections to confirm his life wasn't here in the states anymore.

"I can't tell you how good it is to see you again," was all she trusted herself to say, aware of the guarded but kind smile he returned.

"Same here. Look. I know what I need to do."

"I half-expected you to be on your way back to Scotland by now."

"I gave you my word. I'm committed."

It's not that she didn't expect it. She sensed the heart of a warrior, just like his father. "I still thought you'd change your mind."

"Why?"

She shrugged, looked away. "I'm asking a lot. Plus, Michael didn't look too happy about your decision to help."

"You know my father. If he can't be in control, he gets a tad testy."

"Really? Just a tad?" A small chuckle escaped as she sat at Christopher's side. "I thought he'd go ballistic during our after-dinner discussion."

"Yeah. Sometimes Dad surprises me too. Look. Your patient is an innocent, his whole future stolen by something evil. I know how it feels." He came closer, sank down on the foot of the bed and folded his arms across his chest. "I owe you an apology. It was rude, what I said about your weight."

"No apology necessary. Michael said the same

thing. I don't take offense."

"I know you've been through an awful time. Some things you bury very deep, but they never leave you."

Had it been anyone else, she'd shut them down with a look and a spell that'd have them itchy for days. Then she'd throw herself into work and not come up for air, hoping to numb the feelings. But Lu, the honesty on his face and in his heart had her simply look away. "There's something inside me rooting for him. We have to save him, Lu."

"Do you ever get any response?"

"To what?" she asked meeting his eyes.

"When you rub his arm that way." Not even realizing she had touched Christopher, she pulled her hand away as if she'd just touched a hot stove, quickly folded her arms. "What do you sense about him, M? You can tell me."

A bit flustered, she shook her head. "I don't know. It's not clear."

"He's got the height and the coloring of a warlock. Does he have blue eyes, too?" She nodded once. "I thought so. Maybe that's all the more reason to move quickly and find her."

"I swear. If I dye my hair blond and wear blue contacts, I'd force that damned Gatekeeper to open the damn portal and I swear I'd hunt down the bitch myself."

His expression grew hard as if to hide something he didn't want her to see. "It's not a nice place. Mostly conjured, made to look clean and proper. It's not. Then there's the guards. Pure buckets of filth. I'd have to find you before, God forbid, one caught you and put you in a cell. You'd have to deal with me first, then I'd have to hand you off to my father."

"And *that* would definitely *not* be something to look forward to. Did you mean they have prison cells?'

He looked away before he stood and flexed his fists. "Beneath their palace. It's a… a very scary place."

A wave of pure rage flared around him. *All those years of talking, texting, writing. I never once asked about what happened to him there. He never shared, either. Yeah. I guess some things you really do bury very deep.* She barely whispered, "I'm so very sorry, Lu."

"I've dealt with it," he offered. Then his features softened and he gave a nod. "I'll find her and bring her here. It's as simple as that."

But it wasn't simple. And she knew it. "When are you going?"

"That's the other reason I came here tonight. I mean, I wanted to see you before I left. I meet Draven at midnight."

Taking in a quick, sharp breath, her eyes shot wide. "So soon?"

"The sooner the better." As if glued to the chair and unable to trust her legs to hold up, she reached for his hand. He took it, threading their fingers together. She held on for dear life and he didn't pull away. "No using any car services until this is over, M. The Georgian driver assigned will take you wherever you have to go. You'll be kept safe."

What if something happened to him? *Only dinner and two brief conversations? Oh God! I'd never forgive myself!* "No. Don't go. Don't do it. Let's find another way."

He sank down looking directly into her eyes. Cupped her cheek. "You see into this event, M. Your instincts, that super sixth sense says, in no uncertain terms, this is the only way. It's not just the dark witch. It's the hidden portal. Going after her solves both problems. I swear. It's all good."

Their eyes stayed locked to each other's for a full minute. Then her lids drifted down as she spoke the words her grandmother taught her, engulfing him in a powerful spell of protection. When she opened her eyes, she sensed his courage, his resolve. Everything about him said exactly who he was—the kind of man he had become.

"I have to go," he whispered.

She didn't want to unlace her fingers from his. "Please be safe. By all that is good, so shall it be."

He kissed her cheek, and then the smile he gave slashed through her heart. When he was young, everyone said he had the face of an angel. His face had thinned some, revealing high cheekbones, which made his large deep-blues a most striking feature. Full lips, dimples and a small cleft in his chin. *Now he has the face of an archangel... a warrior ready for battle.* He stood saying nothing more and then walked out of Cubicle Q.

Without thinking she grabbed for Christopher's hand to thread their fingers together. It felt like a jolt, as if her power surged. She whispered the spell of protection again, hoping with all her heart that it wrapped around Lukas ten-fold this time. She'd say that spell over and over again. Her body stayed tense. Her mind stayed focused on the mystical warrior—the only person who could end this nightmare.

****

*I could have pulled her out of the chair, held on tight and really kissed her the way I wanted to,* Lukas thought shaking his head over that pathetic little peck on M's cheek. But the feel of her fingers threaded through his, well, he buried that deep down in a secret place in his heart. What he was about to do required total focus. He walked familiar streets of the city with steady steps. There had been some changes, but by and large, it looked as it had when he was thirteen and hellbent on killing the then mystically enhanced vampire—Michael Malone.

He recalled his last day in the Second Realm. Held in a cell. Allowed a mid-day walk behind the palace with a filthy guard. Then the guard's neck ripped open. His unique father picked him up and ran for the portal. *Yeah. Totally terrified, and finally free.* But deep rage had already taken root. He became a danger to himself as well as his father.

As he walked, he recalled many details of his own private Hell. Now he would go back willingly. He turned down Broadway knowing exactly where he was heading. Passing Times Square, he turned down a side street, not at all crowded like it should be with an after theater crowd. Near the middle of the block, his father stood in the shadows across the street from the club called *Destiny*.

"An ironic name," he said.

"Not if you know Draven. The vampire always had a dramatic flair," his father answered while digging into his pocket and pulling out a disc the size of a silver dollar attached to a thick leather string. "This is from Mary. Put it around your neck and keep it hidden under your shirt." He opened the top button and shoved it down. Next, three small stones came into his hand. "I don't know realm currency. Use the rubies in the event you need to purchase something at the markets." Those went into the front pocket of his jeans.

"I'm really quick with the grab. Merchants won't even know what I take."

"No. No palming a peach there, Lukas. Keep a low profile. Observe and blend in."

He gave a nod. Next, his father handed him more important items. A worn leather sheath holding the trusted broadsword hung tight to his back. A pearl-handled knife slipped into his boot. Both weapons had history—one mystical, the other a part of his ancestry, not only useful, but what he considered good luck charms like treasures to keep him safe. When a long woolen traveler's cloak settled on his shoulders, it brutally yanked him back in time recalling the crafty warlocks in the Second Realm. He started to cross the street, but his father grabbed his arm. "You don't have to do this, son. I'll go in your place."

"No. You won't pass for a realm dweller. Not even the half-breeds who do all the menial work or the ones kept like slaves."

"Why not?"

"Because no one, not one single realm dweller, has longish dark wavy hair and looks as fucking intimidating as you."

His father still looked tense. "We will all understand if you back out."

He knew what his father was trying to do. He'd have none of it. *And we're right back where we started again.* He met the worried expression with confidence. "I won't back out. I know what I have to do and how to do it."

A low guttural growl sounded. "I'm not buying it. This will bring back memories. You can't let them get in the way. You have to be attentive."

"I have to blend in."

"Absolutely, but—"

"Dad. I get it. Look around, get information, and get the hell back out."

"You will only have two hours before I want you meeting Draven at that portal. Then we'll see how it goes."

"I understand." He started to cross the street only to be grabbed by an arm again.

"And be careful around the vampire. He's clever."

"Like your sire was?" he asked with a mischievous grin.

"Not as strong as my sire, but clever, nevertheless. You cannot trust Draven, Lukas. Be on guard. At all times."

"I got it. Now let's go." His father gave a slow nod before they crossed the street together. As they approached, the bald bouncer blocked the door.

"Draven is expecting us. Michael and Lukas Malone," his father said.

The bouncer gave a quick nod. "When you go down it's the—"

"I know the way," his father replied. They went through a long, bejeweled hall and then down a flight of stairs. The music in the nightclub sounded somber and sensual, at the same time like some sexual dirge.

"Wow. This place is packed."

"Lukas," his father said, and quickly refocused as they turned down a hallway passing multiple bathrooms.

The door up ahead stood ajar. When they walked through it, a tall vampire dressed in a black suit, matching shirt and tie, not to mention jet-black hair pulled into a ponytail at the nape of his neck stood behind a glass-topped, carved wooden desk. Eyed up and down like a bug under a microscope, the vampire strode closer to where they stood. "Welcome Michael. This must be your son. Yes. I can see why it is you instead of your father. You could pass for a warlock. Very easily, I might add."

*And you two could pass for brothers,* Lukas thought, a bit taken aback. The vampire tossed a satchel his way, which he caught mid-air with his left hand extended at just the right height.

"He has all your mystical strength and skills, I presume," Draven said to his father at his side. "I'd never suspect a mystical trait would be inherited as if it were genetic."

"Like father like son, many say." his father replied, then placed a hand on his shoulder asking, "Ready?"

"Yeah." Fixing the satchel's thick leather strap across his body, he looked Draven in the eye. "What's in this thing?"

"Second Realm currency should you need to purchase something. I've taken the liberty of having travel documents forged—in the event you are stopped and searched."

"Why travel documents?"

"It grants you access to all villages. There is also a photograph of Aurora for you to show during your inquiries. We doctored her image from the video feed, so it looks like a typical Second Realm portrait. Her name is inscribed underneath the image to lend further credence. There's also a vial in the satchel. It is a potion you may need after portal travel… to relieve nausea. The air is thin there, more so than in the highlands of Scotland. I'm sure you remember."

This time, *he* eyed the vampire. "I know what to

174

expect." He knew to take shallow breaths instead of gulping down lungful's of air. "Can we get on with this now?"

Draven inclined his head in a respectful fashion. "Please follow," he said leading the way to a tall metal door at the other end of the office. In front of it, he punched in a code. Lukas memorized the four tones, sure that his father did as well. The three of them entered a dimly lit room roughly eight by eight.

Immediately, the low vibrating hum pulled at the center of his chest. He took a step forward, but his father yanked him back. Their eyes locked, full of emotions, too deep to express in words. His father's hands came to Lukas's cheeks and a kiss landed on his forehead. "Above all, be safe."

"I love you, too," came out soft, genuine and straight from his heart. As his father pulled away, he gave a slow nod before approaching Draven.

"He will be at my side awaiting your return. I will check every ten minutes until the second hour when you are expected. Should anything go wrong, stay close to where you entered the dimension and look for my hand to appear on the ground. I will pull you back safely. At the end of the second hour, the portal will generate visible energy. Keep sight of the inside of the vault in mind, get a running start and rush through without delay. Good luck and God-speed."

Lukas eyed him again, especially after the last two words. Vampires didn't use the word "God" and Draven had, almost in a reverent way. He got the feeling there was more to this vampire than his father let on. "Thanks," he replied.

Again, the vampire inclined his head. They

approached the portal shoulder to shoulder. Draven's long arms disappeared in the gray swirling vortex that pulled wide like the jaws of a huge dragon. When it reached a specific radius, the vampire stepped back and nodded.

Lukas steadied himself and then took a slow, even breath before he walked through.

****

Michael had almost forgotten to breathe, and as the vortex swirled and closed, he finally filled his lungs with air and blew out a slow, even breath. His pulse raced and every muscle in his body tensed. He didn't need a mirror to see he had become as pale as Draven. In all of his three-hundred-plus years of existence, first as a man, then as a vampire, and now again as a man, never had he ever felt this terrified.

His son. His precious son. A child who faced unbearable horrors at the hands of the Second Realm's sorcerers. Terrifying nightmares triggered by a turn of a phrase or a non-specific sound or scent. And when Lukas raged, only he could bring him out of it. While other kids were growing up care-free, his son had shouldered a heavy burden. And scars. Physical scars of abuse. Something even a father's unyielding love couldn't erase. He recalled the first time he saw his son's back. His reaction had frightened the boy. *Why did I let him go through the portal?* As he stood staring at the swirling gray matter, Draven came to his side. The glistening mist had him lost in memories as if caught in a tailspin and unable to pull out. *Handing my newborn son to someone who could keep him hidden. Years later, jumping through a portal to rescue my raging child from the sorcerers.* How in Hell had he allowed Lukas to be exposed to such danger, such evil again? Why in Hell had he not rejected the plan outright? He couldn't answer either question.

"I've locked my office. We'll keep the vault door open. Here. I've brought over a chair. Sit down," Draven whispered. Yet he didn't move. "I said sit down, or you will fall down, Michael," sounded as if the vampire had an edge of authority. Then Draven stood in front of him, blocking the view of the portal. He didn't see the typical, arrogant smirk nor that bored expression. Draven looked somewhat concerned.

Pushing numbing fear aside, Michael gave a quick nod. The chair stood against the vault's inner wall and next to the door. He settled into it and gripped its wide arms. Then his fingers dug into the plush, padded leather. Each minute felt like an hour. In his head, he said every prayer he knew. At the first ten-minute interval, he watched Draven kneel and bend low. One arm disappeared into the portal and stayed there for precisely thirty seconds.

Michael's heart raced again and sweat beaded his forehead. His unsteady hand swiped it away. *How in God's good name am I going to survive these two hours?*

Chapter 17

Man on a Mission

Entering the Second Realm where their day was his night, the first thing Lukas did was walk into a crop of green flowering bushes. Then he bent forward to grip his knees—and puked his guts out. He took short breaths and stood up slow, walked beyond the bushes and when his palm hit a tree trunk; he leaned against it. Spitting out sour saliva, he then swiped a hand across his lips. The closest description he could give would be like stepping off of a wild rollercoaster ride. It may have been the height of the thrill at age seventeen. Now? He craved anything that would stop the churning in his gut and the tilting landscape.

Reaching into the pouch, he felt around for the vial. Hell, if the vampire hoped to poison him, rather it be sooner than later. Plus, staggering through a village with a sour stomach would call all kinds of attention to him. And *that* was not on his agenda. After swirling it around with his tongue like mouth-wash, he swallowed it in one long gulp. Oddly enough, it tasted very minty. With a hand on his chest, he waited a full minute. No foaming at the mouth. No gasping as the lungs shut down. And nausea slipped gently away. *Yeah. Trust is an awesome thing.* That he was still alive said something about the vampire.

Plopping down, he sat with his back against the tree and pulled the travel papers out of the satchel. "So I'm Wyn Cleaves, a history apprentice from the North Country, whatever the hell that means." But it gave him an idea, which made a lot of sense.

Feeling more himself, he stood. How would he explain the sword at his back, he wondered. *Historians wouldn't carry weapons. But a traveler would. It's plausible enough.* After placing the phony documents back in the satchel, he pulled out an old-fashion pocket watch. The vomit episode and rummaging through the satchel had taken roughly ten minutes, which gave him enough time to explore the nearest village.

He stood and brushed dirt off his cloak. Heading to the road, he started to walk. *Records. Every village has to keep a roster of who lives there.* But there was a better place to start. Because every village had a gathering place like a pub. "God, I could use a cold beer right now," he said as he walked.

****

Aurora straightened Anika's arm under her own. "There. Study how our hands align," she said as they walked down the forest path near her cottage. "Notice how my arm settles over yours. Do you feel it?"

"Yes, my mistress," her servant replied.

"Whenever we walk through the courtyard of the palace, this is how we'll do it. No. No, slow your step to match mine. Commit this to memory. You are always on my right side, and I will always be nearest the wall in the courtyard."

A gust of wind suddenly sent their cloaks into a billow. While Aurora pulled the sides closed with a hand, Anika pulled away with a shriek. "Silly fool! You must

179

never *ever* pull your arm away! What were you thinking?"

"That I'm cold," Anika whined.

She ignored the shiver. "Your needs *never* come before mine! Is this clear? When we return home, you will scrub the kitchen from top to bottom. And that includes the refrigerator. Every square inch of it."

"But it's fully stocked, my mistress!"

Stopping to stomp her foot and turn around, she replied, "And you will do it all while I have a nap!" Holding the rim of her cloak, she pivoted, gave a dramatic twirl and hurried back to her cottage. With a flick of her wrist the door swung open. She unknotted her cloak strings, left it in a heap on the floor before flicking her wrist a second time. Her bedroom door yawned open, and she strutted through, kicking it shut just because she could.

*Perfection is paramount!* "Stupid girl," she murmured as she slipped under the covers in nothing but her undergarments. She'd cast a spell on all the fresh produce and blacken it with hideous mold. Her fingers grasped the locket which had settled between her breasts. Nothing more would rattle her today.

\*\*\*\*

Keeping up with other travelers along the road, Lukas listened to various conversations. Some villagers complained about inflated prices, to which he could relate. Everything cost more these days in his world as well. Many talked about Samhain preparations, things to purchase in the Second Village. At least now he knew where he was. He'd been walking for thirty minutes, which he made sure to note. The village came into view, and his keen sense of smell picked out the scent of ale.

He veered left following his nose. *Ye Olde Village Two Pub* was written atop a squat white building made of stone with a big, pane-glass window at the side of the door. The sign in it read: Open for mid-day meals only. He entered the establishment with a growing thirst, took a seat at the bar.

"Welcome traveler," the barman said. "What can I serve you?"

Reaching into the satchel he pulled out a silver coin roughly the size of a half-dollar. "I'll have a glass of water and a glass of your coldest ale, please."

The barman eyed the coin. "I may not have enough coin in the box to make change. Do you want me to check first?"

*Okay, so what do I do now?* "Please," he replied trying to think. He couldn't possibly eat. First, he wasn't hungry and second, he'd rather have an empty stomach when he went through the portal again.

The barman came back a few seconds later. "I think I'll be all right."

"Then pour away. I may even have a second." When water arrived, he drained the glass quickly. The ale on tap felt good going down, cold and hearty. Then the barman placed a plate of bread and cheese in front of him. "Compliments of the house, traveler. I've not seen you in here before."

Bread usually sopped up those nasty stomach juices, and he broke off a piece and chewed slowly, totally sure he'd forego the cheese. The moldy smell of it stuck in his throat and clogged his nose. After swallowing, he said, "I'm from the North Country."

"Aye, that explains it. You've traveled very far from your home."

181

This could go either way if the barman was testing him. He simply shrugged his shoulders and took another swallow of ale. *What if they have a certain accent? What if they dress differently?* "This bread is delicious," he said as he pulled off another piece and chewed.

"I make it myself every morning. I don't bake the cakes, though. There's a good baker at the market. An old gray-haired woman from the North Country as well." He scratched his head. "Can't recall her name. Do you know her?"

"I may. Don't know," he said before he took another mouthful.

One of the customers came to the bar to pay his bill. "Four and half," the barman stated. "I'll take a bottle of ale to go so add it in," the customer said. The barman handed a glass bottle to the customer. "That'll be five even," he stated. The customer pulled out a paper note. The barman gave no change, and then piled paper notes on the bar.

Lukas added as he watched. *The silver coin is probably equal to a hundred dollars. Good to know*, he thought as he drained the beer glass.

"Ready for another?"

"I think not. Here," he said placing a five note on the counter. "Keep the change and thank you kindly, sir, for the bread and cheese."

The barman looked at him. "This is too gracious, good traveler."

"Think nothing of it, good sir. Your hospitality is appreciated."

"Well, then, do come by again."

He smiled. Leaving the bar, he followed his astute sense of hearing and located the market without any problem. No one looked at him oddly. He simply blended in. Curious about everything, he meandered through the market. The baker's stand came into view at the far end. Either the first or the last table customers would see. *Clever spot,* he thought, approaching an old woman sitting behind the table. Her hair had different shades of gray, a little on the wild side.

"Can I help you, good traveler," she said as she stood.

"Please, good woman, can you tell me about your pastries?" He listened intensely, memorizing the rise and fall of her speech pattern. It sounded closer to his Scottish accent than the barman's, probably why the man didn't question him more about the North Country. After living in Scotland and England for the past sixteen years, his acquired inflections had not been too far off her accent. "Thank you ever so kindly, good woman. I will take one scone, and would you please send the Brandenburg cake to the pub for me?"

"Who shall I say it is from, good traveler?"

"Tell the kind barman it is from the traveler to whom he showed great kindness. Many thanks," he said with his hand over his heart and a slight bow.

"Oh! Such a fine young man of the North Country you are, young sir. I have a friend who has a daughter. She is unmarried," the old woman added with a wink of her eye. He noted they were light-blue, much different than his.

"I am sure she is beautiful, but I am taken." Although he thought of Martine, he pulled out the photograph. "Would you like to see?" He showed her Aurora's picture and watched for a reaction.

"Oh my, what a beauty. Not from this village, is she?

She must be a Sixth Villager. It's the skin tone that always gives them away, so close to the sea and the forest as well."

"You are very wise, good woman." He bowed again and left the market. He'd gotten more solid information than he could have hoped for. He walked down the road until a good mile from the village, then slipped into the tall shrubs at the side of the road. Running as fast as the wind, he jumped fallen boughs and jogged across clear patches of grass.

He had nine minutes left. Sitting by the same bush, he removed the scone from his pouch and left it on the ground. Then he waited exactly where he had entered the realm. As soon as the portal appeared he gave himself enough space to gather speed and at a fast run he pushed through the swirling gray barrier.

Opening his eyes, he became aware of being on the floor of the dimly lit room. Someone untied his cloak. He felt it fall away before being pulled into a sitting position. The broadsword's harness came across his shoulder. His eyelids felt heavy. He was loose-limbed and groggy. Hoisted up on his feet, his arm landed on a solid shoulder with his waist gripped tight. He knew his father's scent.

"Get him over to the couch," he heard Draven say.

Sprawled out, he turned on his side. "I'm gonna be sick," he got out before his father cupped the back of his head over a wastepaper basket. Heaving and coughing, the air stunk of stale ale. A warm cloth, held by Draven, swept gently across his face a few times. His father eased him back against the couch keeping a palm to his forehead.

"Oh God, the room is spinning," he whispered.

"Breathe in and out slowly, little boy," his father

said, using the last two words in an endearing way. Those same words also served as a warning if he stepped out of line, which he often did in his teens, in his early twenties, too.

"The disorientation will stop shortly," Draven stated.

When his eyes eased open, he saw the two of them. The vampire stood with his arms laced across his chest. The man sat on the couch at his side with his arms laced across his chest in the same way. One wore a thin smirk. The other looked full of concern, easy to know who was who. He started to pull himself up and his father stood next to Draven. *Wow. They totally could pass for brothers,* he thought. Funny. They had the exact same worried look on their faces now, both the man and the vampire. On the edge of the couch, he braced his arms deep into the plush leather and stood. Seconds later, he felt steady on his feet.

Guiding the satchel up and over his head, he handed it to Draven. "Thanks for the potion. It did the trick."

"I knew it would. As promised, I checked every ten minutes."

"I felt fine once I got over the nausea." He didn't know how much to share and looked at his father. "When do I go back?"

"You need to rest first," his father said. "And that's an order."

"I would suggest waiting at least twenty-four hours to ensure there is no residual affect. You are, I would guess, mostly human," Draven replied. "Obviously, you had ale. What else did you ingest?"

He shrugged his shoulders and slipped his hands into the pockets of his jeans. "Some bread." He paused for a second and then rubbed his stomach. "You know, I still don't feel all that well."

"I'm taking him home, Draven, no more tonight," his father stated.

"I understand. Drink plenty of water and some sugared tea to settle your stomach. I will see you both back here at the right hour. I shall refill the potion for you, Lukas," he said in a respectful tone.

"Thanks. I really think I need some sleep."

His father locked eyes with Draven, then the vampire held his office door open and they walked through. The music still played, the song a real hip-grinder. The packed dance floor didn't matter, although Draven's club definitely seemed the place to be. His human clientele really had no clue.

Lukas followed his father up the stairs and out into the fresh, crisp autumn night. A car waited for them at the end of the block. He recognized the plates and knew a trusted Georgian would be behind the wheel. They both got in the back and a plexiglass shield went up between the front and back for privacy.

"I really don't feel sick anymore."

"I know."

"I have a lot to share with you."

"Good."

"What's wrong?"

His father stared out the side window. "Nothing. Let's get to the penthouse where you can debrief all of us at the same time."

Things didn't appear all right on multiple fronts. "Does Martine have coverage? I mean, her shift's not over yet."

"No."

His stomach actually soured again. "Well, that's not fair."

"Deal with it," came out a growl.

"I know there's something bothering—"

His father cut him off with, "Drop it, Lukas."

"What happened?"

"Leave it alone," sounded too gruff and low.

"Like hell." More pissed off by the second, he added, "If something's wrong, I need to know. We need to discuss—"

"There's nothing to discuss. Close your eyes and rest."

*Well, that came out clipped and icy.* There sure as hell *was* something to discuss. Martine should be in the debrief. He banged his head against the headrest. *Wait... I know this brood.* It came to him like an arrow racing to a bullseye. His father didn't want him to go back. *Well, too bad, Dad.* He'd been on many vampire hunts with seasoned Guardians over the years. Granted, no mystical mission had ever taken him to different realms.

A hell of a lot rode on his part in this event. *Yeah, if the sorcerers found out I entered their realm I'd be as good as dead.* They didn't take betrayal too kindly. And his father had most-definitely betrayed them big time. You could write that in huge, bold letters. But no one would succeed in getting him to back down or back out. Although his father's reaction wouldn't be kind if crossed, this time it felt necessary. He respected his judgment, followed his lead without question.

But not today. He had made Martine a promise. Plus, Rule Number One: save the innocent meant no cost is too high because each life is a precious gift. And he couldn't live with himself if he didn't see this through to a successful conclusion. *Like any warrior, I'm fully prepared to lay my life on the line.*

No way in Hell would he *not* go back to the Second Realm. He'd contact Draven and go behind his father's back. *Nope. No way do I back down. No fucking way.*

Chapter 18

Debrief Debacle

Seated at the table in the study of the Georgian penthouse, Lukas sized up the players who knew the full scope of the event. Deepa represented the Georgian Council. Mary represented the good witches in the healing circles. He and his father were mystical warriors who did what had to be done. The debriefing began with Draven's cooperation. Oddly enough, his father was succinct, generally pleased with the vampire's cooperation. Should Draven step out of line in a deceitful way, he'd meet eternal unrest in the fires of Hell without a second thought.

Then it was his turn, fully prepared when Deepa requested facts and total disclosure. He pointed to a rather simplistic map of the realm pinned to the wall. It had been found in Georgian archives and hand delivered to the penthouse earlier. Leaving the table, Lukas walked to it.

"The portal left me at the end of the main road in the Second Village, I'd say roughly thirty miles from the edge of it. To the left of the main road is the pub. The silver coins Draven gave me are approximate to hundred-dollar bills. I made change to paper currency, which called less attention. The barman mentioned someone from the North Country selling baked goods right about here. I proceeded to the open-air market and met the baker woman. We had a conversation where she did most of the talking. Again, Draven must have done his homework."

"How so," Deepa asked.

"Apparently each village has a regional dialect. The barman could have passed for an Irishman. My tempered accent is close to the North Country's, and I sensed the speech pattern—how they used their words. It's a bit like stepping back in time, but such is the characteristic of all the villages. I remember that from before."

"Can the air support the average human?" she asked while writing.

"It might take days before the nausea stops, and even then I'm not sure."

"Yet we know for certain that humans have been sent through to the Second Realm as slaves."

"Anyone on a forced march will do as they're told or drop dead," Lukas stated.

"Perhaps a seasoned Guardian could accompany you when you go back," Deepa replied.

He realized his father was most likely behind the suggestion. "We don't have that kind of time to explore the possibility."

"Yes. I see. Too risky, no doubt." Deepa nodded as she wrote.

His gaze slid to his father who wore a neutral expression. But he heard the quicker heartbeats. Although the look on his face probably fooled Deepa, his father was fuming. "When I spoke to the baker woman, she gave me a stellar bit of information about Aurora. Again, this occurred only because Draven had the foresight to include a portrait of her in the satchel."

Praising the vampire had to burn him, too.

"And what would that information be," Deepa inquired with grace.

"The woman made a comment about Aurora's skin tone saying she is most likely a resident of the Sixth Village." His finger slid across the map. "Note the location. The sea to the north and the forest to the southeast. Both border the edge of the realm, which isn't inhabited. If this is where she lives, then she has easy, quick access to both borders. And where better to find a hidden portal?" He paused a moment, adding, "I would bet on the farthest edge of the forest."

"It makes sense," Mary said with many nods.

He tapped the map moving his finger through the layout of the forest to its edge. "This has to be where the portal is—possibly why it has remained unnoticed. It's most likely off a path. Once I have her scent, I can follow it."

"It's been days since she used it," his father stated. "Any shift in weather patterns has wiped her scent clean."

He had a point and a good one. "But suppose there's another marker. Something right in front of our noses but we're missing it."

"Yes," Deepa stated, "Are you referring to the legend?"

"Having read up on it in multiple Georgian documents, the common thread is Gwendolyn and her child disappeared never to be seen again." His finger slid back to the edge of the Sixth Village. "Some accounts place her home, probably a small cottage, near the inner edge of the forest. The conjecture is that Gwendolyn killed the warlock, the father of the baby, and I concur.

Then she walked through a path in the forest with her son in her arms."

"You think that's how she disappeared?" Mary asked.

"Not yet," he said with a mischievous grin. "First she went through the portal and brought her newborn to the human world."

"Which just accidentally landed her in Manhattan," his father said as he sat back in the chair at the table.

"Georgian seers indicate a breach on the night of a crescent moon. I have no idea where the portal landed her."

"So what is your point?" his father asked.

He tapped the map again. "My guess is then Gwendolyn went back through the portal and near it, somewhere in this forest, she killed herself."

Deepa narrowed her eyes. "What makes you say that," and at the same time, Mary said, "But her body was never found."

Taking his place back at the table he locked eyes with his father, feeling somewhat victorious. "Because she did what she had to do—to protect her son. She'd have been forced to say where she took him. And she'd have been found by the guards if she went on the run. You can't hide from realm guards. They find you and torture you until you break."

"Which is why you are not going back," his father stated in a low rumble leaning forward.

"Are we *really* going to do this here, Dad?" His frustration had been festering since the conversation in the car. For the moment, his father stayed silent, but there'd be hell to pay later. He pointed to the map. "There's a mountainous rock formation near the edge of the realm. I'd venture to say Gwendolyn's body is at the bottom of it. Because that's exactly what I would do. Either climb to the top and throw myself off, or if there's deep water beneath it, gladly take a dive."

His father's palms slammed the table, his expression fierce. "Lukas," he bellowed as he stood. Both women jumped, and he could swear he heard Deepa gasp.

Fully defiant, he shot back, "I know where Aurora is. I know how to deal with these guards. I'm no fool," he stated with a quick shrug of his shoulders. "I get her. I force her to show me the portal. We jump through and land in that trashy alleyway between two theaters."

Leaning down and into him, his father hollered, "No!"

Matching his tone, Lukas replied, "Yes! And you won't stop me because you taught me to always do the right thing!" He looked at Deepa, her eyes as big as quarters. "I apologize for this... this family drama, Deepa. With all due respect, whether or not the Georgian's sanction a plan to extract Aurora doesn't matter anymore. Martine was smart enough to know there isn't any other route. And *she* should have been here. She earned a chair at this table! Why isn't she sitting here?"

"Because I told Deepa to leave her out of this," his father stated. Mary looked to the side avoiding his glance. His father righted the chair and sat back down; his arms braced across his chest.

Instantly, Lukas's eyes narrowed. "Why the hell would you do that?"

"Draven can get any information we share here out of her, and it won't be hard. She wouldn't even know she was telling him."

"But she said his charm doesn't work on her," Mary stated.

"He has other ways. I'm sure I don't have to elaborate."

"Ridiculous," Lukas huffed, "Martine would never—"

His father interrupted with a quick, "Yes, she would, and she wouldn't even know how she got there." He paused before saying, "I can survive in other realms."

"Yeah, when you were a vampire," he said as his hands flew up.

"I still have mystical abilities. Just like you."

"Oh, great. Then we'll both be bent over puking our guts out. I've already said you won't pass as a Second Realm dweller."

"But I would pass as a vampire passing through," he said with conviction.

He ramped up... didn't care where it led. "Dad—"

"Now it's your turn to sit and listen," came out sharp and edgy. "Deepa, may I speak," he then said full of respect.

"Of course, Michael," she stated.

"I waited for my son to return safe—which is something I will *not* experience again. Draven wants the portal located and closed as much as we do. Together we shadow Lukas. Lukas goes for the dark witch. We go directly into the realm's edge at the Sixth Village to locate the portal. This cuts his time in the realm significantly, which makes his presence less likely sensed by the sorcerers."

He. Was. Livid. "And how do you plan to disguise your heartbeat, Dad?"

"I'll cross that bridge when I come to it, *son*."

Deepa stopped writing and looked at his father. "It is a valid question, Michael."

"Their realm could do with a few less guards, or warlocks, or dark witches."

After clearing her throat, Deepa said, "Yes. You certainly have proven you don't back down from a fight."

"But I will *not* start one this time, Deepa. Draven and I will be discreet."

"Why should we sanction the vampire's extended participation in this plan?" she asked.

"It ensures that the continent's only known portal remains closed to traffic because he will be otherwise engaged."

The bob of her head said she bought it. Then Deepa captured his attention. He knew the question before she asked it. 'Lukas, are you in agreement with this alteration to the original plan?"

His eyes slid to his father, who purposely kept his gaze averted—he was sure of it, calmly stating, "My main mission is to save the innocent. Getting the dark witch to the hospital so she can lift the spell has not changed."

Seconds of silence where unsettling to all, but then she asked, "When will you leave, Lukas?"

"Tomorrow. Right after midnight. Give me two days in the realm and I'll have her at Christopher's side removing the spell."

"The Georgians will sanction this." Deepa gave a nod. "May God keep both of you safe."

They all stood, and Mary came to his side. "Michael's right. Martine's safety is my first concern."

He touched her arm, softly replying, "I understand."

But he didn't agree. She should have been sitting right at his side like she had when she made the ask.

"You need to get some rest, Lukas."

He smiled to reassure her. "I plan to fall into bed right after a hot shower as soon as I get back to the brownstone."

She whispered, "Don't hold this against him, sweetie. He loves you."

Nodding once, he said, "I know. But I can handle myself there. I don't want to worry about him hanging out with a vampire who could turn on him at any minute."

She cupped his cheek. "I remember how shy and quiet you were at fifteen. Look at you now. You're a warrior just like him. Keep your guard up and we'll send you a truck load of protection, but make sure to call Alana before you go back."

"I will. I promise," he replied with a catch in his voice.

He turned to leave and locked to his father's dark eyes. They walked to the elevator and rode down in silence. As his father held open the car door, Lukas said, "I prefer to walk."

A low, growled, "Suit yourself," really pissed him off before the car door slammed.

****

In many ways, Lukas hated this city. He had walked aimlessly for an hour, something he rarely did. But he had his reasons. The major one—the arrogant pain in the ass waiting up for him at a well-kept brownstone many blocks away from where he now stopped and studied.

There had once been a huge portal in this passageway between two deserted factories somewhere in the West Twenty blocks. He had been born here on a warm May night as the clock struck twelve. Years later, his father carried him through that portal to get him away from the Second Realm. And years after that, he watched his father battle an army of Hell-beasts that marched through that same portal before his father hit the ground. Now Lukas stood on the very same spot where he saw it happen. The rutted pavement at his feet appeared to swim. He blinked repeatedly to clear his vision. Sniffing the air, he palmed his eyes and blew out a sharp breath before he turned around.

"Talk to me, son."

"You diminished me tonight."

"I did no such thing."

"Yeah. You did."

"Change your perspective, little boy."

"Don't call me that because I'm not in the mood to—"

"I mean it, Lukas. Your pride is hurt. You're tired."

"I'm fucking pissed off," he replied, mirroring the signature stance, feet slightly apart and his arms laced across his chest.

"You want to take a swing at me? Good. Get it out of your system."

"Don't tempt me."

"Do you recall the last time we were in this alleyway together?"

"Of course I remember." He'd never forget that night.

"Then you see where doing something alone gets you."

Pointing at his father, he yelled, "This is different!"

"How is it different? Back up is a good thing."

"I don't need it. I don't want it."

"You don't get to deny it when it is offered. You're on your own with the dark witch. I don't care if you flatter her or trick her. You'll reach your ultimate goal."

He stepped closer. "Then why did you dream up some crafty shit to go through the portal with me?"

"I didn't. It was Draven's idea."

"Oh. That's just—like, *way*, *way* out there. Disguising your over-protective nature by blaming it on a vampire."

"I never disguise my over-protectiveness when it comes to someone I love with all my heart. You'll know the feeling one day. Draven suggested we back you up."

Looking at the sky, curiosity tamped down his anger. A little. "Why?"

"He's still an evil bastard, but he's a bit different from the typical idiot who is turned. Cyril sired a particular type of man. In my case, it was my arrogance and fierceness. Draven had different talents, although he has an arrogance about him as well."

"What are you talking about because I really don't have a clue where this is going."

"I know about his life before he was sired. Something he doesn't recall."

"Life memories leave as soon as you are turned. Yeah. I know."

"He retained his musical ability. He was a concert pianist at the height of the Romantic Era. Cyril and I often attended his parlor performances. They were truly breathtaking. He retained a thread of morality. But what he didn't retain is the memory of the son he adored."

His head shook and he rubbed his forehead. "I don't get the connection."

"You should. He made sure you were prepared for this mission. Coins and travel papers. The potion he sent. I never told him you tend to—"

"Puke."

His father nodded. "Which you do. Whenever hyper-anxious."

"Or jumping through a fucking portal." *Like my very own Achilles Heel.*

His father paused, ran his hands through his hair. "I swear to God I stayed plastered to that chair waiting for your return. What you were like when I found you played again and again in my head, and I couldn't move. But Draven stood like a lion at that portal, poised and ready to bring you back safely. He showed more humanity than I expected when he cleaned your face. These are all telling signs."

Somewhat calmer now, he asked, "What kind of telling signs?"

"For all the cruelty in him, there is perhaps more than a little morality. His responses to you were that of a father. He doesn't recall his son. He simply recalls the feeling."

The two of them had a powerful bond—always there, and neither reluctant to show it. "Maybe it's what he sees between us."

"I never meant for you to feel less than you are, Lukas," he said in a low, soft voice. "If you took it that way, then I truly apologize. You've grown into a fine man with a mind of your own. But a little back up is a good thing."

He didn't question the sincerity, saying, "But I do this my way with the dark witch. As for Draven, I sense there's more to him than meets the eye."

A thin smirk appeared. "Perhaps, but he really is a devious son of a bitch."

He sighed and rolled his eyes, not in a disrespectful way. "You'll stay back and let me do what I know I can?"

"Aurora is all yours."

"Good."

"Now can we please go back to the brownstone? I need my rest. Not getting any younger, you realize."

Lukas chuckled. "Did you walk here?"

"Absolutely not. The car's waiting at the end of the street."

"Good. I'll take that ride now," he said as they left the passageway.

With a grip to his shoulder, his father said, "You really need a shower."

"Don't I know it," he replied.

Chapter 19

The Glitch

Aurora sat in her bath grinning wide and fingering the locket she wore. She closed her eyes and focused on Anika in the kitchen. Bags of rotted fruits and vegetables had come out of the refrigerator. Her servant's arms positively strained to their limit. Little cuts on her hands came from trying to scrape off the hideous gunk on the refrigerator walls. Of course, the smell had turned purely putrid! In between hitched sobs and mopping her brow, Anika scrubbed and scrubbed some more.

Up to her neck in bubbles, Aurora imagined the gorgeous gown she'd wear when presenting herself to the immortal sorcerers. *Royal blue with gold and silver strands embroidered in a floral pattern with vines at the hem and lovely lilies at my bosom. The neckline low to flatter my full breasts. Under them is a two-inch band of matching blue velvet, and a gathered skirt that flows when I walk.* Her belly would be nearing its full-swell. Her coif high and regal with exquisite blonde tendrils framing her expression of joy. The scent of roses and jasmine subtle. Her gait simply regal.

Minutes ticked on and on, replaying it all in her mind. She slid out of the fantasy to gloat again over her servant's plight. As mindsight shifted to the inside of the freezer, the grin slid off her face. Her body jerked up and into a forward sit. Her eyebrows knit before her glare went wide. *No. No-no-no... NO!* "What have you done you foolish, *foolish* twit," she hissed. Both hands gripped the tub. Slippery bubbles burst to coat her skin. She pulled one dripping foot out of the water and felt it hit the floor. She did the same with the other and then grabbed her dressing gown, fighting the pink silk as it clung to her wet body.

Panting at the bathroom door, she fumbled to unlock it. Thrusting it wide, she walked to the open cottage door. Her eyes slid to the right taking in a blazing bonfire, the stupid girl throwing a bag onto it. Before she could yell "stop," flames shot high, sparks flew and popped as everything burned. She grabbed the threshold ready to sway. That's when Anika turned and curtsied.

"What did you do," she screamed, "What did you do!"

A happy and proud smile lit the girl's face. "My mistress, I scrubbed the mold out of the refrigerator and the freezer. Instead of having your sense of smell assaulted with the rotten food and vegetables, I burned everything. Mistress? Are you not well?"

It took many seconds to find her voice. "The vial... in the freezer. Where is it?"

Anika looked confused and then pointed behind her. "The vial had crust and mold."

Aurora lifted her hands, and Anika flew through the air screaming like a banshee with her arms and legs flailing. She landed in a scramble of limbs on the forest floor after hitting a tree. Another incantation rose from Aurora's lips. Twigs and leaves on the ground swirled like a tornado, the girl shrieking and crying at its center. Suddenly the bonfire's flames shot high to the sky.

Murder crossed her mind, but she needed this servant. She needed to be pampered as her belly grew. Who would go to market? Who would cook? Who would cater to her every whim?

With a snap of her fingers, the swirling matter stopped, falling instantly and burying the stupid girl. The flames of the bonfire smoldered. Only Anika's wails broke the silence. With one finger, she snared the fool, whispered a different incantation. Anika's body lifted up to hover above the earth. Plunking her servant down before the steps of the cottage, Aurora's voice sank low as her chin lifted high, looking down with hooded eyes. "From now on you will only have enough coin for one day of my meals. You will walk to market and not have access to pony or cart. You will walk, starting today. Now go before I beat you," she added in an icy tone. Jagged breaths came at her. She conjured coin and threw it on the porch watching the bloodied, bruised servant pick it all up and limp away.

Drained of energy, Aurora turned, entered the cottage and locked the door. After strutting into her room, she collapsed on the bed.

\*\*\*\*

Martine closed the book and sat back when her mother walked through the curtains of Cubicle Q. "What the hell is that in your hands?"

She shrugged a shoulder. "Nothing."

"It's not nothing. Is it a book? What book?"

"I took it off the hospital's library on wheels cart?"

Mare's eyes narrowed. "Martine, it's like five o'clock in the morning. I'm too tired to read your mind. Just tell me."

She huffed and shook her head before holding up a

famous sci-fi novel.

"You read that years ago in high school."

"Yep. I bet he did too." Watching the frown deepen, she added, "Well, I got tired of talking about myself. I got as far as my early twenties. Jeez, I was still a wild-child, Mare. I thought reading to him would be fun. Dottie suggested it."

"Okay," her mother said, drawing out the word like she was a nutjob or something. "Couldn't you have picked something a little bit simpler?"

"Like what? A hot romance novel? Or how about your favorite vampire novel? No. Too close to home, right? I mean, maybe the author met … nah. Michael would've mentioned it."

A quick chuckle came at her. "You're getting punchy, honey."

"I usually am on the first shift back after two days off." She stifled a yawn, and then curiosity surfaced. "Did you talk to Lu? Did he go through? Did he come back okay?" She had more questions but stopped at three.

"Yes, and he walked the realm for two hours to see how his body takes to portal travel."

"And…" she said as she sat forward.

"He did just fine."

"Did Draven cooperate?"

"Like he promised he would."

"Did Lu and Michael come over to the brownstone to fill you in?

"No. I saw them at Deepa's for the debriefing."

Her eyes narrowed. "So… I'm good enough to come up with a plan but now I'm out of the loop. You all have a lot of nerve."

"It was Michael's request and Deepa agreed. I do, too. Draven may find a way to get to you and there are many things about this event he doesn't need to know."

"You really don't trust him, do you."

"I know him, Martine."

"Care to share, Mare? A little more back story to shed light on what I'm sensing?"

Her mother looked down at Christopher studying everything about him. "I was young and hell-bent on living in the moment."

"You were a wild-child teenager, too?"

"I didn't start my rebellious stage as early as you. It was the 1970s and I embraced inquisitiveness with a passion. I saw the way my mother looked at Michael. I knew what he was, and I grew overly curious. Maybe in some ways I wanted to know what it felt like… to be intimate without restrictions."

"I could just imagine," she mumbled. Draven had a sexy way about him. She couldn't say it hadn't crossed her mind as well. For a brief moment.

"I saw them together on occasion. I jumped to the wrong conclusion. Very naïve, right? It didn't last long. I'd been warned about Draven more than once."

She understood head-strong. Not listening to warnings. "But it didn't stop you, did it?"

"My mother and Michael *both* came down on me like a ton of bricks. They had every right because I could easily have been one of his victims."

"But you still raised hell."

"For a while. Then I fell in love with your father."

"And then you raised hell together."

She squinted with a smile on her face. "Yeah. We raised hell together. And then you came along."

Martine began to grin. "I'm still not happy about being left out of your pow-wow."

"Can I make it up to you with a mani-pedi?"

"Hmm… This requires a full day at the spa of my choice. It can wait until Christopher is released from the spell and the dark witch-bitch is made to pay. I hope he can hang on. He'll have to be moved to a long-term care facility if this continues any longer."

"I sense your worry. Things should start to move fast now."

"How?" Then she read the look on Mare's face. "I'm not getting anything more, am I?"

"It's for your own safety, Martine. I decided to take a few days off from the gallery. It will be in good hands. The healing circles already have the word out. We'll all send spells of protection their way."

"*Their?*" she said in a whisper. "No, Mom, Michael can't go with him!"

"I've said too much. I'll see you at home."

"Mare… Mom!" she said, but her mother was gone. Her eyes filled and she swallowed even though her throat felt too dry. Guardian Angels, God, Buddha, and Mother Goddess. She began to pray to all of them. *Two mystical warriors are going to risk their lives. What if Lu doesn't come home? What if both of them don't?* Draven remained the wildcard whose loyalty could go either way, each one's fate linked to the other.

She took Christopher's hand and held on for dear life. "What have I done? Why did this happen?" Useless and out of the loop, she could do nothing. Then his hand twitched, as if he wanted to let her know he heard her questions. Another twitch, as if he wanted her to know he understood. The third twitch said the real Christopher

Forbes was still in there.

****

In an hour, dawn would break on a new October morning. Sitting at the grand piano in his music room, Draven executed a breathtaking glissando in the Chopin ballade. His fingers glided over eighty-eight keys with accuracy leading him to the conclusion of the masterpiece in a minor key. He recalled the composer's last days in the arms of George Sand. His frail lungs gasping for breath. His pale skin slick with sweat. *Place Vendome* in Paris was a beautiful street to exit the mortal world.

Of course, he had paid his respects to the beloved poet of the piano long after sunset; after feeding on a vagrant, so there would be no chance of bloodlust overtaking him during the visit. The small token he brought to the lovely George was a gold locket to keep a lock of Frederic's hair as a remembrance. She would wear it close to her heart until the day she joined him in eternal rest.

That had been his last personal contact with a human in the 1800s. Yes, he continued to attend parlor performances with his sire. But that world, which he knew he had been a part of, no longer held an invitation. It had pained him, like a mortal wound to the chest. There were some boundaries as a vampire he flatly refused to cross. Interference with the arts remained one of them.

Many of his own compositions had been based on his idol's masterpieces. He preferred the dramatic chords of the minor key. He preferred the lower strings, not the vibrant tones of the upper brass. His passion remained the piano, which provided him a symphony of sound like no other. To be able to control by the touch of a finger the volume of each note continued to be a thing of beauty. An innate gift.

Both hands returned to his lap. His foot came off the *sostenuto* pedal and met the floor as the last vibrations echoed. Each end to a composition reminded him of a sudden death, shocking and natural at the same time. He pushed off the bench and stood. His fingers brushed the pristine keys without making a sound before he walked to his bedroom. Sustenance had come from a murderer tonight. The man had pushed a young woman into the path of a car with a look of glee on his face. *Gang members... such a joy to hunt and terrorize before the drink and drain.* They liked to run. So did he. It cleared one's mind in a most satisfactory manner.

He lay on his bed after hanging his suit jacket on a cedar hanger in the closet. Naked as the day he was born in 1814 he aligned his body with the exact center, pulled a thick quilt over him, and closed his eyes. Yet his mind stayed active.

Michael's son had been a treasure to behold. A stunning man whose vivid eyes captured you. The body of a warrior, muscular and trim. An air about him brimming with intelligence and vitality. *And Michael? A concerned parent full of love and admiration for his son. His son...*

The two words meandered through his brain like a wisp of a memory just out of reach. Preparing for the young warrior's safety had pleased him. And he had ordered top quality papers to ensure Lukas's alias. Choosing a name that meant "blessed," which the child truly was. Blessed with mystical abilities. Blessed with the love of a commanding, albeit arrogant, father. Fierce in a fight with a vampire, he would imagine. Yet he felt compelled to protect Lukas. Had it been the worry that clung to Michael like mist over a raging sea? Again, the wisp of a memory assaulted his mind. Just out of reach.

Should the Third Realm's sire's get a whiff of his aiding them it would be considered a blatant betrayal. Herodotus wouldn't think twice before slicing off his head with a silver sword. Should the immortal sorcerers sense his part in this it would have repercussions across every dimension. His one saving grace remained locating that hidden portal Aurora had used. But of course, there was also another way to save his well-deserved role as the Gatekeeper who controlled the only active portal on the continent. It would ensure his survival and elevate his status.

He could simply give them Michael.

Chapter 20

The Conversation

"Pull over and wait here," Martine said to the Guardian driving the small black sedan. As soon as the car came to a stop, she rushed out and up a set of familiar steps to Michael's brownstone. Before she could knock, Lukas opened the door, and she entered the foyer quickly. Bare-chested and in a pair of black sweats that hung low on his hips, he was also barefoot. His sandy-blond hair, damp and loose, cascaded down ending just below his shoulders. Her eyes narrowed and her face jutted forward. "What," he said, more a statement than a question.

"Do you... do you crimp your hair?"

Looking at her like she had two heads, he replied, "Crimp my hair? You're joking right?"

"No. I mean, it's a good look on you." *Nope. It's a stunning look on him!*

"I don't...It's natural when it gets this long. That's why I keep it tied when I'm in public."

Her eyebrows shot up. "Oh," she said and swallowed, "Good to know." *Because he'd be mobbed by panting women everywhere with it loose like this.*

"Come on," he said over his shoulder, leading her through the dark living room and into the kitchen. *Wow... the sway of his hips would have them panting as well.*

Refocusing on the reason she came here, she pulled out a chair and sat as he brought two glasses and a jug of orange juice to the table. After filling both glasses, he offered her one, which she took. She sipped it slow while he drained the glass and poured another. The fresh and fragrant smell of citrus worked on her like a strong cup of coffee.

Putting the glass down, he scrubbed his face before saying, "What happened?"

"He moved his fingers, Lu. Not once but three times in a row."

"Are you sure you weren't imagining it? I know you want him to wake up."

"I'm telling you, three times in a row! It's as if the spell weakened ever so slightly and just for a few seconds. That's the only reason this could happen."

"Isn't it possibly just an involuntary motor response?"

Her eyes went wide and her pointer finger poked at the table. "I was talking to myself out loud. Questioning why this happened when I saw not only one, but *three* twitches in a row."

"Drink your juice. It's good for you," he said.

She took a few mouthfuls. He raised an eyebrow, and she took a few more. He drained his second serving, put down the glass, and then relaxed back in the chair, lacing his arms across his bare chest. *And what a gorgeous chest,* she thought and looked away. Depending on your perspective, her glass was either half full or half empty, just like the information she just shared. Then she glanced at his neck. "You're wearing the Kendrick Family amulet. It belonged to my great-grandmother Morgan."

"Nice… some history here, right," he replied as his fingers closed around its circular shape, which thrilled her.

"It's a seven-point pentagram of protection cast in silver with a blue sapphire stone in the center." *Just like the color of your eyes.*

"Dad gave it to me last night before I—"

Holding up a hand, she quickly interrupted with, "Shush! Don't tell me anything I'm not supposed to know. I wouldn't want the evil vampire Draven to suck it out of my swooning mind while he's seducing me and then get you in trouble."

His lips curled into a mischievous grin. "I'd stake him before he laid a hand on you. And I'm very comfortable with trouble. You know that." The grin disappeared as he paused a full ten seconds. "I didn't agree with them, M, and I voiced my dissent. You came up with the initial plan. You should have been at the meeting."

She fluffed it off with a flick of her wrist. "In the long run? Who the hell cares. The Georgians will do what they choose, and they always lean to the right of what's right. I came here to share what I sensed when his fingers twitched. I'll bet the dark witch lost control for a few seconds."

One elbow rested on the table as his chin rested on a fist. "How do you know she lost control?"

"Keeping a spell of this magnitude going takes full concentration. Plus, it's not just controlling what's in front of her. It has to be powerful enough to cross dimensions." Searching for the right words, she added, "Okay… think about poking a hole through a ball of cotton with a pin. Until you push and pull the threads together again, there's a tiny tear in it. The matter is still connected except for an itsy-bitsy puncture." Her cheeks puffed out as she blew out a long breath. "That's the best I can do."

"No. it's good. I can visualize it. What do you think would make a pin-sized hole in the spell?"

"What would make you lose concentration?"

"It would have to be something unexpected."

Planting her arms on the table, one hand rested over the other. She leaned forward. "Just say what you're thinking."

He sat back with a shrug. "I don't know. Pain. Shock. Anger."

"Bingo," she said as she straightened her back. "I can concentrate through pain, and shock would make me loopy. I'm going with anger to the nth degree. Something or someone really threw her off her game."

"You think she's not alone in this."

"Not necessarily 'in' this. I think she's not alone."

"Which means someone's with her."

"Exactly. See where I'm going with this? Anything can make you angry. Breaking a nail. Ruining your favorite sweater. People in general. A driver who cuts you off. Some snooty bitch at the store who cuts in line. That's a normal angry. For a spell by a powerful witch to suddenly have a pin-hole in it, someone made her go right off the charts."

"Male or female," he asked with more interest.

She thought about it before saying what she sensed deep in her gut. "Female. Like a companion."

"Older or younger?"

Again, her sixth sense tingled. "Younger.

213

Definitely."

"A fight?"

"No. An action. Something shaking her to the bone and then some."

"So, I should be on the lookout for two women. Aurora and a companion."

"Yeah. I think."

His one eyebrow rose. "Let's take it a step further. Would Aurora be walking around her village, visiting friends and neighbors?"

"Witches have a highly developed sixth sense. She wouldn't want anyone to know she has a secret or get too nosy."

"So, that's a no. She isn't out and about. When I was young, I stayed far away from Dad when I had a secret."

"Pretty much the same for me with Mare, but I can shield thought." She shook her head. "So if she's staying away from everyone, then she's not running around doing things for herself. That's a definite no-no but a pretty definite yes on younger female as a companion."

"I'm hungry," he said and stood with a stretch.

She watched the flex of his arms before she looked away when he walked to the fridge. *Holy Hell, he has really filled out! I had no idea.* She heard him push things around the obviously well-stocked fridge and then sit down with a loaf of white bread and an open package of roast beef. "Want a sandwich?" he asked, piling at least half a pound of meat between two slices of bread. Then he held it out to her, and she scrunched her face. "Why the look? What? It's just a sandwich."

"The size of that would take me a week to work through."

"I could make you a smaller one. M, you have to

eat."

"No. I'm good." But her sixth sense did that tingling thing again. "Wait. Who gets her groceries?"

"What do you mean," he said before he took a healthy bite.

"A female companion who gets her groceries."

He swallowed before saying. "They don't have grocery stores there. It's pretty old-school like modern meets medieval. They have open-air markets in every village."

"Where a servant would shop—by herself. Maybe something the servant did or didn't do made Aurora go ballistic, and maybe she hit her. Which means she might have bruises."

"I'm not about to strip a girl down and check." With that said, he poured another glass of orange juice.

She eyed him. "Seriously, Lu, switch to water, because your blood sugar level is going to soar."

He gave an adorable, charming grin, complete with deep dimples. "I have a really fast metabolism. Besides, you would know what to do if anything happened to me, right?"

She cleared her throat. Changed the subject. "Maybe she slapped her face and left a mark."

"Oh. Okay," he said. Then he totally inhaled the last of the sandwich and drained the glass.

*His grocery bills have to be enormous*, she thought. "Wait. Open-air markets. Medieval villages. It's like you're stepping back in time."

"In more ways than one," he mumbled.

Her concern grew. "This is dangerous, Lu. When are you going back?" He looked at her and she shook her head. "I'm sorry."

"No. It's okay," he said very softly.

*What is it about him and his father? Once their tenderness comes at you, it's as if you're hugging a teddy bear—and everything really does feel okay.* She leaned back in the chair, and he whispered, "M" until he had her attention.

Nodding once, he said, "After midnight." As if able to read her thoughts, added, "And don't even think about showing up at Draven's in a blond wig and blue contacts."

"But, Lu—"

He held up his hands. "It's a total no. I know how stubborn you get. Besides, portal travel is a bitch. I puked my guts out going in and coming back out. Christ," he said, rubbing his chest, then swallowed with a sour expression. "I hate to puke."

Giving a slight grin, she replied, "Ginger ale helps." Then her grin slid into a frown. "Please be extra careful. What if something goes wrong?"

"Dad and Draven are going with me."

"Mare told me," she whispered. Seeing his serious expression, she shook her head. "Some line up, right, with mystical man and vampire, it's like having two paranormal superheroes as wingmen."

His broad smile reassured her. The honesty in his dark-blue eyes, not to mention the goodness in his brave heart, couldn't be disguised. Years ago, why had she chosen regret over reaching out? Why so many cruel last words instead of "I really need you"? Then his expression turned serious again. "I wrote you a letter. Just in case," he whispered with a slow shrug.

She sensed a sureness in him that hadn't been felt before. "Our letters and texts used to check off the 'dear friend' box, didn't it?" *Oh God, you have to come back.* Taking in everything about the man he had become, her heart suddenly fluttered. "I'll send one protection spell after the other beginning at midnight, Lu. By all that is good, by all that is right, may you be blessed."

They both stood, walked side-by-side to the foyer. He touched her hand and when she turned around, he wrapped her in his strong arms. She wanted to stay this way, with the soft hair on his chest against her cheek, taking in his scent as if to always remember—whispering the ancient spell to protect. To heighten his already keen mystical abilities. To ward off danger of any kind.

"I swear I'll tell you everything when I come back. And I *will* come back, M, I promise," he said in a softer tone.

She pulled away slow. Had to swipe the corner of her eye. His face tilted down, and their lips brushed before he sweetly kissed her cheek. She kissed his as well, seconds longer than she should have. Feeling the lick of his breath on her face, her heartbeat pounding like an insistent knock on a door. When they pulled apart, she sensed strength in the tender warrior standing before her.

Yet she flatly refused to say good-bye. It felt too permanent. "We'll talk again soon," she whispered. He opened the door and held it for her. If he looked in her eyes again, she was afraid of what he might see. Once in the car, pulling away from Lukas, Martine's finger brushed the spot where he kissed her. She brushed her lips. Something felt just out of reach—so obvious yet so elusive.

Chapter 21

Worries

*Exhaustion seems to have become a habit*, Martine thought entering her bedroom. Not so much physically drained, but mentally. Emotionally. So many issues had her out of focus, but she needed to be super-sharp not only tonight, but until Lukas returned. Once in her purple pajamas, tossing and turning more than usual, it seemed like forever to get comfortable. With black-out curtains over the windows, insomnia didn't occur because the room needed to be darker. Her room felt cozy and warm against the early October chill. She whispered words of protection again like the chant had turned sacred.

*Unable or unwilling to turn off your mind? Definitely both.* She worried about Lu, the task before him a tricky one. She worried about Michael. What would Alana and the twins do without him? Without them both? *Oh God... Alana.* Michael's soulmate was a strong woman. They'd been through so much together, always rose above challenges thrown at them. Plus, she loved Lu as if he were her own son, had helped turn him into the good man he had become. *And what about the twins?* She had been thirteen when her father died, but Michael filled that hole in her heart. Who would fill theirs?

As for Christopher Forbes? If he turned out to be

Gwendolyn's son, then he had unique, untapped powers and didn't even know it. *How overwhelming is all of this? Very*, she thought as she turned onto her right side and hugged a pillow. One man lay helpless in a hospital bed. The other man about to risk his life because of her ask. She connected them both. She connected them all.

****

Mary dried her hands on the kitchen towel, folded it as she always did and placed it on the granite counter to give it a slow glide-over with her hand. The clock on the stove read five in the evening, and she made a fresh pot of coffee. Closing her eyes, she sensed her daughter already dressed for work. Soon she'd come down the stairs and they'd go through a ritual she highly valued— some mother-daughter time. Alone and together.

*Maybe it's time to sell the gallery and think about retirement. Seventy isn't too far away. Maybe it's time to explore other interests.* Or cut back and shadow Martine's schedule, so they'd have the same days off to spend together. *Either way,* she thought as she pulled two coffee mugs off the hanging rack, *family is everything.* "As it is, so shall it ever be," she murmured bringing cups to the table before returning to the stove to stir the stew.

"Did you add extra potatoes," her daughter asked as she came into the kitchen and grabbed the coffee pot to fill their cups.

"I sure did. It's mostly potatoes and beef, not too heavy on the carrots, string beans or lima beans. And yes, I used baby carrots."

"Oh. Super. I'll set the table." Mary brought over a loaf of fresh baked bread and caught an obvious bounce in her daughter's step. "Wow. You kept busy today,

Mare."

"Just like you, I have a lot on my mind. Cooking calms me down some. We'll start a vigil of protection at midnight when they go through the portal. Word has gone out to other healing circles and the covens, too."

She brought the pot to the table and set it down carefully. Then grabbed the ladle on the counter before she sat. They ate in silence. Obviously, both of them tense, thinking about the same thing. Shocked that Martine finished a healthy plate of stew, sopping up the aromatic juice with a good chunk of bread, Mary sipped her coffee. 'Your appetite is coming back. I noticed it last night at dinner when Michael fixed your plate." Her daughter gave a nod. "Those were some wonderful Sunday dinners we shared with your grandmother doting on him."

"One very loving but extraordinarily odd-ball family, which no one questioned."

"You didn't get home until 8 a.m. and you didn't sleep well."

"No." Her daughter brought the plates to the sink and then sat back down at the table. "I went to Michael's and had a really deep conversation with Lu."

Her eyes narrowed, her brow knit. "You went to see Lukas this morning?"

"I had to, Mare. Something happened last night with my patient."

She listened to the way Christopher moved his fingers, then a play-by-play of the conversation with Lukas. Except for a few 'uh-huhs' and 'then-what-did-you-say's" she kept quiet, very aware of animation in someone who had stayed stuck in somber for years. It thrilled Mary to see her daughter's eyes light up every time she said his name. She knew how hard it is to give yourself permission to side-step overwhelming sadness. It gave Mary hope.

"I'm glad you went there," she finally said.

"It was easy to talk to him, like we fed off each other's ideas to make sense of what I saw." Her daughter paused. "I can't get over the way Christopher moved his fingers. I swear I'm missing something."

*Maybe more than you realize, my dear daughter,* Mary thought. Unless Martine brought up what she sensed, she wouldn't prod and poke. "But you discovered a trigger for Christopher. It'd be a blessing to have the dark witch go over-the-moon crazy-nuts so you can worm your way deeper through that spell."

Martine's shoulders slumped as she said, "It only happened for a split-second, Mom."

"More like ten or twenty, Martine."

Her daughter shook her head. "That's not enough time. I'd have to stay in his mind and be ready. I can't do that and send thoughts of protection Lu's way at the same time."

"Kinda makes you want to whip up a hurricane or some freak thunderstorm with threads of lightning in the Second Realm, doesn't it?"

"I wish I knew a daughter of chaos who'd do it for me."

"That's mostly fantasy, Martine. It may work on television but it's not real."

"What if we harness our powers and send our own spell to trap her."

"And how do you propose to do that?"

Her daughter's eyes went wide. "Through Christopher's mind."

221

She leaned forward with a soft, "Go on."

"Why can't we weave some chaos for her through him? She's connected through the spell."

"You can't lift the spell, Martine. She has to do it."

"We can get her a little flustered, Mare. The two of us can. Maybe even Sharon can lend a hand."

The look on her daughter's face read stubborn determination. "Whether or not it works, I'm in and I'll talk to Sharon. We'll come tonight, but it has to be well before midnight because once they go through, all focus has to be on protecting Lukas and Michael."

"What about Draven? Gonna send some protection his way," her daughter said with a smirk.

"It's not on my to-do list," she said less than kind. Without a doubt, at the first sign of danger that vampire would save himself. "I have some pastries left over from last night's dinner," she said as she stood. Lifting the pink box out of the fridge, she brought it to the table, waited for the usual "I'm full" that was sure to happen. Martine went to the counter and came back with the coffee pot, freshening both of their cups.

Her daughter lifted the lid and seemed to take her time, as if she'd actually eat one. "Ooh! I didn't see this one last night." Pulling a petit-four iced with dark chocolate out of the box, her daughter bit into it and swooned with a slow roll of her eyes. "Jeez, I love these!"

"I'll make a note of it and stop at the bakery tomorrow morning, just for you."

"Really?" The rest of the small cake went into her mouth. Then she took a gulp of coffee.

"Lukas told you the truth. He stood up to his father and Deepa for you."

That soft look claimed her daughter's face again. "He is such a sweetie. I told him not to divulge anything I shouldn't know. And he didn't."

"I think Michael's very uneasy knowing his son has to take the lead and go it alone."

Martine put down her coffee mug as her expression grew serious. "I'm whispering words of protection for him every chance I get. Alana has to be worried sick. I'd have loved to be a fly on the wall when Michael told her they were both going."

"I called her earlier this afternoon."

"What did she say?"

"That she had spoken to both of them."

"And?"

"She understands the mission and she understands the danger."

"So she's okay with it?"

With a deliberate flick of the wrist and a hearty 'pfft" Mary replied, "Not in the least. And she doesn't trust Draven, either. It's the importance of the mission that won out on this one. Always save the innocent. It's the Georgian way." She paused a moment before adding, "Can I make you a plate for later?" She got up and went to the counter praying for the response she wanted to hear. Whatever had sparked the change in her daughter, it needed to continue. Fiddling with the dishtowel again, she thought, *Please, please, please...* and eyed the plastic container on the counter seeing herself fill it.

"Mostly potatoes and lots of juice. I'll take a chunk of that bread, too."

She closed her eyes, let out a silent breath. How long had it been since her daughter ate like this? And two nights in a row? Not since before the loss of her baby.

Her grandchild. The hole in her soul that would never mend. Regaining her appetite meant a step in the right direction.

*What's changed? Having Michael here again?* Check. *Being focused on helping her patient?* Check. Always a dedicated nurse, she'd go the extra mile no matter how lost she felt. *Having Lukas here to talk to?* Now an eyebrow raised. Last night at dinner, her daughter's mood shot skyward when they laughed together. *The easy banter clearing the table... Not to mention the way they fell into each other's arms and stayed that way a little too long. How could she not see it? Not feel it?*

Their conversation meant more than her daughter realized, because a phone call or text after a thirteen-hour shift would have been easier. More convenient. More impersonal. No. Martine had *wanted* to see him. Lukas had started to pull her out of the abyss. *It's a hard climb out. But Michael had thrown me a lifeline when my Lawrence died.*

"Where'd you go, Mare," her daughter asked standing next to her.

"Eh… sometimes the mind wanders," she replied keeping her thoughts shielded. She snapped the lid on the container and cut off a large chunk of bread, placing both in an insulated lunch bag.

"Ooh. I forgot my phone upstairs. I must be in a fog or something," her daughter said leaving the kitchen.

Mary leaned against the counter as a small grin began. That hadn't happened in a long time, either. It reminded her of happier days. Normal days.

When Martine came back in, she took the lunch bag from the counter. "See you around ten p.m.?"

"You can count on it. Be safe."

"Like anything is going to happen with a slew of Guardians hiding in all the nooks and crannies at the hospital. Not to mention my very own car and driver."

Mary reset the alarm in the foyer lost in thought. Had her daughter finally turned a corner? She spent too much time alone reliving a tragedy. *Isolation never heals. It keeps you stuck in the rut of what-ifs.* Now, nudged out of that gruesome place, her daughter could find her footing back in the world of the living. She might even find room in her heart to care about someone again. It was long overdue.

Chapter 22

A Little Help

Hours into her shift, Martine changed Christopher's IV bag, Dottie came through the curtains of Cubicle Q. "I don't believe it! We've been totally slammed again! I thought this crazy flu would let up by now. I've seen more pale people holding their stomachs than I can count and it's not even close to mid-shift." She took the empty IV bag from Martine and threw it in the red bin.

"Thanks. I've given him a sponge bath and a shave tonight." she replied while straightening white blankets around Christopher.

"He looks like any minute he'll open his eyes and start a conversation with us. And of course, it isn't going to happen. Hey. I've got a treat for you." Dottie placed three small candy bars on the overbed table. "Did some early Halloween shopping last night. Thought you'd like a little chocolate pick-me-up."

She chuckled. "Oh wow. These are my favorite."

"I know. That's why I picked them out of the variety bag just for you. Sugar power for a shift like this goes a long way." Dottie fixed the blanket over his feet. "Never mind the vitals, do you sense any changes in him... either way?"

"Not a one," she replied. "We just have to have hope." What else could she say? Definitely not *'Until two very important people in my world put themselves in a strange sort of danger in a different dimension to locate the bitch who did this to him.'* If they didn't succeed, would he come out of this? Hell. No.

"Our job comes with loads of hope," Dottie replied as Jose entered the cubicle. "You want some sugar power," she asked reaching into her other pocket. Four chocolate kisses landed in Jose's open hand.

"Ooh, I love you, Dottie," he replied with a laugh, already unwrapping one to pop into his mouth.

"To what do I owe the pleasure of your presence," Martine asked with a grin.

"We just got a readmit from last week. She was here the night your patient arrived, and we got no room except for your Cubicle R, *Emita*," Jose said, unwrapping another.

"Really," Martine replied, and they all laughed.

"You called it right. Cubicle Really it is. I'll wheel her in, but I can't get her into the bed. I'm slammed over on the other side," he said as he left.

"Not a problem," Dottie said. "I'll help you with her."

She shook her head. "Go help out on the other side. I'll keep the curtain opened between the two so I'll have eyes on both." She went over to the wall and pulled the curtain to the foot of Christopher's bed. When Jose wheeled her in, her sixth sense tingled, quickly smiling at her colleague to hide the shiver that ran up her spine to the base of her brain.

"You'll be fine," he said to the old woman in a caring tone before winking at Martine and leaving them alone.

She fixed both curtains so that the corridor wasn't

visible and went over to the wheelchair. "Hello, my sister. Not feeling well tonight," she said as she helped her out of the chair and into the bed.

The old one motioned her close. "I'm clear as the tinkle of a little silver bell. Tonight, I'm here to help." Her voice sounded wispy and brittle with age.

"I don't know what you mean."

A smile slid across the old one's lips, the wrinkles around her eyes didn't dissuade their intelligence. "When I'm lucid my craft is still powerful. You have a troubled mind, child. Whereas I have nothing to drain my power. I knew your grandmother. In our day, we could bring about controlled disruptions when we put our minds together. You have powers like Martha. I sensed it when I met you and you have stayed on my mind."

"Then you know tonight is a crucial one on two different fronts."

The old one gave a grave nod. Her gray hair lay in crinkled strands across the pillow, her eyes bright with intent. "Don't bother explaining details. I won't remember, anyway. But it is my homage to my old friend Martha to join with you. As it is, so shall it be."

"Blessed be." Martine closed her eyes and saw Granny Martha as clear as day. "It is our honor to have you with us tonight, old one."

"Your mother arrives. Bring me next to him." She undid the breaks on the bed and positioned hers next to Christopher's. Sensing the request, she placed his smooth hand in her wrinkled one, careful so as not to impede the IV line. "You're right. He doesn't know his power born of witch and warlock. Gwendolyn had goodness within. Not the warlock. You must tell him." She went to the other side of Christopher's bed and took his other hand. She leaned close to his ear and whispered it to him. Then the old one said, "Feel the power within him stir, " and a brief jolt of energy raced up Martine's arm.

"What are you doing?"

Martine looked up with a start. Her mother and Sharon were at the foot of his bed, and Sharon's mouth formed a perfect letter 'O'.

Her mother looked shocked as well, saying, "Isobel? Is it really you?"

"It's been a long, long time, Mary Kendrick."

"What on earth are you doing here?" her mother replied with her hand over her heart, almost breathless.

"She's the old one admitted the night they brought Christopher in," Martine told them. Before saying anything else, she placed a spell around the two joined cubicles to ensure no one heard or disturbed them. Although the invitation to join in had not been verbalized, Sharon and her mother did the same.

Mare went to Isobel's side with Sharon right behind. While her mother stroked the old one's hair in a caring way, Sharon rubbed her arm. As her eyes grew glassy, Isobel whispered, "Let us join hands, my sisters, to form a bond. We welcome the young warlock to our circle."

Energy channeled as their minds linked. Martine searched for another pinhole. None could be found. His blood pressure didn't change. He didn't move a muscle. Not even a millisecond of a twitch. They rested often and tried again and again.

On the verge of a headache, Martine finally pulled her hand away from his. "I'm sorry. I have to stop." Disappointment etched her face. She bent her neck forward and rubbed the back of it thinking about popping two aspirin. Mare and Sharon stayed next to Isobel while she sank into the chair beside her patient. Then she looked at the clock on the cubicle wall. "I didn't realize we were at that for an hour."

"Neither did I, Mare, we have to go," Sharon whispered.

"Take me with you," Isobel said and started to push the white cotton blanket down.

"No, Isobel," Sharon said in a very sweet voice, "Stay and rest."

"Nonsense. I can protect..." When her eyelids fluttered before staying down, they all knew she was lost, somewhere in her befuddled thoughts. Martine rubbed her neck again as her mother and Sharon put on their coats and picked up their handbags.

"She's all alone. I wish we knew where her sister went," Sharon whispered.

"Her and her sister were always inseparable until she remarried," her mother answered.

"I never liked that arrogant warlock, taking her away from Isobel, " Sharon hissed.

"I'll keep her with Christopher for now. She can't go home alone in this state. Want to run it by Deepa, Mare? Maybe the Georgians have a social worker in the city who can find her a rest home or something when this is over." She studied Isobel's wrinkled face before looking up.

Her mother's eyes locked to hers. "I'm sure they'll help. It's good we tried this tonight. Maybe you need to sew a few seeds of chaos in Christopher's mind for Aurora to pick up."

She gave a nod. "Good one, Mare. I'd like to see that dark witch-bitch handle something crazy thrown out of left field. Maybe the healing circle can drum up a little chaos as well."

"It's a thought. Anyway, the car's waiting. You should sit and close your eyes for a few minutes if you can." Her mother touched her shoulder and she put her hand over her mother's.

"Let's just keep them both safe. Blessed be your healing circle."

Mare and Sharon echoed, "Blessed be," and then her mother said, "just take care of you. Promise me."

"Will do. See you a little after dawn."

When they left, she noted her patient's vitals in the electronic patient file on the tablet before picking up the three square candies left by Dottie. Sinking into the chair at his side, she peeled each miniature chocolate delight and chewed them. *Lu has a sweet tooth, too.* She recalled some witty texts where they renamed favorite candies. *These little chocolates were Stitchers and the other ones were Milky Whys, The rainbow of little round chewy things? Lu came up with Thistles.* She began to smile. *Memories are treasures. Any including Lu are precious.* Then she closed her eyes. She had fifteen minutes before the clock struck twelve.

****

"You're worried about her," Sharon said, settling into the back of the car.

Mary sank into the seat unable to relax. "Yes and no," she replied as the plexiglass partition between passenger and driver closed.

"How could it be both?"

"I'm worried because I sense growing concern for her patient and losing an innocent. She's hell-bent on Lukas bringing that dark witch back here to lift the spell." She took a moment before adding, "I'm not worried because Martine knows her limits. She'll pull back before falling over another edge of despair. For the most part, she always does."

"Martine is skin and bones, Mare."

She held up a hand. "I don't want to jinx it, but since Michael and Lukas arrived, she's eating more. I wish I could bottle their special brand of love so I can keep spoon-feeding it to her when they leave. Even before cancer took my Lawrence, Michael helped with her."

"I remember those wild-child years."

"He watched her like a hawk, Sharon. He's still the only one who can shut her stubborn down and snap her back to normal with just a look."

"It's too bad she still so closed off from everyone. No girlfriends. No healing circle."

"I really couldn't stand that pitiful excuse for a man. A full year of misery with that jerk before he walked out on her and his unborn child. He had her arguing with everyone. Martha wanted to whammy him. But I said no, that everything would work out the way it should in the end."

"You still can't tell Martine to let go of anything."

"Oh don't I know it. She's still lost in the loop of loss. I mean, I can relate. But at some point, she has to move forward and make room in her heart for life again." Not wanting to say it out loud, she touched Sharon's knee.

Sharon sucked in a breath before a long, dramatic, "No."

"Yep."

"Oh thank the high heavens and the good Mother Earth!"

"The looks on both of their faces when he hugged her was a sight to behold. He sat right next to her at dinner. Instead of pushing the food around on her plate— as if a mother doesn't notice— she actually ate. And tonight, she even had dessert."

"Maybe she's turned a corner," Sharon said, ever the optimist.

"I sure as hell hope so because she can't continue on like this. I'm always afraid she won't want to bounce back." Needing to change the subject, she said, "And what about finding Isobel there tonight?"

"It's a sign. But it's so sad to see her like that."

"She was one of the most powerful among my mother's generation."

"She sensed the need and held it together long enough to help."

Mary sighed. "Did we help? Did we get through?"

"We tried. And we should try again with the healing circle."

"Our focus has to stay on protecting Michael and Lukas. The Georgians give them two days to get her here."

Sharon replied, "I'd still run the idea of disruption by the healing circle. We'll take shifts, so protection is continuous around the clock."

"I agree." They both got out of the sedan and walked up the stairs to the brownstone. Mary turned off the alarm as Sharon closed the door. The living room was already set up. The coffee pot, placed on a timer, had the aromatic blend wafting through the first floor.

She went up to use the bathroom, and when she came down Sharon stood at the open door like a one-woman welcoming committee. The gathering of witch and warlock had both living room and dining area overflowing. She didn't have enough chairs!

At midnight, tokens representing the five elements were placed in front of the fireplace. Spirit. Water. Fire. Earth. Air. The room had been cleansed with burning sage and windows cracked open. Mary and Sharon took their places. Chants of protection, ancient and ancestral, blended together to form one powerful call. She saw the three realm travelers in her mind's eyes and shared it through the concentric circles.

Sixteen years ago, many of these same witches and warlocks had gathered together to protect Michael and Lukas Malone. As they linked again for much the same purpose, energy shot through Mary as it had that fateful night. This link couldn't be broken, a mystical chain connected to all others like them in the human world. Some called it praying. Some called it chanting. They all hoped for the same result. Two mystical warriors and a vampire would remain safe and shielded from harm while wandering around the Second Realm.

Chapter 23

The Second Realm

Dressed in a faded-blue muslin shirt and black jeans tucked into brown leather boots, Lukas placed the leather satchel across his chest and settled it on his left hip. His father's trusted broadsword and the pearl-handled knife were already in place. His steady hands tied the black woolen traveler's cloak, which swung across his shoulders and ended just below the knee.

He stood across from his father and Draven, who both looked pretty much the same except for faded-brown muslin shirts. Knowing the physical effects of portal travel on him, this time his senses stayed on high alert to the process. He had kept his stomach empty but had polished off a tall glass of ginger ale before entering the club called *Destiny*.

"I've calibrated our entrance so that we step into the edge of the Fifth Village," Draven said as he locked his office door. Walking toward the vault, he added, "We will skirt the edge of the realm heading southeast. I'd advise you to procure a horse. There's additional silver coins in your satchel for that purpose."

"Thanks. What about you and Dad?"

Draven gave a thin smirk as he tugged at his traveler's cloak. "Care for a bit of a run, Michael?"

"I'm up for it," his father replied in a confident tone.

"Good. We'll stay on foot until the Sixth Village's perimeter, perhaps persuade a farmer to part with a gelding or two, which we will, of course, return before we depart." They entered the vault, which Draven locked behind them with a different four-digit code.

Under the dim light they linked arms with him in the center. Lukas pressed tight to his father and for a brief instant, his body shivered, yet very much willing to face the unknown with total focus on the mission. The swirl of the portal, the hum that vibrated through his chest like a low rumble, a variation of hues within the moving gray matter—he memorized every aspect.

"Get ready," the vampire said, and then came, "Step through now."

As one entity linked by flesh and bone, they did. Pulled through a void, pressure slammed against his chest. Holding on tight to two hands, one warm, one cold, he had no sense of up or down, nor north or south until he felt his feet on solid ground.

Disorientation claimed him, but his father had a hand at the small of his back. He bent forward gripping his knees, less nauseous than the time before and breathed through his nose, slow and controlled until the feeling passed. They entered the realm on the side of some dirt road in a dense patch of high grass with dull-brown plumes that stunk something awful.

"Talk to me, Lukas."

He shook his head to clear it, blinked repeatedly as he stood up straight. "I'm okay, Dad." His father's arms wrapped around him in less than a second. He could care less what Draven thought, resting his head on his father's broad shoulder, a place of comfort and a singular privilege to have such a bond. "Please be safe and cautious. I love you more than you'll ever know, little boy," his father whispered.

He gave a nod and grinned at the term of endearment, whispering back, "I love you, too. Stay clear of the guards, Dad. Mom can't lose you." She'd be beyond devastated; would probably never come back from the loss of her eternal love. And his sisters? He quickly shook his head to erase the thought because he couldn't handle it. Pulling out of the hug, he eyed Draven standing off to the side with his face turned away, probably allowing them the private moment. And he felt grateful.

The vampire finally came over, his face expressionless. "The livery stables are on the outskirts of the villages. Go now with Godspeed," Draven said like a calm, focused order. "You will have daylight for several hours. Do not linger in the Fifth Village. Do not enter the pub. You have small change in your satchel. Purchase some drink, bread, and cheese for your travels. Then make your way east with haste. With any luck, the open-air markets are still open. You should start your search there. Forty-eight hours are all we can chance."

Lukas eyed the overcast sky, shielding a weak sun. "The day is not a problem for you here, Draven?"

"No. Especially not with this thick a mist. Neither realm has strong sun in any season. Autumn and winter are very easily managed. It is the growing period in the spring and summer when I need to be cautious. Oh," he said as if it just came to mind, "purchase a blanket. You may be more chilled here with the air being thinner."

He gave a nod and an honest, "Thanks." Grabbed his father's shoulder. His father did the same to him. "Later," he said. "I'll find you in the forest at the edge of the realm."

"Be careful," his father said.

The low rumble of his baritone voice held emotion, and he took in a quick breath, blew it out just as fast. "I learned from the best. Always," he replied as their gazes locked one last time. Turning to the road that led to the village, he peered through the tall weeds looking up and down, noting travelers far in the distance. He stepped out onto the road with a steady boot.

Lukas didn't look back. He simply put one foot in front of the other and fell into the rhythm of a brisk walk. Every once in a while he went off the road and through the tall smelly weeds to break into a run, his speed as fast and controlled as ever. Weaving back onto the road and keeping every sense on high-alert, he slowed his pace long before approaching other travelers. When he matched their step, he inclined his head as he saw others do, but he spoke to no one. Sensing the Fifth Village very different than the Second Village, he trusted innate intuition, and proceeded with caution.

****

Draven led the way through the tall weeds shadowing the road. His step stayed vigorous and sure. Michael was right behind him—perhaps three feet back. "This shit stinks. What the bloody hell is it?" Michael grumbled.

"The Second Realm's version of Indian grass which grows rather high enough to keep us hidden. It will begin to lessen in density as we approach the edge of the realm." He began to smirk. "Am I too fast for you?"

"Not at all. Just hanging back so I can take in the lay of the land."

"I could slow my step."

"Keep doing what you're doing. I'm fine with it."

He heard no huffs or puffs of breath, which told Draven the vampire-turned-human-again had impressive physical skills. He recalled their recent meeting after many years, in the space between the two theaters when he went back to see or sense the portal. Specifically, that pointy piece of wood aimed directly at his unbeating heart. No doubt, the mystical man had enough strength to push it clear through. Which meant he'd always need to keep his guard up against such a formidable human.

A mile later the tall grass began to thin. "We are almost there."

"I noticed," his travel companion replied.

As if they were of the same mind, they both broke into a run, the ground beneath them flat and solid. As they entered the boundary of dimensional gray mist, both of them stopped at the same time, shoulder to shoulder. "We'll turn east here. The ground is firm and the foliage thin. Once we reach the edge of the Sixth Village we'll go inland and find a farm."

"I'm fine running—although I'd love a cold drink right now."

"Sorry. Not on my list of necessities."

"How do you control your bloodthirst here?"

Of course he could reply with the obvious. Michael's blood would be extremely potent. He licked his lips at the very thought. "It is minimal in this realm."

"Which means you fed before we left."

"What do you think?" He turned to face someone he had known throughout all of his undead existence. Studying the man who could pass for his brother, both in life as well as in undeath, he couldn't deny the hint of jealousy, especially considering Michael's healthy complexion, not overtly pale like his own. "Gang members and murderers are plentiful in the city if you know where to look. I rather enjoy the hunt of a healthy gang member. Their blood, after a good chase, is thick and rich. Murderers are a different story. It's pasty. Coppery. Most don't run as fast. I'm sure you remember."

"Vividly." Michael paused, perhaps recalling his previous existence. "Since when did you limit your drink and drain to criminals?"

A wicked smile began. "I limit the drain to their kind. I said nothing about the drink." His arm extended outward. "Shall we?"

"After you," Michael replied with a bland expression on his face.

Draven walked out of the tall grass at the end of the Second Realm road. He'd never admit how the smell stuck in his nostrils like rotting rats—if he decided to take in a breath for no particular reason. Crossing the packed dirt, he slipped into the brush and withered foliage and then broke into a run. He heard the drumming of Michael's healthy heart wondering just how long the mystical man could keep up with a vampire.

****

After some ten miles, the brush thickened again, and Draven stopped running. Michael stopped next to him. *No sweat on his brow. No erratic beats to his heart. Quite composed.* "We are nearing the Sixth Village. Let's move inward and find a farm."

"Is it really necessary?"

The question merely laid claim to Michael's ego, and he replied, "You need a drink. Of that, I am certain. As for procuring horses, yes, it is necessary because I have no idea how dense and how far the forest at the end of the realm really is. It's not like we had a topological map to study before this adventure."

"Is that how you see this, Draven. An adventure? My son's life is on the line, damn it!" Michael sank to a fallen tree trunk and sat with his hands gripping his knees. It was the first noticeable human action since they came through the portal.

He walked over. How long had it been since he experienced fear for another? A flicker of a feeling nudged at him and then slipped out of reach. "Your love for him is fierce."

"It's immeasurable," Michael replied.

"I understand," he answered.

"You can't possibly."

"Why?"

"Because you cannot remember him."

His eyes narrowed. "Remember who?"

"Nothing. Let's get a move on." Michael stood. Draven grabbed his arm. Their eyes, both dark and determined, locked. "Let. Go."

He didn't, and before he could stop himself, said, "Explain to me what you are feeling." Michael continued to stare at his hand until he pulled it away. Then Draven stood with his arms at his sides like a statue in the middle of nowhere.

"My son was kept hidden and safe, away from me until he was nine. Then the sorcerers' bastard of a liaison found him and brought him here. I found him at the tender age of thirteen, terrified and raging with hatred. But you never stop loving your child, be he a boy or a man."

"A strong man with heightened senses like yours,

241

Michael, a warrior," Draven said aware of the flood of emotion in his every word.

"But he is still my son. My child. He'll face unknown danger again in a realm where ugly memories haunt him like ghosts in this bloody gray mist." Michael's pulse began to race but his words came out a low hiss. "You want to know what I feel? Terror. Absolute terror. So much so that should you get on my nerves, I just might stake you." He began to walk north toward the village. "Let's find that farm. I need a drink."

The self-assured gait, the determined strides so like his own, Draven fell in step with Michael. The land slowly became growable with rich soil. After a solid half-hour, they both stopped and sniffed the air. Hay that had been baled. Manure and horse piss fresh and ripe. They followed the scent to three barrel-chested horses standing in a corral. The scent of two males grew stronger.

"Let me do the talking," Michael said just above a whisper. "We don't want anyone to accidentally see a fang or two... should you open your mouth wide."

"I'll concede, but if you are asked, you are a half-breed emancipated slave from the North Country. Think back to the century after you were turned. I believe it will serve your disguise well enough."

"Anything else I should know? And as hard as it is for you, be honest."

"The villagers love coin more than life itself. Pay them well or they'll give you up to the guards without a second thought. One or both are warlock, so shield your mind. Keep your hood up and your eyes averted. You will not pass for someone from the realm."

Michael stopped and looked at him. "Then we have

a change of plans." He turned and headed back into the thicket, and Draven followed. Once hidden again, Michael spun around and grabbed him by the throat. "Nice work, vampire. I wondered how long it would take. Was that your plan all along? Allow me to get caught, and then I'll have to wait, bound and gagged, until they send for guards to take me to the sorcerers. Do I look like an idiot."

When Michael let go, he said with a haughty edge, "I beg your pardon."

"You have hurt my feelings, Draven. You're taking advantage of my thirst, and that's not nice. Now let's talk about *your* thirst because this is most likely the truer scenario. Two farmers find me suspicious, about to call for the guards. Then you play hero, saving my ass from capture. Fast-forward to two drained farmers lying in tall smelly grass. No one would find them for weeks, if ever, knowing how meticulous you are. No. We do this the right way. We wait until dark. Steal two horses and leave twelve pieces of silver for them."

"They will tell the guards their horses were stollen," he said as he straightened his cloak over his shoulders.

"No. They will go to the livery and buy two magnificent beasts they can work to death. Come on. Think like a man, not a vampire. I bet they simply say the horses died and they are now food for the winter."

He raised an eyebrow. "Very good, Michael. I commend you on your wit and wisdom."

"You should. Now let's find a stream. I believe if you listen closely with your vampire ears you'll hear it, too." Draven watched his typical long strides taking him deeper into the tall grass again, and then Michael turned back to face him. "Get a move on. I've got a thirst to die for."

He gave a sarcastic smirk, but followed.

Chapter 24

Friends

Well past mid-day, the open-air market still looked packed with merchants and villagers. Lukas kept his hood up, as many travelers did, and walked the main street of the market slowly, stopping at this or that tent, looking carefully at the types of items sold, figuring out how much things cost. He found the dairy vendor. After tasting various cheeses, decided on something akin to a mild cheddar. At another booth he purchased a leather saddle bag, and then stuffed the cheese into one side before slipping it under his cloak and over a shoulder. On the other side of the street, he found bottles of ale and juice for sale, purchasing three of each. With both sides of the saddle bag bulging, he walked to the end of the market to purchase bread. Everything, including the desserts, looked delicious. His empty stomach growled. One thing he'd never deny was his love of sweets. Then he heard, "Welcome, young traveler. Oh my! It is so good to see you again!"

The excitement in a familiar voice forced an easy smile. He bowed with his hand over his heart. "How fare thee, good woman? It is my pleasure to see you as well."

"You didn't say you were traveling to the Fifth Village," she chided and clicked her tongue. "I would have saved my best Battenburg for you. I would have hidden it aside."

"Thank you kindly, good woman." Thinking on the spot, hoping she wouldn't question him further, added, "Sadly, my horse could go no further the day before this morn."

She all but cackled. "But our home is in the other direction, young sir."

He threw her a charming smile. "I was on my way to the Sixth Village when I saw you the other day."

Sucking in a quick breath and with a hand to her heart, she replied, "To fetch your lovely lady? Oh! I adore romance. I recall her well. She is truly enchanting!"

"Something like that," he replied and then leaned down close enough to hear her heart skip a beat. "I mean to surprise her."

He held a finger to his lips, and she clutched her heart. "How very romantic!"

"But now I require a horse. Do you know of a reliable livery in this village," he asked with wide eyes and a bit forlorn, "I have been walking for close to a day now."

Reaching for his hand, he gave it to her, and in a motherly fashion she patted and rubbed it gently. "You poor child. The terrain can be treacherous in the Fourth Village." He had no idea but gave a nod. "Many travelers lose horses through the mountain pass. It's a wonder you didn't freeze to death."

"Such truth you speak. I mean to purchase a blanket as well."

"Say nothing more. Some will not sell you top quality goods." She leaned over the breads on display and glanced to the right. "Three booths down. Moira is known for her weavings. She is highly reputable, which as you know is not often the case in this particular village. Nonetheless, go now and then come back." He hesitated, but she shooed him, saying, "Off with you."

"I hoped to purchase some of your bread."

"I will put two loaves aside. Go on with you, now."

At the booth he made reference to the sweet baker woman. Moira produced a heavy woven blanket of black and gray. Paying her, he added an extra coin and a sincere thank-you. He gave a slight bow with his hand over his heart. The zaftig weaver blushed and returned a curtsy. Then he walked back to the baker, who positively beamed.

"I told you, didn't I? Moira's work is one of the best in the realm. It will keep you warm when you sleep, as if curled in your woman's arms."

He let that remark slide with a small grin, instantly thinking about holding Martine. Reaching aside, she produced two round breads wrapped in brown paper, which he took. Then he eyed the desserts. Everything looked and smelled delicious. Before he could ask, she collected two of each kind of cookie on display. "For your love of sweets, young sir," she said with pride as she wrapped them in brown paper, tied them with string as well.

*Christ, have I read her wrong?* Could she, in fact, be a dark witch like Aurora? Able to read his thoughts? Before he could shield his mind, she clicked her tongue again. A sliver of caution shot through him and feeling color drain from his face, grabbed at the amulet under his shirt. *Please Lord, don't let it be so.*

"I sense your sweet tooth, but no, I am not a dark witch. Many of us in the realm prefer to use our power for good, not greed. My name is Bronwyn."

Still skeptical, he reached into his satchel and placed a silver coin in her hand. "Pleased to make your acquaintance, kind Bronwyn."

Her light-blue eyes shot wide. "Oh, no. I cannot make change, young sir."

"I don't expect any. You have shown me kindness and concern. I value that above all else. I'm sure you can put the coin to good use."

"No," she replied with a shake of her head, "I will not take your coin." She looked both ways before again motioning him closer, placing it back in his hand. "Listen carefully. Do not show such a large sum of money around this realm. Villagers get suspicious and call the guards. Go to Malcolm's livery. At the corner of the street, make another right. Tell him Bronwyn sent you. He will have a fine horse for your journey. I will be in the Sixth Village in three days to sell my goods. Should you need assistance, find me in the open-air market."

"Thank you," he whispered as he slipped the coin into his satchel and stuffed the bread and cookies into the saddle bags. Yet he continued to study Bronwyn sensing goodness, knowing he'd never see her again. He didn't have three days to find Aurora.

"One more thing," she whispered, "Your lady has not been seen for weeks. She sends her servant to shop. The girl is called Anika."

"You recognized her then," he said, a bit surprised.

"Yes. And I sense more about you than you say. Be cautious. Be clever."

"My name is Wyn," he whispered back.

"No, it is not, but Wyn is a fine pseudonym because you are truly blessed and protected. God-speed, my charming Wyn." She reached out her hands and he took them in his own. "Yes, indeed. You are blessed and protected," she said as she squeezed them. He felt a jolt of energy rush up his arms, and for a second, didn't want to let go. When he did, he cleared his throat and straightened his shoulders.

"God-speed to you as well, gentle Bronwyn." With a bow and his hand over his heart, he took a step back. She pointed the direction to the livery stables.

\*\*\*\*

Run down and totally a barn in need of repair, Lukas spotted a huge man, as broad as the stable door, bending over to rake out a stall. Sloppy, rust-red curls ringed his huge head. The smell of hay and fresh manure filled the musty air. "Good day, sir. Are you Malcolm?"

"Aye. Tis who I be," came after a grunt. When the man stood up, Lukas took a step back. If angry giants existed he surely stared at one. Most likely six-foot-seven, barrel-chested with logs for arms and legs, not to mention a rust-red unkept beard! "An hew migh be askin."

Letting nothing show in reference to the odd pronunciations, he replied, "Uh, um, Bronwyn the baker woman sent me?"

The fierce expression turned soft and open. "Och! Ye should ha said tha first, yoong laddie. Whatcha be needin' then?"

"A… a horse, sir, I have silver coin to pay."

A belly laugh followed as he put down the rake. "Well, now, wha else would ya be buyin' at a stable, laddie? Och. Follow me," he said with a thrust of his arm, "I've gut one oot back that's sure ta please ya." He passed six stalls, three on each side before they reached a dirt path that led to the corral. Malcolm gripped his shoulders, eyed him every which way. "Yepyepyep, he'll do ye fine." He put two fingers in his mouth and the whistle that followed started at a low pitch and ended on a high one. What trotted over looked a sight to behold. "He be a dapple grey, buh I call 'im Splotch."

The magnificent beast nuzzled Malcolm who scratched him behind the ears. It was love at first sight, but then he thought about it and approached, standing next to the wooden fence. "He's beautiful, Malcolm, but I have limited funds." The horse's ears perked up and he whinnied, nudging Lukas's shoulder.

"Funny," Malcolm said as he rubbed his beard. "He doon't take ta too many o' yer kind. Usually kicks and bucks. Tis why he's still here."

Petting the horse's ample jaw, he asked, "What do you mean, my kind?"

"Yoong warlocks, lad. He doon't like em. Tries ta eat em all the time. Tis a fierce bite old Splotch has." His light-blue eyes narrowed. "Ya sed Bronwyn sent ye?"

"Yes, sir, I did. How many coin for him?"

Scratching his beard again, Malcolm shook his head. "Well now, seein' as I canna get rid o him. An I'm no' about ta sell him for meat, so what can ya afford?"

He felt around the satchel grabbing a fistful of silver, and then took them out to count. "Will you take ten coins, sir?"

Malcolm's bushy eyebrows lifted, his eyes as large as quarters. "Ya got yourself a horse, laddie. I'll tro in saddle and blanket as well." Lukas handed him the coins, and after glancing left and right, Malcolm quickly pocketed them. Bringing Splotch into the stable, he threw over a thick woven blanket and set the saddle, which looked to be close to a Western one. A small sack of oats landed on the horse's back. "Just a treat for old Splotch here an yer all set." Malcolm walked the horse out of the barn and into the open area between stable and corral.

Sensing it custom in the realm, Lukas gave a slight bow with his hand over his heart saying, "Thank you, good sir." Malcolm stepped back with a friendly wave.

Putting his boot in the odd-shaped stirrup, he mounted with ease. Although he hadn't been on horseback recently, sense memory took over. He settled the saddlebags, made a clicking sound, and Splotch left the stable area in a slow walk.

Heading for the open road, he stroked the coarse main and mumbled, "How could anyone call such a magnificent beast Splotch." The horse nodded its head as if it understood. And agreed.

Chapter 25

Enemies

Seated comfortably in the slightly weird saddle, Lukas grew more confident—until he approached a wooden barrier across the Fifth Village road. With no place to hide, turning around wasn't an option, either. He'd already been spotted. Pulling back on the reins, Splotch quickly slowed its step.

Simply the sight of the two guards who rode their horses out of the tall grass and up to him made his stomach spasm. Their uniforms had not changed, dull-gray shirts with sleeves that billowed, loose-fitting black pants and boots with spurs. Thick black belts at their waists. His grip tightened on the reins as his gut clenched again. *Had I stayed in the fields, they wouldn't have seen me. Too late now.* And what the hell was the proper protocol when encountering realm guards? For once, he wished he had the ability to read minds.

He brought the horse to a complete halt and studied them. Each had a hand raised. Miss-matched eyes and off-color hair said they were half-breeds, the lowest in the chain of command. Not powerfully built and probably dim-witted, so he murmured a quick, "Thank you, God," under his breath.

Yet they dismounted and approached like they owned the realm, full of themselves and obviously not too bright. "Dismount," one ordered.

Which he did.

"Papers," the second guard ordered with one hand on his sword and the other outstretched.

Lukas rolled the cloak over his left shoulder and dug through the satchel to produce them. Snatching the documents from his hand, one studied them while the other circled his horse.

"Name," the guard with the papers ordered.

"Wyn Cleaves of the North Country," he replied, respectful and soft.

"You're a long way from home. Why might that be, Wyn Cleaves?"

"I travel to the Sixth Village to pursue a woman."

They both snickered before the guard holding his papers said, "None of the sluts good enough for you in the North Country? So you go to fuck a creamy Sixth Village lady?"

"I do, sir," he answered with caution. "We have corresponded through letters."

"Show us the letters," the guard said.

"My girlfriend got jealous, sir, and burned them," he replied with a hint of sadness in his voice. "Therefore, I beg your understanding, because I cannot produce a one."

"I know this horse," the guard who circled him said, "It's the oddball dapple from the half-breed mutant Malcolm's livery. I wouldn't be caught dead on such an ugly thing."

"It was all I could afford, sir."

"Just purchased, eh?"

"Yes, sir."

"Then how did you make it to the Fifth Village from

253

the North Country? Are you so smitten that you walked?"

"No, sir. My horse did not make it through the mountains of the Fourth Village," he lied praying the tidbit of information would be accepted.

"Eh, like many others. You're a fool to pollute the rest of the realm with North Country bumpkin ways. Stick to your own kind."

With daylight fading, he needed to move on, quickly losing patience with this charade. He knew how cruel guards could be. Knew it firsthand and had the scars to prove it. And if they laid so much as a fingertip on him… Vivid recall of his captivity dislodged the rage that sizzled right below his skin. When the guard folded his travel papers and shoved them in a pocket, Lukas said as respectfully as he could, "I need them back so I can travel, sir."

The other guard shoved him further away from his horse. "Raise your hands and spread your legs." He accepted the pat-down, which lingered between his legs far too long, showing nothing on his face. The other one rummaged through his saddle bags before slinging it across his own horse.

"Remove your cloak and don't put your legs together," came next. Like a stoic, he complied. Untied the cloak and let it fall to his feet. But as the guard pulled his father's trusted broadsword out of its leather holder, every muscle in his body tensed. "Nice piece of ironwork," one said to the other as their filthy hands touched it.

"No… not steel. It's pure *silver,* this one is! There's enough here to keep me in coin for the rest of my life." Then eyeing him added, "How did you come by something as unique as this in the realm?"

"Why bother to ask? He's nothing but a common thief. Probably killed its rightful, rich owner and then dipped his cock in a lot of sluts after showing off this much silver."

"We could have some fun before we do him. Leave him bleeding out for the buzzards to feast on. No one would be the wiser."

A gruff laugh sounded. "Then split the coin when we melt this down."

"You go first."

The rage that raced through his veins felt primordial. Lukas spun around punching one in the stomach and the other, who called him a thief, in the jaw. The sound of small bones splintering didn't faze him, and he caught the trusted broadsword before it hit the ground. Without so much as a flinch the tip of the heavy weapon went clear through the guard's heart. He pulled it out and leered at the other who grunted and cupped his broken jaw.

"I am not a thief. I don't dip my cock, filthy fucking bastard," he bit out. Dropping the broadsword, he grabbed the dead guard like a bag of garbage and flung the body far into the tall grass alongside the road. Picking up the weapon, he approached the other with menace in his steady step. The idiot's eyes looked about to pop their sockets. His left hand flexed in its hilt. "You're the one who took my provisions. In some cultures they slice off a hand for stealing." The idiot stepped back, but before he could run, Lukas skewered his heart, just as he had done with the first one. He squatted next to the body, pulled the weapon out and wiped the blood with the guard's shirt. After returning it to its sheath, he stood and dragged the second piece of garbage to the side of the road before tossing it into the high grass. Then he took back his saddle bags before slapping both horses on their rumps, sending them at a trot through the high grass and into the distant forest.

Rubbing his hands down his jeans, he kicked at the dirt in the road to cover the blood splatters just in case anyone happened along. With flexing fists he looked at Splotch. The dapple-grey stood perfectly relaxed as if blood and violence didn't bother him. That no one else travelled the road seemed odd, but he chalked it up to either fate or Martine's protection spell.

"Thank you, M," he whispered. Settling his cloak on his shoulders, he mounted his horse and pulled off the road, riding through tall grass, which smelled as putrid as an open sewer. By the time he reached the thick of the woods, he couldn't stand the stink on his clothes from the brush of its feathered plumes. He closed his eyes and barely breathed, picking up a faint sound before pointing Splotch its way.

After dismounting at a stream, Splotch went to the water's edge and drank deeply. So did he. With fresh cool water in his cupped hands, he scrubbed his face. He had to eat something before his stomach cramped again. Before sitting down, he pulled two bottles of juice, the bread and cheese from a saddlebag. Settled cross-legged beneath a tree, he leaned back popping the cap off the juice. It tasted like a blend of berries and apples. Ripping through the brown paper, he pulled off a big chunk of bread and tore into it. The cheese had a waxy film around it, so he used the pearl-handled knife from his boot and sliced out a hearty wedge. Although it didn't fill him, it took the edge off hunger.

He had to get closer to the Sixth Village before nightfall. After mounting Splotch, he made his way through the forest. Surrounded by tall pines, he thought about what he had done on that road. Second Realm guards had slapped him around and dragged him by the hair more than a few times, even though he was just a terrified kid. Their filthy, smelly hands had lingered where they shouldn't. He had run away dozens of times during the last months of captivity. That's when they started using their belts on him... after they finally caught him, after greedy realm dwellers took their dirty coin and led them to his hiding spots.

"A terrified kid at the mercy of mad dogs," he whispered, feeling every scar on his chest and back. Now the realm had two less torturers. "Not even a dent," he muttered as he rode through the trees.

Chapter 26

Frenemies

"Don't you need to come up for air," Draven quipped as Michael again scooped water into his hands from the stream in the forest.

"First off," he said after he swallowed, "I'm thirsty. Second, we've got nowhere to go until nightfall. Relax. Go hunt a couple of squirrels to drink and drain. It'll take a slight edge off your arrogance."

His lips settled into a frown. Tips of his fangs dug into his bottom gums. One eyebrow arched as if he were somewhat amused rather than annoyed, which in fact, he was. "No thank you. I'm good, as they now say. Unless you're hungry. How long has it been since you've dined on skewered squirrel over an open fire?"

"Not long enough," Michael replied before closing his eyes with a groan.

Not about to watch the man rest with his back to the tree with one leg straight, the other bent at the knee, Draven started to walk away.

"Don't stray too far. And do *not* revisit the farmer."

"I am a vampire of my word, Michael,' he replied, not at all insulted.

"So you say... until the old bloodlust surfaces."

"You would know. I believe your drink and drain had been legendary. Really... how many multiple kills in one night?"

"None of your business. Go romp through the forest, will you already?"

He did just that, following the running stream in a slow, pensive gait, the solitude refreshing. He continued on another four hundred feet, and when he picked up a scent, he stood perfectly still. His eyes scanned the forest floor moving closer to the objects with a slight tilt of his head—already familiar with the human's unique scent. Bending down, the smell of cheese, bread, and a mixture of apples and berries swirled up his nose. He lifted the tin lid the size of a quarter and put it in his pocket along with a torn piece of brown paper.

Then he continued walking many more hundreds of feet and farther downstream. He sniffed the air again, the scent stronger than it should be. Picking up speed, what his eyes rested on could be considered *very* good fortune. But.. the reaction he'd surely get if he approached wouldn't be a good one, so he turned around and raced back to Michael. He kicked a boot, which elicited a grunt as the man's eyes flipped open. "Do you know you snore?"

His travel companion cleared his throat before saying, "So I've been told."

Draven pulled out both items, then threw them on the ground. They landed right beside Michael who barely sniffed saying, "My son's scent is all over them. Where?"

"About half a mile from here. And I believe Lukas has a dapple grey. Get up. I scented two horses farther downstream."

Michael pocketed the tokens, stood and brushed off his cloak. "Which means we don't have to revisit the farm. Why didn't you simply save us time and bring them back?"

"I have never liked glamouring a horse. It disturbs me."

"More likely they don't like *you* and may have spooked."

"As someone once told me… tomato-tomahto… shall we?" He broke into a run with Michael on his heels. When they neared the horses drinking from the stream, Draven leaned in with the whisper, "I will stay back. They are all yours."

Like a true equestrian, Michael approached them calm and steady, his footwork as intriguing as a choreographed dance. Both beasts came over and nuzzled him as if they were long lost friends. The softly cooed words sounded like a lullaby of reassurance. With one fluid motion, Michael grabbed the black horse's mane, pushed off the ground and swung his leg over. He took the other horse's reins in hand and rode over.

Draven's eye's narrowed. "There is the scent of your son and blood on them."

"I smell it, too. But it's not my son's blood, which is a good thing. You know this realm. What is the stamp on the saddles?" Although Draven approached slow and steady, both horses reared and whinnied anyway. "Bloody hell… it's like something out of *Young Frankenstein.*"

Taken aback, he huffed, "I've read Shelley's book. There is no young in the title." The uncharacteristic laugh made Draven huff again.

"Don't you watch old movies on that big-screen of yours? Honestly, Draven. Get an undead life. So tell me. How long has it been since you've ridden?"

The arrogant bastard had full control of the horse! "I preferred the carriage back in the day."

"All those decades with Cyril… you rode perfectly fine."

"And I despised every second of it."

"Well, you don't have a choice. We conserve energy on horseback. Just tell me what the symbol on the saddle is." Michael reached out to hand him the reins of the other horse, which he took with lips locked tight and hooded eyes.

Standing motionless next to the other beast, which thankfully, did not rear, he replied, "The stamp indicates they belong to the realm, most probably ridden by guards. If your son encountered them, then he is in trouble."

"My son can handle himself when it comes to not-so-innocent men. I'm sure he's fine—physically at least."

"And psychologically?" he felt compelled to ask.

With an unreadable face, Michael replied, "Either they're already dead or in the process of dying."

"You taught him well."

"As a father should." After a pause, he added, "Search your saddle bags, will you? I want to see what's in them."

Draven reached into the right one and pulled out a wrapped clump of something that had a pungent odor. He handed it to Michael. "I think it is food."

"Thank the good Lord," Michael uttered as he unwrapped a fistful of beef jerky. He tore into a piece and then another until nothing was left. "Let's get a move on. We have moonlight tonight. I'll cross first."

Draven followed through the stream. Neither spoke

as the horses moved sure-footed through the trees. His mind wandered through the monotony of the moment. As for Michael? Certainly the man's mind stayed focused on his son, somewhere alone in the vast forest between the Fifth and Sixth Village. One bit of knowledge bothered him. *Should dead guards be found, the entire realm would be put on high alert. Which makes staying out of sight all the more important for Michael and son.*

Obviously, the sorcerers would know they weren't killed by a vampire.

Chapter 27

Reflections

Lukas made good time using the rest of twilight to his advantage. When he reached the rim of the Sixth Village, his sense of smell immediately picked up change in the air. Very humid for an autumn night with a mix of sea and forest scents. Balmy almost. He breathed deeper and felt refreshed.

The tall pines had wide trunks, the low foliage still more green than orange or yellow. No sign nor scent of the tall grass with its putrid plumes. As his horse walked, he untied his traveler's cloak laying it across the horse and in front of him. He pushed up his sleeves and reached into a saddle bag for his last bottle of juice, chugging it down to quench a nagging thirst. His body stayed in a relaxed sway with the saddle while thinking how none of this looked familiar.

He had never gotten this far on his run-aways from the sorcerers' palace. With it being the farthest village, hopefully there would be less guards patrolling this part of the realm. It would be his good fortune. The filthy guards' as well. Bypassing a babbling brook, Splotch crossed its rocky floor slow and steady. Heading deeper into the forest, wondering just how close he had come to the Sixth Village, a larger body of water appeared. He decided to make camp. Little moonlight reaching the forest floor would serve him well. He took a careful sweep of the site he chose, found it to be perfectly shielded.

With Splotch tethered to a fallen branch jutting out of the water, he removed the saddle—memorizing in reverse the way it needed to be mounted in the morning. His hands brushed down the warm, smooth dapple's multi-colored hair on its sides from neck to rump. His reward was a long nuzzle and a few good snorts. He left a decent treat of oats from the sack.

It had been a long day. His hand sluiced through the water with a sigh as he crouched down. Shrugging off both satchel and leather sheath complete with trusted broadsword, Lukas lay them carefully away from the water's edge yet close enough should they be needed. His butt hit the ground to pull off boots and socks so he could wiggle his toes.

Untying his hair, he shook it free. Then he removed his shirt and rubbed his chest before dipping the itchy muslin thing into the water. With any luck, the loose weave would release the streaks of blood. He wrung it out before laying it on the forest floor. Then he stripped off his jeans, leaving them at the water's edge. Walking into the ice-cold water with his arms bent at the elbow until it lapped against his hips, he took a gulp of air and sank down. The shoot up came very quick. Both hands threaded through his unruly hair to get it off his face. Ten seconds later he headed to the river bank and wrapped himself in the heavy blanket he had purchased. Bathed in the humid air, he stretched out to dry off.

It took longer than expected, the humidity heavier now. Dressing quickly, even though the coarse muslin shirt was still drenched, he gathered his wet hair before tying it back with a strip of leather. Then he finished off the cheese, bread, and delicious cookies washing it all down with bottles of ale.

Wrapped in his cloak and blanket, he stretched out again. Tomorrow would be an important day. Would he find this servant girl? And how would he handle her? Using his charm, he'd put her at ease. She'd give up everything he needed to know. If he got forceful, she'd be so scared she'd give it up faster. Either tactic would do the trick.

But then Martine came to mind. What would she say when he told her he scared a helpless servant girl half to death? Of course, he wouldn't be proud of his actions, but he wouldn't lie about it. *What will she think of me? Is she thinking about me now? Sending me protection?* He hoped so—with all his heart.

Seeing her again stirred old feelings buried deep in his soul. No one knew he'd had a crush on her for years. Hell, Martine didn't even know, and they had been very close, often finishing each other's witty comments. They shared a secret love of words, had taken the old-fashioned art of letter writing to new heights. *But then that asshole pulled her away from me, played with her mind and brought it all to an abrupt stop.* Yet, he said nothing. Did nothing.

Staring up at the dark cloudy sky, he thought about their differences. He'd been late to the party with hormones. Martine looked curvy, fully developed at seventeen. Now, he had lean muscles and she looked boney and frail. Back then, she lived up to the title of wild-child while he came off moody and quiet. Yeah. These five years apart had changed them both. He embraced open and friendly while she seemed more than guarded. Matured mystical skills made him a fierce fighter, yet he preferred intellectual pursuits. Martine thrived in the hands-on profession of nursing. *That kiss last night… Oh Christ, I wanted more.* Holding her tight made him feel like a broken part of him had been put back right. *Distance is a living, breathing thing. And I never want to feel it again.*

He rolled onto his side on the forest floor as if changing his position could change the past. *Sure. Loss is a living, breathing thing as well. She wears it in her eyes.* He'd never be able to take it away, to ease her sorrow. And he worried about her. She looked to be totally fading away. He didn't miss her curves. He missed that healthy lust for life he didn't sense anymore.

*She can't ever know how I feel about her.* He'd keep it tucked away, the spectrum of emotions between low level guilt to high level rage. Between being mildly amused to being overjoyed. *Internalized but never truly digested. It's my way of coping.*

Seeing her last night again had forced him to look deeper within himself. *Her 'ask' had been for the mystical warrior, the confident, fierce and focused side.* Not the one he kept hidden. That side of Lukas Malone felt totally different. Too vulnerable to expose. Too complicated. No. He'd never feel good enough for Martine.

****

The dawn of dim daylight didn't concern Draven as, once again, he kicked his traveling companion's boot. It elicited the same response as the last time. Michael sat up in the middle of a snore and cranked his chin upward. Naturally, there came no "good morning," or other nicety. Something Draven shrugged off as small talk, anyway.

"What is that?" Michael asked, his voice gravelly from sleep.

"Breakfast for you," he replied, walking away. He pulled off one of the horse's blankets and laid it on the ground. Then placed his goodies on it and pointed to his offering. "There. Fit for a king."

Already on his feet, he knew why Michael walked away from their camp, preferring the privacy of nearby dense bushes to relieve his bladder. *Ah. The human body is such a wonderful machine.* Before approaching the feast, Michael went to the water. After scrubbing his face and running wet hands through his hair, he approached, using the brown muslin shirt like a towel. "My word, a feast for me. Thanks," the man said—almost politely. "Where did you get this? Or rather, *how* did you get this?"

"The apples are from an orchard about a mile north. The bread and cheese are from a farm right past the orchard. Don't worry. Both occupants of the cottage were in their barn probably milking cows or something. Their well-stocked larder was around back. But alas, I did steal an empty milk bottle. Thought it might come in handy to have water with you... to perhaps assuage your thirst as we ride." A shred of humanity poked through his composure. "Please eat. Your color is off."

As Michael sat cross-legged at the edge of the blanket, he sliced the apple and put a wedge into his mouth. Had he been a normal man, he'd have already devoured the apple in a few bites. Such control seemed extraordinary to Draven.

"And your hunger, vampire? Are all the cows still alive?"

"How gracious of you to inquire of my well-being. I found a deer with an unfortunate gash down it's leg. I put it out of its misery. Not my normal sustenance."

"But blood is blood," Michael replied ripping off a chunk of bread, placing a slice of cheese on it.

His eyes narrowed and then he raised one eyebrow. "How do you know I'm telling you the truth?"

Michael prepared another slice of bread and cheese. "Lies sound different. I'm sure you know what I mean."

Draven gave a slight shrug before walking to the water's edge. "We should leave soon. The dead guards may have been found. More will probably comb the forest for the killer. Hopefully your son has not dawdled. Fifth Village dwellers are notoriously greedy. They'll give up anyone for much less than one silver coin."

"He'll be fine."

"You say that so nonchalant. If he were mine own, I would be beyond worry."

"I know my son. I taught him well." Then Michael paused. "Now I will repay your kindness for bringing me this nourishing meal. You were a good father to your son, Henri."

He whirled around with fire in his eyes, his shoulders back and his spine straight. "Do not use my Christian name. I am Draven, Gatekeeper of the portal."

"You are now, but you weren't then. And don't try to tell me you don't want to know more."

Immeasurably, he did. The pull of his humanity had always set him apart from Cyril's other progeny. He'd become a master at disguising it. Otherwise, he'd have been beaten before Cyril sliced off his head with a silver blade. He whispered, "tell me."

Michael brushed off his hands and after a long drink

of water from the stolen milk bottle, said, "Besides playing the piano brilliantly, you were a fine composer and a magnificent performer in the parlor circuit in Paris." Michael stood, reached down for the leftover bread, cheese, and apples, walking over to his horse, placing them in a saddlebag.

"I already know that."

Then he picked up the milk bottle and drained the water in it before replenishing it at the stream. Draven followed, full of interest. "Your compositions sold well long after you were turned. Enough to leave your family in a decent financial state. Your disappearance was quite deeply felt by your friends, they contributed to your wife and son's well-being. They were both devastated, leaving Paris immediately, which turned out to be a blessing. Months later, when we returned with Cyril, there was no trace of them—thank God."

Draven said nothing, showed nothing. They readied the horses and mounted before heading southeast until they shadowed the rim of the realm. Kept a steady trot where possible and slowed to a careful walk when necessary. When the air smelled of sea and humidity, Draven said, "We are in the Sixth Village. The land should open up a while before we find the thick forest at the end of the realm. I don't know how many more miles that will be. I've never been this far."

Riding alongside him, Michael gave a nod but did not continue talking. Yet everything he had learned tugged at Draven's brain. He had fathered a son! He had been a good man.

He had to know more. Needed to, as if it were an endless craving. Yet the arrogant bastard divulged nothing more. *Very clever. Should I not stray from the trustworthy path Michael expects, I'll be rewarded with more. Very clever, indeed.*

# Chapter 28

## Servant Girl

Aurora awakened itchy and hungry, as if she hadn't eaten in days. Literal days. She reached down under the covers and scratched a thigh, then a knee, and finally her right calf. She scratched her neck and left elbow before jumping out of bed and throwing off the covers. Nothing. Yet it felt as if ants crawled over her skin. She looked out the window to see a *second* day of heavy, overcast skies. It looked as if the clouds geared up for one of those rare storms she had read about in journals of witches who had fled the human world. She wondered what such a gushing downpour felt like or even looked like. This realm didn't have extremes of weather, barely cold enough in winter to produce a puny snow squall, if any.

Today, she needed a change. She'd visit the seashore, the salty mist considered excellent for the skin. She waltzed into the kitchen with a flounce and sat at the table. "After you serve me, you may put the pony and carriage together."

"But my mistress, I… I don't know how everything fits," Anika whined as she placed a plate of yesterday's fruit and one poached egg on toast in front of her.

"You were ordered to watch the groomsman when he comes to check the pony. Have you disobeyed me?"

The girl winced. "I will never use those skills in the

palace."

"Suppose we need to flee to save our lives." Both hands slammed the table, which caused the plate and silverware to bounce before a resettle. "Get the carriage ready. And it better be done properly or I will whip you—as if you need any more bruises," she spit out as an afterthought.

"Your egg will get cold."

Her face screwed, her eyes became slits. "Where is the "my mistress"?"

Anika's chin quivered as she curtsied low with teapot in hand. "Forgive me, my mistress."

"Leave. Prepare the carriage," she ordered.

****

*Why did I agree to do this*, Anika thought in the barn staring at the pony in the stall. Aurora had *never* been so mean or bossy. Just weeks ago they had laughed together like sisters. "I was only gone three days. And I came back to a shrew," she mumbled under her breath. Tears clouded her vision and she swiped at them with her apron as her breath hitched once. Being sent whirling through the air and into that huge tree still stayed in mind, one hip and arm barely useful. And her face had cuts and bruises. The shame she felt going to market this way. She even told a lie to a sympathetic vendor, saying she had tumbled down a ravine while picking berries in the forest—one of many more lies to come, she figured.

She placed the leather halter on the pony where she thought it should be and tightened every strap that looked like it kept the animal tethered to the wooden contraption with a seat and two large wheels. Then she stood back, studied everything again. Tying the reins to the porch-post, she went back inside.

Aurora called from the bedroom and as she limped into the room, the meanie said, "Is something wrong, silly girl? Stop acting like an invalid and help with my dress."

The tone of voice sounded just like another insult. She approached to pull up the zipper, and as Aurora held up her hair, Anika narrowed her eyes. Whether rash or an allergic reaction of some kind, Aurora's back and neck had hundreds of tiny pink spots. She said nothing, fixed the clasp at the neckline.

"I want fresh fruits and vegetables today. And a leg of lamb roasted with potatoes and parsnips. And bring me a creamy, chocolate dessert." She turned with an odd grin. "I have a craving,"

"Yes, my mistress," she whispered, watching her leave the bedroom.

She picked up the nightgown and folded it neatly as the door to the cottage closed with a loud *thwunk* that made her blink. Rubbing her sore right arm, her eyes filled. The room blurred. The lump in her throat made it hard to swallow. Sinking to the bed, both shoulders slumped forward, and her head hung low. "What have I gotten myself into?"

\*\*\*\*

Lukas hid Splotch deep in the forest leaving a good portion of oats and access to water, far off the main road to the Sixth Village. Thinking it better to check out the village on foot, he stayed hidden in the thick bramble bushes that lined the sandy dirt. The day had a deep haze, denser than yesterday, and it was already mid-morning. The main road looked full of travelers. As he walked, he noticed very few half-breeds and wondered if this particular village had a higher population of warlock and witch. Pulling his hood up, he waited to cross the sandy road before the fork up ahead.

The humid air brought a sense of confinement with it. His blue muslin shirt itched around the collar and down his back, his skin coated with sweat. He wanted to push up his sleeves and ditch the cloak, but it was clearly not an option. He swiped an arm across his brow on the edge of losing patience with the wait. The silver talisman plastered to his chest with his sweaty skin strangely heated up. He clutched it through his shirt.

A heavy gust of wind suddenly swirled, causing those on the road to turn or cover their faces. Even the horses neighed in unison and shook their heads becoming skittish. He darted out of the brambles and sprinted across the road with mystical speed. Low to the ground and ready to run, he stayed as still as a statue for a full minute. Running north, the out-lying orchards gave off a clear citrus scent. He passed acres of root vegetables tended by half-breed workers. The ripe scent of sheep irritated his nose when the wind blew from the west.

Entering the village on the street full of livery stables, Lukas counted a half-dozen. He wiped his brow and settled his cloak and hood before stepping into the road as if he had come from one of them and headed east to the open-air market. The first booth he visited sold ale and juice. He purchased two juices, flipping off the tin lid of the bottle, gulping down a citrus-blend that tasted of orange and pineapple. It quenched his thirst and cleared his mind at the same time. He shoved the other bottle into his satchel.

He strolled among villagers, listening to their conversations. Observed their pace, which seemed to be slower, more hospitable. Less haggling with customers and more smiles, too. The produce looked rich, the meats fragrant and varied. Walking further, he saw tents with clothes and bright colored fabrics from silk to cotton. Not too many wool products, which confirmed a warmer climate. The Sixth Village actually had small stores, an apothecary, one full of dry goods, and another sold kitchen supplies. As he reached the end of the street, his eyes narrowed. He quickened his step to the wagon with a shocked smile on his face. "Hello, good baker woman. I didn't expect to see you today." *Or ever again,* he thought.

Bronwyn's face lit up instantly. "I had the good fortune to visit Malcolm yesterday. He swapped my two ponies for quarter horses and a larger wagon, then decided to take the reins himself for a brief holiday at the Sixth Village Sea. We made excellent time on a road I never knew existed," she said with a laugh.

He eyed the cookies. "You have little left to sell."

"Not one cake left after the morning rush. I shall return home heavy with coin on the morrow." Then her eyes slid to the side, and she motioned him close with a jerk of her head. He leaned down and in. "Anika the servant girl is here today. She is limping—so much so that it is noticeable. Yet her grocery list is long, dear Wyn. I listened to the gossip earlier." She clicked her tongue with a sad expression. "She says she tripped and fell into a ravine. Everyone knows it's a lie. There are sand dunes here, but no ravines."

"Why would she lie," he asked, more curious.

"To cover an unnatural truth. And she has been sent to the market on foot—and in her condition, the poor child. So cruel, I tell you." She studied him before saying, "Find another to woo, dear Wyn. Your woman is not kind. She may have powerful skills but does not use them for the good of others. Hers is a dark, dangerous soul. Self-serving and cunning."

"She is not like you, dear Bronwyn."

"I remember the human realm," she whispered. "Didn't always use my power for the good of others in my youth."

"And you chose to jump through the portal years ago during the great exit?"

She gave a slow nod. The wrinkles around her eyes and mouth grew more pronounced. "For the love of my warlock. Now he is gone. I left behind someone very dear to me in the city. It is the burden I will carry to my death as well I should."

The amulet warmed against his chest. "May I ask the city you left?" Her eyes shifted right then left, the tremble visible as if saying it out loud was too dangerous. He wouldn't want to see her hauled from the market and imprisoned, or worse yet, tortured, so he leaned in as if he were going to kiss her wrinkled cheek and whispered, "Did you see planes fly into the two tall towers before they burned and fell?" Her lips immediately began to quiver as tears filled her light-blue eyes. He cupped one cheek and pressed his lips to her ear. "Please don't cry. I didn't mean to upset you. All will be well."

Her mouth turned down and she sniffled, taking his hand from her face and then kissing his open palm. "She is at the butcher's stand and will pass this way soon. Be at your ready, gentle Wyn. Right the injustice."

"Believe me when I say there is more than one. It is an outrage in the human world. Aurora will pay for what she's done."

"And that is why you are here. But how will you get back? There is danger here. Guards will detain you."

"I'm faster than them," he said with a mischievous grin.

"You are not fully human."

"I assure you, I am, with inherited mystical abilities."

Her eyes went wide, and she studied him as both of her wrinkled hands closed around his open palm. A look of wonder crossed her face. Barely an utter under her breath, she said, "You are the Champion's son! Oh blessed be!"

"I must go," he quickly said.

But she held onto him. "Malcolm and I will camp at the third stable tonight. Come if you need us. You will be protected."

"Thank you, dear Bronwyn," he said as he pulled back, grabbing a cookie with a charming smile. Her focus shifted and then he felt an elbow poke his lower back. He heard a high-pitched shriek, turning and catching a girl before she hit the ground. Potatoes rolled out of her cloth bag. Eggs crunched. A wrapped leg of something flew up before hitting the packed sand. Every villager stopped and stared before they turned their backs on her.

"Oh, many apologies, good miss," he said, honestly embarrassed. Tears slid down her bruised cheeks. Her long red hair disheveled; her petite stature reminding him of a pixie. He grabbed the potatoes, stuffing them back into the soggy bag, which he slung over his shoulder before picking up the meat, scenting it, identifying it as lamb. She stood there as if buried knee deep in sand, quaking with tears drip-drip-dripping to the ground like little sprinkles of a spring rain.

"Please don't cry," he said in a gentle tone. With his free hand he grabbed her left elbow and guided her to the corner very aware of her limp. He turned them onto the side street, then into an alley, sitting her down on a high step of some store's back door.

The tears kept coming. He pulled his shirt out of his jeans, squatting down in front of her to gently pat her face with a soft, "Hush, now, no more tears. I will make it all better, I promise." She folded into herself and he recognized the sign of abuse without having to ask. But those silent tears ripped at him, recalling that feeling. "I am truly sorry this happened. Stay here while I—" She grabbed for the leg of lamb and held onto it as if it were a stuffed animal for comfort. "Your bag is saturated with broken eggs. Don't move. I'll be right back."

At the open-air market, he purchased a new cloth bag from the fabric tent and filled it with fresh eggs, replacing turnips, potatoes, and everything else that dripped of runny egg. Luckily, the piece of cake didn't have any liquid on its wrapper, but the potatoes sure did. With an easy gait, he turned the corner and then jogged to her. "Everything's replaced. Everything's good," he reassured. He pulled the bottle of juice from his satchel, popped the tin lid, and offered it to her.

She didn't take it. "I insist. Now drink." Tentative, she took it, and when she handed it back, fresh tears slid down her pale cheeks. "I want you to stop crying," he said in a soft, but firm voice. "We've had enough tears now. You're fine. Your goods are replaced, and I will personally carry them home for you." With a sound resembling a swallowed gasp, she struggled to her feet wincing and shrieked, "No!"

And here came the choice. He knew the tone he had to use. But she looked so frail, probably didn't weigh a hundred pounds soaking wet. "Do not be ungrateful. I refuse to accept your no."

"You... you have to," she sputtered on the verge of more tears.

"Stop crying right now," he firmly stated. Then he took her chin in hand. "Look at me. Come on. Open your eyes and look at me." When she did, he gave a charming smile with a soft, "That's better." His hand brushed down her arm and she jumped. "You're injured."

"Are you warlock?" she asked as her lips quivered.

"Not quite, and no tears anymore, do you understand?" he said in a gentle way. "I'll take that leg of lamb now," and he did, after a comical tug of war. "Now I'll hook your waist and we walk into the brush together. You'll lean on me and keep the weight off your right side." Very slowly he gathered her to him, and they made it to the brush unnoticed. Stopping about ten feet in, when they came to a tree he settled her against it. "Stay right here while I fetch my horse."

"I can't," she said, still shivering. "I... I have to be on my way or else—"

"Or else, what," he interrupted, raising an eyebrow and holding her gaze. "How were you hurt? And don't lie about some errant ravine. I want the truth." He didn't think a person's shoulders could slump any further, but hers did. Plus, she looked ready to cry again.

"I did something that made my mistress very angry."

"Did she beat you?"

She shook her head with a wobble, "I threw something into the fire, and she...she made a...a....a frightening swirl of wind and... and I flew through the air and hit a tree."

Outrage flickered within him. This girl looked petrified! *What had Martine called Aurora? Oh yeah… the dark witch-bitch—now she definitely pays.* "How did you get the cuts and bruises on your face?"

"The harsh winds made leaves and sharp twigs twist into me. Kind sir, I have said too much. I must go. My mistress—"

"Is a bitch. Under no circumstances do you leave this tree," he ordered, abrupt and tight. He turned in the direction of his horse and jogged until out of sight. Placing the new cloth bag carefully on the ground, he'd grab it on his way back. Then his pace ramped up to an unnatural speed. He jumped fallen limbs, sprinted across open fields in spite of the thick humid air pumping through his lungs.

In a flash he untethered Splotch and galloped back through the open meadow. The dapple grey walked through the forest and brush, opening up to a trot where possible. Picking up the bag, he proceeded to the girl. But she was gone. "Fucking hell," he cursed under his breath.

Chapter 29

Mystery Man

Clutching the leg of lamb, Anika limped as fast as she could toward the cottage. Just her luck it was still more than a mile away. Her side hurt so bad that she could only take shallow breaths of humid air. Her empty stomach hurt, too. She'd keep off the sandy road, shadow it through the dense trees until her usual turn onto the path that led her home. "Home. Pfft! This isn't my home," she muttered, alone in this lousy place at the edge of nowhere. "How will I explain no turnips or potatoes for the roast? No sweet chocolate dessert." Her eyes filled and she sniffled again. "You've already cried a bucketful today, you idiot. *He* probably thinks you're a simpleton or something."

*He*. Who is *he*? Not quite as tall as the warlocks in the realm, but the most gorgeous man she'd ever laid eyes on. The dark-blue of his eyes, like royal gemstones. The plains of his friendly face perfectly symmetrical. Even when he simply spoke one's eyes drew to those dimples. His lips were full, very kissable. And talk about strength? *Oh, heavenly realm, he was pure muscle!* She clutched her hip and had to stop. Leaning against a tree trunk she closed her eyes. His face would forever be engraved in her memories like a dream-lover. The way he pulled her to his side, his scent like a fresh-running stream and pine. His manner so kind. Confident yet gentle. She closed her eyes and hugged the leg of lamb. Yet all she had to look forward to was a litany of mean, cutting words. The sound of twigs snapping and a quick snort from a horse made her stiffen against the tree trunk. Her eyes went wide and stayed that way as she held her breath.

"I told you to stay put and you didn't listen," she heard along with his dismount. "Come here, Anika."

"How do you know my name?"

"It doesn't matter. Do as I ask."

The tone he used didn't sound like an ask. She pushed half-way off the huge tree, peeking around it before leaving. He stood next to an odd grey horse with his hands on his hips. *Why do I want to run to him like in those spicy forbidden novels?* With little dignity left, she forced her chin up and started to lurch. When her side cramped, she let out a gasp. Immediately scooped up before hitting the ground, her head rested against his shoulder. He pulled the treasured leg of lamb from her arms and flung it aside.

"Why didn't you just stay where I left you? Damn it. You shouldn't be walking."

"I don't have a choice! It's my punishment for throwing some moldy vial into the bonfire with rotten vegetables." So flustered over trying to explain it, she shook her head. "Oh, why did I leave my father's farm? Why didn't I see the cruelty in her? Now, she's hellbent on doing something I could be tortured and put to death for if the sorcerers find out! I'm a total failure!"

"You're not a failure. Just caught up in something no one in their right mind would do. In any dimension."

She pushed off him until he put her down. Then she

looked him in the eye. "Who are you?"

"Call me Wyn, and I'm here to stop her."

Her mouth fell open and her eyes went from narrow to wide. "You have no idea what you're up against."

"I know exactly what I'm up against. She's a dark witch with a fantasy that isn't going to happen."

"What fantasy? What was in that moldy vial?"

"Her back-up plan."

He didn't make any sense. "I have to get home," she said and started to walk away but he grabbed her arm. "Please. Let me go."

"Not until you hear me out."

"Let me go first. Then I'll hear you out." The wilting leg of lamb wouldn't help her against someone with a broadsword at his back. Someone so strong. If she had to she'd defend herself, but with what? She'd worry about that later. When he let go, she backed away rubbing her right hip.

"Your dark witch friend—"

"She's not my friend anymore."

He rolled his eyes and frowned, in a very attractive way. "Okay. Your dark witch ex-friend plans to get pregnant by someone in the human world."

Her lips quirked to the side and her eyebrows knit. "That's ridiculous."

"She found a hidden portal and slipped into the human world. She has a man under a dark magic spell," he said with an edge to his voice. "That man is an innocent. He is going to die."

"What? There are no hidden portals!"

"She fu… uh, had sex with him and I think that vial was insurance, just in case she didn't get pregnant." The light-blue hue of his shirt made his eyes a darker blue—

as if it were even possible. She could stare at him for hours. "Anika? Are you following me?"

She blinked. "How do you know all this?"

"Not important," he said with a shake of his head. "I'm here for Aurora."

A jolt of fear ran through her. "Are you a spy for the guards or... or the sorcerers? Oh no! Please don't torture me!" She sank to her knees. One hand flew to her heart clutching at her blouse.

"Why would you—? I hate those bastards. Just trust me."

Both hands flew into the air with a grunt. "I've got a lunatic on one side and a mysterious hero on the other who wants my trust. Aurora will kill you before you lay a finger on her."

"Can she walk your mind?"

"No. I don't think so. But she can glamour with the best of them—and she sees things."

"That's good to know. Wait. Did the bonfire you spoke about take place a few nights ago?"

"Yes. But it wasn't nightfall yet."

"Right... day is night, but the timing fits," he whispered.

"No. Day is day, and it was just about sunset."

"When you made her go ballistic she lost concentration. I'm thinking it happened when she conjured up the swirling wind, like a tornado, to punish you. He moved his hand," he said looking at his left one, which didn't make sense. "For a few seconds, her spell wavered."

"You aren't from around here, are you," she said, planting her hands on the forest floor, to crawl away.

"Whoa, hey, I'm not going to hurt you."

"I've heard of those who escape from the Third Realm and come here to drink."

"Oh, good Christ," he muttered. "I'm not a vampire. *Really?* You were just up against me. I'm not as cold as ice and you heard my heartbeat. The truth is—I... I might have heightened senses like one but..." He shrugged.

He didn't look dangerous, but that answer didn't make any sense, either. "You won't stop her. She's become more powerful."

"Yeah. I will. Have you seen her keep something hidden? Maybe another vial?"

"I don't know."

His hands clipped his trim waist and then he palmed his face. "Can you snoop around?"

She shook her head. "I've already said too much. I've got to get back to the cottage. I've got to roast the lamb! She'll be livid if she gets there before me."

His gorgeous eyes narrowed. "Why? Where did she go?"

"Probably the sea." she said. Trying to stand was brutally hard—until Wyn helped her to her feet. He handed her the leg of lamb and stood next to his horse.

"I swear by all that is good, Anika, you have to trust me. Show me the cottage. I'll even let you down a good ten yards from it, just in case she's already there." A second later she was in his arms and lifted to his horse. A second after that, he mounted behind her. She showed him the way to the last cottage deep in the forest but offered nothing more about Aurora. He carefully set her down before dismounting—far enough away, just as promised.

She looked up memorizing the good-looking

mystery man. "Thank you for helping me."

"Promise you'll come to this exact spot tomorrow? I have a plan, but I need your help." He handed her the grocery tote, then touched her cheek and held her gaze. "She takes advantage of your loyalty, Anika. That says she was never a friend. Keep your thoughts guarded. Do not believe for one second that she isn't the most dangerous dark witch you've ever known. I'll be right here tomorrow—two hours before noon. Please be safe."

"You too," she whispered and watched him mount. The charming smile that came at her before he rode away made her heart flutter. Then she pushed him right out of her mind. Closing her eyes, she made up a totally different tale about her market activities today. The story grew like a fantasy in her head. By the time she entered the cottage and put her goods down in the kitchen, she realized that it felt like rewriting history. Simply erase what you want to keep hidden.

Chapter 30

Sacred Spot

Instead of heading back to the Sixth Village, Lukas took a detour. He rode north, but after the smell of sea air became heavy, he turned his horse around and headed south. He closed his eyes and listened. Deep in the forest and many miles later, the sound appeared close and he followed it.

"Wow! What a magnificent thing of beauty." The horse whinnied as he dismounted. A huge flat black stone some feet away looked as if it had been sliced in half to offer a place to sit and think. But this waterfall's rock formation literally disappeared into the misty sky with angry water creating a huge lake. Splotch approached to drink. At the water's edge, Lukas sank down on his knees and sluiced ice-cold water over his head and face. The air seemed thinner here, far less humid. He pulled his shirt off and swished it around in the lake.

"Remind me never to wear muslin *anything* ever again, old man." As if the horse understood, it gave a loud snort and a long raspberry. He sat back on his knees and chuckled. After filling the empty juice bottle with water, he secured the tin cap on it and placed it back in his satchel. The cold, wet muslin shirt brought a shiver to his body, but he couldn't take his eyes off the impressive natural rock formation, sure that this hidden lake was likely very, very deep.

The legend of Gwendolyn came to mind. So did the years he'd been held in this realm by the sorcerers. All three of them had terrified him, but one more than the others. Torturous screams from other prisoners in cells also terrified him. And when dead bodies were dragged past his own cell, the miserable guards took their time so the stench of blood and burnt flesh would be branded in his sinuses.

He sat and pulled his knees to his chest, the same way he had as a frightened kid. He'd rock and shake. His stomach would sour and he'd vomit up what he had been fed. He had breathed fear in and out with short breaths through clenched teeth until he felt light-headed, then he'd fall on his side and curl in a ball on the cell's cold stone floor.

His eyes were open, but they weren't clear anymore. His heart pounded with the recall of the internal war between fight and flight. He scrubbed his face with his hands, blinked and breathed to steady himself. Had he found this lake on one of his run-aways, he'd have taken his own short life rather than be dragged back to that cell.

As if he could sense Gwendolyn standing next to him, he whispered, "They would have found you. Done unspeakable things to make you talk. If you'd have given up where you took your son, they'd have swept the human world to find him. Then kill you, anyway. You did the right thing. What any good mother would do."

Reaching back, he untied his hair. He pulled out the pearl-handled knife and sliced off a generous lock of it, placing it under the leather strip and on the ground near the water's edge. "It isn't much of an offering. But I give you a part of me. Rest in peace. I will help your son get his life back or die trying. This I vow."

Before he stuffed his shirt down his jeans, he used the pearl-handled knife to cut a strip off the hem. Grabbing his hair, he tied it at the nape of his neck. Then he mounted his horse and rode back to the Sixth Village. He had a plan, but he needed Bronwyn's help.

One way or another, he'd drag that dark witch into the human world and save Gwendolyn's son.

\*\*\*\*

Riding for hours, Draven finally said to Michael, "Pardon the cliché, but this is like trying to find a needle in a haystack. A very large haystack."

"My ass is sore and I'm getting grumpy. Make your point," Michael replied in a low monotone.

Draven pulled back on his reins. "You cannot go on. The air is thick with humidity. Your shirt is soaked on your skin. Need I say you smell ripe."

"Yeah? What else?"

He kicked his horse, brought it next to Michael's and grabbed a rein bringing both animals to a halt. "The glare is unnecessary," he said, clipping each word— because the man had to listen. "You need rest and food. You need to dip yourself in fresh water and have a much-needed bath."

"Draven—"

"Don't interrupt, you arrogant bastard. Now *I* am losing patience with *you*. We've been at this for hours. It's like working a grid. Back and forth. Back and forth," he said with his eyebrows touching each other as if they'd been sewn together. "Listen to reason."

Michael blew out a long breath. "I hear you. Two more times. I promise. If we find a stream, we stop."

"Not good enough." The thought of a nip at Michael's neck looked better each passing moment.

His insane travel companion held up a hand. "All right. You win. Let's head north. As soon as we find water of any kind, we stop."

"And I hunt."

"Don't stare at my neck. I know what you're thinking."

A thin smirk began. "It's all the rage in the Third Realm. Feeding off each other, except you cannot bite back."

"I have long, sharp canines, like a reminder of my past. I'm guessing in the event I ever need to bite someone back—in a pinch."

Now that made him laugh, indeed, an extremely rare occurrence. "I promise to bring you something edible, brother." The last word slipped out easily, and no rebuke came. They headed north and many miles later they stopped to listen. Draven took the lead through the dense trees. The sound grew louder, and they rode in silence.

When they saw it, they both stopped. "I have never come across anything like this in the realm," Draven said, admiring the mountainous structure. They rode on for some unknown reason, not stopping at the edge of the lake and skirting it to the left. Michael pulled ahead, which irked him. As much as he hated to follow, he did. Then he picked up a specific scent, certain that Michael had as well. He kept his horse steady and still, watching Michael track it. Hundreds of feet later, Michael leapt to the ground.

Draven dismounted and walked his horse over. "Lukas was here," he said with more emotion in his voice than he intended to show. "What is in your hand?"

He couldn't explain why he asked, his vision and scenting ability as acute as ever. Perhaps he wanted to hear the emotion in Michael's voice when he said what he now held—to experience the sight and sound of something he had lost so long ago. Yet he heard nothing come from the worried father. Michael's fingers brushed a strip of leather and a thick lock of rippled blond hair. He looked up to the sky and the expression on his face was simply indescribable. Beautiful, in a way. Tight jaw. Lips a thin line. Nostrils flaring with each intake of air he needed to breathe. But it was the look in his eyes that stirred something in Draven. They were misted with tears he knew would not fall. He heard the tight swallow, the pounding of Michael's healthy heart as his chest rose and fell. The familiar stance with his legs apart—barely holding him up. Every muscle tense in the man.

He grabbed Michael's arm. The man didn't pull away. In a soft, calm voice, he said, "We are going to walk just a few feet. I will guide you down onto that rock." Getting no response, he proceeded to do so. Then he ran back to the horse, grabbed the empty bottle from the saddlebag and filled it with fresh water from the lake. Determined steps brought him back to his brother in blood. "Drink slowly," he ordered and placed the bottle in Michael's hand closing his fingers around it. "Your heart is racing too fast. Bring it down. You know how to, I'm sure." Each command was followed. When the bottle of water emptied, the man's pulse turned slow and even.

"Thank you," Michael whispered.

"You are welcome," he replied. He walked back to the horse and unrolled the blanket, placing it around his shoulders.

Their eyes met. Neither looked away. They were

different yet the same. How often had they walked together among humans at different gatherings—picking and choosing their next unsuspecting victims? Often thought to be human brothers. Michael broke the connection first. Lost in thought, Draven stepped away and stared at the water.

"My son sat right where you're standing. Thank God he's not been injured."

"You would have scented his blood."

"Absolutely."

"So we know he is safe. And he is close. It is a good sign."

"Yes, a very good sign."

Draven folded his arms across his chest and turned to the man, whose hands gripped his knees, his legs apart and his head hanging down. "I will leave you to hunt. Perhaps you might fish so you can eat."

"I don't fish. I'm fine."

Draven knew better than to believe him. "I will unsaddle the horses a half-mile away, should they be discovered."

"Good."

"Keep your sword at the ready, Michael. I don't know this part of the realm."

Without further small talk, he walked off toward the village. Not only would he hunt. Like a thief, he'd steal something palatable for his travel companion. For himself? There was always the possibility of running into an unknown criminal along the way.

Chapter 31

Rescued

The first thing Lukas noticed was the empty streets of the Sixth Village before sunset. The second? Every single road in and out of the village full of guards. *The side streets are probably full of them as well.* So he had backtracked several miles shadowing the main road.

Guards were strategically placed at half-mile intervals. When he happened upon empty wagons and multiple travelers, he led his horse out of the tall bushes to blend in as if he were one of them, and then made his way across the road and back into the forest to avoid the next checkpoint. Roaming growing fields, he had picked oranges from a grove and devoured them. He stayed to the far-side of the farms and rested his horse wherever possible before going back to the livery stables.

The sun began to set but humidity still hung heavy in the air. A mist formed which provided cover. Seeing the corrals in the distance, he dismounted and walked his horse. Bronwyn's wagon stood off to the side, which told him he had found the right one. He pulled Splotch into the back barn door of the third livery stable. With most of the stalls occupied, he took the empty one near the front, hung his saddlebag next to others and unsaddled his horse. The stable office looked empty, the front barn door slightly open. From what little he could see, a guard stood at the end of the street. He wondered if it was the same on every street. *Why here? Why tonight of all nights?*

"A bucket of fine oats awaits you," he whispered as he patted Splotch's neck in the stall. Checking the office again—still no one to be found. Nevertheless, he dug a silver coin out of his satchel and placed it on the cluttered desk before leaving, still wondering why no one tended the horses.

Grateful to be off the road and out of the saddle, after taking care of Splotch, he had more to explore. With his senses on high alert, he eyed the loft and then climbed up the ladder leading to it. The hay door in the upper gable stood open, and he avoided it, not wanting to be seen by anyone outside. Finding the darkest corner, he shrugged off the leather sheath with broadsword intact and buried it in a mound of hay. Then he laid himself down wrapped in his cloak, and covered himself with hay, leaving a small space clear to see the ladder.

Now he fully understood the meaning of the word weary. His body ached from using muscles he hadn't even thought about. His stomach growled like an irritable lion. The smell of hay and horse, everything coated in humid air, assaulted his sense of smell. As uncomfortable as he was, he needed sleep.

****

The bang of the barn door and muffled voices jarred Lukas awake. Light came from the stable below. The sky was dark, but how long had it been since sunset? He hadn't a clue. When he heard, "That's his horse. I recognize it from the half-breed mutant's stable," come from an unfamiliar voice, a sliver of fear pricked him like a splinter.

Heavy footsteps sounded on the wooden floor below. Booted footsteps. The smell of sweat and ale clogged his nose. "Look here. I found me a silver coin right there on the desk."

He knew it would be pocketed. *Taking what is not yours. The sound of booted feet. They're guards.* He mouthed a curse but made no sound.

"Nobody here," one said.

"Nah. Probably cowering like other half-breeds in some hellhole. Shaking and shivering."

"Check the loft."

"Check it yourself."

"You got the coin, don't ya?"

"Yeah and I worked for it. I checked the last loft. You do it." A scuffle followed. Punches thrown and one of them landed with a thud. The ladder wobbled and clanked against the lip of the loft and then crashed down. Horses whinnied and kicked the walls. Then came the draw of a sword. He knew the sound.

"Get up off your ass, you lazy lout, or I'll skewer you right through the heart and say the murderer did it to another one of us."

Cursing loud and long, the one on the ground took his time pulling himself upright with a grunt. Lukas estimated most of the guard's weight to be in a mid-section paunch. But then the ladder hit the edge of the loft. Ever so carefully, Lukas reached down for the pearl-handled knife in his left boot, fully prepared to use it.

The guard was half-way up when the other one shouted, "You! Ya half-breed mutant. What are you doing in the Sixth Village?"

"Aye, sir, 'tis me, aw righ, sir," Malcolm answered. "I come for me horse."

"The one you sold to the murderer? This ugly piece of horsemeat is scoffing down oats like there's no tomorrow."

"Aye, sir, one and the same. 'Cept I did no sell it, good sir, it be gone from me corral on yester-eve before I ken sell it fer slaughter. I tink it knew it weren't long for this realm."

The ladder bucked and shook until the other guard hit the ground, probably to participate in the menace of Malcolm. "Don't believe a word this one says. Let's arrest *him* as the murderer of our fellow guardsmen. Let *him* swing from the castle wall for all half-breeds to see."

"Och! Nay, good sir, I did no a thin' wrong. I be good folk."

"Mutants are scum. Not worth the juice in my mouth for a spit. You're lying. Liars get their tongues cut out."

"Why would he lie, good sirs?"

*Dear God, that's Bronwyn, and they'll kill her!* His grip on the knife tightened, but his hand tingled as if it had just fallen asleep.

"You are mistaken, good sirs. You came in looking for someone who is not here," she said in a soft, calm voice that made Lukas think he was dreaming. "Both of you fine gentlemen checked the entire stable. You found a treasure to keep you in pints of ale and good food for your bellies. Nothing more in here interests you. Not even the mutant. Your shift throughout the night is uneventful. Now you will go with the satisfaction that you have done your job, and all is right in this stable. You will not enter again."

Lukas shook his head thinking his brain had been scrambled for a few seconds. Then a guard said, "Nah, there's nothing here of interest. How about we get us a good dinner and a couple of pints of ale at the best pub? I found this coin on the street, didn't I?"

"Aye. I saw you pick it up. No. Nothing out of the ordinary here. Good eve to you, good woman."

"Good eve to you both, good sirs."

The barn doors closed. A block of wood dropped into place, on the back doors as well. "It's safe to show yourself now, young man."

Lukas brushed off hay and sat up to replace the knife in his boot. Grabbing his broadsword in its leather holder, he slung it across his back and made his way down the loft ladder. Bronwyn and Malcolm had their backs to the front barn door as he stood at the bottom of the ladder. "I could have gotten you both killed. I'm so sorry. It was a mistake to come here."

"No mistake, laddie," Malcolm said in a serious, soft tone. "Ye be needin' us. The good witch knew and that's why we come back here."

"Many guards arrived this afternoon," Bronwyn said. "Two guards have been found dead and thrown off the road in the Fifth Village. They are after the murderer."

Feeling the flush creep across his face, he whispered, "They are after me."

"Ye kilt em, laddie?" Malcolm asked.

"And I'd have killed again in this stable had they touched either of you. I know how guards operate in this realm. The sadistic bastards like to torture the innocent."

"Aye. Tis true," Malcolm replied before going into the office.

"And you have the scars to prove it," Bronwyn said. Lukas looked away. "Some here tell tales of a boy brought here to suffer and taught to hate."

"You know it's not a tale," he whispered, not embarrassed, but uncomfortable.

"No. It isn't. You're truly Michael's son."

"You're as powerful as the Kendrick witches," he replied.

"My sister and I knew them well. You're Martine's age." His heart skipped a beat at the mention of her name, and Bronwyn's lips curled into a smile as her light-blue eyes almost twinkled. She rubbed her hands together as she approached. "Blessed be your future. Now tell us what you need."

"I have less than a day to get the dark witch and find the hidden portal. I need a potion. Something strong to cloud her brain for two hours."

Bronwyn's face lit up. "Very clever of you to come to the good witch for such a thing. Rest a bit more. Malcolm will stay here, just in case anyone enters. When you wake from a nap, you'll find food in the office. Eat well and then return to the loft to sleep. You must be very alert when you take the next step." Before he could say thanks, she added, "You are truly welcome, Lukas."

Chapter 32

Bonding

As weak sun lit the realm, Draven stood over the sleeping man. Wanting to wake him immediately to share pertinent information, he also knew the need to have Michael rested and well-fed before continuing deeper into the forest to find the hidden portal.

He had already fed well. First on a buck, then on an old man close to death on the side of the road quite far from the village proper. *And humans think vampires are cruel. We kill to satisfy need. Humans kill each other for sport.* Beaten beyond recognition, the old man smelled of guard.

As quiet as he could, he placed the package of goodies down on the ground and then stood. At the edge of the lake, he sank down on his haunches and swirled his fingers through the water. Small waves swelled and dissipated. It felt as if he were touching something that lived, yet just as cold as he. Hearing the change in breathing patterns, he turned his head. "Are you rested from your sleep?"

Throwing off the blanket, Michael replied, "Yes. What is all this." He walked to the water's edge and washed his face, then ran his wet hands through his brown wavy hair.

"Your breakfast. Juice. A decent slice of ham. Three

boiled eggs. A loaf of bread. Cheese and oranges for our travels." He stood and met Michael sitting cross-legged on the ground unwrapping the feast he had proudly procured.

"Plus a tablecloth. How kind of you. Who did you kill for all of this?"

"No one. I raided the kitchen of the pub when the cook left to relieve himself. I could not get silverware, but I'm sure you'll make do. The oranges are freshly picked, by the way."

"Thank you," Michael said as he pulled the shell off an egg. "It's overcast again today."

"We must talk." Draven sat the same way, directly across from him.

"I talk first. I owe you this and more." Michael paused. "Before I left the Georgian Estate in England I read up on Henri LaVigne. Your father was a winemaker. Your mother was a good Christian woman, and you were raised very well outside of Paris in wine country. The vineyard's owner had a pianoforte. His son, about the same age as you, taught you how to play. You led a good life, and you were a kind, moral man. You studied composition at the age of seventeen with composers in Paris." Michael pealed a second egg and ate it. He drained a bottle of juice, ripped off a chunk of bread. Draven sat there in silence, watching him eat. Not even a thread of a memory came into his mind. "At eighteen, you married Marie Dupont, a Parisian who played the cello. You both went on to have stellar reviews and careers. Marie gave birth to a healthy baby boy."

"My son," he whispered. Not a memory—but a feeling tremored through him.

"Julien LaVigne idolized his father. He was gifted, artistic like you and your wife. You taught him piano. Marie taught him cello. Both of you continued to perform. Later in life, he became a violinist who played in a variety of symphony orchestras. He adapted many of your works for small ensembles. They are all dedicated to you. The Georgians have Julien's original scores. Yours as well."

Unable to digest it all, he whispered what worried him the most, "You said yesterday that after my... undeath... Marie and my son left Paris immediately."

Michael nodded, cut a square of cheese, popped it in his mouth, chewed, then swallowed. "She and Julien went to live with your parents. Although she mourned you, she eventually married the owner's son, the same one who taught you piano. He was a good father to Julien. They left France to open a vineyard in Tuscany." One question haunted Draven. As if Michael read his mind, he stated, "You were sired at the age of thirty-two. Julien was about to turn thirteen, the same age as Lukas when I came to this dimension and found him a very broken child."

He absorbed it all, then whispered. "You must truly hate being here."

"No. I hate that my son came back here. I cannot begin to fathom how it must make him feel. I don't care how old he is. I know the boy and I recall every nightmare. He's learned to live with it. I have not." Michael stood and walked away, shaking his head. After a minute, he said with less anger, "Now it's your turn to talk."

"Sit back down. I have much to say." Thankfully, Michael complied. "There are guards on all the roads and

301

on every street. Two guards were found dead in the Fifth Village. Both took a sword right through the heart. They were in the tall grass, many feet from the road, apparently. A hunt is on for a murderer. I assume it is Lukas."

"He knows to go for the heart. It's a sure kill—whether human or demon. Was there a description of him given?"

"No. Only that it is a young warlock reportedly riding a dapple grey. We cannot go back to any village, Michael. We cannot go back through the portal we came from. We'll all use the hidden portal—today. It is no longer safe. Should Lukas be recognized by anyone in the realm, they will arrest him for murder and take him prisoner." Already on his feet before Draven finished the last sentence, Michael reached down and fit the broadsword's leather sheath across his back, then bundled the leftover food and threw it far into the lake.

"Let's go, Draven. I'll get the horses."

"Villagers will recognize the logo on the saddles."

"Then we ditch the saddles, sink them to the bottom of the lake."

"I'm sure they know their own horses. Most probably branded somewhere."

"We'll worry about that later if need be, but not right now. I've ridden bareback. How about you?"

Although hating the idea, he replied, "I was never as proficient a rider as you and Cyril. But I will try."

"Good," Michael said as if he were still lost in a fog.

They broke into a run, sprinting through the forest side by side, and then drew to a silent halt two hundred feet shy of four guards circling their horses. "We can take them," Michael whispered.

Keeping his voice barely audible, Draven replied, "Four more bodies for them to find."

"Not if they're at the bottom of the lake with the saddles. We need our horses, should we not—"

Quickly, he whispered, "We *will* find the portal today, Michael."

" My son may be near. I say we take them."

"No. Please allow me the privilege."

"I hate those fucking bastards more than you."

Getting irate, he hissed a curt, "No. There could be a mistake, you can be injured and I don't know first-aid." The tiny drop of sarcasm slipped out before he could stop it.

"What are you going on about? I still self-heal," Michael murmured.

"One doesn't self-heal in this dimension. Doesn't your son have scars on his body from his time with the sorcerers?" Sensing the quicker pulse, strained silence gave away the answer.

"My son is the one in more danger then."

"Lukas already knew the risks," he replied. "Stay here. Stay hidden. Please allow me." Not only because he could take all four before they knew what 'bit' them, but mostly out of a sense of gratitude for the snapshots of life he now treasured. Answers to questions with no one to ask. *Marie. Julien. I loved my wife and my son. So much lost, never to remember.*

Chapter 33

It Happens Today

Dragging two dead guards with their throats ripped open, Draven turned to Michael, who dragged the other two. "They were slower than I would have thought. Definitely drunk." At the edge of the water, Draven sank down and rifled through their belongings, taking coin and paper currency.

"This one has my son's papers on him," Michael said as he read the documents. "They know the name you gave him, damn it," he mumbled as he shoved the papers in his pocket.

Draven stood and removed his cloak. One by one, bodies were tossed far into the lake, landing midway to the far waterfall. Michael matched his throw each time. Then both of them stood shoulder to shoulder at the water's edge, feet slightly apart and arms locked to their chests.

"Great minds think alike," Draven stated with a smirk.

"Did I ever tell you I hate clichés," Michael replied, crouching down to rinse his face and hands. "Let's get the saddles in the lake as well, then get the hell out of here before more come our way." He inhaled deeply, adding, "You reek of ale. You might be too drunk from the alcohol in their blood."

"I have great stamina," he replied as much-needed sustenance raced through his veins, eager for a good run. Of course, Michael stayed right on his heels, and they made it back to their horses without hearing anything but birdsong in the trees. After mounting, they walked their horses past the lake toward the other end of the realm. Less than a mile later, they stopped in the densest part of the forest. No chirping birds. Just a strange stillness as if warning man or beast to turn back. Shadowing the misty edge, they continued on. The air became heavy, more humid, the mist exceedingly thick.

Michael pulled on his reins and listened before cursing under his breath. "Do not say it."

Happy to further annoy him, Draven said, "We've gone very far out of the way."

"I told you not to say it."

"I never cared for sand or sounds of rough waters." Hearing the dismount, almost afraid to ask, he said, "*Now* what are you doing?"

"Stripping. You said I smelled ripe."

"You could have bathed in the lake."

"Shut up and deal with it."

"Make it quick."

After hearing running footsteps the man made body contact with rolling water. He shifted on the horse. Not about to dirty his boots with even one grain of sand, Draven ticked off the minutes as if he were a timekeeper as well.

****

In the loft, Lukas woke with a start. Seeing out the loft door, the day looked overcast again, and the mist appeared thicker to blanket his movements today. He wondered if chants of protection in another dimension had anything to do with it. As the broadsword settled on his back, he eyed a small brown bottle with a cork stopper by the loft's ladder. Picking it up, he read the note it stood on: Seven drops will do the trick.

Bronwyn had come through! Leaving the loft, he thought about the dinner she had provided last night. A thick slice of ham with honey sauce and roasted potatoes. A dessert of creamy thick custard with glazed berries on top. She had also left two glass bottles of water.

He walked over to Splotch, knowing the time had come to part ways. He said a quick prayer asking that the loyal horse would live out his years in green pastures and with plenty of oats. Leaving the saddle bags, he took only the satchel, placing the small brown bottle safely within, then refilled one glass bottle with fresh water, wrapped it in a cloth and replaced the tin top. It went in the satchel as well. He nuzzled Splotch once more before leaving through the back barn door. Slipping into the thick mist, it reminded him of heavy London fog, a real 'pea-souper,' and offered another prayer of thanks.

With mystical senses on high-alert, he darted past the corral and the farms. A mile later, he smelled the guards before seeing them. Untying his cloak, it fluttered off his shoulders as he grabbed the sword with his left hand. The satchel hit the ground without a sound as he began to move toward the scent. Laughter erupted about ten feet away.

"Can we just tell them the half-breed old scum we beat up last night was the murderer?

"The commanders won't buy it without a body. How much coin did he have?"

"Just enough for a roast-pig dinner is all."

More laughter erupted as Lukas waited for the right

moment. One stepped away, and then peed like a horse. The other stretched with a yawn. His broadsword ran through the guard's heart. When the guard sank to the ground, he pulled it out.

"Drop your weapon," came from behind, the tip of a blade poised at his lower back.

"Make me," he replied, perfectly balanced on his feet with the tip of his own weapon still pointed to the ground. The guard grunted as his sword eased away. Lukas turned, saw the sneer, the lean look of his next victim. Younger and eager as hell. It wouldn't matter. He'd go for the sure kill as he had been taught.

He jumped back just as the guard's broadsword swung, and innate skill took over. The blade had missed him by a hair and although a good fight would be nice, he had someplace to be. The next lunge missed as well, and with a sweeping motion, his blade tore through the guard's shirt and midsection. Grabbing his gut, the guard sank to his knees with wide eyes, the perfect 'oh-shit' look on his face. It didn't matter, either. His sword went right through the heart.

"Nothing but murderers," he bit out before cleaning his broadsword and returning it to the leather sheath on his back. "Burn in Hell, fucking bastards." The satchel settled across his body. The cloak settled on his shoulders. He walked away as if leaving a picnic. Rage was back in its cage. And he'd bring it out again when necessary.

At the orchards, he pulled oranges from the trees; sat and devoured two of them. He picked two more for later. The main road had no traffic, the fog thicker here creating a milky-white blackout. He pulled the cloak's hood low and slipped in far from the posted guards to cross into the brush. As if by magic, reaching the forest the fog thinned. Heading to the cottage with mystical speed, to the exact spot where he had put Anika's feet back on the forest floor, he thought about nothing but capturing Aurora and getting the hell out of this realm.

****

Aurora slept in this morning. Pulling on a pink silk robe, she stared out the bedroom window while scratching her neck. *Such strange weather for October. Humid and foggy like never before.* She fingered the locket between her breasts. Perhaps next week she'd visit the sea again—once the fog was long gone and the autumn skies visible. She scratched her neck, still strangely itchy.

With a dainty yawn, she settled at the table for breakfast. "Good," she said with her nose in the air like the Mother-Queen she'd soon be, "You sensed me awake."

Hearing the respectful reply of, "Yes, my mistress," she added while scratching a knee, "I don't know why I am cheerful today. Perhaps the sea made me mellow. You will not go to market, most likely get lost in the fog and then who would serve me? Pick greens from the garden and berries from the far bushes for my mid-day meal."

With a deep curtsy, Anika replied, "Yes, my mistress."

She ate slowly with care. Was she eating for two? She had very high hopes.

Chapter 34

Zig-Zag Along

Anika cleaned up quickly and thanked the heavenly realm that Aurora decided to bathe herself before retiring back to her bed. She pulled a basket from the counter and headed outside to pick plush, plump greens, and then limped to the farthest berry bushes to pick the ripest ones.

Her mind stayed in the fantasy about the gorgeous hero with the face of an angel and the strength of a warrior. She stepped deeper into the mist with a grin on her face, entirely engulfed in humid fog, hoping to find the exact spot where wonderful Wyn would be waiting.

A hand clamped her mouth. Another had her waist. The smell of stale ale and sweat assaulted her nose. Unable to fight and dragged deeper into the forest, she knew the brute wasn't Wyn. The basket flew off her arm as she kicked and clawed whatever body part she could reach. "I like a feisty little bitch once in a while," her assailant said. When her back hit a tree, the pain in her right side screamed—but *she* couldn't, staring with terror at two realm guards.

"Look what I found. Hold her arms up while I do her," he said with a nasty grin. Her wrists squeezed tight before slamming into rough bark above her head. A hand snaked up her dress clawing her. She squeezed her thighs together with every ounce of strength she had, but when the guard dug his hands into her right leg, the pain shocked her. Tears ran freely down her face with her nostrils flared wide to breathe. A rough hand pawed her again, and although she jerked and twisted there would be no escape.

Through a new swell of tears her wrists fell loose. Then the guard's eyes went wide with a gasp—before his head left his neck and his body collapsed at her feet. Hugging the tree behind her, she felt ready to faint. The hand at the end of a muted-blue sleeve cupped her cheek, then her neck, pulling her to his chest. He smelled of oranges as she tried to suck air down her sore throat.

"Okay. It's okay. I've got you; I've got you." He stroked her hair. "Breathe slow and steady. That's it. Good girl. I've got you… but you have to listen very carefully. The forest is crawling with guards. When I ease you away, you can't make a sound, okay?" Her head bobbed as she swallowed easier now. "Here we go, nice and slow." He held her an arms-length away. Streaks of blood ran down his shirt. His deep-blue eyes, kind and full of concern, searched hers. Those full lips stayed drawn down in a frown.

"Thank you," she whispered, wanting to say more, but thought she'd cry again.

"I'll find your basket, okay? Stay where I put you down and be totally quiet." He lifted her over the dead bodies and moved her many feet away. Minutes later, he hooked the basket over her good arm with the whisper, "Everything's there, salad greens and berries, too." Wyn ducked his head down to be eye to eye. "Now listen carefully again. I'm giving you a potion in a bottle. Sprinkle seven drops on some berries. Make sure Aurora eats all of them as soon as possible. Keep the bottle hidden on your person and wipe what you did from your mind. She should become sleepy. Get her to bed and then open the cottage door."

She nodded. "Like a secret signal?"

"Exactly. Once she's asleep, think about where she'd hide something she doesn't want found. Tell me when I enter the cottage. Do you understand?"

"Yes."

"Because this is all very important. An innocent life depends on it. Are you ready?" When she nodded again, he whispered, "Great."

She took the small brown bottle from him, slipped it down the neckline of her blouse. His one eyebrow rose as he straightened his back with a nod. She stepped away, wringing her hands as if that would make her stop shaking. After a resolute breath in and out, said, "I'm ready."

"You'll do fine. I know it."

Limping back to the cottage, the conviction that Aurora had to be stopped grew stronger, especially if an innocent life was at stake.

The attack rattled her to the bone. *He's an innocent victim. I am as well.* No. Aurora had to be stopped. She'd eat every berry coated in the potion. As Anika entered the cottage, she decided to use nine drops instead of seven. Like her mother had always told her, more is better than less.

Lukas watched her leave. After disposing both bodies deep in the bramble bushes, he cleaned his broadsword with his cloak. Already sweating, he didn't put it back on. Once Aurora ate those berries, he'd take her back to the waterfall by the lake. Surely his father and that vampire had already found his scent there. If not, he'd wait for them. When the dark witch woke up, the three of them would force her to reveal the portal. Then he'd be out of this realm, never to return again.

As the mist thickened, he silently made his way to the huge oak tree closer to the cottage. A gust of wind blew revealing the wooden steps. He had planned perfectly. Sitting underneath it, he ate an orange and drained the last bottle of water in his satchel. Then he leaned back, stretched out his legs, and waited.

****

Irritated beyond belief, Draven walked with Michael at his side. They had encountered more guards. This time, *both* of them made quick work of killing them. This time, they left their horses, sensing it better to go on foot. Between the fog and the high bushes, they were easily out of sight. Once back on track, they made their way to the edge of the realm at the waterfall fully alert. "Look over there," Michael said as he pointed. Draven followed. Michael crouched down and brushed at fallen leaves. "It's a path. With a female's scent."

It was very narrow, and they stayed silent as they walked. About a mile later, they both stopped and listened to a distinct hum. Both of them recognized it. They walked closer, but three feet from the source of the sound, Draven grabbed Michael's arm.

"I'm not about to throw myself through it. Let go," Michael hissed.

He didn't. "I know you're not an idiot. And I doubt you would leave this realm without your son."

"Correct on both counts, vampire."

"We are back to name calling so soon?" Just as he let go, Michael pulled his arm away with such force that he landed on his ass. "How satisfying. It's almost comical. What's the old saying? If looks could kill?"

"Asshole," Michael muttered, quickly on his feet, brushing off his cloak. "Why did you grab my arm?"

"The hum is different."

Michael's shoulders shrugged slightly. "And what would that mean?"

"It is the slightest tear. I'd say no larger than a dime. My guess is it only widens with magic."

"You *are* kidding, right? We get this far only to learn we cannot bloody well open it ourselves? Perfect. Where are we going to find a witch or warlock we can trust in this fucking hellhole of a realm?"

"Aurora must open it. That's all." The litany of foul language spewing from Michael's mouth seemed to him just as comical as the arrogant bastard landing on his ass. "I applaud your colorful command of the English language, but cursing won't make it grow any larger." Michael wrenched the cloak off his shoulders and as it hit the ground, he walked away. "Where are you going? I demand an answer."

He stopped walking, turned to Draven with murder in his dark eyes. "I am following the scent of the woman. Obviously it belongs to the dark witch. *Obviously* we follow the scent, we find her, and then we go from there."

"We held up our end, Michael. Let your son take care of his."

Michael walked back to him with eyes blazing like dark expensive liqueur in a cut-crystal glass, his eyebrows knit tight, his lips a simple slash. "It doesn't work that way, Draven. Think for a moment. Put your ego aside and your hurry to jump through that thing on the back burner. Chances are, Lukas already knows where the dark witch lives. I'm guessing she doesn't take five-hour hikes, which means her house isn't many miles away from where we are. I'm guessing Lukas has a plan, already somewhere close, watching and waiting for the right moment to grab her. I'll let him do his thing. But as his father, I absolutely will do mine as well. Now. Are you coming with me or are you going to stand guard over that damn thing?"

Although Draven hated to admit it, his angry companion was right. Perhaps a quick ounce or two from her lovely long neck would hasten her desire to open the portal for them. Then, in the event the deceitful woman tried to escape, he'd be able to find her quicker than either Michael or Lukas. "Lead the way, brother," he replied as he removed his cloak, "I'm right behind."

Chapter 35

Execution and More

Steadying her hand before replacing the little brown bottle inside her blouse, Anika put the healthy salad and a bowl of berries in front of Aurora. "These are especially ripe today, my mistress."

"Hmmm. I may save them for later."

"Yet they do such wonders for your beautiful skin. Plump blackberries are rich with vitamins. How could something so sweet and tasty be so good for you?" She gave an eager smile.

"Very well. But they are too large. Cut them up and place them over the greens for me."

"Yes, my mistress." Anika took the plate back to the counter. She used a knife to cut them and a spoon to place them strategically on top of the greens, very careful not to touch them. With a curtsy she returned the plate to the table.

Aurora took a forkful of berries, then looked at her. "These are beyond delicious. You may try one."

*What!!* "Oh! Oh no, thank you, my kind mistress. They are for you and your beauty."

"I insist."

"I may be allergic, which would take my breath away and then I could not serve you."

There came a pause. A long one. "Very well." she

finally replied and took another mouthful of berries.

After reaching the counter, Anika blew out a slow, silent breath… and waited. She scrubbed the sink before facing Aurora again. *Now for part two.* "Might I suggest a nap after mid-day meal to further enhance the vitamins in the blackberries, my mistress? It is such a lazy, humid day."

With no berries left and the greens half eaten, Aurora leaned back in her chair. "For once, you make a good point. Perhaps we have turned a corner on your insolence."

****

It seemed to take forever for the cottage door to open. When it did, Lukas was ready to grab Aurora and meet up with his father and Draven to get the hell out of this realm. He stood up and adjusted the broadsword against his back. He pulled the satchel across his body and walked to the cottage.

Coming up the path he turned to the left. Shocking pain shot through his right thigh. His lips drew back as his teeth locked. Looking down, he saw a hunting knife buried deep into the muscles. He pulled it out unable to stifle a yelp of pain. Dashes of light claimed his vision as he bent forward. He blinked and breathed through his mouth.

"Nailed you good, fucking murderer. I knew there was a good reason for us to split up. I get to keep the coin reward all to myself now." The guard let out a whoop as he approached with a swagger, the idiot so full of himself that he hadn't bothered to draw his sword.

Rage raced to the surface as Lukas pushed off with his left foot at just the precise moment. Their bodies vaulted through the air together, but the guard absorbed the weight of the landing. He had the bastard tackled on the ground, straddling a wide chest while slamming his fists into the guard's ears, enjoying every yowl of pain.

"You have no idea who you're dealing with," he hissed. After a brutal jab to the throat, he grabbed the guard's head and twisted. The body stilled. He rolled off, grabbed his right thigh and moaned before planting his left foot on the ground to haul himself up. Waves of pain shot down his right leg and back up to his groin. He spit in the guard's face and then with his hand pressed to his bleeding thigh, he turned and limped to the cottage. Nothing would stop him. Nothing could. Holding tight to the railing, he hopped each step and made it inside. Anika's eyes went wide as her hands flew to her face. "I'm okay," he got out. "Where is she?"

"In here," she said grabbing his arm.

His right leg felt like jelly and allowed her to take a little of his body weight like a crutch, wincing as they limped and lurched. The wound hurt like hell, but once he eyed Aurora, stone-cold determination resurfaced. The devious bitch looked like a sleeping beauty with one arm bent above her head on the pillow, her face turned to the side with her lips partially open. In a slinky pink nightgown, the lowcut neckline gave a glimpse of her full breasts. He shook his head, then poked her shoulder. She was totally out of it.

"Give me the bottle," he ordered. It came to his hand, and he shoved it into his satchel.

"I put an extra two drops on the berries," Anika said with a quiver in her voice.

"Good girl. Very clever. What did you find?"

"Nothing out of the ordinary. You're bleeding," she added.

"I'm fine. It will heal very soon," he lied. "It has to be here. Something she never lets go of."

Anika rummaged through dresser drawers before a hand swept under the mattress, but then she sucked in a gasp. "Look, look, Wyn," she said pointing to Aurora's graceful neck. He hooked a finger and pulled up the chain, which had a five-sided amulet of silver attached.

"Has she always worn this?"

"No. In fact, I never saw it before I left for a few days. Aurora ordered me to go, and when I came back… Wyn, it hasn't left her neck!"

"Makes sense," he said as he turned it around to study it. Not about to see what could happen if he yanked it loose, he tucked it between her breasts again. A sharp pain shot through his thigh, and he grit his teeth. *And where in hell is that guards partner?* "Look. I've got to hurry. Get to the market. Find the baker woman named Bronwyn. Tell her Lukas sent you. She'll keep you safe."

"Lukas," she said like a question.

"That's my real name. I don't have time to explain. Go now. Be safe."

"I'll take her. The roads are crawling with guards." With a quick turn of his head, he welcomed the sight of a familiar face. His father eyed the wound but said nothing as he came closer. Grabbing a pink robe off the bed, his father tore a wide strip, winding it around his upper thigh many times before tying it with a sturdy knot. "Get her to the portal with Draven. I'll meet you there."

"I gave her a sleeping potion that Bronwyn made."

"Bronwyn," his father whispered.

"She knows the Kendricks, Dad. We can trust her."

"How long will she sleep?"

"About two hours."

Anika tugged his arm. Lukas leaned in. "I… I gave her nine drops, not seven."

He met his father's eyes. "Oh. Right. Maybe longer. Get her to Bronwyn and keep her safe." But Anika gripped his arm tighter, shaking her head. "Don't be afraid. He's my father. He's strong like me." He peeled her fingers off as she eyed his father as if very suspicious. "Honest. I swear he'll protect you, won't you, Dad?"

"Absolutely, son," his father replied with a rare open smile directed at Anika. "Come on, honey. Give me your hand. I'll get you to safety. There's a pony in the barn, correct?" She nodded, but when she didn't budge, he added, "I have two daughters a bit younger than you at home waiting for me to return."

"Go on. And thank you," he said to her. To his father, he whispered, "A guard assaulted her. I stopped him before—" Her arms shot around his neck and her lips pressed to his. His eyebrows lifted high, but he'd not have her feel awkward by pulling away.

When she did, she sighed and said, "Thank you, Lukas. I… I—"

"You're very brave to have helped me. I couldn't have done this without you. Bronwyn will care for you. You can trust her. But we'll keep this kiss a secret." Her smile lit the room like a pretty paper lantern. He swiped a tear off her flushed cheek with his thumb. "Now go with my father."

She stood and took the extended hand. Before they left, his father turned in the doorway. Pride and concern lit his eyes. "Get a move on, Lukas. Draven's waiting."

"Right, " he replied.

As soon as they were out the door, he prepared

himself for the agony of what needed to happen next. He grabbed Aurora's arm, slinging her over his left shoulder. As he stood, he hissed, then moved as fast as he could through the cottage and down the steps. A few feet into the forest, he came upon Draven standing over a dead guard, his tongue rimming his lips.

Lukas jerked his chin. "His partner's already taken care of... right over there."

Eyeing his leg, the vampire said, "Let me take her from you."

"Just keep your fangs in your mouth, okay?"

The look Draven gave made him chuckle—because the eye-roll with both hands flying into the air said it all. Draven had her over a shoulder, then reached out and hooked his waist. Lukas tried to pull out, but "I insist. So deal with it," came at him as an order.

"Did my father tell you to say that?"

"Just walk," the vampire replied.

## Chapter 36

Rage

Far down the path, Draven veered off heading south at a slower walk. A mile or so later, he sank down on the flat-topped rock at the edge of the lake, scenting his father, knowing he had been right here. How safe would he be alone with Anika on the road? His stomach cramped, his leg twinged with pain, and his anxiety level rose, mopping cold sweat off his brow.

Draven dropped Aurora on the ground like a rag doll. "I would have gotten her off my shoulder a bit more gently. But then I thought about it again." Looking down at her, he added, "She's out cold. Hopefully, we can quickly revive her—convince her to open the portal before we're out of time."

His entire right leg started to throb. Touching his thigh, he felt his temperature rising. But then his eyes narrowed. "Wait. What? What did you just say?"

"I know you have the same ability to hear the softest murmur." After an egotistical smirk, the vampire added, "I have located the portal, but Aurora needs to open it. It appears to be locked."

"Like hell," he bit out, then mumbled, "fuck," under his breath.

"How else do you propose we get her back to our world? I don't do magic."

"I thought all she had to do was lead us to it. You never said she has to be awake. You never told me that! Christ! She'll be out for hours, and this fucking realm is crawling with fucking guards." Rage simmered below his skin as sweat trickled down his temples. "Then let's forget about the portal. We go back the way we came."

"You just said the realm is crawling with fucking guards. We cannot risk it."

The scent of the dried guard's blood clogged his nose as particles of fear prickled his skin. His gut lurched again and he swallowed hard. Less in control, he bit out, "You knew there would be an army of guards coming after us, didn't you."

"I didn't expect you to kill two and leave them where anyone could find them. That was your mistake. And keep your voice down."

"What did you do, huh? Collude with the shithead sorcerers or something?"

Draven suddenly stood over him, looking down with his arms laced across his chest and his feet slightly apart, his facial expression tense and tight. "You are dripping with sweat, flushed, and bleeding from an injury, so I will ignore your comments assuming you close to delirious."

"Fuck you," he said loud and clear. "What deal did you make? What's your secret plan? Turn us in? Save your own ass by giving us to the sorcerers? They'll pay a fortune for me. Then they can finish the job they started when I was a kid. As for my father, he destroyed their links to the human world and over-populated their realm with witches, warlocks, half-breeds and human slaves to live in this shit-hole! They'll have a field day on him. Like fucking hell. I'll kill myself before they take me back!"

"Lukas! Don't talk nonsense."

The vampire sounded just like his father. "Don't," he yelled, threw up a hand, finding it difficult to breathe the hot, humid air.

"Keep your voice down. I don't want the taste of guard in my mouth again."

"Yeah. Cross-contamination of human blood with the likes of those bastards must be a bitch. I hope you choke on it." He leaned to the side on an elbow, ready to puke as blood dripped down his leg. "Let it fucking stick in your throat like a fist."

"Lukas. Stop."

"Who the fuck are you to tell me to stop?" he yelled.

Just about to go at it again, Draven cuffed his upper arms, pulling him up and off the rock until they were eye to eye with his feet barely touching the ground. The vampire's eyes flickered amber before quickly returning to a natural state, still ablaze like roaring fires and just as intense. "You are crossing a line far too quickly for an intelligent young man." This close up, Lukas noted his long fangs. "Out of respect for your father, I am asking you nicely—to stop."

With a mischievous grin, he said, "Well, since you ask nicely." Then he kicked hard. Draven's footing faltered and he let go, which sent Lukas's right knee into the sharp edge of the rock before landing hard on his injured leg.

A groan of intense pain shot up his throat. No dashes of light this time. A whole galaxy of stars appeared! His eyes filled and his nose dripped. "Fucking bastard," he bit out through the brutal pain. "You re nothing but an undead thing! A cagey, crafty undead thing! You deserve

a friggin' stake through your heart. Fucking bastard."
Sniffling and swiping at his eyes, he rolled over in pain.
Seconds later he felt himself pulled up. His ass slammed
down hard on the rock. Nauseous and hurting, he bent
forward to hug his knees with a long, low groan and
biting his lower lip. The leather sheath and broadsword
came off his back and hit the ground.

# Chapter 37

Hidden Portal Home

"Do not dare open your mouth. I see you've met the other side of my son. The side I do *not* tolerate."

"Shit," he muttered.

"I said not one more word." Lukas's chin stayed hooked with an unyielding hand, forcing him to see the no-nonsense expression on his father's face. "Draven is not about to sell us to the sorcerers. He'd be dust and bone before you could count to three."

Still ready to fight, he jerked out of that tight grip. "Yeah, right. Keep telling yourself that. Just let me get my hands on him. Fucking bastard."

"Draven told you to stop. Now I am," his father stated in a sharp tone. "Your wound is probably infected, the guard's knife most likely not clean. This is a nasty gash on your knee, and your jeans are ripped. I know. Your stomach is cramping and you're sweating profusely as if fighting off an infection."

Draven handed him a glass bottle of water. He turned away, muttering, "Like I trust you didn't poison it."

"Drink," his father ordered.

He grabbed the bottle from the vampire and chugged it down, breaking into a coughing and wheezing fit afterward. The bloody bandage came unwrapped from his leg and his stomach really rolled! After soaking it in lake water, his father wrapped it tight again.

Now the knife wound stung like hell. "I fucking hate this place. All of it."

"I said enough," his father yelled.

When Draven moved aside, the 'fuck you' stuck in Lukas's throat. Bronwyn knelt next to Aurora. She caught his eye, and he quickly looked away.

His father rummaged through his satchel, threw his last remaining orange to Draven who caught it mid-air. "Peel the skin off a wedge. Soak it in the potion and rub it over her lips and teeth to keep her asleep. Bronwyn will open the portal," his father stated handing the vampire the little brown bottle.

"Don't fucking trust him," he mumbled, swiped his sleeve across his hot forehead. Then they locked eyes, and Lukas definitely wasn't prepared for *that* particular look. "I will warn you one last time. Stop right now, little boy," his father growled.

"Just had to use those two words for *him* to hear," he said pointing to Draven.

"Absolutely. Tuck away that temper. I don't care how sick you feel. It's no excuse. Injured or not, I will get parental."

*Just an empty threat,* Lukas thought but didn't dare say. Yeah. He really did feel sick. Dizzy and nauseous, too. And this was going nowhere fast.

"Did you hear me?"

"I hear you," he whispered.

"Good. Now let's get on with this." His father helped Bronwyn to stand.

"She'll be asleep for hours, Michael. I'm positive I'll be able to link to Mary's healing circle for help."

"Perfect. Let's get to the portal, shall we?"

When Draven picked up Aurora, handed her off to his father, Lukas scoffed with a snicker. "What, afraid he'll take a bite?"

"Well there's that, but I told you, not one word. He's all yours, Draven."

"He's not touching me," Lukas yelled, struggling to stand, "Oh hell no!"

"Oh hell yes," Draven growled handing his broadsword to his father. "Ready? Up and over."

Pulling his arm back with his fist tight and ready to swing, his father grabbed that fist, bit out his name in that low, menacing tone. "Now you are *very* far out of line. Stop it!" Turning to Draven, added, "Get him over a shoulder. If he utters one word—*one* word—smack him good and hard." Grabbing his chin once again, stated, "Am I clear, little boy? He has my permission." Woozy, hurting, and now insulted as shit, he didn't dare speak. Landing over Draven's shoulder, an unmovable arm hugged the back of his thighs.

They began to walk. "My dear Bronwyn, please stay between us for your safety. If you need to stop and rest, we will oblige."

*Wow... from menace to charming in seconds, another talent*, Lukas thought. He felt achy all over, hot and cold at the same time. Not liking this position at all, he seethed but kept his mouth shut.

"I'll be fine, Michael," Bronwyn replied as if talking to an old friend.

"Will Malcom take care of the girl?"

"He will bring Anika to her family as soon as it is safe to travel."

His father didn't reply, and both man and vampire

kept their pace slow and steady on the narrow path. Then suddenly lightheaded, Lukas felt an odd pressure in his chest. The low hum of a portal clawed at him. When they got even closer, the vibration buzzed in his ears and his stomach fully soured.

"Come with us," his father whispered. "The Georgians will find your sister. I promise."

"It is too much to ask, Michael."

"Martha wouldn't want me to leave you here. And I owe you much more than a jump through a portal for helping my son. Please. For Martha."

"But it wasn't part of your plan," she said with a quiver in her voice.

"Live out the rest of your years where you belong. Then I can truly repay this debt. You will have every comfort, four very different seasons…Chinese take-out—"

"Please, dear woman, say yes already," Draven said with a hint of irritation. "Here's the small tear, the opening. Do you see it?"

"I do," she replied, "Now we must all stand tight together. Draven on my right and you, Michael, on my left. Both of you tighten your hold on Aurora and Lukas. Once we link arms, both of you must concentrate on the place where Aurora entered the prime dimension. Hopefully, what I sense to say will open it wide enough for all five of us. When we jump through, please hold on to me. I don't want to end up somewhere in New Jersey."

"Will you be able to close it," his father asked.

"Yes. Once in the human world, I will link to Mary's mind. She will link to the healing circle and we will seal it shut. But once I start, think of where we will land." All Lukas could think about was Martine. Only Martine as he fought through pain, shivering with sweat.

"Hear me, portal, where I stand. Feel me, portal, brush my hand. When we travel let us through. Then to seal, ne'er open anew. Blessed be good. Blessed be right. Take us home to where it is night."

The hum grew louder, drumming in his head before surging to deafening. The ground trembled, and Draven's grip on him tightened. Almost incoherent, he panicked in the void unable to open his eyes as he felt pulled every which way. He grabbed onto Draven's belt trying to suck in a full breath of air. His chest grew tight as his heart hammered. Then he curled on the ground, cold and hot at the same time, his leg throbbing like a sonofabitch. His body jerked as he moaned. His shoulders lifted and he leaned back as a warm, steady hand came to his forehead.

"Bronwyn has her, Michael. Aurora is still unconscious. I'll run to the club and have the limo driver bring me back. Your son needs medical attention."

"Run fucking fast, brother."

A heavy thud sounded. He turned to the side and coughed repeatedly before he threw up. A strong familiar arm brought him to a place of comfort. "I've got you, little boy. Dear God, you're burning up."

Lukas's world went dark.

Chapter 38

Home, Not Safe

Martine felt a lurch of her heart. Then the cell phone buzzed in her pocket. She pulled it out to see Draven's name and the word: EMERGENCY!!! She sucked in a breath and then read the full text. Shooting out of the chair, she ran to Dottie in Cubicle S. The look on her face must have been pure panic because Dottie left her patient's side, ran over and grabbed her shoulders. "I need help. I think I need help. Can you leave," she said looking past her friend to the patient in the bed.

"Sure. Jose can cover."

"I... I need two more beds. We can move your patient to the other side."

"Sure," Dottie replied, running out and over to the other ER corridor.

*Breathe. Stop thinking about Lu and just breathe.* She paced with the curtain wide open in case Dottie's patient needed her. Jose came running around the corner. "I got you, M." he said.

When Dottie appeared, Martine knew she had to say something. "What you see next has to stay between us. Everything will be smoothed over with administration. This all has to do with Christopher. I can't explain any further. If you aren't comfortable, I'll make other arrangements."

Both of their heads bobbed in unison.

"I'll move the patient over to the other side. We have open beds tonight," Jose whispered. He unlocked the rolling bed and maneuvered it down the hall. Thirty seconds later, he rolled an empty bed into Cubicle S. "Juan from maintenance said this wing of the ER is closed off. Some special patients might be highly contagious."

"You don't need to suit up with any sterile gear or masks. Things may get weird, but just go with it. Dottie, keep all the curtains open and stay with Christopher. Jose, get Isobel in the farthest bed by the back wall. The two patients coming in, Lu, uh… the male goes in S, which means the female goes in R for now."

"And Isobel is in T. Right?" Dottie asked.

She gave a quick nod. "Jose, can you stay with Isobel?"

"Whatever you need."

"Thanks. Some private nurses will be arriving. Maybe even a doctor we don't know. It's okay. All approved. Get bags of saline hung up. The female may need her stomach pumped… not now… but eventually." Then her eyes began to tear, and she swiped at them with her fingers. "I'll need a suture kit and penicillin for the male going into S, ready and waiting." She turned and ran to the ER entrance just as a limo screeched to a halt.

Pulling out her phone, she texted her mother: It's begun. Aurora here. Lu injured. After hitting send, she pocketed the phone and turned her head both ways. The hall was empty except for the Georgian standing next to a DO NOT ENTER sign on a hospital stanchion. He gave her a nod. Then her attention turned to three individuals walking through the doors and the two being carried.

Bitterness rumbled inside when she saw Michael carrying Aurora. His nostrils flared, his long wavy hair all askew, and his lips a thin line. Murder stood in his dark eyes. Dried blood covered his shirt. He looked like hell. Draven had Lu limp in his arms and cradled to his chest. The tourniquet on Lu's right thigh looked soaked with fresh blood. The vampire's dark hair was still bound at the nape of his neck and neat. But the look on his face... the same as Michael's, and blood covered his shirt as well.

Her gaze drifted down to the wrinkled woman with a head of wild gray hair looking like she'd just come out of a wind tunnel. Her face locked in an expression of concern, her eyes light-blue and sparkling. Martine dipped into her mind and shivered. "Oh," she said, "Welcome, sister."

"I'm Bronwyn. Me and mine knew Martha long before you were born, Martine Kendrick. Blessed be."

Her sixth sense clanged like cathedral bells. Now she shivered from head to toe, so much so that her cheeks tingled. She took Bronwyn's extended hands in hers. *Full power of a good witch.* "Dottie," she called louder than she had wanted to. Dottie ran to meet her. "Please take her to your dementia patient and stay with her. Check her vitals immediately. Send Jose to Cubicle R to monitor the female they just brought in. I'll take Cubicle S," she said as her heart raced. "But as soon as the other nurses arrive, I've got to ask you and Jose to leave. I'm sorry."

"No worries, M. We'll go to the other side of the ER," Dottie said with a grave nod.

"Thanks," she replied.

Thirty seconds later, all blood pressure machines

were in use. Monitors beeped like a mechanical music ensemble, the staff moving like one entity. No matter how hard she tried to distance her emotions from the warrior in the bed, her heart pumped wild in her chest. *Blood on his face, hands, and shirt. High fever, injured knee and thigh... Unconscious... Oh God, Lu!*

Draven stood over him like a bodyguard. "His personal physician is on-route. Michael called him in the car. He should be here shortly."

"I need more," she quickly whispered.

"He was stabbed by a guard. Is it the fever that renders him unconscious? Was he poisoned by the knife in his thigh or is it an infection? Shouldn't he be awake already?"

"Too many questions, Draven. Why isn't he self-healing," she asked as if thinking out loud.

"No wound occurring in the Second Realm will self-heal. Unfortunately, like the scars on his back and chest, it will mark him."

*Scars? What scars?* Maybe she didn't hear correctly. She picked up a surgical scissor from the prep tray and cut the bandage off his upper thigh. The wound looked an angry bright red, but how could it be infected already? How long ago had he been stabbed? Just about to ask, a hand came to her shoulder. She expected it to be Draven, but it was Marsha, the Georgian nurse with a doctor she'd never seen before.

"Doctor John Baker," Marsha whispered to her.

He took the surgical scissors from her hand. "Thanks," he said in a friendly tone. "You must be Martine. I'll take it from here." Martine nodded to Dottie and Jose, who left immediately, and pulled the cubicle curtains closed. She cast a quick spell so that no one

M. Flagg

would hear them and then zeroed in on the doctor. A quick probe of his mind told her many things. He'd known Lukas since the event with Michael some sixteen years ago. Memories of a jet, scars on a terrified boy as the doctor examined him. It all swept through Doctor Baker's mind like drifting snow in a blizzard. Marsha pulled Lukas's right boot off as the doctor began cutting away his jeans from the ankle up. "He's in excellent hands, Martine. Paige will be in soon to assist," Marsha said, which also meant she should leave them now.

"Draven," she said as she walked to the curtain. The vampire stood there with his hand on Lukas's shoulder as if he didn't want to leave. She called his name again, and he followed her into the cubicle with Aurora.

Bronwyn's eyes, red-rimmed when she looked up, were just as powerful as her sister's. "No words necessary, Bronwyn," Martine whispered.

"Destiny brought Isobel to you and led your Lukas to me."

Not about to try and explain her relationship to Lu, she whispered, "Blessed be."

"Aurora is asleep with an opioid compound. She's heavily dosed." Bronwyn's fingers grasped the amulet hanging around Aurora's neck.

"Is it the apex of the spell?"

"I believe so," Bronwyn replied.

"How's my son," Michael asked, jarring her from further probes of Bronwyn's mind.

As if in a trance, she replied, "Doctor Baker and a Georgian nurse are with him."

"Good," he simply replied. Worry came off him like leaves raining down to the ground in a gust of wind. She could relate. "I want to rip that thing off her neck,"

Michael growled in a low tone, ripe with disgust.

"No, you mustn't touch it," Bronwyn said. "She must be awake. Cognizant of her crime. Only then will it open."

Draven, standing on the other side of her bed, growled low. "Let me have a taste and I'll tell you how much is in her system."

"Like hell," Michael shot back.

With his arms folded across his chest, Draven's eyes slid to him. "It will serve another purpose besides giving us medical information."

"Yes. I know. Once bitten, always found," Michael said with a nod. "I need your word it's a taste and not a deep draw."

Martine's jaw dropped and her eyebrows shot up. "You're not actually going to let him bite her, are you?"

"I know what I'm doing, Martine," Draven said.

"No. I won't let you."

"You won't stop me," Draven replied in an even tone.

"What if it dopes you up? How the hell do I explain a sleeping vampire to my colleagues? What if it has the opposite effect and you go all, uh, fangs and no reason."

"Do you seriously think I don't know the effects of an opioid?" His voice sank to just above a whisper and he leaned over the bed to her. "I'm not taking a pint. I'm taking a sip. To serve a higher purpose. What if she casts a spell and decides to bolt? Drugged or not, she has mastered many dark arts to pull this one off. Use your head, Martine."

"He has a point," Michael said as if he agreed.

"What!? I thought you didn't trust him," came out a tight low whisper.

"We've bonded," Draven said in a casual way. Michael glared at him but didn't reply. "Please leave us."

Stubborn and shocked, she said, "Hell no! I stay right here."

With an incline of his head, he replied, "As you wish," and lifted Aurora's wrist.

His fangs looked long and sharp. The legendary beast-within didn't surface, his warm-brown eyes remained the same. Was it a glamour or self-control? She truly hoped the latter—as his fangs pierced her skin. A shiver shot through her, witnessing what she never expected to see. Suddenly he was licking the tiny punctures. *Incredible!* He locked his lips as his tongue worked his mouth. "She'll be out for hours."

*Wow!* She had to ask, "It's that strong a dose?"

"But her heartbeat is strong and steady."

She cleared her throat. "Then we'll pump her stomach."

Michael gave a solid nod. "Johnny will do it when he's finished with my son."

Everything appeared set and ready out on the tray. Thank heavens, because she really had to sit down after what she had just observed. The pull to her psyche when his fangs slipped into Aurora's wrist gave a sensation she'd never experienced. Sensual in an odd sort of way. Now she fully understood why Michael ordered her to stay away from Draven. If a vampire tasted you, you were forever his. Invisibly branded with nowhere to hide.

Chapter 39

Who Am I?

Her heart remained wrapped around Lu, but her feet took her to Christopher. At the foot of the bed Dottie stood with the patient tablet in hand. "Doc Forster wants his vitals." Martine sprawled in the chair at his side, scrubbed her face and after a full intake of air through her nose, her cheeks puffed out with a long, slow exhale. "You look exhausted, M."

"And I've got hours to go, Dottie." She appreciated the concern, and someday she might even tell Dottie what was really going down in this ER wing. *Someday. Not tonight.*

"That young nurse who relieved you yesterday came in. She went directly into Cubicle S for the man they brought in."

"Thanks, Dottie." *Paige is with Lu instead of me? Okay... A little jealous here.*

"My God," Dottie whispered, "I know this is on the inappropriate side, but I've *never* seen so many gorgeous men in this ER at the same time. First there's this one, our very own handsome sleeping beauty. Then, that tall piece of eye-candy with a ponytail who carried the cutie pie in like he weighed nothing. Ooh, he is something to look at, M, with a face like a young Brad or that cute quarterback in Kansas City. Except he's got some head of hair!"

Martine's lips curled into a quick smile. "You nailed it, Dottie."

"And that other tall, dark and handsome hunk carrying the woman? Those mussed up waves? Good God almighty," she said with jazz hands over her head as if she were on Broadway.

Perfect descriptors like that deserved a bit of info. "Lukas is the blond cutie carried in by Draven, who is very much off limits, so get him out of your head *completely*. Michael, the totally gorgeous hunk is an old family friend." *Like hundreds of years old.* "He's Lukas's father, and very happily married." *Thank goodness she didn't ask about Aurora.*

Dottie's hands clipped her hips and simply stared at her. "Any more friends like that unattached and available? How about the doctor? He's pretty handsome, too," she said with a laugh.

"I've never met him before. So, wait a minute. Tell me. Are you ready to date again?"

"Not really. That cutie pie is too young for me, but the other two and that doctor? Are there *really* men in this world who look like that—that aren't air-brushed models or in movies?"

"Michael is as good-hearted as he is good-looking. So is Lukas. I call him Lu. We've known each other since we were teenagers."

Dottie's eyebrows shot up. "And you let him get away?"

What she wanted to say is that she had been a fool to cut him out of her life in such a cruel way, but instead, Martine shrugged a shoulder. "He was scrawny and shy. I was a wild-child. We were like opposite ends of the spectrum, but good friends for a long time."

"And now? You better not let him get away again. I mean, assuming he's single and unattached," Dottie said bobbing her head.

"I don't know," she said in a nonchalant tone. *Is he? Oh, God, is there someone missing him? Waiting for him? Loving him?* The roll of her stomach ended up a lump in her throat. "I'll stay with Christopher until Paige gets here."

"You sure? Want to maybe take a break? I just took his vitals. No change. He's stable."

"No. I think I'll just keep him company. You go." Dottie left, resettling the curtain so it was fully closed. She took Christopher's hand and leaned into him with the low whisper, "We have her. It won't be long until you'll have your life back. Please stay strong. You'll be released from this spell even if I have to choke it out of her myself."

Without question, she felt guilty. Very guilty. Lu had been injured. He'd have a scar on his body with her name on it. Stab wounds could take weeks to heal. The infection would have to be monitored. He'd need meds and daily care for that wound. *Alana must hate me for putting her eternal love and Lu in danger. She'll make sure neither of them ever come back to the city.* Lu could be gone before she had a chance to... *Add it to your list of uncomfortables.*

Minutes ticked by. She kept looking at the clock, straining to hear anything being said two cubicles away. Her thoughts became so very muddled that her sixth sense seemed too remote to access. In her mind, she saw this as a fork in the road. One led to possibilities. One led back to her idea of self-preservation.

\*\*\*\*

An hour later, Paige said as she walked through the curtain of Christopher's cubicle, "They've released him."

Martine shook her head. "I'm sorry. Released who?"

"Lukas. He's still pretty out of it, so Doc Baker sent him home in a private ambulance."

*Oh God! He's already gone!* "Back to Scotland?"

"No. Michael wants him in the security of his brownstone under personal, private care. They just left."

Still dazed, she asked, "Michael went with him?"

"No. Marsha did. Your mom's meeting the ambulance at the brownstone. Doc Baker's pumping Aurora's stomach now. I came to relieve you. Michael's waiting for you outside the ER. Put your sweater on because the wind's suddenly howling like a pack of wolves out there." Paige bent down and handed over her purple sweater, which she took with an added 'thanks' before she left the cubicle.

He leaned against the brick building about twenty feet from the ER entrance. Martine pulled the sweater close, pulled up the hood, and hugged her arms as she approached. His shirt, streaked with blood, fluttered in a gust of wind. He ran his hands through his wavy hair and then he crossed his arms. Standing in front of him, the chill went right through her and shifting her weight from foot to foot, stared at her sneakers.

'None of this is your fault, so get that right out of your head before I shake some sense into you," he said in that low, calm baritone voice, more gravelly than usual.

"Michael, I—"

"Nope. I don't want to hear you're sorry. You will

340

listen and not interrupt because I'm on my last nerve and I'm tired as hell."

She closed her mouth and rolled her eyes, which he couldn't see because she still looked down at her feet. *Here it comes. And I deserve it after putting them both in danger.*

"I've known you since you were born, Martine. Even before your father died, I watched out for you. Through the arguments with your mother about the piercings, the first tattoo, the crazy boyfriends you found only God knows where. You settled down somewhat after I left the city. But when you stepped out of line, it only took one phone call because you knew I'd come here to personally reel you back in. You once had a close friendship with Lukas. Alana and I always looked forward to your visits in England. So did my son."

Now she *really* couldn't look at him.

"When tragedy had you in its grip, you pushed everyone out of your life when you needed us the most. My son took off for Scotland like a bat out of hell, and he refused to discuss, or even hear about you again. Martha and Mary visited us, but not you." He paused before adding, "You need to hear this. And if it hurts, it hurts. That's life. You've suffered a great loss. You will own it alone forever. She rests at peace in your soul. You cannot live in loss. Starving yourself hasn't brought her back. You are truly skin and bone. Your face is drawn, and your scrubs hang off you in a very unhealthy way. Stop it, honey. Come back to the world of the living."

He pushed off the wall and took her in his arms. She shook from head to toe and not because of the cold wind. He kissed her hair and held her tight in a gentle sway. Her body stayed loose as if he alone kept her on her feet.

"My son didn't think twice about putting his life on the line. Because *you* asked. He'd walk through the fires of Hell—if *you* asked. Open your eyes, Martine," he said, the rumble of his chest a blessed comfort. "Now *I* have an ask. Will you go to the brownstone and monitor Lukas after this bitch let's your patient go?" She nodded against him. "Good. Now let's go in there and get one Christopher Forbes back to the world of the living, too."

The wind swirled like an angry banshee around them as they walked back in. His arm stayed around her like the fierce protector he had always been, whether vampire or man.

Chapter 40

Break the Spell

Martine pulled off her sweater and shoved it under Christopher's bed. Then she met Michael outside the curtain, and they walked into Cubicle R together.

"She's just about to wake up," Doctor Baker told them as they entered. "I'll be waiting down the hall should you need me," he added before leaving.

Martine looked at everyone as Aurora's fingers and feet twitched. She was uncovered, the silky pink nightgown mid-calf and low-cut showing the rise and fall of full breasts. *She may look like Glinda, but she's truly the Wicked Witch of the West.*

Paige opened the curtain between the two cubicles to put the beds side by side. Bronwyn motioned her over, saying to her mind, *We are shielded from the outside world now. Nothing will be seen or heard.* Then Bronwyn whispered, "Please bring my sister. She's awake and able to sit in a wheelchair. We will need her powers."

Of course, she complied with Paige's help. Once Isobel was at her sister's side, Martine said to Paige, "You need to leave now. Please wait outside with Doctor Baker. Take a break if you want."

"Sure. Just text if you need an extra hand?"

"Will do," she replied.

Isobel looked alert, beaming from ear to ear when she took her sister's hand. Draven stood at Aurora's feet, Michael at her head. Martine took her place next to Christopher and watched Bronwyn place his hand over Aurora's. Isobel's palm rested on Aurora's lower abdomen where her womb would be. They linked their minds to the healing circle through her mother, the chain complete.

Aurora's lids fluttered before staying open. Then she looked around. "Where am I? Who are you?" she said eyeing Bronwyn. "You fools, I am powerful," she hissed and started to mumble.

Lights flickered. As if the hospital walls were no longer there, icy autumn wind gusted around them in thick swirls. She uttered more unrecognizable words and her aura glowed giving off a ghostly light. Like they had a will of their own, everyone's hands flew off Aurora. Michael and Draven lifted high off the ground before crashing down just as suddenly. Martine fought to shield her eyes from the onslaught of wild wind.

As Aurora's body floated up off the bed, her right hand shot to Christopher. "I claim you as mine! Awake and rise to do my bidding!" The IV line burst free. Blood spurted and began to run down his arm. Every piece of medical equipment touching him flew free and sizzled. Sucked into the swirling wind, Martine's face and arms stung as if cut, but she grabbed onto the collapsed bar of the bed and hung on for dear life!

"Collective powers to me gather, linked together make evil shatter," Bronwyn chanted. Isobel and Martine took up the chant, fighting against the whipping wind. In a trancelike state, Christopher rose from the bed, his face aimed upward to the dark witch floating above like a cloud. Martine grabbed his forearm and then once at his back, locked her arms around his chest.

Dragged in an unnatural way, Martine shouted, "By all the power of good within you, by all the power of good within us, unlock your powers! See your mother! See her sacrifice!"

A roaring screech came from the floating dark witch. Stubborn as hell, Martine repeated her chant, and Isobel and Bronwyn joined in. Christopher's somnolent march faltered.

Martine screamed, "Open your mind! Find the pinhole, warlock!"

His body abruptly jerked and collapsed, bringing her down on top of him. Fighting the unnatural element of swirling wind, Michael and Draven crawled over to turn him over as he began to convulse. Another unearthly screech came from the dark witch.

Bronwyn shouted, "You will not keep him! You will not succeed. End this aberration and reverse the dark spell. Reverse it now!"

"Never, old witch," Aurora's voice ringing around them.

Michael rolled off to the side, held onto the bed, fighting unknown forces to haul himself up. He grabbed her ankle yelling "You fucking bitch!"

Her body slammed down on the bed. The howling wind stopped, the ER lights flickered once before coming back to full power. Bronwyn ripped the talisman from her neck, closed her hand tight around it as Draven and Michael wrestled Aurora to the bed. She struggled and writhed like someone possessed.

Holding Isobel's hand Bronwyn chanted, "By all that is good, open you must." Martine joined in as she took Christopher's hand, sensing the link to her mother and the healing circle grow even more powerful as she took up the chant.

Aurora screamed, "Give it to me! Give it back! You can't stop me!"

"Ah, but they can," Draven said in that low, menacing tone. "You broke unwritten laws, dark witch. There is a price to pay."

"I hold the future of our realm in my womb. I hold the secrets of dark magic," she said in a voice that no longer had any power.

"You hold nothing, evil one," Isobel said in a forceful tone. "Your womb is an empty vessel."

"No. No-no-no, old witch! I will rule as Mother-Queen. I have seen it, so shall it be!"

"Dark witch, dark witch, where are you," Isobel sang like an old nursery rhyme. "Tell me, tell me, tell me true. Did you grab beyond your reach? All good witches come to teach."

Her body arched as she struggled. Her head jerked from side to side, "Stop it! Stop the screaming in my head! I will destroy you!"

"Silly brat," Isobel hissed.

"I have dark magic power," she shrieked.

"You have nothing. It is a conjure. A charade! An *abomination* that you take an innocent's will from him. An *abomination* that you break Unwritten Laws. There will be a very significant price to pay. And you will pay it! Own the chaos you have created," Isobel said, her voice all authority and goodness. Her words true and wise.

When Bronwyn placed the talisman on Aurora's forehead. It burst apart. "Free thy hair, thy saliva, thy seed. Free thy future. Blessed be." The talisman and all that had been held hostage turned to tiny black particles and disappeared.

The shine of Aurora's beautiful blonde hair dulled. The bloom on her cheeks faded. Discolored blotches appeared on her skin. Shrieks turned to sobs. Untouched on the bed, she curled on her side and moaned.

Christopher gasped. His chest heaved and his mouth fell open as he tried to take in breath. Draven lifted him off the floor and placed him back on his bed.

"Get him out of here quick, Martine," Michael ordered.

She unlocked the wheels and threw back the curtain. Her patient needed medical attention... the human kind. The Georgian maintenance man grabbed the end of the gurney and they ran him to the other side of the ER just as Dottie came out of a cubicle.

"Get Paige. Call for Doctor Forster. Stay with him, Dottie. I'll come back later." Dottie gave an affirmative nod, didn't ask a single question. Then Martine met Doctor Baker's eyes and without having to say a word they ran back to Aurora's side. Bronwyn gave a slow nod as she pushed Isobel's wheelchair back to the last cubicle.

"You'll need to wait a few minutes before examining her, John," Michael said.

Doctor Baker stepped feet away and pulled out his cell phone. "I'll text Deepa," he said.

"We are not done with her, Michael." Draven quickly locked to his narrow glare.

"This is over," Michael answered.

"No. It is not."Draven grabbed Aurora's chin. "Look at me. How did you know about the portal?" Her eyes dulled and she cowered. He repeated the question much angrier this time.

"I don't know," she cried.

"You are lying. I will tear into your throat slowly, painfully if you lie again."

*Pure menace.* Martine saw it first-hand. *He most certainly can be cruel.* Martine went to the side of the bed and touched Draven's hand. Without a word, he released her and stepped away. Blood trickled from Aurora's nose and ears. Martine settled her on her back, rubbed an arm and smoothed her dull, brittle hair. "I see the words in your mind. Say them. Tell him the truth."

Aurora closed her eyes, whispered, "A vision came to me. Only me." Of course, Draven heard every word and she looked at him. Then, as if she could read a vampire's thoughts, she turned back to Aurora. "Did you tell anyone about the portal?"

"No. It is my secret to keep."

"You have your answer, now back off," she said to him before replacing monitor leads on her new patient. The beeps became erratic. She knew the signs, knew what was happening as Doctor Baker moved the stethoscope around Aurora's chest. Martine's shoulders drifted back until she stood up straight. Then she walked over to Draven by the curtain. "You can't kill her," she whispered.

"Really. Let's ask Christopher how I should proceed. She stole his life."

"You won't kill her, Draven," she said with a shake of her head.

"And why the *hell* not?"

"Because she's dying."

The menacing look turned to a questioning one.

Michael walked over and stood eye-to-eye with him. "You won't have to dirty your hands with a kill."

"Michael," Draven hissed.

"No one will ever know another portal existed now."

*And there they go again*, Martine thought. *The same signature stance like two bulls not sure if they want to tangle with each other so they have to stop a minute and think it over.*

The monitor's beep went erratic before the flat-line tone sounded. Doctor Baker switched off the machine himself, pulled the sheet at the foot of the bed over her.

"Brother," Michael whispered with a slow shake of his head. "It is done. Let it go."

Draven walked to Aurora's bed and stared down, his face like a blank sheet of paper. Seconds passed before he said, "I have much to attend to. I will take my leave. Good night, dear Martine."

"Lose the dear. And forget you ever met her, or I swear I will find you and stake you," Michael said with murder in his eyes.

Draven's mouth slid into a thin grin. Then he put his hand over his unbeating heart. Face to face with Michael, he gave a slight bow, a soft, "brother," before leaving the cubicle.

Pulled out of the strange scene, Martine studied the covered body on the bed. Dark magic had taken one hell of a toll.

"John, make the arrangements with Deepa," Michael stated. "We don't want a record of her in the city morgue. I'll meet you at the Georgian Estate in England later today."

As Doctor Baker pulled out his cell phone, Martine asked, "Aren't you going to stay a while and look in on

Lu?"

"I know you'll take good care of my son. I need to be with Alana and my girls." He pulled her into a comforting hug. "Take two weeks off, honey. This has been intense."

"I have to take care of Christopher. He'll have questions and I should be there."

"Let the Georgian nurses care for him. Christopher Forbes will need time before he can handle anything."

"But you know who he is."

"The Georgian's will help him understand his heritage as well as his powers. Visit with him in a few days. You'll know just what to say to prepare Gwendolyn's son for a new life. It certainly will make you think twice about legends."

Her right eyebrow rose as she pulled out of his hug. "You're awfully chatty lately. And what's all that brother stuff with Draven?"

"We have a bit of history… often passed for brothers back in the day."

"*Way-way* back in the day, like what, one-hundred-fifty years ago?"

"Something like that."

"About Lu—"

"He executed your plan perfectly. Everything worked out, and I will say no more," he stated. "Remember our little chat outside. Don't force me to come back to this city." He kissed her cheek, and she barely whispered, "Bye," as he walked out of Cubicle Q with confident, singular strides that set him apart from all others.

Doctor Baker spoke to two Georgians who entered the cubicle to prepare the body for removal, then he met her at the curtain. "It's nice to finally put a face to the name, Martine. You're a gifted nurse, a gifted woman."

"Thanks. It's my pleasure to meet you as well," she replied in a professional tone.

"Oh. About Isobel and Bronwyn. Michael reached out to Deepa earlier tonight. A Georgian social worker will be arriving shortly for them."

Her smile broadened. "He's something, isn't he?"

"So is his son."

She had to ask. "Have you heard anything about Lu?"

"Marsha texted. He woke up when they settled him in bed. If you sense anything serious that warrants my attention, I'll fly back in. The thigh wound is deep but didn't hit the femur. I prescribed a heavy dose of penicillin and pain meds. He's got a nasty gash on his right knee as well."

"Stitches?"

"On his thigh, but I sealed the gash on his knee with surgical glue."

"He was unconscious."

Doctor Baker smiled and shook his head. "Yeah. It's his body's unique way of coping. High fever and loss of consciousness. It's happened before. Give him a little leeway, but make sure he takes the antibiotics."

*One more bit of information to fit into the puzzle of Lukas Malone*, she thought as he followed the gurney out of the cubicle. Martine looked around, a bit lost in the silence of the ER wing. Bronwyn stood at her sister's side in whispered conversation. Walking around to the other side of the ER, the curtain was open with Doctor Forster notating his exam on the patient tablet. He looked up with a loose grin. "Christopher is doing fine. We'll send him over for an MRI just to be certain. Normal blood pressure and good oxygen levels. He'll be here a few days under observation."

"Great," she said with a smile. "I'll get him back to Cubicle Q now."

"Good idea. No quarantine anymore?"

"No. Just a false alarm with all this crazy flu. Didn't even have to admit them." She released the break on the bed and got a bright smile from her patient.

"Hi. I'm Martine."

"I know," he replied.

With no one in the hall or waiting to be seen, the move went fast and smooth. She settled the bed back against the wall. "Feeling better, Christopher?"

"Please call me Chris. A little stiff, but pretty good." She swept his mind and he studied her with tight, light-blue eyes. "Dottie said you were mostly by my side like my own personal nurse."

"I was. A private organization felt it best you stay at St. Francis. Their nurses will continue your care until release."

"But you were here every night. I know. I felt your presence. I think I—"

"You need to rest. I'll come back and we can talk in a few days."

"You have to know, I heard everything you said. I just couldn't respond."

She entered his mind, guided him to a restful place. "All in good time. No worries."

Paige walked in. "Hi, Chris. I'm one of the nurses who will be on this case until you're well enough to go home. Oh. Your friend Trev comes every day before he goes to work. I shot him a text to let him know you're awake. He'll be here later today." The look on his face when hearing his friend's name meant he had full recall of his life. But the way he studied Paige made Martine grin.

"How about we get you to sit up a little. Would you like that," Paige asked with a sweet smile.

"Sounds good," he replied as she adjusted the bed.

Glancing at her, Paige said, "The social worker took our two older patients a couple of minutes ago. She said she'd reach out to you tomorrow. Marsha's taking your shift for the next two weeks."

"Oh," she simply said. No doubt, Michael had something to do with it.

"The prescriptions and supplies have been sent over for your patient at that brownstone." Before she could reply, Paige held up her sweater, waiting for her arms to go through. Then Paige handed over her handbag. "The car's waiting outside. I was told you should leave for your new assignment ASAP."

Really at a loss for words, she replied, "Oh. Well. I'm on my way then."

"Thank you," her former patient said with a nice smile. "I don't think those two words are enough."

"You're very welcome. I'm relieved to see you awake."

"Yeah. About that." He rubbed his forehead.

"Just relax and let Paige take care of you. Give yourself time. And when the detective comes to talk with you, tell him what you know. But don't stress, okay?" She looked at Paige, who gave a knowing nod, then left Cubicle Quirky and the ER.

Outside, the air felt crisp. Not even a hint of howling wind in the pink morning sky above. A black sedan idled a few feet from the ER entrance.

Chapter 41

Aftermath

When the driver pulled in front of Michael's brownstone, Martine sat with her hand poised on the door handle and took a moment before stepping out into the sunshine. Seeing Lu unconscious had frightened her. Knowing he'd have more scars on his body made her feel guilty. And facing him meant no turning back. As her foot hit the top step, the front door opened.

Without reservation, she accepted a hug from her mother. "I'm so proud of you. You made the right call and didn't back down."

Thoughts of Lu stayed with her, but the much needed hug felt like heaven. "Thanks, Mare," she said in a tired whisper. "I feel so responsible."

"He's a big boy, Martine. He'll survive. And how's your patient?"

"Christopher Forbes has his life back." She shrugged out of her sweater and Mare hung it on the brass hook in the foyer. Her handbag already rested on the small peddler's bench. Now for the words she didn't want to utter. "How is he?"

"Sleeping and snug in the master bedroom." She recalled the upstairs layout, pretty much similar to Kendrick House. But long before she was born, Michael had broken through a wall to create a large master suite out of the two back rooms. The second bedroom had dressers and a twin bed. The bathroom had been expanded and turned into a truly exquisite one.

Her mother touched her arm. "Before you go up, have a cup of coffee with me."

Heading through the well-designed and furnished living room and dining area, she followed, remembered walking in here with Lu three days ago. Facing him would be grueling, even though she couldn't wait to assess his condition for herself. She sat at the classy kitchen table that screamed of Michael's innate sense of design. The counters were black granite, cabinetry dark cherrywood with gold hinges and handles. Everything said top of the line down to the dark, glossy wood floors and every modern appliance.

Her mother placed a hot mug of aromatic coffee on the table—fixed the way she liked it. The plate between them had blueberry scones and croissants. She reached for a scone, ate some of it in silence. After another mouthful of coffee, she asked, "Have you heard from Michael?"

"He knows Lukas is in good hands."

"Did he tell you I have two weeks off?"

"I admire the way he thinks of everything," her mother said with a small grin. "He's a singular character. Always has been."

"I put them both in danger. Alana may never speak to me again. Lu got hurt. And it's going to leave scars. Jeez, Mare, what was I thinking?" she said as she shook her head and looked away.

"Hey. What's the matter with you? The moment Christopher ended up in your ER you sensed the dark spell. That hidden portal is sealed shut. You knew it would take extraordinary individuals to end this and you were right. Look what's been accomplished in a little over a week. And then there's Isobel and Bronwyn, reunited after sixteen years. Look at every angle of this event. It's serendipity."

"You know Aurora's dead," Martine whispered.

Her mother gave a loose shrug. "Dark magic demands a high price. I'm not surprised. Now everything's back in sync with the universe as it should be." Her mother studied her. "You've made a habit of beating yourself up for things no one can control. As Michael would say, stop it. Stop it right now. When will you open your eyes?" Her mother stood, took her coffee mug to the sink.

"If I hear 'stop it' with the ever-irritating 'right now' one more time, I swear I'll throw my version of a wild-child fit. Not to mention the ever-loving open your eyes!"

Her mother turned around and Martine glanced up. "I'm going home now. The key is on the bench in the foyer. The alarm code is 1928. You have a patient waiting. Go to him."

After the front door closed, she pushed off the table and stood. Facing her biggest fear seemed harder by the second. She faltered at the bottom of the stairs before taking them. In the doorway of the master bedroom, she came to a complete stop.

Lukas was fast asleep. She walked over to the armchair on the other side of the nightstand, sank down without making a sound and studied the peaceful look, his brow relaxed, full lips slightly apart. His loose hair framed his face like a halo, shoulders lean yet strong.

*How long has it been since he slept? Since he had a*

*good meal? How had being back in the Second Realm affected him? Is he in pain? How will he heal?* As the hours passed, she'd lean forward when he moaned. Did he dream about what he'd just been through? Or did he dream about a special someone waiting for him back in the highlands of Scotland? *What am I going to say when he wakes up?*

****

Lukas's eyes fluttered open at the scent of her so close. The bedside lamp lit the room. He had no idea what time it was, and he didn't care. All that mattered? Martine had her fingers on his wrist. His heart quickened. Her heart beat faster as well. A slight blush crept up her cheeks. He swallowed, knowing he had a lot to tell her.

She had been foremost on his mind since before being carried through the portal by the vampire. Setting down his wrist, she handed him four huge pills and a glass of water. He sat up a bit, put two at a time in his mouth and washed them down with a few gulps. She took the glass from him, and after his head hit the pillow, he turned his face away.

She sat closer, hooked his chin, and studied him. Worry and concern stood in her eyes. Yet a flood of memories about being back in that realm and how he had killed without mercy hammered his brain like a migraine. Rage surfaced real easy. So did regrets. Wanting to tell her everything, he knew he couldn't. Just like he couldn't control the tremors, the tight expression on his face as too many hidden feelings rushed to surface.

Her thumbs caught his tears as his chest heaved. She kissed his forehead and stroked his cheek. Christ, he hadn't cried like this in years. But she didn't leave, pulling tissues from a packet in her scrubs to dry his face with a tender touch. He had buried that trauma deep, and yet being back there left a different kind of mark. This time, he killed instead of cowering before being beaten. Finally able to palm his eyes, he whispered, "Sorry... I don't usually—"

"I'm the one who's sorry. So very sorry," she replied with a slow shake of her head.

"No, M. Please don't be. It's not your fault. I'm really okay. Just don't leave me?" Her head settled under his chin, his arm came around her back. That he sensed her so upset turned him into a puddle of slush. "I'd walk through the fires of Hell if you asked me to."

She stilled. Almost stiffened. Then pushed off his chest. He captured her eyes, the tiny flecks of gold, the loveliest shade of brown he'd ever seen. "This is horrible. You'll end up with more scars," she said far too serious.

"So what?"

"I don't care if the earth falls off its orbit. You are never going to that horrid realm again."

"Oh yeah? Think you could stop me?"

"You know I will."

"The reason for my mystical gifts is the same as yours. Protect the innocent. We did this together. And we'd do it again."

"I want to see your back."

*Christ, what a way to change the subject.* "You've seen me shirtless before."

"Yeah but I wasn't looking."

"Oh. Good to know," he replied. Maybe he had read her wrong. Because he would have memorized every skin cell on her back if given the chance. Before his body reacted to the visual of her naked, well, he closed that down fast.

"Your back, Lu," she whispered.

"Oh... right," he answered rather sheepishly.

He didn't share this part of his life. Didn't talk about it, preferred to ignore it. But this ask came from Martine, so he rolled onto his stomach, relaxed his shoulders and kept his face turned away. The bed covers resettled at his waist. There were many, and she traced every single one. He kept his eyes closed and his breaths even. Yet each brush of her finger soothed and excited at the same time.

"You were just an innocent kid and then, you went back there. Relived it all and put yourself in danger because I asked. The scars on your leg are a new reminder with more ugly memories."

"Come on, M. I'm really okay." He wanted to turn around, hoped the quilt thick enough to conceal his body's reaction to her touch. But he had to know. *No time like the present... either she kisses me back or slaps my face.* He pushed off an elbow and as soon as they were face to face, his lips slammed into hers.

Her hands ran through his hair pushing it away. Then she gripped his shoulders leaning into the kiss and straddling his waist. Their tongues danced together. He reached under her baggy top and unhooked her bra, breaking the kiss just enough to whisper, "I want you."

"I want you, too," she replied, then locked tighter to his kiss.

He pushed the top up. She grabbed it, and for the seconds that their lips parted, he studied the outline of her ribs, the lines of veins up her arms. The tattoo above her left breast of a heart with a sword through it. The one between her breasts an exact image of the seven-pointed amulet he had worn. She tried to look away, but he held her chin and devoured her mouth. Both of them breathing hard, their heads swiveled one way and then another as if each new taste a different discovery. Lukas had to pull back. Gasped in quick breaths. He shook his head to get rid of the wide-eyed look, telling his hips not to jerk because underneath the thick quilt he was as hard as stone.

Her shoulders drifted back; her hands resting on the bed too close to his hips. Cracking a smile, she said, "I can't believe we're doing this."

"I can't believe it took us so long," he replied, trying to slow his body down. "I don't want to stop, M. I want you. That first night at dinner, I knew I wanted you. Getting back here to tell you is all I thought about."

She didn't fall back into his arms with another hot kiss. He closed his eyes and shook his head. *Did you really call this one totally wrong?*

"No, you didn't. Jeez, I'm sorry. You're very easy to read. Look. There are stitches in your thigh. Your knee's pretty banged up. You stayed unconscious and feverish for hours, and penicillin can make you groggy. You need rest."

*No chance of that.* "I want you. I have for a long time. I should've been on the first plane to the city and at your side years ago, no matter what you said to push me away."

"I know why you never came back here, Lu. It was too much of a risk."

"Fuck the risk. I let you down," he said in a whisper. "Because loss is like a demon, and I didn't run to save the one person I care deeply about. I ran the other way."

Her right eyebrow rose. "So now here we are. In a bed. Both of us half naked. Talking about the past. Where do we go from here, Lu?"

"You tell me because I know what I want. I want you." He folded his arms under his head and stared at her. Now came the war of stubborn glares. A stand-off between stop and go. Her hand was on the switch because he'd never force her. They had too much respect between them, too much history. Maybe not enough love... which would totally crush him.

"Hand me my top," she said. He did, and she slipped it over her head without bothering with the bra. He closed his eyes, and when she came off his waist, he resettled the covers thinking, *I really know how to kill the mood, don't I.*

Martine wanted to pour out her heart. She wanted to be under the covers feeling his body against her. She stood at the foot of the bed and carefully pushed up the thick quilt. His knee had a huge gash and a hematoma, the color a rich purple, which she put a fresh bandage on. His thigh remained an angry dark red. Without further conversation, she picked up the clipboard and notated his medical chart. The last reading of his temperature had been normal. *Well, not now after those heated kisses and an erection.* Placing a hand over his bandaged thigh, she closed her eyes to see beneath his skin. The knife went deep but did no major damage. Just muscle. Lu was more than physically fit and his wounds were already healing, but she'd make sure he took antibiotics on schedule.

Notating the chart, her hands shook. So did her focus. She knew full well what her body looked like. Every rib showed and her breasts were small now. She really didn't need a bra but wore one anyway. *Passionate kisses. The smell of him so masculine. The feel of him so very right.* She had been aroused as well. *How many times had he said I want you?* That hadn't been some throwaway line to get her in bed. *I should be riding him full of need and desire instead of looking at his chart.* But her twisted notion of self-preservation had shut him down cold.

"Am I going to live, nurse," he said with a hint of sarcasm.

Unwilling to look at him, she bit her lower lip as her shoulders drifted down. Placing the medical chart back on the nightstand, she turned, but he grabbed her hand. Like some strange 'scene-one-take-two', she sat at his side.

"Come put your head on my chest. I'm sure you're exhausted, so let me hold you. I swear… just come to me and I will hold you." His voice held tenderness and strength at the same time. *But that's Lu—never mean. Never abusive. Never anything but honest.*

Too stressed to talk, she stretched out next to him with her head over his heart. She loosened her bushy bun and let her hair fall where it wanted. He brushed it to the side while she played with the soft hair on his chest. His embrace tightened. *Safe and secure. Such a perfect fit.* The rise and fall of every even breath. The sound of his heart beating along with hers in an intense duet. He kissed her hair and her eyelids lazily fluttered before they closed.

Chapter 42

Truth

Martine awoke alone in the bed. Sunlight poured through the window. She shielded her eyes blinking, trying to focus. Obviously they had slept straight through the night. The yawn snuck out as she ran her hands over her face. About to get out of bed, Lu came in wearing a pair of black boxers. His uneven gait, a pronounced limp, had the water in the glass he carried sloshing over the sides.

"You shouldn't be on your feet and you're off schedule with your meds," came out of her mouth.

"Yeah. I guess."

"Penicillin needs to be consistent in your system."

He shrugged his shoulders. "They pumped me full of the stuff yesterday morning. I took four pills when they brought me home and then with you—before you got in bed with me." A crooked smile complete with deep dimples appeared on his face. "I took four again when I got up at six, like an hour ago."

"With food? Did you eat something?"

"Two croissants. I talked to my parents and then I came back up and hit the bathroom. Brushed my teeth, shaved, and washed up a bit."

Her hand went to her chest. "How the hell did you make it down the stairs?"

"I held onto the banister."

"You shouldn't have any weight on your leg. Let me see if it's bleeding again."

"I'm not bleeding, See? " he argued, lifted the cotton boxer leg up higher.

"Get in bed."

"I brought you a glass of water."

"Thanks. Get in bed," she said as she went to him, hooked his waist to take weight off it. They slow-walked across the magnificent, masculine bedroom.

"I want to shower," he said as she set the glass down before helping him into bed. "Can I? Please?" Her lips turned down and she looked at him. "What! I said please."

"Not yet. Later you'll sit in the bathroom, and I'll help you wash up again."

"I can wash myself, M."

"Fine. But you can't put pressure on your leg. You should have eaten a whole meal while you were downstairs. Made yourself one of those huge sandwiches."

"I'm not hungry."

She narrowed her eyes with a "pfft" and a jerk of her head. "Really?" She felt his forehead and took his pulse. He let out a laugh with his eyes focused on the ceiling.

"The bathtub is a jacuzzi. Maybe you'd want a bath?"

"I smell that bad?"

"Not at all. But you can't be comfortable in those scrubs. I untied your sneakers and got them off your feet for you."

"I was wondering about that. Thought I was too tired to remember doing it myself."

"See? I said you needed to rest. And I loved holding you while you slept." She avoided his eyes as he kept trying to capture her gaze, his head bobbing one way then the other. "I could give you a clean shirt and a pair of my sweats. I swear I won't get out of bed or anything," he said as she fixed the bulky quilt around him again.

"Is there shampoo?"

"Sure."

"I'll take you up on the offer. I must stink like hell," she said—and she meant it. No matter what he said. Plus, she needed some alone time.

"My clothes are in the spare bedroom. Take what you need."

"Great. And don't get out of bed again. Close your eyes and go to sleep. Let the medicine do its work. Where are the pain meds?"

"I threw them down the sink. I don't need them. Don't want them in the house."

"Okay. But aren't you in pain?"

He looked her straight in the eye and said, "Aren't we all?" His deep-blue eyes were clear and wide. She gave a small grin and ran her hand down the side of his cheek. He nuzzled against it before she gently pulled it away.

**** 

It had been years since she had been in Michael's brownstone. Only used the bathroom, which was also right out of a home design magazine, a couple of times. In the small bedroom, Martine rummaged through an open suitcase and pulled out a dark-blue cotton shirt that matched the color of Lu's eyes and a pair of charcoal-gray drawstring sweats. The shirttails ended above her knees when she held it against her. Maybe she'd be able to get the drawstring tight enough to keep the sweats up.

Her eyes slid to the dresser. She went to it, turned over the pearl-handled knife in her hand before she picked up the broadsword on top of a carved leather sheath. It felt very heavy, very masculine. Three M's were engraved just under the hilt. She placed it down carefully and then picked up the Kendrick Family amulet. The one her mother gave him. The one he wore pressed to his chest in the Second Realm. The thick leather ribbon had been cut to get it off him in the ER.

With clothes in hand, she peeked in on Lu, already fast asleep and snoring. *He's truly a beautiful man, both inside and out,* she thought as she continued down the hall. Deciding against a bath, the rainwater showerhead seemed an additional perk. Showers helped her think. Even about things she didn't want to face.

Yeah…She had spent too many years crying and blaming and then destroying her curvy body, an inherited trait among Kendrick women. They used no special diets or exercise regimens. Morgan's lovely full-bodied figure could be seen in an ornate frame displayed at home on the mantle. Martha had been petite and curvy while her mother was statuesque and curvy. Martine's figure had once been somewhere between mother and grandmother—and curvy. Not anymore. What she'd purposely done to herself wasn't the elephant in the room. It was the way she let loss lead her to an empty garden where nothing grows. *Thank God it hasn't ruined my professional life… that's one blessing in disguise.* Four years ago when she took the position at St. Francis, meeting Dottie had been another. *You only come alive at work because you aren't wrapped up in you, and there's no time to blame yourself, or cry.* But she had wanted to cry in Lu's arms. And she wanted to drown in more sensual kisses. What burned within lit a fire in her soul.

Questions ran rampant in her head until she rinsed off. What had Michael said? *Step back into the world of the living and open your eyes, Martine.* Her mother had said it as well. She turned off the water and it finally clicked. *I've ignored the signs instead of exploring them.*

Toweling off, she knew she had to do something. Yeah, the shirt looked like a sack and the sweatpants barely stayed up, but dressed and determined she went downstairs to the kitchen. Made a fresh pot of coffee. Waited for it to stop brewing then poured it into a mug. She added a little milk before sitting down at Michael's classy kitchen table. Slowly ate another blueberry scone. Then she pulled everything out of the fridge she needed and went to work. On a tray found in the small pantry she fixed everything a certain way, then went back upstairs to the only man she wanted in her heart. Not just until he healed. But forever.

Chapter 43

Nothing but the Truth

He stirred with various aromas racing up his nose. He could list everything on the tray before opening his eyes. But the utmost, special scent that excited him was Martine.

"I know you're awake. Come with me on a picnic?"

He opened his eyes and immediately chuckled, which ended with his most charming smile. He knew how to turn it on, and with the way he felt about Martine, well, he gave it his all.

A tablecloth was under the tray on the king-sized bed. The sandwiches looked to be his kind of heaven— full of meat and not a hint of any condiment or crispy lettuce. Two tall glasses of orange juice and a plate of chocolate cookies complimented the menu. Yeah... She remembered his need for sweets—and it had been one hell of a week. Sitting cross-legged on the other side of the tablecloth dressed in his favorite shirt and a pair of sweats, Martine was his version of total loveliness. Kind of sexy, too, knowing she wore his clothes, sitting on his bed and in his life, he hoped. He sat with pillows piled against the carved wooden headboard, repositioned his weight as well as the quilt. As if sensed that he'd need to stretch too far, she handed him the glasses so she could bring the picnic closer. But Martine still sat out of his reach.

"Listen, about what happened before," he said.

"Nope. We're starting fresh. Wanna play a game?" she asked as she often had years ago.

"Is it one we played before?" Because she always came up with some unique ones.

"Nope. It's new."

"I need to know the rules first." Certain it wouldn't be her weird version of Twister, *one way or another, you'll be in my arms tonight and every night*—and he instantly hid that thought.

"It's simple. I take a bite and you talk. You take a bite and I talk. But we both have to be totally honest, or you have to take three bites in a row before you get another chance."

"Can I ask questions?"

She turned her lovely face to the side as if deep in thought. "Yes, only if necessary."

He'd play along. "What if I want to take a drink?"

"You can only drink your juice during a pause."

He had to wonder where this was heading, but said, "Okay… who goes first?"

"I do. Because I thought it up and I made the sandwiches. Ready?" she asked with wide, pretty eyes, her long black hair pulled over a shoulder dampening his shirt.

He took a bite as she cleared her throat. "I've missed you like hell. I didn't realize how much until I saw you again. When I came into your arms something stirred. I really knew I missed you when I came over to talk to you the next morning. I loved it when you held me. When you kissed me, my whole world turned upside down. Because you were here. Because you were always in my heart. I just couldn't see it. And take smaller bites or you won't be playing fair."

"Sorry," he said after swallowing. "Okay. My turn. And don't pick at your sandwich or we'll be a year older before we finish." With a wide, open mouth, she took a healthy bite. Her cheeks puffed out like a chipmunk's stuffed with acorns. He almost lost it watching her try to chew. "I was thirteen the first time I saw you with my father. He had just gotten me away from the sorcerers and I stalked him. That night, he had you by the arm, but you fought him like a whirlwind until he picked you up and carried you to Kendrick House. I liked your feistiness. I still do." *Oh shit… she's still chewing.* "I saw him do that lots of times that year. If I thought he had hurt you, I would have staked him right then and there. Before you ask, I stalked him almost every night, and when he caught me, he couldn't hold on." He took a refreshing gulp of juice, thinking *thank God she swallowed.* "Okay, Your turn." He took a bite and chewed.

"I pushed you away when I met that asshole, and I said some nasty, horrible things on purpose to hurt you. He *really* hated our friendship, Lu. Said you had no place in my life anymore. Like a fool, I agreed. Then I blew off Mare and left the healing circle, like I could bury my gift, my sixth sense. I moved into his Brooklyn apartment when I got pregnant, and I felt so far over the moon. But he started taking longer business trips and rarely came home. I stuck it out for months until he said he didn't want a baby and had taken a position in the company's LA location. That's when I knew it was over for good. I made peace with Mare, now very pregnant, and I planned to move back to Kendrick House before the baby came. I wanted to call you. But I couldn't. I knew I had hurt you very deeply." He handed her the glass of juice. She took a sip and studied him before saying, "Why didn't you ever tell me about the scars?" She took a bite.

*Christ... the one subject I share with no one.* But he'd not deny her ask. "I was held in the palace by the sorcerers for four years, and they fed me lie after lie about my father. After I turned twelve my defiance became my defense. I got curious about what was outside the palace walls, so I started sneaking out. Got very good at stealing food and hiding. At first, the guards had orders to simply bring me back. I found passageways that led farther outside palace walls and used them more and more. By then, I could steal anything I wanted and it was fun to cause a little craziness in the open-air markets. But realm dwellers are greedy bastards. Guards offered coin to rat me out."

"Is that how you got the scars?"

*Now for the more difficult words.* He nodded once. "One of the sorcerers tolerated my defiance less and less. Ordered me locked below in a cell. When the guards caught me, they got rougher. The sorcerer looked the other way and let the guards beat me. That's how the filthy bastards put scars on my back and my chest, using the wrong end of a belt."

"Oh Lu," she whispered with a hand over her heart.

"It hurt like hell. I screamed and bawled. Laid low for a while, but I got out again. Hate was my constant companion and rage got me days of freedom before the fucking bastards found me." He looked away and then at her again. "This time, I killed every realm guard I saw, including the one who stabbed me." He drained the glass, took a bite of the sandwich thinking, *Christ, I hope that's enough because any more honesty and I'll be a total mess.*

"Oh God. No wonder you were raging when Michael found you."

He shrugged and then swallowed. "I embrace rage like a friend. I know my father bargained with those stupid triumvirate of evil idiots in our world, to give me a normal life while he planned his revenge, and then he destroyed them."

"That started the mayhem in Manhattan," she said with a serious nod.

"Maybe the next year of not remembering tempered me enough to see exactly who my father was. But slipping into a rage is very easy for me. Dad tolerated it—up to a point."

"I can just imagine," she said with a smirk.

"He'd warn me, tell me exactly where I'd end up, but I'd just defy him. Then my butt would sting for hours."

Leaning forward, she said, "But he loves you so fiercely."

"I love him fiercely, too, and I know exactly how to push his buttons. It took a while for me to finally understand the meaning of self-control. I told you the type of mischief I got into. I just didn't tell you what happened after I got caught."

Martine shook her head. "I don't get it. You were always so shy and sweet."

He shrugged before admitting, "Yeah, with *you.*"

"You were always like an A-plus student." She took a small bite of her sandwich.

"I did great in school. But it took me years to finish

my PhD. After that last phone call from you, I don't know, just couldn't concentrate. I took the historical research assignment for the Georgians in the Scottish Highlands—to be left alone." *Because I missed you so very much.* He paused, looked away. "Talk to me, M. Tell me what happened."

She sighed, pushed back her long black hair and relaxed with her hands on her knees. "My mother and I started talking. More and more."

"How far along were you?"

"Twenty-six weeks. I decided it was time to go back home. I packed a bag and got in a taxi. It happened so fast—I cramped and felt a gush of fluid. The driver took me straight to St. Francis. I begged the doctor to save her. I begged my mother to save her. They couldn't. They said they did everything they could, but she didn't survive. I held her as she took the last breath, named her Madeline." He handed her the glass. She took a sip of juice. *Words beyond painful,* he thought and whispered her name. "She's at rest with Morgan and Martha, my grandfather and my father. I don't recall the burial service at the Kendrick crypt."

"I should have been there. Why didn't you let me come."

"No. I couldn't face it. That's why I said all those terrible ugly things when you called. Only Mare and I buried her. But I had already shut down. Like a slow stroll down a dark and empty road."

"I'm here now. For only you."

Her eyes filled. He wanted to hold her, but handed her the sandwich, instead. She took a small bite, and full of tenderness, he whispered her name. He'd feed her every day for the rest of his life if that's what she needed.

He'd kiss every sorrow from her heart.

"I never should have said those things. Now you're scarred because of me."

*How do I answer that?* He sensed that he had to let it rest. She'd talk about it more in her own time. "You were always in my heart, M. In the Second Realm, I knew I had to come home to you. Only you. Look. I don't talk about my scars. I don't let anyone touch them."

"You let *me* touch them."

He smiled. "I'd never deny any ask you give."

"And what about your life, since we stopped talking," she asked in a whisper.

"I'm an open book."

"Is… is someone waiting for you in Scotland?'

He slowly shook his head. "No. I've had relationships and friends with benefits. But I keep who I am and what I've been through private. You took a chunk of my heart when you hung up on me. I stayed far away when you lost Madeline to honor your request. I should have understood and read into your pain. Last week, when my father called, I drove like a fucking maniac to that airport. I wouldn't let you down again. I've never told anyone how I feel about you, because it's deep. Real personal. If your next ask is for me to leave you alone and return to Scotland, I will. But what I feel for you will never stop." He studied the turn down of her mouth, the slow blink of her beautiful eyes. The way her shoulders lay low and how her hands rubbed her knees.

"Losing Madeline hurt so bad. I called you a thousand times in my head to apologize. I couldn't ever hear your voice again. There's solitude in loss. I mean, who really wants to know how you feel when they ask? No one. No one knows what to say and conversations get awkward. Friendships die. Mare poked and prodded, but her heart was broken, too. Just like mine. You lose your footing and one day it doesn't matter anymore. Like treading deep water but you have no desire to make it to shore. You're just... shattered."

"Enough. Let's stop."

"I needed your help and I couldn't even make the damn call. I forced Mare to handle it. I knew Michael would come, but I never expected to ever see you again. Then you were standing right in front of me. For the first time in a long time—your kiss, your hug. Such comfort. Like I didn't have to ask you to understand. You just did. Then I go and put you in danger. Dredge up terrifying feelings. I know how they hurt when they surface..." Her voice faded away before she added, "When you kiss me, I want it to never end. When you hold me, I feel home in your arms. No one else's arms... No one."

"This game is over." In a totally rare, firm tone, he added, "Get this stuff off the bed or I will do it with one swipe of my hand." She blew out a haggard breath, stood up and put the tray on the dresser.

"Come to me, M." And she did, sitting at his side as he took her hand. "I want you. You want me. What are we waiting for? And don't ever again say it's your fault I got hurt. Hurt just happens." Their fingers threaded together when he whispered, "What is your next ask? I want you so bad right now, it better be the right one."

"Will you take me in your arms?"

"That's a yes, but it's not the right one. Try another."

"Will you kiss me again the way you did before?"

"That's another yes, but it's not the right one, either."

"Will you finish what you started?"

"Christ, I thought you'd never ask," he said and pulled her into his arms.

He captured her lips. Let their tongues tease each other's as he unbuttoned his favorite shirt. She moaned, massaging his chest, only removing her hands to get her arms free. He cupped a breast as she guided his other hand to the drawstrings of his sweats. He untied them to touch her. As the sweats slid down, she pulled her body up so he could get them off.

Still locked in a hot, heated kiss, he explored her. She rimmed the waistband of his boxers with one finger. He wiggled out of them, springing free and heavy. Kisses graced her neck, her breasts, her stomach, thrilled by every gasp and moan he heard.

"Let me love you," he whispered. Her hips moved in a restless way when his next kiss met the tip of her and produced a soft cry. Every sigh echoed through his heart. His tongue traced her, excited her, and the palm of his hand held her locked to the bed. Her fingers ran through his hair. Her quick breaths, her last wriggle against his tongue made him buck. Digging his elbows into the mattress, he pulled himself up until they were face to face. Her parted lips inviting, the look in her eyes soft as they captured his. They both said, "I love you," at the same time. She brushed his hair off his face and on the next heated kiss, he entered her.

Martine's body hummed with passion, the feel of him entering her incredible. She knew they said those three little words at the same time because they had been waiting a long, long time to be said. For many, many years… With every text, every letter, every phone call. The sensation of him going deeper and pulling back rocked her soul. He was a sensual lover—in so many unexpected ways. The scent of him, strong and intense. The way he kissed her... as if time could stand still. Every touch like a secret language saying to her soul I've missed you—I want you—I need you. This type of desire, this type of surrender she had never felt before. And when they climaxed together, she sensed more than their bodies had become one, as if their souls had joined as well.

She opened her eyes mesmerized by the expression on his face. The slack jaw, his full lips loose as his breathing slowed. Just a glimpse of those hooded, dark-blue eyes, an erotic look—so very personal. So very real. When he settled at her side, he kissed her immediately. Her hand slid down to stroke him. He kissed her again, more passionate than before—as if it were even possible.

He brushed her hip, grabbed her bottom, slid down her thigh until he guided her knee high up on his chest. With a grin on her face, she felt comfortable resting her head right under his chin. She was just at the right angle for him to explore, so she took the opportunity to reach down and tease him as well. Craving the length of him inside her again, when his thumb found that hidden spot at the tip of her core, her body jerked and trembled. She pulled back to see the sexy way he bit his lower lip. He moved his fingers again and she gasped.

The mischievous grin he wore made her shiver. "Don't you dare move your hand off me, but come a bit—"

"Oh I'm coming all right," she said in a pant.

"Yeah," he said as he ran his fingers over her core in such a way that she curled like a ribbon across his chest. But the tip of his erection straining for her touch sent a different type of thrill through her. The rise and fall of his chest so very thrilling, so very hot.

He groaned. Her body hummed. He reached down for her hand and repositioned it, which made her ready to orgasm again. "This is where I want it," he said in a very sexy way.

"Come into me again," she barely whispered.

He caught her hips and swung her over the tip of him. He held her there as she panted in anticipation. With a naughty twinkle in his eyes, he brought her down as his hips thrust up. Martine threw her head back and gripped his arms totally lost in the pleasure he gave. As if her body could splinter into a million pieces, every single one of them marked by Lu, this time, her orgasm felt far beyond incredible.

****

Lukas had her in his arms, his good leg bent at the knee as she rested at his side pleasantly rubbing his chest. "You're too quiet, M. You okay?" A soft "ummm..." was his answer. The tight snuggle against him with her thigh over his hip produced another satisfied groan. He took in the heady scent of their physical love and treasured it. Committed it to memory. Pulling the thick quilt up and over her, he welcomed the feel of her skin against his. He could stay like this forever with the love of his life tight to him.

His right thigh throbbed something fierce. His knee hurt like hell. It was expected. This time, he'd heal like an ordinary man, not a mystical warrior. All things considered—it didn't really matter. The jump-start to his future had been a strange event. The irony of such synchronicity had played its part once again. Just as it had years ago. Inherited mystical gifts took him down a singular path. To hone each skill to perfection. To use his astute intelligence in research for a deeper understanding of all things out of the ordinary. To be steps ahead of evil that existed, unseen by most. And for good reason.

He kissed her hair and she stirred. "Where are you, Lu?"

"Right here as I'll always be, M." When she pulled off and cupped his cheek, he kissed her palm. Christ, he felt incredibly blessed. In so many ways. But what he felt for Martine completed him, plain and simple. "Can I shower yet or what?" he asked. "I know. It's a mundane question."

"Not yet. I'll sponge you down."

"Your hands roaming around my body? Christ, I'll be hard and ready to go again immediately."

Her eyes sparkled and her lips turned up into a come-on grin. "Ooh. This could be fun. It's a deal." She stood, and he started to get out of bed. "Then you have to sleep for a while and I have to go to St. Francis and talk to Christopher."

"Okay… why?"

"He knows he's different. He has questions. I can at least ease his worries about being crazy. He has to know, Lu. He has the gift."

"If you feel you can help, then sure. But I don't want you alone out there."

"I'm sure the Georgian driver is sitting in the car right outside scrolling through his phone."

"And that's the only way you travel from now on. You're very important to me. And what you do to me? I mean, just looking at you—" he said as he sat on the bed and took her hands in his. A healthy blush replaced the paleness of her skin.

"Let's get you to the bathroom so I can have my way

with you," she said helping him stand. "Lean on me," she added, held him around the waist. "Does your leg hurt?"

"Nah. I barely feel it."

"Sure," she drew out. "You'd be taking three bites of a sandwich if we were still playing that game." He started to grin. "What's so funny?"

"I finished the sandwich. Game over."

"Okay. Fine. You win." *Yeah, because you're mine.* He sensed it in his soul.

Chapter 44

Visits

Even before she pulled back the curtain to enter Cubicle Q Martine heard his laugh. Paige sat on the bed at Christopher's side. Her senses tingled noticing their fingers touch. A small smile began thinking, *well what do you know and blessed be.*

Paige sprang to her feet with a soft, sweet, "Hi, Martine."

She gave a wave and, naturally, picked up the tablet lodged in its holder at the foot of the bed. All tests normal, her former patient now fit and lucid as if none of this ever happened.

"Hi," he said. The tray of food in front of him, no longer broth and green gelatin, suggested he had turned another important corner. Christopher's eyes followed Paige as she left. Martine knew that look and hoped the lovely nurse had found her eternal love—the way she had.

"Hi, back." She pulled the chair close and sat. "I'm not going to ask how you're doing—"

"Because you sense it."

Her head bobbed. "Has the detective been here?"

"Yeah. I told him the truth. I remember nothing about that night. He chalked it up to a random attack, which isn't too rare these days in the city."

"But you sense that's not why I'm here." *It's too early to switch to non-verbal communication.*

"I heard that in my head, but until I get a grip on how this all works, let's keep it verbal."

*He has a warlock's air about him already—a good thing.* "I linked to your mind briefly at times. What had been done to you is considered one of the worst crimes against anybody. Those like us will continue to protect you and assist you on your journey. It's inherited through your mother. She was very powerful. Literally the stuff of legends in our world and hers. Many of us who know our heritage come into our powers at a young age. You were deprived of that."

"My adoptive parents were the best. They loved me and I loved them."

"Thank God, because had you been abused, believe me, we'd be in a very different place right now. The power of family, love, and goodness is something we revere. We don't pry. We do no harm. Many of us believe in the synchronicity of events. We seek the deeper connections. Like the fact that your ambulance diverted to St. Francis. That I was on shift and met the transport. See where I'm going with this?"

He gave a thoughtful nod. "How long does it take you to know, uh, to sense things?"

"It varies. Look. The Georgians will help you understand a lot of this. They'll have answers to all your questions."

"What exactly are they?"

"The Georgian Circle isn't found in any directory. They protect the innocent in this world and go where they're needed. Some are researchers. Some are warriors. Most are everyday people. Professionals, like

Paige. We aren't part of them, but we've worked with them during paranormal events. They're really good people, Christopher."

"Chris," he corrected with a charming smile.

"Chris," she said, with a gracious nod. "Deepa Chandra, their representative on the North American Continent is a close friend of my mother's. You're in good hands."

"What about my life? My career?"

She sensed his worry. "Your life is going to change. I mean, how could it not? Look. Just take it one day at a time."

"What about Paige?"

She fully smiled at the question. "She's a Georgian. Need I say more?"

He grinned. "No. So. When do I get out of here?"

"Probably very soon. You'll go to a private house under Georgian care and protection. You should request that Paige be assigned your private nurse."

"They can do that?"

"And much, much more. Their network is worldwide. And don't kid yourself. You'll need their protection. Accept it and learn what they have to teach you. You'll be fine."

"I want to thank you, Martine. For holding my hand. For caring. For seeing into me and pulling me through. Yeah. It's a lot to sort out. We had a connection, didn't we?"

"We sure did. And we'll keep in touch. Although I'm guessing you're probably powerful enough to link to my mind without any help."

"The Kendrick witches," he whispered.

"There you go. Another warrior in the fight against

evil is always welcome."

She stood and he took her hand. "I'm sensing some incredible power here, Martine," he said with a nod.

"Oh you have no idea," she replied to the handsome man sitting in the bed before she broke the connection. Some thoughts were private. Hers alone to own. Plus she had somewhere else to be.

\*\*\*\*

Martine sat across from her mother at the kitchen table in her ancestral home. She had eaten a yummy pastry before taking the last sip of coffee, shielding her thoughts like a pro. This had to be said out loud and not between mouthfuls of a cannoli. Sitting back, rimming the empty mug with a finger, her gaze slid to the side. "I know you're over the moon that I ate every last crumb, Mare."

"Damn right," her mother answered in that low, smoky voice of hers.

"I've put you through hell these past five years. I'm sorry. I know you'll forgive me because that's what mother's do. My health is a number one priority now, so slow your roll." She met her mother's dark, intense eyes. "You were grieving, too."

"Grief is a thief that takes over your life. I had hoped you'd snap out of self-destruction sooner. Thank God you're snapping out of it now."

"I had help. And I told Lu about Madeline. I didn't cry when I said her name, as if she was telling me it's okay to love again."

"She's always with you, honey."

"I know. Alive in my soul forever." She paused. "Did you know what would happen when I saw him? Be honest, Mom."

Her mother folded her arms and her chin went down. "After the look on his face when he pushed off the dinner table and took you in his arms, I mean, Michael and I stared at each other—both of us in some strange new level of shock. That comical cartoon of tiny little hearts floating overhead comes to mind."

"He's very special to me."

"I met your father when I was sixteen."

She had to ask. "When did you know you loved him?"

"I was in my thirties, just like you. As sure as I'm sitting here, that first kiss echoed through my bones."

"What I feel is powerful. I sense it's the same for Lu."

"He's not going back to Scotland."

"No. He says he's wherever I am. I believe him. This connection between us feels so natural."

"Because it's right. Take it slow or take it fast. Either way, you both have my blessing. I think he'd walk through the fires of Hell for you."

An easy grin began. "What is that, like an old saying shared by Kendricks and Malones or something?"

Her mother nodded with the reply, "Close to a hundred years in the making."

"How so?"

"In the 1920s, Morgan, my grandmother, awakened something in Michael. Ever since then, he's been a part of us. My mother had him in her life since she was five. He's been in all of our lives. We have a bond, a deep bond to him. His bloodline is probably more powerful than ours."

"Do you sense it destiny that we came together?"

"Call it destiny or whatever you want. That bond

that began almost a century ago continues through you and Lukas."

Her hands slipped over her mother's. Martine sensed it as well.

Chapter 45

New Perspectives

The past two weeks had flown by. Boxes of personal items as well as books and a high-tech, high-speed computer had arrived from Scotland. Everything had found their proper places in Lukas's new home. His right leg continued to heal. The Georgian Council honored his request to stay in the city... with Martine. A security detail of Guardians were assigned to him.

His father had graciously signed over the brownstone, even though his trust fund was enormous and growing every day through sound investments. He and the love of his life didn't need to change a thing, with the exception of purple towels in the bathroom. He could live with it.

This house held memories for him. The first? Full of fear, misgivings, and mistrust as he hid from his father's enemies here some sixteen years ago. The most recent? Permanency. The gnawing desire to put down solid roots with the woman who now knew many facets of his life, both as a boy and as a man. Above all, he truly understood loving and being loved in return.

As twilight faded to the dark of night, Lukas sat in the living room dressed in his favorite blue shirt and a pair of jeans. Against his chest rested the Kendrick talisman on a long, thick silver chain, right over his heart and out of sight. Martine had already been driven to her first night back on the in-between shift at St. Francis Hospital. He had made her dinner.

A Guardian ushered in his special visitor, dressed in an expensive black suit, black shirt and tie. A large, thick manilla envelope lay on the coffee table in front of the roaring fire on this chilly October night. With a smirk on his face strikingly similar to his father's, Draven sat on the sofa across from him.

That little worm slithered through his stomach knowing what he had to say. He cleared his throat, and even though he wasn't a kid anymore, he felt like one. Lukas leaned forward and rolled his eyes. "I'm sorry for going off on you in the Second Realm. I'm *really* sorry for what I said and the way I spoke to you. I was way out of line, and I sincerely apologize."

"How long did it take your father to convince you this was necessary? And apology accepted, for the record. Which I am sure you will note for the Georgians."

He laced his arms across his chest and his shoulders settled back with a loose shrug. "Not long. Never does," he added under his breath.

The vampire threw back his head and gave a very uncharacteristic laugh, which allowed his long fangs to show. "Ah. My brother in blood raised you well. Yet it amazed me how long it took for him to put a stop to that bratty side that still exists in you."

"Those were extreme circumstances. But we're good—you and I, right?"

"Yes, we are good. So. I hear you're a new resident in the city. No doubt ordered to keep an eye on me as well."

"Yeah. Very perceptive. Look. I really couldn't have done this without you, Draven. You have my respect."

"Duly noted and appreciated."

"That doesn't mean you have license to drink and drain. I'll be watching and I'm quick with a stake or silver sword. Like you said. Dad taught me well."

"You have many of his qualities. Straight forward, a hint of arrogance. Quite fierce when backed against a wall."

"You know it."

"Well, perhaps I will further explore my moral side. Sometimes. When the mood strikes me."

"One could always hope, I'm guessing. Should you need a shove in the right direction you know where to find me."

"Likewise, if my assistance is needed, I can be reached… if necessary."

"Good to know." He glanced at the manilla envelope. "This is yours. Dad said you more than earned it." He leaned down to push it forward.

When Draven opened it, his face softened. Blood tears welled before receding. Then his lips drew tight, his chin dipped down, an unusual expression for a vampire who didn't have a soul and as close to human as one could imagine. Enough so, that Lukas felt compelled to whisper, "Are you okay?"

"These… appear to be some of my original manuscripts, and their ensemble arrangements composed by my son Julien." After studying a daguerreotype, Draven handed it to him.

"Is this you?"

"No. It is my Julien… at age thirty."

The likeness was incredible. Lukas memorized it, and then handed it back. "You must be very proud of him."

"Immensely," he replied, the word rumbling in his chest as if struggling to be said. "I must leave." He abruptly stood, the thick envelope clutched tight with both hands. Lukas stood as well. "You make your father proud, Lukas, a fierce warrior, a good man. I expect an update on this new relationship with your soulmate from time to time."

He gave a mischievous grin. "I don't have to ask how you know."

"Her scent is all over you. As it should be. Love is a treasure very few find in the world today. I wish you both all the happiness your hearts can hold."

"I'll tell her I saw you tonight," he said, not at all worried that the vampire would dare approach or touch her, *or ever* feed her again. He led Draven to the door and opened it out of respect. "Take care, vampire."

Eyeing him, Draven replied, "You as well, little boy."

Lukas rolled his eyes, then watched him hurry down the steps and take long familiar strides to the car. His tall frame folded into the back seat of the limo. A grin began as he closed the door. They shared a strange world. A world hidden from the innocents. As it should be.

****

Martine sat in the breakroom eating a thick roast beef sandwich, which had been prepared for her with love. Dottie sat across eating a yogurt. "You really look good, M. Two weeks off and you're like a different person. Sooo…" Dottie said, twirling the plastic spoon.

"I'm with someone."

"Does he have long blond hair, a killer bod and the deepest-blue eyes I've ever seen, by any chance?"

She swallowed and then smiled. "He totally does."

"I knew it! I mean, the look on your face when you saw him carried in said it all."

"Thanks for everything you did to help."

"And Christopher Forbes came out of it okay."

"One hundred percent fine," she said with a smile.

"So about that hottie?"

"Lu? Right. He has a clean bill of health, too." She wrapped the half-eaten sandwich. "He made this for me."

As the last lick of yogurt began, Dottie's nose crinkled. "I could do my jazz hands again. It's about time."

"I totally agree. Healthy meals every day. Plus, he keeps these scrumptious chocolate cookies in the kitchen."

"So you see him every night," Dottie asked—as one eyebrow did a little lift.

"I know this sounds like we're moving fast, but we're living together at his brownstone." Before her friend could ask, she added, "Mare adores him. And I'd love for you to meet him. Mom makes these terrific Sunday night dinners. We'll have you over soon."

Dottie's eyes filled as she smiled and gave a nod. "You look so happy."

"That's because I am. Really happy."

"I'm sure you sensed how worried I've been."

Martine tilted her head and studied her wonderful friend. "I did."

"You can read people like no one I've ever known. And what do you read in Lu?" Dottie's hand immediately shot to her mouth.

"No. You're not being nosy. I've kept so much in for so long, but I'm ready to share." She leaned in close to her good friend, met her half-way across the break room table. "This story needs tons of time, but for now... Let's just say a wild-child and a quiet shy kid met a long time ago. Something happened and that wild-child, now a woman, made an unbelievable ask of that shy kid, now a man. He came back to the city and made everything all right. Then she opened her heart, and he stepped in. All because of what happened on the night of the crescent moon." Martine added with an open smile, "It's amazing what you see when you finally open your eyes."

The True Legend of Gwendolyn

Gwendolyn of the Second Realm stood still in the shadows of evergreens, guarded by the crescent moon high above, wrapped in a magical mist so strong not even the sorcerers could penetrate.

Such was the love of a mother. Such was the desire to free her son, her beloved baby, from the life destined by birth. She'd protect him against the ways of the Second Realm. Snuggled and swathed to her chest, she took shallow breaths so as not to reveal her mission. With hands still coated with the blood of the child's sire, the one chosen to bond with Gwendolyn had been a cruel warlock. Bonded to him against her will. Forced by her bloodline to fulfill a destiny. He was of no consequence, a mere tool of the sorcerers. Her one blessing was conception. And yet, this child would someday be sacrificed to renew the sorcerers' powers.

But serendipity intervened. She found a portal deep in the forest as if put there by good magic and revealed to her alone. A way to slip into the human world with ease, as it should be.

The newborn stirred, and without pause she bared her left breast. He latched on with need. This act of motherhood pleasured in a way she would always remember. Fortitude guided her steps. The feel of firm needles now lifeless beneath her feet foreshadowed the sorrowful task that lay ahead. Anything worthy held both pleasure and pain. He would thrive in the human world, not be slated for death like a sacrificial lamb. Gwendolyn knew this from visions that occurred nightly throughout her pregnancy.

As birth approached, Gwendolyn's path became clear. The what, the why and the how coalesced. Nurture the child within with care and love. Kill the child's sire. Take the child to safety. She trudged on, weary from birthing alone in the secluded cabin. Blood oozed from her womb, placing her on the precipice of exhaustion. Gwendolyn stopped at the hidden lake, its waterfall flowing from a rocky ledge far above. She whispered words of gratitude, reveled in the icy water, sluicing it over her hands to palm her face.

Tears welled in her eyes. Never to hold him, to see his smile. Never to nurture one so precious. She prayed life would be kind to him. She prayed with the deepest love a mother holds that good magic would someday fill his soul.

The portal came into view. Although obscured, a mother's determination cleared her senses, her vision, her magic. She saw her destination. A red-brick chapel. With sureness her footsteps neared the portal's rim. Gray matter swirled and she focused her magic on opening it wide enough for safe passage. Swaddled close, she nudged the sleeping babe from her breast. A second later, her bloodied nightgown was covered by a simple midnight-blue cloak that fell mid-calf. Her long blonde hair contained under its hood. The air felt crisp this October night. The crescent moon above shone bright to light her way to the chapel door. Chants of prayer hummed through the stone walls giving glory to their God, the Supreme Being.

A simple roll of her hand brought the child into a soft blue blanket. The first steps toward his destiny in this dimension came without hesitation even though the pain in her heart felt a new form of torture. Tall and resolute, she pulled open the chapel door, the narthex cool with dim light from sconces on the inner wall. The spicy scent of incense hung heavy in the air. Gwendolyn sought the one mind she had sensed in her last vision, the elderly one called Mother. Placing the blanketed babe on the stone floor, she swallowed the pain of separation that rose from her womb to clench her heart. After a gentle kiss to her son's forehead, Gwendolyn left.

The slip back into the Second Realm took little effort. In both her head and her heart, she knew she had done what was necessary. The blue cloak melted from her skin. Alone she walked with purpose until she stood at the edge of the icy pool once again. A huge rock formed. With a flick of her wrist it split. One part would be a place to rest. The other, her freedom. She conjured a coarse rope of hemp to circle the heavy rock as well as her ankles.

Her soul screamed in misery. Why? Why did this happen to me? And what about the next boy-child conceived and delivered on the Night of the Crescent Moon? How would that mother feel about giving over her son to the sorcerers?

Legends. Legends like prophecies can kill. Gwendolyn's misery turned to rage. "Never," she hissed. "I curse the prophecy. Let no boy-child be born on the Night of the Crescent Moon. Let no witch conceive by warlock on that night." Power surged through her body, enough to make her quake with unbridled energy as fierce as a mother's love. "As I say, so mote it be," she intoned.

The placid water from the towering waterfall churned as if it absorbed her misery. Her hands reached out over the lake as the tied rock soared far beyond the water's edge. When Gwendolyn dropped her hands, her body dragged across earth, air and then water sinking to the farthest depths. As she plunged down, her last thought was of her son's safety in a world where no such prophecy could touch him.

Thus it is stated. Thus mote it be.